"It would bring dishonor upon my family and myself if my child were born out of wedlock," Rafe said.

Violet shouldn't have been surprised by this. She had basically guessed it when she'd looked up information on his country.

That didn't mean it was what she wanted to hear seconds after one of the best orgasms of her life. She sagged against his chest. "Do we—will we have to get married? Is that what happens in your country?"

He paused. "In my family… we do not have a choice. We are married for power, we bin Saleeds. Love…"

She closed her eyes. Love. They had talked about a lot of things, but love was not one of them.

Rafe cleared his throat. He began to rub his hands up and down her back. "It is something to consider, yes. But I have made you this promise, Violet. I will not force you to do something you do not wish to do."

"Oh. Okay." But honestly, did she know him well enough to believe he'd keep that promise?

* * *

A Surprise for the Sheikh
is part of the series The Texas Cattleman's Club:
Lies and Lullab
a scheming she

A SURPRISE FOR
THE SHEIKH

BY
SARAH M. ANDERSON

First Published in Great Britain 2016
By Mills & Boon, an imprint of HarperCollins*Publishers*
1 London Bridge Street, London, SE1 9GF

© 2016 Harlequin Books S.A.

Special thanks and acknowledgement are given to Sarah M. Anderson for her contribution to the Texas Cattleman's Club: Lies and Lullabies series.

ISBN: 978-0-263-91856-4

51-0416

Our policy is to use papers that are natural, renewable and recyclable products and made from wood grown in sustainable forests. The logging and manufacturing processes conform to the legal environmental regulations of the country of origin.

Printed and bound in Spain
by CPI, Barcelona

Sarah M. Anderson may live east of the Mississippi River, but her heart lies out West on the Great Plains. Sarah's book *A Man of Privilege* won an RT Reviewers' Choice Best Book Award in 2012.

Sarah spends her days having conversations with imaginary cowboys and American Indians. Find out more about Sarah's love of cowboys and Indians at www.sarahmanderson.com and sign up for the new-release newsletter at www.eepurl.com/nv39b.

Prologue

This was really happening.

Ben's hot body pressed Violet against the back of the elevator. Something hard and long bumped against her hip, and she giggled. Oh, yeah—this was *so* happening.

She was really doing this.

"Kiss me," Ben said in that sinfully delicious accent of his as he flexed his hips against hers. She didn't know where he was from, but his accent made her think of the burning heat of summer sun—because boy, did it warm her up.

Violet ran her hands through his thick black hair and lifted his face away from where he'd been sucking on her neck.

He touched his forehead to hers. "Kiss me, my mysterious, my beautiful V." Then—incredibly—he hesitated just long enough to make it clear he was waiting for her decision.

Power surged through her. This was exactly why she was riding in an elevator in the Holloway Inn up to a man's room—a man who did not know she was Violet McCallum, who did not know she was Mac McCallum's baby sister.

Her entire life, she had been Violet. Violet, who had to be protected from the big bad world. Violet, the lost little girl whose parents died and left her all alone. Violet, who still lived at home and still had her big brother watching over her every move to make sure she didn't get hurt again.

Well, to hell with that. Tonight, she was V. She was mysterious, she was beautiful, and this man—this sinfully handsome man with an accent like liquid sunshine— wanted her to kiss him.

She was not Violet. Not tonight.

So she kissed him, long and hard, their tongues tangling in her mouth, then in his. She did more than kiss him—she raked her fingers through his hair and held him against her. She made it clear—this was what she wanted. He was what she wanted.

She hadn't come to this hotel bar a town away from Royal, Texas, with the intent of going to bed with a stranger. She hadn't planned on a one-night stand. She'd wanted to get dressed up, to feel pretty—maybe to flirt. She'd wanted to be someone else, just for the night.

But she hadn't counted on Ben. "You have beautiful eyes," he said in his sunshine voice, his hands sliding down her backside and cupping her bottom. "Among other things, my mysterious V." Then he lifted, and it was only natural that her legs went around his waist and that the long, hard bulge in his pants went from bumping against her thigh to pressing against the spot at her very center.

Violet's back arched as heat radiated throughout her body. Ben held tight to her, pinning her back against the elevator wall as he pressed his mouth to the cleavage that this little black dress left exposed. One of the hands that was cupping her bottom slid forward, snagging on the hem of her dress as he stroked between her legs. The heat from his hand only added to the raging inferno taking place under her skin.

"If you leave this elevator, you will be mine, you understand? I will lay you out on the bed and make you cry out. This is your last chance to take the elevator down."

A shiver of delight raced through her. Respectable Violet would never let a man talk to her like this. But V? "Is that a promise?"

"It is," he said in such a serious tone that she gasped. "Your pleasure is my pleasure."

That was, hands down, the sweetest thing anyone had ever whispered to her. Her entire life had been one long exercise in telling people what she wanted only to have to listen to the litany of excuses why she couldn't do what she wanted or couldn't have what she wanted. It was too risky, too dangerous. She didn't understand the consequences, she didn't this, she didn't that—every excuse her brother could throw at her, he did.

If Mac knew she was in this elevator with a man whose pleasure was her pleasure—well, there might be guns involved. This was risky and dangerous and all that stuff that Mac had spent the past twelve years trying to shield her from.

She was tired of being protected. She wanted something more than safety.

She wanted Ben.

"Why are we still in this elevator?" she asked in as

innocent a tone as she could muster, given how Ben's body was pressing against hers.

"You are quite certain?"

"Quite. But don't stop talking." The words hadn't even gotten out of her mouth before Ben hauled her away from the wall of the elevator and out into the hall.

"Are you this adventurous in everything?"

He was carrying her as if she weighed nothing at all. She was as light as a feather, a leaf on the wind, in Ben's arms. She was flying and she didn't ever want to come down.

She also didn't want to cop to her relatively limited experiences in the whole "pleasure" department. Every time she got serious about a guy, her brother—her well-meaning, overbearing brother—came down like the hammer of Thor and before Violet could blink, the guy would be giving her the it's-not-you-it's-me talk.

Violet may have had only a couple of boyfriends, but V was knowledgeable and experienced. She could not only handle a man like Ben, she could meet him as an equal. And so help her, no one was going to give her the let's-be-friends talk tonight. "Why don't we find out?"

He growled against her neck.

A door opened. "What's—" an older man, voice heavy on the Texas accent, said.

Ben stopped and, without putting Violet down, turned to stare at the old man in the open doorway. He didn't say anything. He didn't make a menacing gesture. He just stared down the other man.

"Ah. Well. Yes," the older man babbled as the door shut.

"Whoa," Violet said, giggling again. "Dude, you are—wow." So this was what exuding masculinity looked like.

"'Dude,' eh?" Ben said with a sexy chuckle as he

began walking down the hall. Every step made Violet gasp as Ben's hard length pressed against her sex. "For a woman as beautiful as you, you often talk like a man."

"I don't always wear little black dresses."

Ben stopped in front of another door. "Hmm," he said as his hands stayed on her body as he set her down, which effectively meant he hiked her dress up. "Are you sure you won't tell me your name?"

"No," she said quickly. She didn't want this fantasy night of perfection to be ruined by something as mundane as reality. "No names. Not tonight."

He got his key out and opened the door. Then his hands were back on her body, walking her backward into the room. "Who are you hiding from? Family?" He pulled her to a stop and turned her around. His fingers found her zipper and pulled it down, one slow click after another. "Or another lover, hmm?"

"I'm not hiding from anyone," she fibbed. It was a small fib because, no, she did not want Mac to know she'd done something this wild, this crazy. That's why she was in Holloway instead of Royal.

"We are all hiding from something, are we not?" Ben began to pull the dress down, revealing the black bra with the white embroidery that she wore only when she was feeling particularly rebellious. Which, in the last few months, was almost every day.

"I just—look," she said in frustration, taking a step back and pulling free of his hands. "I won't ask about you, you won't ask about me, and we use condoms. That's the deal. If that doesn't work for you…" She grabbed the sleeves of her dress and tugged them back up.

Ben stood there, his sinfully delicious lips curved into a smile. Oh, no—he wouldn't call her bluff, would he?

Because she wanted to strip him out of that suit—and she didn't want to walk out of this room until she was barely able to walk at all.

"I just need a night with you," she said, the truth of that statement sinking in for the first time since she'd walked into the bar at the Holloway Inn and laid eyes on this tall, dark and handsome stranger. She'd thought she just needed a night out, but the very moment Ben had turned to her, his coal-black eyes taking in her lacy black cocktail dress, her wavy auburn hair, her stockings with the seam up the back—then she'd needed him. And she wasn't going to rest until she had him. "That's all I'm asking. One night. No strings. Just…pleasure."

Ben stepped into her, cupping her face in his hands. "That is really all you want from me? Nothing else?"

The way he said it, with a touch of sadness in his voice, made her heart ache for him. She didn't know who he was or why he was here—he wasn't local, that much was obvious. But she got the feeling that in his real life, there were always strings.

She knew the feeling. And for tonight, at least, she didn't want to be hemmed in by other people's expectations of her. Good idea or not, she was going to take Ben to bed. There would be no regrets. Not for her. "No. Your pleasure is my pleasure," she whispered against his lips, turning his words back to him.

"Kiss me," he said against her skin.

So she did. She tangled her hands in his hair and pulled him roughly against her mouth, and then they were flinging each other's clothing off and falling into bed and she couldn't tell where her pleasure began and his ended because Ben was everything she'd ever dreamed a lover could be, only better—hotter, sweeter.

She fell asleep in his arms, listening to him whisper

stories to her in a language she did not know and did not understand, but it didn't matter. She was sated and happy. She'd started this night desperate to do something fun, something for herself.

Ben—no last name, no country of origin—was an answer to her prayers.

One

Four months later

This was *not* happening.

Dear God, please let this not be happening. Violet stared down at the thin strip of plastic. The one that said in digital block letters, *PREGNANT*.

Maybe she'd done it wrong. Peed on the wrong end or something. Yeah, that was it. She'd never taken a pregnancy test before. She hadn't even studied. She'd failed due to a lack of preparation, that was all.

Luckily, Violet had bought three separate tests because redundancy wasn't just redundant. It was confirmation that her night of wild passion four months ago with a stranger named Ben had not left her pregnant.

Crouched in the bathroom off of her bedroom, Violet carefully read the instructions again, trying to spot her mistake. Remove the purple cap: check. Hold the other end: check. Hold absorbent tip downward: check. Wait two minutes: check.

Crap. She'd done it right.

So she did it again.

The next two minutes were hell. The panic was so strong she could practically taste it in the back of her throat, and it was getting stronger with every passing second.

The first test was just a false positive, she decided. False positives happened all the time. She wasn't pregnant. She was suffering from a low-grade stomach bug. Yeah, that was it. That would explain the odd waves of nausea that hit her at unexpected times. Not in the morning either. Therefore, it wasn't morning sickness.

And the low-grade bug she was fighting—that's what caused the positive. It had absolutely nothing to do with that night in the Holloway Inn four months ago. It had nothing to do with Ben or V or...

PREGNANT.

Oh, God.

One was a false positive. The second? Considering that she'd had a wild night of passionate sex with a man in a hotel room?

What the hell was she going to do?

She didn't have a last name. She didn't have his number. He'd been this fantasy man who had appeared when she'd needed him and been gone by morning light. She'd woken up in his room alone. Her dress had been cleaned and pressed and was hanging on the bathroom door. Room service had delivered breakfast with a rose and a note—a note she still had, tucked inside her sock drawer, where Mac would never see it.

Your pleasure was my pleasure. Thank you for the night.

He hadn't even signed it Ben. No name, no signature. No way to contact him when she had a ràpidly growing collection of positive pregnancy tests on the edge of her sink.

She was screwed.

Okay, so contacting Ben was out, at least for the short term. She might be able to hire a private investigator who could track him down through the hotel's guest registry, but that didn't help her out right now.

"Violet?" Mac called out from downstairs. "Can you come down here?"

She was going to be sick again, and this time she didn't think it was because of morning sickness.

How was she supposed to tell her big brother that she'd done something this wild and crazy and was now pregnant? The man had dedicated the past twelve years of his life to keeping her safe after their parents' deaths. He would not react well.

"Violet?" She heard the creak of the second step—oh Lord, he was on his way up.

"Give me a minute!" she called through the door as she grabbed the two used tests and shoved them back in the box. She hid everything under the sink, behind her maxi pads. Mac would never look there.

She needed a plan. She was on her own here.

Violet stood up and quickly splashed some cold water on her face. She didn't normally wear a lot of makeup. She had no need to look pretty when she was managing the Double M, their family ranch. The ranch hands she'd hired had all gotten the exact same message, no doubt— hitting on Mac McCallum's little sister was strictly forbidden. Which irritated her. First off, she wasn't hiring studs for the express purpose of getting it on in the hayloft. Second, she was the boss. Mac ran McCallum Enterprises, the energy company their father had founded, and Violet ran the Double M, and the less those two worlds crossed, the better it was.

Because Mac did not see a ranch manager, much less a damned good ranch manager. He didn't see a capable businesswoman who was navigating a drought and rebuilding from a record-breaking tornado and still making a profit. He didn't see a partner in the family business.

All he saw was the shattered sixteen-year-old girl she'd been when their parents had died. It didn't matter what she did, how well she did it—she was still a little sister to him. Nothing more and nothing less.

Violet had wanted so desperately not to be Mac's helpless baby sister, even for a night. And if that night was spent in a stranger's arms...

And here she was.

She'd just jerked her ponytail out of its holder and started wrenching the brush through her mane of auburn hair when Mac said, "Violet?"

She jumped. She hadn't heard Mac come the rest of the way upstairs, but now he was right outside the door. "What?"

"An old friend of mine is downstairs. Rafe."

"Oh—okay," she said, feeling confused. Rafe—why did that name sound familiar? And why did Mac sound... odd? "Is everything okay?"

Ha. Nothing was okay, but by God, until she got a grip on the situation, she was going to pretend it was if it was the last thing she did.

"No, it's fine. It's just—Rafe is the sheikh, you remember? From college?"

"Wait." She cracked the door open and stared at her brother. Even though she'd hidden the evidence, she intentionally positioned her body between him and the sink. "Is this the guy who had the wild younger sister who tricked you? *That* Rafe?"

"Yeah. Rafiq bin Saleed." Mac's expression was a mix of excitement and confusion.

"What's he doing here right now?" Violet asked. "I mean, correct me if I'm wrong, but didn't he blame you for his sister's—what did you call it?"

"Compromising her innocence? Yeah."

"So why do I have to meet this jerk?"

"He's in town. He's apologized for his behavior years ago."

Violet stared at him. Men and their delicate attempts at friendship. "And you're okay with that?"

"Yeah," Mac said with a shrug. "Why wouldn't I be? It was a misunderstanding. His father was the one who was mad. Rafe is making amends."

After twelve years? That seemed odd. *Men.* "And you're warning me in advance because…"

"Because I know you, Violet. I know you're liable to shoot your mouth off. He's a sheikh—they have a different set of customs, okay? So try to be polite."

She gave him a dull look. "Really? You think I'm so impulsive I can't even make small talk with a man from a different culture?" She shoved the door open. Her hair could wait. "Thanks, Mac. I appreciate the vote of confidence there."

Mac grinned at her. "Said Violet, impulsively."

"Stuff it. Let's get this over with." She pushed past her brother and stomped to the closet, where she grabbed a clean shirt. If she was going to be meeting—wait, what was a sheikh? Were they royalty? Well, whatever he was, the least she could do was make sure she was wearing a shirt that didn't have cow poop on it. "I'll meet your rude sheikh friend and then make myself scarce, okay? I've got stuff to do anyway." Like maybe tracking down her one-night stand and figuring out her due date and, well, her schedule was just *packed*. She started unbuttoning her work jeans.

The wheels of her mind spun. This was going to change everything. She'd had plans—she'd been slowly working on convincing her brother to buy the ranch to the north, the Wild Aces. Violet had loved the Wild Aces for years. She wanted out of this house, out from under Mac's overprotective roof, and the Wild Aces was where she wanted to be.

They were already leasing the land. The Double M's water supply had been compromised by the tornado last year. But Wild Aces had plenty of water. Violet had thought that would be the motivation Mac needed to sign off on the purchase, but because she was the one who'd suggested it instead of his assistant, Andrea Beaumont, Mac had said no. Eventually, the two women had convinced Mac to at least lease the land.

But now? Violet was pregnant. How was she going to manage the Double M, much less the Wild Aces, with a huge belly or a baby on her hip?

Mac didn't say anything for so long she paused and looked up at him. "What?"

"Everything okay?" he asked.

She tensed. "Why wouldn't it be? It's fine. Totally fine."

Mac wrinkled his brow at her but before he could question her further, she said, "Shouldn't you be downstairs with your sheikh friend or something? So I can finish getting changed? Maybe?"

Mac paled. He may have stepped into the role of father figure after their parents' deaths, but he was still a big brother. An irritating one at that.

Okay, so she had a plan. She was going to pretend everything was just hunky-dory for the foreseeable future while she thought of a better plan.

Where was Ben? And even if she could find him, would he be happy to see her? Or would he claim that their night had had no strings attached and a baby was a huge string and therefore, she was on her own?

What a freaking mess.

"Sorry about that," Mac said, strolling back into the room. "Violet's…well, she's Violet."

Rafe sat in the center of the couch, surveying the room and the man before him. Mac had most certainly aged in the past twelve years, but he didn't have the haunted look of someone who had betrayed his best friend.

Rafe was not surprised, not really. At the time Mac compromised Nasira, he had exhibited little regard for Rafe's family's name. He did not look guilty because, more than likely, Mac McCallum was incapable of feeling guilt.

Revenge was a dish best served cold. But Rafe couldn't overplay his hand here. He put on a warm smile and said, "Yes, your younger sister—I remember. She was still in high school when we were at college, correct?"

"Yeah, that's right." Mac shrugged apologetically. If Rafe were capable of being sympathetic with a person such as Mac, he could sympathize over wayward younger sisters. "So," Mac went on, changing the subject. "Tell me about you, man. It's been years! What are you doing in town?"

Rafe shrugged, as if his being in Royal, Texas, were

some sort of happy accident instead of entirely premeditated. "My father is dead," he said.

Mac's cheeks reddened. "Oh, dude—sorry about that."

Rafe smiled—inwardly, of course. The last person to say "dude" to him in such a way had been V, the beautiful woman at the inn a few months ago. It had seemed so odd coming out of her perfect rosebud mouth. It was much better suited to a man like Mac.

Where was V now? That was a question that had danced at the edge of his consciousness for months. He had gotten better at putting the question aside, though. It was almost easy to not think of her. Almost.

"I appreciate your concern, but there is no need for sorrow. He was a…difficult man, as I'm sure you know."

Mac nodded sympathetically. In fact, before Mac's betrayal of Rafe's family, Mac had been one of the few people Rafe had confided in about his "difficult" father. There had been a time, long ago, when Rafe would have trusted this man with his very life.

Rafe did not trust people. He had learned that lesson well. Years spent locked up by his father had taught him that.

"With his passing," Rafe went on, "my older brother Fareed became the sheikh and I became more free to seek my way in the world." He tried to make it sound carefree and, in truth, some of it had been. Fareed had turned his attention to the modernization of their sheikhdom and released Rafe. Fareed had even entrusted Rafe with control of the family shipping business. All things considered, the reversal of fortune had been breathtaking.

But just because Rafe had no longer had to deal with Hassad bin Saleed did not mean he was free. He was still a sheikh. He had his people's honor and pride to preserve.

And if that meant waiting twelve years to exact his revenge, then so be it.

"I had meant to seek you out much earlier," Rafe went on, bending the truth until it was on the verge of breaking. "But my brother gave me the shipping company and I was quite busy turning the business around. You understand how it is. I am expanding my company's holdings and was looking to get into energy. The worldwide demand is rising. Naturally, I thought of you. I remember how fondly you spoke of this area and its many resources."

That was his story. Secretly, Rafe had been buying up land all over Royal, Texas, under the front of Samson Oil, a company he had created ostensibly to purchase the mineral rights and whatever remaining oil existed underground.

But Samson Oil was buying lands that had no more oil and no valuable mineral rights to speak of. The land was good for little else besides grazing cattle, and the entire town knew it. He had hired a Royal native, Nolan Dane, to act as the public face of Samson Oil. The townsfolk had been easily swayed by the outrageous offers and Nolan's down-home charm. They were happy to take his money—except, of course, that no one knew it was *his* money. By the time they figured out his scheme, it would be too late.

Rafe would own this town, and he would do with it as he saw fit.

Mac snorted. "Tell me about it. McCallum Enterprises has completely taken over my life. I can't even run the ranch anymore—Violet handles that for me."

"Your younger sister does a man's job?" But he was not truly surprised. Mac had always spoken of how outlandish his baby sister was—a tomboy, he'd said.

"She does a damn good job, too," Mac said in a thoughtful voice.

"I had thought she was going to follow you to Harvard." That had been the story Mac had told him all those years ago. But had that just been a lie to earn Rafe's trust as they bonded over difficult younger siblings?

"That was before our parents died. They went out for a flight on Dad's plane and…" Mac sighed heavily. "She was so lost after the accident, you know? I hated that I wasn't here for her when it happened."

"I had not realized," Rafe said sympathetically, even though of course he had realized. The McCallum family had suffered a terrible blow when Mac's parents' plane had crashed into an open field. There had been no survivors.

It all happened right after Rafe had been pulled out of Harvard by his father for daring to let his younger sister consort with the likes of Mac. Rafe had not found out the details of the accident for years afterward—after his own father had died and Rafe had suddenly had the means to investigate his enemies.

It had been a missed opportunity. If Rafe had been aware of the McCallums' deaths at the time, he could have moved swiftly to buy Mac's land out from under him or take over McCallum Enterprises. Instead, Rafe had to settle for watching and waiting for his next best opportunity to exact his revenge. He had not rushed. He was, as the Americans often said, playing the long game.

His patience had finally paid off when, last year, a tornado had torn through Mac's hometown of Royal, Texas. The town's economic base was weakened, which was good. But what was better was that Mac's water supply had become compromised.

It was a particularly good scheme. Rafe would not only cut off Mac's water supply and essentially strangle his ranch, but under the guise of Samson Oil, he would also buy up large parts of Royal. Mac had always spoken of his love for his hometown.

When Rafe was done with him, Mac would have nothing. No town, no land. That was what Mac had left Nasira with when he had betrayed Rafe's trust and ruined Nasira.

Thus far, Rafe had been operating in secrecy. But when his scheme came to fruition, he wanted Mac to know it was he who had brought about his destruction.

Which was why he was here, pretending to be concerned for the well-being of his former friend's sister. "Was it very hard on her?"

"Oh, man," Mac said with a rueful smile. "I moved back home and tried to give her a stable upbringing, but never underestimate the power of a teenage girl. Hey, listen," he went on, leaning forward and dropping his voice a notch. "I know that things didn't end well between us…"

Rafe tensed inside but outside, he waved this poor excuse for an olive branch of peace away, as if he'd truly left the matter in the past. "It was all a long time ago. Think nothing of it."

"Thanks, man. I never meant to hurt Nasira, but I swear to you, I had no idea she was in my room that night. It wasn't what it looked like."

Rafe's mask of genial friendship must have slipped because Mac's words trailed off. Rafe rearranged his face into one of concern. "It's fine. She was able to marry a man who was more to her liking." It was time for a subject change. "Your sister, Violet? It has been a long time."

"Yeah—that's what I wanted to talk to you about. I

try to keep her out of trouble, but if you, you know, could just keep an eye on her while you're in town, I'd really appreciate it."

Now this was ironic. Here Rafe was, doing everything within his power to avenge the honor of his sister and his family, and Mac, the source of all his troubles, was asking Rafe to look after Violet?

That would be a new layer to Rafe's revenge—corrupting Mac's sister just as Mac had corrupted Rafe's.

"But of course," Rafe said as he bowed his head, trying to look touched that Mac would extend him this much trust. The fool. He was making this too easy.

"My ears are burning." Rafe heard the soft feminine—and familiar—voice seconds before its owner entered the room. "What are you two…talking…"

She stood in the doorway, her mouth open, all the color draining from her cheeks.

Rafe's body responded before his brain could make sense of what he was seeing. His gut tightened and his erection stiffened and one word presented itself in his mind—*mine*. The reaction was so sudden and so complete that Rafe was momentarily disoriented. This woman was lovely, yes, but her body was not the kind that usually invoked such an immediate, possessive response from him.

Then the conscious part of his brain caught up with the rest of him and he realized exactly who she was.

She looked different in the light of day. Rafe had not known her in such mannish clothing—jeans and work shirts. Her hair was pulled into a low ponytail at the nape of her neck and her face was scrubbed clean.

But he recognized her nonetheless.

V.

His mind spun in bewilderment. His mysterious, beautiful V was *here*? The woman he had been unable to put from his mind was…in Mac's home?

Mac stood and Rafe stood with him. This was an… unexpected development. He would have to brazen it out as best he could. "Ah, here you are. Violet, this is my old college friend, Rafe bin Saleed."

"*Bin* Saleed?" she said, her eyes so wide they were practically bursting out of her head. *"Bin?"*

"Um, yeah," Mac said, his gaze darting between the two of them. "Rafe, this is my little sister, Violet."

V was Violet. V was his mortal enemy's younger sister.

Destiny had a twisted sense of humor.

Inwardly, he was kicking himself, as the Americans said. Rafiq bin Saleed did not randomly bring a woman back to his bed. He did not seduce her and strip her and he most certainly did not send her love notes the next morning. He was a sheikh. He had no need for those things. His one night of passion with the exact wrong woman could threaten twelve years of planning.

Outwardly, however, he kept his composure. Years of facing his father's wrath had trained him well in remaining calm in the face of danger. He had to put a good face on this. His scheme had not yet come to fruition, and if Violet placed him in the greater Royal area four months before his "arrival" today, everything could be at risk.

All his schemes could fall apart in front of him, all because he had been unable to resist a beautiful woman.

Unless…a new thought occurred to him. Unless Violet already knew of his schemes. Unless she had been sent by her brother to find him all those months ago. Unless Mac had anticipated Rafe's attack and launched a counterattack while Rafe was distracted by a beautiful smile and a gorgeous body.

But she had insisted on no names. He had never used his real name, just as she had hidden hers. Was it possible that she had really just been looking for a night's passion?

He had no choice but to continue to play the part of the long-lost friend. He couldn't show his hand just because he had accidentally slept with this woman. "Violet," he said, letting the hard *T* sound of her name roll off his tongue, just as so many other things had rolled off his tongue. He bowed low to her, a sign of respect in his culture. "It is an honor to finally meet Mac's beloved sister."

"Is it?" she snapped.

Mac shot her a warning look. "Violet," he said quietly. "We talked about this."

"Sorry," she said, clearly not sorry at all. "I was expecting someone else entirely."

Rafe wanted to laugh. Truthfully, he had been, as well. But he did no such thing. Instead, he said calmly, "Have I come at a bad time?"

Americans had an expression that Rafe had never heard before he'd attended university at Harvard— "If looks could kill." In his sheikhdom of Al Qunfudhah, no one would dare look at a sheikh with such venom— to do so was to risk dismemberment or even death at the hands of Hassad bin Saleed, who had ruled with an iron fist and an iron blade.

But he was no longer in Al Qunfudhah, and if looks could kill, Violet would have finished him off several minutes ago.

He notched an eyebrow at her. He was more than capable of controlling himself. Could she say the same? Or was that why Mac had gone to speak to her privately— were they getting their stories straight?

You were *capable of controlling yourself*, a small voice in the back of his mind whispered. *Until you met her.*

"No, no," Mac said warmly. "Violet, maybe you should get us something to drink."

She turned her wrathful gaze to Mac and Rafe decided that, even if Mac had sent Violet to him, she had not told her brother the truth of their evening together. "Excuse me? Do I look like your maid?"

"Violet!" Mac sent another worried grin toward Rafe. "Sorry, Rafe."

Rafe waved his hand as if Violet's attitude were nothing. "We are not in Al Qunfudhah," he said, trying to set Mac at ease even as he enjoyed his old friend's discomfort. "I remember how things in America are quite different than they are back home. I do not expect to be served by the women in the house."

But even as he said it, he casually sat back in the middle of the sofa, spreading his arms out along the back and waiting to be served by someone. He took up as much space as he could. *I am here*, he thought at Violet, catching her eye and lifting his chin in challenge. *What are you going to do about it?*

Oh, yes. If looks could kill, he would be in extreme pain right now. "That's where you're from?"

The bitterness of her tone was somewhat unexpected. The last time he had seen her, she had been asleep in his bed, nude except for the sheets that had twisted around her waist. Her beautiful auburn hair had been fanned out over her shoulder, and even as she slept, her rosebud lips had been curved into a satisfied, if small, smile. She had looked like a woman who had been thoroughly pleasured, and Rafe had almost woken her up with a touch and a kiss.

But she had only asked for a night, so he quietly let himself out of the room, arranged to have breakfast sent up and then met with Nolan to go over his plans for purchasing more of the land around Mac's Double M ranch. He had tried mightily to put his night of wanton abandon with the beautiful V out of his mind.

Which was not to say he had succeeded. Not for the first time, he replayed their evening together. He had not coerced her—no, he specifically remembered several points where he had given her a respectable out.

It had been her choice to come to his room. Her choice to make it one night. Her choice not to use names or places.

As far as Rafe was concerned, Violet had nothing to be bitter about. He had made sure she had been well satisfied, just as he had been.

"I'll get us something to drink. Violet, can I talk to you in the kitchen?" Mac said, forgoing subtlety altogether.

"I'll take some lemonade," Violet responded, ignoring her brother's request and sitting in a chair across from Rafe. "Thanks."

Of course Rafe knew they were not in Al Qunfudhah anymore, but it was something of a surprise to not only see a woman give a man—her guardian, no less—an order, but to see that man heave a weary sigh and obey.

Perhaps if Nasira had felt freer to assert herself as Violet did...

Well, things might have been different. But knowing his father, things would not have been better.

Rafe pushed away those thoughts and focused instead on the woman before him. Violet was seething with barely contained rage, that much was obvious.

Once Mac was out of the room, Violet leaned toward him. "Rafiq *bin* Saleed?"

He would not let her get to him. She may be a slightly hysterical female, but he was still a sheikh. "It's lovely to see you again, V. Unexpected, yes, but lovely none-theless."

"Oh, it's unexpected all right. What the hell?"

He ignored her outburst. "You are well, I trust?"

Her eyes got wide—very wide indeed. "*Well?* Oh, you're going to care now?"

He bristled at her tone. "For your information, I cared that night. But it was you who asked for just that—a night. Just one. So I honored your wishes. No names, no strings—that was how you put it, was it not?"

She continued to glare at him. "What do I even call you? Not Ben, I assume."

"Rafe will do for now."

"Will it? Is that your real name? Or just another alias?"

"My name is Rafiq," he said stiffly. He did not enjoy being on the defensive. "Rafe is a well-known nickname in my country."

Her nostrils flared, as if she were getting ready to physically attack him. "Well, Rafe, since you asked, I am not well."

"No?" Against his will, he felt a plume of concern rise through his belly. He should be glad she was not well. That would only cause Mac more suffering.

But Rafe was concerned. He wanted to pull her into his arms and feel her breath against his skin and make her well. He was a wealthy man. There was nothing he could not provide for her. "Not because of something I have done, I hope."

She was breathing hard now, as if she were standing on the top of a tall peak and getting ready to jump. "You could say that. I'm pregnant."

Rafe blinked at her, trying to comprehend the words. Had she just said—*pregnant*? "Mine?"

She looked much like a lioness ready to pounce on her

prey, all coiled energy and focus. "Of course it's yours. I realize we don't know very much about each other but I don't normally pick up men. That was a one time thing. You're the only man I've been with in the last year and *you* were supposed to use *condoms*!" She hissed the word but quietly. It was for his ears and his ears alone.

Before he could come up with something reasonable to say—something reasonable to think, even—Mac strode back into the room, carrying a tray with a pitcher and glasses. "Lemonade?"

Two

Rafe just...sat there. For Pete's sake, he didn't even blink when Mac walked back into the room. Violet's whole world was falling apart around her and Rafe looked as though she'd announced she liked French fries instead of the fact that she was carrying his child.

She couldn't take it. She needed to go. If she could make it back to a bathroom, where she could throw up in peace and quiet, that'd be great.

"Actually," she said, forcing herself to stand. "I'm not thirsty. Thanks anyway, Mac."

The father of her unborn baby was not just some nameless stranger she'd met in a bar. Oh, no—that would be getting off easy. If that were the case, she'd merely be pregnant and alone. Which is a terrifying prospect, but comparatively?

The father of her child was a sheikh. And not just any sheikh. Her brother's former friend, the one who had blamed Mac for seducing his sister and ended the friendship under no uncertain terms.

Oh, she was going to be so sick.

She willed her legs not to wobble as she stood. Ben or Rafe or Sheikh Saleed or whatever his name was stood with her.

In the past thirty-some-odd minutes, her perfect fantasy night had somehow become an epic nightmare. Had she been dreading telling Mac she was pregnant before? Ha. How the hell was she supposed to tell him now? *I'm expecting and by the way, the father is your old friend. Isn't that a laugh riot?*

Mac already treated her as though she was still a lost little girl of sixteen. What would he do now that she'd proven how very irresponsible she was?

Oh, God—this was going to change everything. It already had.

She turned and headed for the door, but due to her wobbly legs, she didn't get out of the room fast enough. "Violet," Rafe said in his ridiculous voice, all sunshine and honey, and damned if the sound of her name on his lips didn't send another burst of warmth and desire through her. Her head may have been a mess, but her body—her stupid, traitorous body—still wanted this man. Hell.

It didn't matter. She couldn't let his accent melt her from the inside out, because what had happened the last time? She'd ended up pregnant and unmarried. Violet did not often think of her parents—the loss was too painful, even after all these years—but right now, what she wanted more than anything was her mother.

"What?"

Mac winced and Violet could almost hear him adding, *Said Violet, impulsively.*

"I would like to know more about Royal and catch up with my old friends." Something about the way Rafe said *friends* hit Violet wrong, but before she could figure out what it was, he went on, "Would you both join me for dinner tomorrow night?"

What had she done to deserve this? Because the torture of sitting through dinner with both her brother and her former lover at this exact moment of her life and pretending that nothing had changed was right up there with being stepped on by a herd of stampeding cattle.

"Well, damn," Mac said. "I'm going to be out of town. But Violet can go with you."

That was just like Mac, to assume that she spent all her free time painting her nails and listening to Backstreet Boys. She rolled her eyes at Rafe, which must not have been something people in his country did, given the way the color on his cheeks deepened.

Still, Rafe forged on, by all appearances completely unbothered by her impulsiveness or her pregnancy— except for that blush, which only made him look more sinfully handsome. Damn the man.

"Ah, that is acceptable. That way I can keep an eye on you." His gaze never wavered from hers. "Shall we meet tomorrow, say at seven?"

And Mac, the rat bastard, nodded his approval, as if they were having this entire conversation about her without remembering she was in the room.

She was totally going to blame this on hormones, this mix of rage and self-pity and the sudden urge to cry, all folded in together with desire and relief until she was so mixed up she couldn't think straight.

But had Mac already asked this man to keep an eye on her? Violet *so* did not need a babysitter at this point.

In six months or so, yes, she would need a babysitter. But before she had an actual baby, she did not. "I don't—"

"Sure, that'd be great," Mac said warmly, as if Violet were incapable of having dinner on her own without getting into some sort of trouble. "I have a meeting with Andrea scheduled that I can't get out of—Andrea's my assistant," he added, seeing Rafe's quizzical look. "But you two can go on and have a nice time."

A nice time? Oh, she had some things she wanted to say to her brother—about Rafe—but the fact was, she did actually need to talk with Rafe. Alone. "Yeah," she said, trying to sound at least a little bit excited about the prospect. Four months ago, another evening with her mystery man, Ben, would have been too good to be true. But now? "Sure. Dinner."

Rafe gave her a small smile that absolutely did not appease her. She hated him right then, because her entire world had just blown up in her face and the father of her child stood there looking as sexy as he had the night he'd taken her to bed. This pregnancy was going to change everything for her—but for him?

Yeah, they needed to talk. Preferably where no one would interrupt them to offer lemonade. "Tomorrow, then," Rafe said.

"Sounds good." Mac was staring at her, so she dug deep for something polite to say. "I look forward to it."

Rafe tilted his head down but kept his gaze locked on hers. "As do I."

"Say, Rafe, in two nights, I'll be at the Texas Cattleman's Club—we've got a meeting. If you're interested in setting down some roots locally, you could come with me."

Violet started choking. Somehow, the air had gotten

very sharp in her throat. She couldn't have heard that right—could she have? "What?"

Rafe inclined his head at Mac, but he spoke to Violet. "I have been considering branching out into the energy business, so naturally I sought out my old friend."

"Oh, naturally. That makes total sense." She tried to smile, but it must have looked more like teeth baring, because both men recoiled slightly.

Something didn't add up here. But her head was such a hot mess right now that she had no hope of figuring out what it was.

"I shall see you for dinner tomorrow night," Rafe said, and she didn't miss the particular timbre of his voice that seemed designed to send a thrill through her body. Then he turned, giving Mac a big smile that seemed less than sincere, Violet thought. "And I would be delighted to see this club of yours."

"Great," Mac said, clearly missing the forced smile. "It's a plan!"

Morning sickness was a lie. This was what Violet had concluded after a night and a day of suffering with a roiling stomach.

Of course, there was also the possibility that it was not morning sickness. A quick web search revealed that most people were only sick for the first three months, and Violet was safely in her fourth month. After all, she knew the exact date of conception.

Just thinking about that night in Ben's—Rafe's—arms again made her stomach turn. Frankly, she defied anyone to not have an upset stomach in a situation like this.

She stood in front of her meager closet in nothing but her panties and bra—her regular bra, not the black-with-white-embroidery number she'd been wearing when she met Rafe. This was a smooth white T-shirt bra. Not a danged thing sexy about it.

Because that's who she was—functional and dull and not terribly sexy. If Rafe thought she was going to show up for dinner tonight as V again, he had another think coming.

Besides, her one fancy cocktail dress—black with the lacy sleeves—well, it didn't exactly fit right now. She'd already tried it on and she couldn't get it zipped.

All those little changes her body had been experiencing—the slight weight gain, the nausea, the overwhelming urge to nap—she'd written off each and every little bump in the road as exhaustion or a bug or the changing of the seasons or stress or, hell, the phases of the moon. But now?

Not a bump in the road. A baby bump.

She had a plan. She had an appointment with an obstetrician in Holloway in two weeks. It was ridiculous that she felt she had to go to the next town over, but she hadn't exactly decided just yet on how she was going to tell Mac about this "bump in the road." She kind of had it in her mind that once she had a doctor's official… whatever, it would be easier to talk to Mac. But if she went to the local doctor in Royal, word might get back to Mac before she could gird her loins. So she was just buying a little time here.

And as for Rafe…okay, she was still working on that part of the plan. She'd done another quick internet search on his country, Al Qunfudhah. The Wikipedia article had stressed that, compared to some of the neighboring countries and kingdoms, women enjoyed a great deal of freedom in Al Qunfudhah, but the article had hit Violet funny. Why would anyone make such a big deal about women being able to drive as if it were some wondrous gift?

She did not know what Rafe intended to do. He really was, according to that same article, a sheikh. His brother ruled the country. His father had died a few years ago. But beyond that?

It had been bad enough when she'd been pregnant with some random stranger's baby. But a sheikh's baby?

She was getting ahead of herself. Dinner first. And that meant she needed to put on clothes.

She finally settled on one of her few dresses—the fanciest dress she'd owned, until she'd bought the black one on a whim. It was an olive-green cotton dress with tiny pink flowers printed on it, and it had a pink satin bow at the scoop neck. It was just a little bit girlie but also, due to the darker color, not so girlie. Plus, it was a forgiving cut and it still fit. She paired it with her jean jacket and her nice pair of brown boots, the ones with the pointed toe. She twisted her hair up and pinned it into place, but she decided against dangly earrings. This wasn't a date. This was a…negotiation, really.

That didn't stop her from putting on small hoops, as well as mascara and a little blush, though. Not enough that it looked like she was trying, but every little bit helped.

At least Mac wasn't here. If he saw her in any dress at all, he'd start asking questions. Outside of weddings and Easter services, she was not known for busting out the dresses.

She was debating the merits of her regular tinted lip balm versus actual lipstick when the doorbell rang. Crap. Violet started to hurry, but then thought better of it. She was not at Rafe's beck and call. She was pregnant. She would not hurry to accommodate him. He'd better get used to doing the accommodating around here. She slowly applied a light layer of a deep pink lipstick and then grabbed her jacket. She was cool, calm and collected. No reason to be nervous, right? Just dinner with the father of her child. Easy peasy.

But by the time she got downstairs, she was on shaky legs and it only got worse when she opened the door to find Rafe standing there, a devilish grin on his face and a single red rose in his hands. And then he took her in, her dress and her boots and her jacket, and she wished in that moment she'd tried a little harder to get the zipper up on her black dress.

"Ah," he said in a voice that sent a shiver through her. The voice was so unlike the way he'd spoken to her yesterday that she stared at him. This was the man she'd met in a bar. This was the man who'd taken her to bed.

"Hello," she said, feeling unsettled because it was so hard to reconcile this man with the one who'd sat in the living room yesterday and looked at her as if she were a deer and he were a wolf.

He still looked as though he wanted to devour her, but the difference was so startling that she was helpless to do anything but stand there, gaping.

He held out the rose. "A beautiful flower for a beautiful woman."

She couldn't help it: she wanted to kiss him again. She wanted to feel the way he'd made her feel, beautiful and sensual and desirable. But now that they knew who the other was, she didn't think chasing that little bit of happiness was the best idea. "Look—is this a date? What is this?"

There was that hardness in his expression again and she had to fight the urge to step back. She was *not* imagining that. "I would never force you to do something against your will, Violet. If you would like to go to dinner as friends, then we may do that. If you would like to consider this a more romantic evening..." His voice trailed off as his eyes warmed.

She took the rose and set it down on the foyer table. "The last time we had a romantic evening, things went wrong." Two-positive-pregnancy-tests wrong. "I think we should get a few things settled before we do anything else."

"Yes, that is a wise choice. It would be too easy to... well." She could be seeing things but he might have actually blushed. "Shall we? I made reservations at Claire's."

"Oh." Claire's was one of the nicest restaurants in town and she was wearing a jean jacket. Crap. She looked down at her outfit. "Maybe I should change?"

"You look beautiful," he said, stepping toward her. Before she could react, he had cupped her chin in his hand and lifted her face. "You were beautiful that night and you are beautiful now. And anyone who would deign to criticize you will face my wrath."

Wow, that was the sexiest-sounding threat she'd ever heard. Violet was speechless. Even if she could talk, she had no idea what might come out of her mouth. Something impulsive? Something stupid? Both?

Or, worse, would she tell him how much she'd missed him, how much she'd savored their night together?

Because it would be terrible for him to back her into this house and carry her up the stairs the way he'd carried her down the hall of his hotel. It would be awful if he laid her out on her own bed and did all those things he'd done before.

Yup. It would simply be the worst.

"Ah," he breathed, so close to her that she could have tilted her head just a little and brought her lips against his, "you asked me what this evening is about. But now I ask you—what is it you want this evening to be?"

Violet was used to dealing with men. She did a man's work, day in and day out. She dealt with cowboys and her brother, and didn't spend a hell of a lot of time in a beauty salon, gossiping with other women. She could more than hold her own when some jerk got it into his head that she, a delicate female, shouldn't be fixing fences or branding cattle or any of those manly things men liked to think they were the only ones capable of getting done. Men who decided they were alphas and she had to fall into line either got their metaphorical butts handed to them on a platter or a black eye as a souvenir of the experience.

So, really, Violet should not have felt this urge to give in to Rafe, to tell him that whatever he wanted, she wanted. But she was tempted. The masculinity coming off him was so strong, so potent, it was almost as if she could see the air shimmering around him, like heat off a highway.

All those men before—they'd been all talk. They had to tell people they were the boss because otherwise, no one else would know it. But Rafe? Jesus, he was in a different class. This was not just an alpha man, this was a man born to power, a man who breathed it as easily as he breathed air.

This was a sheikh. *Her* sheikh.

But just as she was about to succumb to his sheer machismo, she remembered their situation.

So she forced herself to lift her chin out of his grasp and she forced herself to stare into his eyes—dark and warm and waiting on her to say the word so he could strip her right out of her dress—and she said, "I want to figure out how we got here and what we're going to do next." Dang it all, her voice came out as something closer to sultry than businesslike.

Rafe heard it, too, and his lips curved into a knowing

smile. "Ah, yes. How we got here. I seem to recall carrying a beautiful, mysterious woman to my room and—"

"No, stop." Heat flushed her body, but she was not going to fall for him a second time. She had enough going on right now. "I mean more along the lines of what happened afterward. I'm pregnant. We need to be taking this seriously."

That worked. Rafe straightened and, sighing, nodded. "Would you like to discuss this over dinner or somewhere more private?"

Private was good. Private was great. But private also meant more of those smoldering looks and hot touches from this man and again, she was totally going to blame the hormones on this one, but she didn't know how strong she could be if she had to fend off those sorts of advances all evening long. "Dinner," she said decisively.

Rafe, to his credit, didn't use all of his innate power to overrule her, just as he hadn't coerced her into doing anything she hadn't wanted that night. Instead, with a nod of his head that veered closer to a bow of respect than anything else, he said, "Dinner, then."

Three

Rafe and Violet were shown to a secluded table tucked into a small alcove in the back of the restaurant. Perfect.

He needed this dinner to be in the public eye because he had little doubt that word of it would make its way back to Mac, and Rafe wanted everyone to see him acting like a gentleman. But he also needed to be hidden away enough that he and Violet could discuss things like pregnancy and plans without being overheard.

He held Violet's chair for her, which gave him the opportunity to admire her from the back. There'd been a moment earlier this evening when he'd wanted nothing more than to sweep her off her feet and carry her to a bedroom. Any bedroom would do. In this outfit, she was not the seductress V had been all those months ago, but she was also not the angry cowgirl who, just yesterday, had informed him she was carrying his child.

Yesterday, she had not been so very hard to resist,

between her shell-shocked appearance and her perhaps justifiable anger. But today?

As she sat, Rafe had to physically restrain himself from leaning down and pressing his lips against the exposed nape of her neck, right next to where a tendril of hair had escaped her updo and lay curled against her fair skin like an invitation.

He managed not to kiss her there, but he must have stood too still for too long, for Violet turned and looked up over her shoulder at him and said, "Yes?"

Rafe didn't answer immediately. He took his time circling the table and taking his seat. "I do not think I have told you how glad I am to see you again."

Violet notched an eyebrow at him. "Seriously? You didn't act all that glad yesterday."

"True. But I think that, given the surprising nature of our reunion, we can both be forgiven for being less than enthusiastic at first."

Her eyes narrowed and he got the feeling he'd said the wrong thing. "Oh, really?"

This called for a tactical retreat. A fast one. "Let us plan, as you have requested. How long have you been aware of your impending blessing?"

Because he needed to know that she was being honest— that not only was she expecting, but that it was his child. The four months between that evening and this one left plenty of time for her to have taken other lovers.

Her cheeks colored. "Well, since yesterday. I was in the process of peeing on a stick when Mac came to tell me you were in the living room."

Rafe coughed over her coarse language, which made her eyes narrow again. "I did not realize," he said. "Just… yesterday?"

"Yes." After a pause, she said, "I had been feeling a

little off for a while—super tired all the time, gaining a little weight. I had thought maybe I just had a stomach bug that was hanging on, but then my friend Clare started asking about how I was feeling and suggested..." She swallowed, staring at her water glass. "And I bought a test. A three-pack, just in case, you know?"

"I see," he said, although he was not entirely sure he did. "How many tests were positive?"

"Two. I didn't believe the first one. But two that said the same thing..." Her voice trailed off sadly. "I guess I was maybe a little rude yesterday, but I had gone from suddenly realizing I was pregnant and wondering how the heck I was ever going to find you and tell you, to walking into the living room and finding you. Except you weren't who you said you were."

"Yes," he said sympathetically. "I can see why that would have been a bit of a shock. It was quite unexpected to see you again."

She wrinkled her nose. "Why did you say your name was Ben that night?"

This was dangerous territory because the truth would endanger his scheme. So he turned her question back on her. "Why did you go by V?"

She did not answer immediately and then, just as she opened her mouth to respond, the server came up to take their orders. Rafe did not often drink. In fact, he had not drunk wine since that night. Perhaps that was why he had taken V to bed, because his inhibitions had been lowered.

But tonight, he decided he needed a glass of wine to get through this evening. Otherwise, he might overreact the way he had to Violet's announcement yesterday and if he enraged her again, it would put his whole scheme in danger of collapsing.

He did not know if Violet was his friend or his enemy.

What she was, at this point, was a former lover, and those relationships could go either way. But no matter how this played out, Rafe knew he needed to keep her close.

So he ordered a bottle of sauvignon blanc to accompany his filet mignon and her chicken dish. In the past several months, he had grown quite fond of Texas beef. Even the barbecue was delicious and quite unlike the way beef was prepared in his country.

But when he placed their orders, Violet narrowed those beautiful eyes at him again. It was only when the server was safely out of earshot that she leaned forward and said in a tense whisper, "I can't drink."

"Oh?"

"Because I'm pregnant?" she said, although it was clearly not a question. "I'm not supposed to drink." A look of panic flared over her face. "Do you know anything about pregnancy? About babies?"

Rafe rolled his hand. "Of course not. I do not have any children and, if I did, we would have nannies to care for them. That is how I was raised."

Had he thought this declaration would relieve her anxiety? If so, he had guessed wrong. The color drained out of her face and, if anything, she looked more worried than before. "Nannies? As in, plural? I didn't—I mean, that's not what I had been thinking for our child."

"Let us not get ahead of ourselves," he cautioned, because that look of terror on her face made him strangely uncomfortable. He should be reveling in her panic— thrilled, even, that he was striking such a blow against Mac's sister. This was revenge at its finest.

And yet, it wasn't. If her pleasure had once been his, her terror was also his. It was a weakness he did not like because weaknesses could be exploited.

"Okay," she said softly.

"Let us start at the beginning," he went on, more gently than he had planned to. But it worked because she took a deep breath and sat back in her chair, looking almost calm. "I did not realize who you were that night. And I assume, based on your statement earlier that you were wondering how you'd find me, you did not know who I was?"

"No, I didn't. No names. That was the deal." She cleared her throat and began to fiddle with her silverware, arranging the knife and the fork in perfect alignment. "I was V for the same reason I was out in Holloway instead of Royal. I wanted a night out where word wouldn't get back to Mac." She looked up and he could see in her eyes that she was pleading with him. "He wants what's best for me, I know that. But sometimes…he can be suffocating. I mean, he doesn't think this is a date because he asked you to keep an eye on me, didn't he?"

"This is true," Rafe confirmed.

She exhaled heavily. "That's how he is. Every man is either a threat to my innocence or a babysitter."

"But you have reached your maturity," Rafe noted. "You are not the same little sister he told me about when we were in university twelve years ago."

She snorted. "Try telling him that. He still treats me like I'm sixteen and lost without my parents. But I'm not. I'm a grown woman now and I'm capable of running half the family business and…okay, so getting pregnant wasn't my finest hour, but I can do this, Rafe."

Rafe thought this over as the wine was served. Violet asked for a Sprite instead. "I must ask—your innocence?"

"Lord," Violet said, rolling her eyes toward the ceiling, and Rafe couldn't tell if she was praying for strength or something else. "Fine. No, I was not a virgin. You?"

Rafe almost glared at her because this line of questioning was not something sheikhs had to endure. But as she watched him, he quickly realized that, to Violet, he was not primarily a sheikh. He was, first and foremost, a man to whom she would be forever tied. "No. And before you ask, I am not currently seeing anyone else. In fact, except for our evening together, I have been celibate for some time."

Her lips quirked into something that was almost a smile. "Celibate, huh?"

He shrugged, trying to keep it casual. "I have been busy. My brother is the sheikh of Al Qunfudhah and I run the shipping business owned by our family. While our sheikhdom was originally founded on oil, we have diversified and my shipping business now accounts for thirty percent of the gross domestic product."

"But celibate? You're a sheikh," she said, clearly puzzled. Then her gaze drifted over his face, his shoulders, and down his chest before she looked back at him. "And you're gorgeous."

Rafe felt his face warm. "So I have been told. But just because I could have any woman I want does not mean I should."

"And modest," she added in a mocking tone. But she smiled when she said it. "That's a refreshing attitude, I have to tell you. Most men would take whatever they could get."

"I am not 'most men.'"

"No," she agreed, her smile warming. "You're not."

Rafe was pleased. He should have been pleased because Violet was opening up to him and the more he drew her in, the more complete his revenge would be.

But that was not why he leaned forward and placed his hand on top of hers, stilling it in the middle of adjusting the precise placement of her soup spoon. "And you? Are you involved with anyone?"

"No," she said in a breathy whisper. "Most guys don't last too long before my brother scares them off."

"That must be frustrating."

She tried to shrug off both the sentiment and his hand and, given that they were in public, he had no choice but to sit back in his seat. "It is, but it's also a blessing—I guess. If they can't stand up to Mac, how could I expect them to stand next to me, you know?"

Rafe thought about this. He knew, without a shadow of a doubt, that standing against Mac would not be problematic. "Indeed."

Their meals arrived along with Violet's soda. She sipped at it gingerly and took small bites of her food. "Is it all right?" he asked, concerned. If she was expecting, shouldn't she be eating more?

"It's fine. I just—well, I've been dealing with morning sickness—which is a lie, by the way. My stomach's most upset in the evening. And for a lot of people, it ends after the third month, but I think it's actually getting worse."

This news was alarming. "Have you seen a doctor yet? Do you think everything is all right?"

She looked at him, trying not to smile and not quite succeeding. "I'm fine. According to the internet, this is all normal. I scheduled an appointment with a doctor in Holloway and the quickest they could get me in was in two weeks."

He set his knife and fork down a bit harder than he meant to, given how the beverages danced in their glasses and Violet's eyes widened. "That is not soon enough. I can have a private doctor here tomorrow—Friday at the latest."

"Rafe," she said, her soft Texas accent caressing

his name like a lover's hands. She'd said *Ben* that way, but not *Rafe*. Not like that. It was enough to make him pause as he typed in the password to his phone. "It's fine. There's no danger."

"I merely want what is best for you and the child," he said, his voice getting caught somewhere in the back of his throat. And he was surprised to realize how very much he meant it.

"Yeah," she said in that quiet voice, "about that. Okay, so I'm not seeing anyone and you're not either. Which doesn't mean that we're together."

"I would not make such presumptions," he assured her.

"It just means that, for once, there's one less complication to deal with."

"Agreed. And I would not be outside of bounds if I asked you to refrain from starting a relationship with anyone else while you are carrying my child, would I?"

What started out as a smile progressed into a full giggle. There was simply no other word for it. Violet McCallum was giggling at him. "Out of bounds. Not outside."

He should have been insulted that she was mocking him. What was it about this woman that made him not only accept her teasing, but crave it? "Ah, I see. Thank you. I shall remember 'out of bounds' in the future."

"No," she said, wiping a tear from her eye. "You are not out of bounds. Dating is a challenge in the best of times. Right now, I can't see how it'd be anything but impossible. I am not looking to start a relationship right now."

A new thought occurred to him as Violet settled down and sipped her soda. Rafe's original plan, once he had realized that Violet was V, was to use and discard Violet much as Mac had done to Nasira. That was the ultimate revenge, a sister's honor for a sister's honor.

But now that Rafe was spending more time with Violet, he wondered if he would actually be able to do that to her. She was, after all, carrying his child—if she could be believed. And Rafe desperately wanted to believe her.

What if, instead of treating Mac's beloved little sister as Mac himself had treated Nasira, Rafe instead just *took* Violet? Not a kidnapping—nothing so brutish as that—but Mac had dedicated the past twelve years of his life to protecting his sister. If Rafe were to marry the mother of his child and move her far away, would that not be avenging his family's honor—while preserving his own bloodline? Violet was already tired of Mac and his interference in her life. It would not be that difficult to turn her against her brother completely.

This was an idea that had much merit.

"That is good," he said, trying to keep his voice level. "We should come to an agreement upon what is best for the child."

He must not have kept his voice as level as he would have liked, for Violet's eyes widened. "That sounds…"

He put on his best smile, his American smile. He did not smile like this at home. He had no need for it. But here, in Texas, this situation required finesse. It was tempting to just tell her they would get married and that she would bear his child and live in Al Qunfudhah. If he were at home, that is all he would have to do.

But Violet was not one of his people, and he knew enough about her to know that any such broad proclamation would have the opposite effect. Violet would refuse and, as long as she was in Texas, she *could* continue to refuse him. That was her legal right in this country, he was reasonably sure.

He would ask Nolan, but his lawyer was no longer his lawyer and, at times like this, Rafe missed the man's counsel. He wished mightily that Nolan had not quit Rafe's employ because he had fallen for a local woman— a woman with another man's child, no less. It had been another betrayal, one that stung.

It did not matter. He had promised he would not force Violet to do something she did not wish to do and he would keep that promise, for the sake of his child if for no other reason.

No, what he needed to do was convince her that she wanted to marry him. It should not be difficult. They were attracted to each other and they already had electric chemistry together. All he had to do was push that electric attraction and make her love him.

In the back of his head, he heard the severe voice of his father berating him. There had never been a time when the sheikh had not told Rafe what a worthless son and worthless brother he was. His father had held Rafe personally responsible for the loss of Nasira's innocence and Rafe had been punished accordingly. He had not been allowed to finish his American university studies. He had not been allowed to live abroad. He had been forcibly returned to Al Qunfudhah and confined to the basement of the family compound like a dog that had to be broken. Nasira, at least, had escaped into a marriage that suited her. But not Rafe.

Much like his siblings, Rafe was supposed to have been married off to a bride of his father's choosing, the daughter of another warlord or royal. The marriage would further cement Al Qunfudhah's position in the Middle East, and a suitable bride would bring honor to the bin Saleed bloodlines.

But after Nasira had been compromised by the one man Rafe trusted with his very life, Rafe's father had refused to allow Rafe the escape of marriage. Nasira had been ruined, so their father had not cared when she had married an Englishman and left the country. For all intents and purposes, Nasira had been dead to the old sheikh. Rafe had not been so lucky. He had been stuck in a hell that was not entirely his own making. The only thought that had sustained him during those first years was that of exacting his revenge on Mac McCallum.

It had been a relief for all of them when his father had died.

Now, years after the man's death, Rafe could hear his ominous voice again. *A true sheikh does not play games. A true sheikh would not concern himself with the wants of a woman. A true sheikh would have already carried this woman back to Al Qunfudhah and put her in a harem.*

Not that the bin Saleeds had harems. They did not. But in times past, the sheikh would have kept many women as his concubines. It had always been Rafe's opinion that his father lamented this cultural loss more than anything else.

"You got quiet there," Violet said, pushing what was left of her meal around her plate.

"I was thinking," he said truthfully. "There is something of a cultural gap between us that we need to bridge. My child will be a bin Saleed and I would like him—"

"Or her," Violet interjected.

Rafe let a grin play over his mouth. "Or her," he amended, "to know our people and our ways."

Violet frowned slightly, as if he had once again said something out of place. "I was trying to do a little reading on your people. The article I read made it sound like Al Qunfundaha—"

Now it was his turn to correct her. "Al Qunfudhah."

"Yeah, I'm probably going to screw that up a few more times," she said, forcing a smile onto her face. "But—I mean, what I'm trying to say is, what I've read makes it sound like your country is trying to be progressive toward women and minority rights but…it's still not like it is here."

What was she talking about? Rafe gave her a look and she threw her hands up. "I'm not making sense, am I?"

"Not entirely." He followed this up with another warm smile. This time, it was not as forced. Perhaps the wine was loosening him up. "But you are concerned about your place and the place of our child in my country, no?"

"No—wait, I mean yes. That's exactly what I'm concerned about. I'm not this world traveler like you are. I've hardly left Texas. I was supposed to follow Mac and go to Harvard, but then my parents died and we had to run the business and…" She smiled again, and Rafe thought it looked like an apology. It was. "I'm sorry. I'm just trying to process everything that's happened and I'm hormonal and you're being wonderfu,l but I'm making a fool of myself—again—and it's still a lot."

He was being wonderful? He should not be pleased with this statement. But he was.

He leaned forward and cupped her face. Her eyes widened but she didn't pull away as she had earlier. Instead, she leaned into his touch. Her skin was soft as silk against his palm, but warmer. "Ah, I am the only fool here."

She looked up at him, her eyes wide and deep and beautiful. "You are?"

"I am." Dimly, he was aware he was leaning in, that her face—her lips—were getting closer. "I find I wish to give you anything your heart desires. Tell me, what is it you want?"

She looked down at her dish. "I like it here. This is my life. But I am so tired of living with Mac, you know?

There's a ranch to the north of us—the Wild Aces. The Double M is leasing it because our water supply got compromised in the tornado, but I wanted to buy it outright. It's a beautiful piece of land and the house on the property is almost a hundred years old—one of those grand old homes. I've always loved it." She looked up at him with much confidence in her eyes. Rafe was certain her bravado was not entirely honest. "If I'm going to have a family—and that does seem to be the plan—I'd love to have my own house, my own land."

"The Wild Aces, you say?" He said it as if he had never heard of such a place before but, in truth, he knew exactly where the property was. The owner had been reluctant to sell to Nolan in large part because she was leasing the water to the Double M. Unlike many of their neighbors, she already had a steady stream of secondary income and was not as tempted by Samson Oil's generous offer.

But the Wild Aces was key to his scheme. If he owned that land, he owned the Double M's water supply. And if he owned that, he owned Mac McCallum. His revenge would be complete and nothing could stop him.

Nothing except a beautiful woman who was carrying his child. "You wish to have this land as your own?"

"I tried to get Mac to buy it, but he always reacts to one of my ideas the same way he reacted back when we were kids—oh, isn't that cute, Violet's trying to think like a big girl!" she said in the high-pitched, nasal voice many Americans used when speaking to small children and animals. Then she rolled her eyes. "It's so frustrating. I have to come at him sideways. He'll at least consider any idea his assistant brings up, so I have to ask Andrea to ask Mac. If I bring it up, he shoots it down,

like I'm not smart enough to make wise business decisions on my own."

This was at odds with the way Mac had described
Violet's management of the Double M, but Rafe did not
show his confusion. "And if you had this land, you would
raise our child on it?"

He was very careful not to make it a promise, because
he was a man of his word and if he did something foolish
like promise Violet the Wild Aces, he would be honor
bound to keep that promise and that would mean all of
his work was for naught.

Besides, he had no intention of staying in Royal or
any part of Texas. And being Mac's neighbor? Out of the
question. Rafe had to convince Violet that she belonged
with him and that they belonged in Al Qunfudhah.

But making Violet think he would do something so
grand as buy her a ranch without actually promising to do
so—well, that was tailor-made to his scheme, wasn't it?

"I would love that," she said, her face lighting up with
joy.

So much joy, in fact, that Rafe was horrified to hear
himself say, "I will see what I can do." Which was not the
same as promising her the ranch. He had merely promised to investigate it. He was still operating with honor.

"Really?" Her eyes were wide and she was looking
at him with what he could only describe as adoration.
"You'd do that for me?"

He had lost control of the situation—of himself—
that much was clear. And it became clearer when he
said, "I would."

"Rafe…"

And he was powerless to do anything but lean forward, to bring himself closer to her, to see how she

looked at him. To be the man she saw, not the man he was. "Violet…"

"Will there be anything else?"

At the sound of the server's voice, Rafe shook himself back to his senses. Had he really been about to kiss Violet? In public? In the middle of this restaurant?

Yes. Yes, he had been. Which was not a part of the plan. He was here as a chaperone to Violet, not a seducer. "No, that will be all," he said, his voice harder than he meant it to be. The server left the bill and hurried off.

Rafe glanced at the bottle of wine—he had consumed perhaps two glasses, at most. This was the problem with abstaining from both women and wine for so long. His tolerance for both was quite low.

"Come," he said, paying the bill with cash. "I shall take you home."

Four

What she would *give* to be able to read this man. That was what occupied Violet's thoughts as she rode in Rafe's very nice sports car. Because he shifted between hard and soft and cold and warm and—yeah, she was going to say it—scary and sexy so fast that she was getting whiplash just watching him.

"This land is quite beautiful," he said conversationally.

Right now was a perfect example. Minutes ago, he'd leaned over and touched her face and told her he wanted to give her whatever she wanted—no, that wasn't right. He wanted to give her *her heart's desires*.

That was the man she'd spent the night with four months ago—sensual and sexy and whispering sweet nothings to her.

But then the waitress had interrupted them—which was good because if word got back to Mac that Rafe had been on the verge of kissing her in public, things would have gotten ugly fast—and all that sensual goodness had flipped off like a switch and suddenly Violet was sitting with an ice-cold man who had terrified the waitress with a few words and a hard look.

Violet didn't know which version of Rafe was in this car with her. But she did know that she vastly preferred the sexy sheikh to the domineering one.

The silence in this car—this very, very nice car that was probably a Lamborghini or a Maserati or some other exclusive brand of vehicle that was expensive and rare and designed to throw other men into a jealous rage— was deafening. She didn't belong here. Not in this fancy sports car, not with a sheikh.

She was just Violet McCallum. Nothing really that special here. She got crap on her boots every day and she was pregnant. Big freaking whoop.

Except…except when Rafe looked at her and spoke to her with that voice of sunshine. She almost felt as if she could do anything she wanted. *Be* anyone she wanted. Which was exactly how she'd gotten into this fine mess in the first place.

He wanted to give her whatever she wanted. Well, what did she want? She knew the answer to that—she wanted the same kind of happy family for her child that she'd grown up with. She'd told him about the Wild Aces—but did she want him there with her? Did she want to go to his country—even if she went as a member of the royal family?

It was all too much, too soon. She wasn't going to do anything stupid like marry Rafe. First things first. Soon she'd be a mother. Which would be wonderful, she had to admit. Now that she and Rafe were getting a few things straight, she was starting to feel more excited about this new adventure. She'd loved her mother—both of her parents, of course, but Violet and her mother had always had a special relationship.

"Now it is you who is silent," Rafe said and thank God, he didn't sound regal about it. "What is the saying? A dollar for your thoughts?"

She grinned, feeling some of her tension melting. "A penny. But you were close!"

Rafe tilted his head in her direction. "I assure you, your thoughts are worth far more than a penny. Do not undervalue yourself."

Coming from anyone else, it would have sounded like a load of manure. And maybe it still was. But the way the words rolled off Rafe's tongue...

"I was just thinking of my mother."

"Ah," he said softly, but he didn't barge into the silence as Mac did every single time Violet had tried to talk about their parents.

Her brother had always had some statement ready to go about how her grief was normal and they were going to get through this together and she was going to be *just fine*. Then, before she could get a danged word in edgewise, he'd pull her into a bear hug and tell her how proud he was of her and how he was going to take care of her and then he'd hurry out of the room, as if she didn't know his eyes were watering. As if they weren't allowed to have feelings in front of each other.

Instead of telling her how she was supposed to feel, Rafe waited for her to talk.

How weird was that?

"I was sixteen when the plane crashed," she said simply. "But I assume you know that?"

"Yes," he replied.

"I mean, I still miss them, but it's been twelve years. Bad things happen and people move on. Or we try," she added, thinking of Mac's overbearing version of love. "But this pregnancy—I was just thinking how much I'd like my mom to be here for this. If that makes sense." If anyone could talk Violet through an unplanned pregnancy, it'd have been Mom.

They'd had their share of fights—Violet had been a teenager, after all. But she'd always known her mom would be there for her. Until she wasn't.

"You were close to your mother?"

What an odd question. "Isn't everyone?"

"Ah," Rafe said, and the regretful tone in his voice made Violet glance over at him. He looked pained—not as though she'd kicked him in the shins, but a deeper pain that spoke of a lifetime of loneliness.

"Oh, right," she hurried to say, remembering what he'd said earlier. "Nannies. I'm sorry."

"I will, of course, defer to you," he said in a not-at-all seductive voice. He sounded more like a businessman and she didn't particularly like it. "If you wish to be more involved, then by all means, I will make that happen."

"How?"

"Excuse me?"

"How?" she repeated. "Look, my life is here. I run the family ranch. I know you told Mac you'd go with him to the meeting at the Texas Cattleman's Club because you were thinking of relocating but honestly? I don't know what your plans are. I don't know why you're here now and I don't know when you'll be leaving. I don't…" Her words trailed off and she suddenly felt like a teenager again, so sure of everything when, in reality, she knew very little. "I don't want to move to the Middle East. Even if your country is progressive."

"I see." Rafe pulled into the driveway of the Double

M. "I can safely say that my plans have recently been revised."

"You want this baby? I mean…" she quickly corrected, because all of a sudden an image of Rafe carrying her child onto an airplane while Violet stood in the terminal, watching them go—powerless to stop them—oh, God. No. "What I'm saying is, you want me to have this baby? Because I want to keep the baby."

"The child will be a bin Saleed. Of course I want you to have the baby," he said with a significant edge to his voice. "I will, of course, need independent verification that I am the father."

"What?" The word rushed out of her like that one time when a bucking calf had caught her in the gut with a hoof. "You don't believe me?"

"I do believe you," he said, the honey back in his voice. "We were together and I can only guess that, at some point, the condoms failed. I did use them because I gave you my word I would. But clearly, something went wrong and my brother, the sheikh of Al Qunfudhah—he will not be satisfied taking the word of an American woman. If the child is to have all the rights and privileges of the bin Saleed family, we must prove that I am the legitimate father."

"Oh." She hadn't considered that. She'd been so focused on what Mac would do when he found out that she hadn't considered Rafe's family obligations.

A family of sheikhs at that. "What will your brother do? When he finds out?"

Rafe slid a sideways smile at her. It was not terribly reassuring. "Calm yourself, my dear. Fareed is not my father and I am no longer powerless. He will most likely insist that the child be cared for and raised to honor our traditions, but," he added with what could only be described as a twinkle in his eye, "I do not think this will spark an international incident."

There was something there, something just below the surface of what he'd said that tugged at her consciousness. But she had a more pressing question she needed answered before she tried to unpack what he'd really meant. "Will you want custody?"

That's what she said. What she meant was, *Will you take my baby away from me?*

Rafe pulled up next to the ranch house and parked before answering. "Ah, yes. We must work out an agreement. This is why my plans have changed. I do not want to be away from my flesh and blood for too long."

So, yes, it was an odd way to phrase it. But the sentiment was what she needed to hear. He wouldn't take her baby and disappear in the middle of a different continent. "Okay, good. I know you said you were interested in expanding into energy—are you thinking of living in Royal? At least part of the time?"

He regarded her for what felt like an eternity. "I am thinking of many things," he said, his voice low. So low, in fact, that she had to lean forward to catch all of his words. "But if I stay here—even part of the time—we would have to have an...understanding, if you will."

"What kind of understanding?"

His gaze traced her face and she felt her cheeks warm. "I know we have agreed not to see other people while you are expecting, but I do not know how I could be around you and see you with another man. It would cut me," he added, placing his hand over his heart.

"Oh," she breathed. What was he saying? If he stayed in Royal, he'd expect them to be a couple? Together? "You mean...what do you mean?" Because if he meant that they were to live together—or get married—she didn't know how she was supposed to feel about that. Panic? Yeah, that was an option. Panic was always a good backup. She was barely coping with being pregnant— how was she supposed to throw a marriage into that mix?

But then another thought occurred to her. Because the one physical thing she hadn't gotten out of Rafe the first time they were together was waking up in his arms. That wouldn't be a hardship, falling asleep with Rafe by her side every night and waking up with him every morning.

Rafe's gaze was burning her in the best way possible. There was so much going on in his eyes—which was at least something to go off, as he was otherwise completely unreadable. Then he reached over and picked up her hand, leaning into her space to press his lips against the back of it. "I have not stopped thinking of you since our night of passion, Violet. I cannot tell you how many times I almost went searching for you. You…" He looked up at her, his voice raw. "You have graced my dreams and haunted my waking hours, a ghost of a woman I could see, but not touch. And it has been torture. The sweetest torture I've ever known."

Oh, my. Was he serious? God, how she wanted to believe he was, that their night together had been more than a one-night stand. "I thought of you, too. I…I still have your note."

He hadn't let her hand go. He was still holding it close to his mouth, where she could feel the warmth of his breath against her skin. Oh, that smile—all of her panic about the future dimmed in the light of his smile. God, Rafe was such a handsome man. "I am pleased to hear that. But I had made a promise to you—one night, no names—and I was honor bound to keep my promise. So I did not search for you. I did not try. I accepted my fate— that one night with my beautiful, mysterious V was all

I would get. And now I have this opportunity to know you—not just as V, but as a woman. As Violet. This is a second chance. I would be a fool to let this—to let you—slip through my fingers a second time."

"Oh, Rafe." She had never heard such a romantic speech in her life—and she'd certainly never been the subject of one. "Is that what you want? A real relationship?"

He turned her hand over and kissed her palm. "I want many things. But you are the one who carries the child. It is you who must be satisfied first." When he looked at her again, she felt as if she were falling into his eyes and she might never want to climb back out. "I think it is time for you to tell me what *you* want."

The air between them suddenly felt very warm, and she had a flashback to the way he'd bought her a drink at the bar at the Holloway Inn and then joined her. At some point between the first drink and the third, he'd leaned over and said those exact words to her. *I think it is time for you to tell me what you want.*

And what she'd wanted then was to be swept off her feet. She'd wanted to have fun; she'd wanted to feel beautiful and special. She'd wanted to be wanted because she was Violet, not because of her brother or her family name or her ranch. Just her.

And she said to him now what she'd said to him on that night. "Why don't we talk about this someplace else?"

One dark eyebrow notched up. "Are you inviting me in?"

She looked back at the dark ranch house. Mac was gone for the next two nights. She knew it. Rafe knew it. She had the run of the place.

"We're not done talking," she said. Although she

wasn't speaking loudly, her voice filled the small space between them.

"Indeed, we are not."

Violet started to undo her seat belt but before she could get her door open, Rafe was out of the car and hurrying around to her side. "Allow me," he said in that honey-and-sunshine voice as he opened her door and extended a hand to her.

She let him pull her to her feet, but he didn't let go of her. Only a few inches separated them. Despite the spring breeze, Violet could feel the warmth of his chest.

"This is just to talk," she heard herself say. "This doesn't mean anything else." Which was possibly the most pointless thing she'd ever said in the history of talking because of course Rafe's coming into her empty home meant something. It might even mean everything.

"I would make no such presumptions," he readily agreed. But his words were directly at odds with the way his thumb was now stroking over her knuckles. She was reading him now, loud and clear. "So tell me what it is you want. What are your dreams for the future? What part do you want me to play?"

"You're being too perfect," she told him. Because it was the truth. Everything he was saying—everything he was doing—was exactly what she needed, when she needed it.

He tilted his head to one side. "Has no one ever asked you what you want?"

"Oh, sure. What do I want for dinner, whether we should castrate the calves today or tomorrow, that sort of thing."

Well, that was some award-winning conversation right there. But Rafe was caressing her hand and looking down at her exactly the way he had when he'd pinned her in an elevator four months ago. Yeah, her mouth and her brain weren't exactly operating on the same wavelength at this point. Heat poured through her body, loosening her limbs as she melted into him, and all she wanted was for him to pick her up and carry her into that house.

"A crime, to be certain," Rafe murmured, cupping her face with his other hand. "I am asking you now. Tell me what you want."

He lifted her face and gazed deeply into her eyes and she was right where she'd been four months ago. She shouldn't do this. She shouldn't have done it last time. She should push Rafe back and cross her legs at the ankle and try, for once, to be the prim and proper sort of girl who was absolutely not swayed by a beautiful man with a beautiful voice.

Rafe was not going to let her go, though. He leaned in closer, so close she felt his breath on her lips, and said, "Because what you want is what I want."

And she didn't want to push him away any more than she had wanted to push him away in the elevator. In his arms, all those months ago, she hadn't been Mac's little sister and she hadn't yet been a future mother. For one glorious night, she'd been who she wanted to be.

It wasn't wrong to be that—to be herself. She could do that with Rafe—and only Rafe.

"Kiss me," she said.

His lips curved into a smile—one that warmed her from the inside out. "Are you sure? Because when it comes to you, I do not know if one kiss will ever be enough."

"I'm sure," she whispered, making her decision. "So kiss me."

Five

Judging from the way Violet threw her arms around his neck and pulled him down roughly into a searing kiss, this was all going perfectly according to his revised scheme. Making Violet fall in love with him would be an easy task. All he had to give her was exactly what she wanted—and, as far as he could tell, what she wanted was a passionate lover and freedom from her overbearing brother. Those were two requirements he could meet easily.

But any thought of revenge went flying out the window as Violet's tongue traced his lips. He had not lied to her—his thoughts had rarely been far from her and to suddenly find her back in his arms was almost more than he could bear.

"Violet," he groaned against the delicate skin of her neck. "Are you quite sure?"

"I want you," she said, her voice practically a growl, which sent an uncharacteristic shiver down his spine.

This was why he had not been able to put Violet from his thoughts—she made him do things that were out of character, such as kiss his enemy's sister because he wanted to do nothing but feel her body against his.

He lifted her against his straining erection and began carrying her toward her house. Every step drove him against her soft heat and there were no thoughts of revenge. There was only this burning need to bury himself in Violet's body, to make her cry out with pleasure.

When they got to the ranch house, he set her down and turned her around so she could open the door. And if she couldn't get it open, he'd break it down. Anything to get inside. But as she fumbled with her keys, the situation grew dire. "Violet," he groaned.

She finally managed to get the door open and then they were safely inside, away from any accidental witnesses. He pulled her back against him, letting her feel what she did to him. "Your room," he whispered against the base of her neck.

"This way." She pulled away and he let her go just enough that she could lead him up the stairs, but he couldn't keep his hands off of her. He traced the outline of her bottom through the thin cotton of her dress, which made her giggle.

When she cleared the top stair, and Rafe was certain they wouldn't tumble to their doom, he gathered her in his arms. All at once she was kissing him and he was kissing her back and pushing her jacket off her shoulders. Dimly, he thought he should be going more slowly, taking his time to savor her—her taste, the small noises she made when he did something she liked.

But he could not take his time. He needed her right now.

He tried to back her toward the right, where an open

door beckoned with the promise of a bed, but she corrected their course and led him left. Then her fingers began to work at the buttons on his shirt as she walked backward into her room.

At least he assumed it was her room. It was dominated by an enormous canopy bed with four tall posts holding up a drape of sheer light blue fabric.

"Kiss me," she said again, grabbing his face in her hands and pulling it down. "Please, Rafe, please."

"I cannot refuse you," he said, carrying her toward the bed. In one swift motion, he peeled her dress off and she was nearly bare before him.

Her hands stilled against his chest. "I've changed. Since that night." She said it as if she were afraid of what his reaction to her body would be.

But Rafe was staring down at the luscious curves. "If anything, you have changed for the better." He lifted her hands away from his chest and guided her back onto the bed until she lay before him. He could not be so thoughtless as to take her roughly, not when she was already nervous. Their first time, she had shared the wine with him and there had been no hesitation. But this time, he knew he needed to reassure her.

"Oh, Rafe," she moaned as he kissed down her neck to the valley between her breasts. Yes, he thought that perhaps they were slightly larger—fuller, he decided as he cupped them in his hands and slid his thumbs over the cups of the bra, right where her nipples should be.

"Take it off," she whispered, threading her hands through his hair and lifting herself up off the bed.

"Your wish is my command," he said, reaching behind her back and deftly removing her bra.

"If anyone else said that to me, I'd think they were full of it," she giggled. "But when you say it…"

"It is because I mean it." He lowered his head to her breast, letting his tongue work her nipple into a stiff peak. "I cannot help myself," he murmured against her skin as he moved to her other breast. "When I'm with you..."

"I know. I feel the same way. I—oh!" That was as far as she got before Rafe kissed his way lower, pulling her innocent white panties down until she was completely exposed to him.

After that, there were no more words to be said because he was busy bringing her to the heights of pleasure with his mouth and she was busy moaning and writhing under his touch. She kept her hands buried in his hair, guiding him in the direction that she most needed him to go.

Their first time, she had climaxed when he slipped his finger inside her. He would hate for her to think that he had forgotten what she liked best, so he repeated the move.

"Rafe!" she cried out as he lapped at her body, her inner muscles tightening around his finger.

And he could not wait anymore, not for her. He could not even do this properly and remove all of his clothing. He unbuckled his pants and grabbed the condom out of his back pocket and somehow managed to get the thing rolled on before he was against her, covering her body with his as he thrust into her warmth.

"Violet," he groaned, wanting to hold himself back—to hold himself apart from her because that was the smart thing to do, the calculated move that would contain whatever emotional havoc she wreaked. But he couldn't, not when she looked up at him with eyes that were glazed with desire, with want—with need.

"Yes," she said in a hoarse whisper as she tried to undo the remaining buttons on his shirt. "Yes, Rafe—*yes.*"

He grabbed her hands and held them against his chest, where his heart beat beyond his control. Then he began to move into her and she began to rise against him, meeting him with her own desire, thrust for thrust.

Mine, he tried to say over and over, but his words had left him and all he could do was hold himself together until she cried out in the throes of her pleasure. When she did, when her body tightened down on him, he gave up all hope of holding himself together. He leaned forward and drove into her harder, deeper, until his climax drained him so completely that he fell forward onto her.

They lay there, breathing hard, their bodies still intertwined. Violet worked her hands free and wrapped her arms around his waist, holding him to her. "Wow, Rafe. Just…wow."

He managed to roll to one side. "A compliment, I hope?"

"Oh, yeah." She giggled again, a light sound of joy.

It made him want to laugh with her. He grinned down at her, tracing the curve of her cheek with the tip of his finger. "When we marry, it will always be like this, I think. You and I…"

His words trailed off because her mouth had twisted off to one side and her eyes had narrowed. "Violet?"

Silently, she sat up, and then stood and walked away from him. Far too late, Rafe realized what he'd said.

Married.

He had overplayed his hand.

Violet sat on the toilet, trying to figure out what had just happened. She found herself reciting the known facts.

Fact: She was pregnant.

Fact: Rafe was the father.

Fact: Sex with Rafe was, unbelievably, even better when she was stone-cold sober than when she'd been mildly buzzed.

Fact: He had just said, "When we marry."

Her brain had gotten stuck on that last word. Okay, Rafe was kind of perfect—sweet words in that liquid sunshine accent of his, hot touches that melted her. He'd even promised to look into the Wild Aces for her. Throw in the sex…

This did not mean she wanted to get married. Even if that vision of her waking up in Rafe's arms every single morning was a warm and fuzzy vision. Even if that meant raising her child—their child—together as a family. Even if…

She dropped her head in her hands, trying to get her muddled thoughts back into some semblance of order.

Not that she got far. Just back to fact number four.

When we marry. It was a statement of fact, a foregone conclusion. There was no uncertainty, no will-she-or-won't-she. Just a fact.

"Violet?"

Oh, God—the concern in Rafe's voice on the other side of the bathroom door was not making this any better.

"Are you well?" he went on.

Violet opened her mouth but closed it again when she realized she had absolutely no idea what she should say. This was all too much, too soon. A mere twenty-eight hours ago, she'd been the same woman she'd always been, one with a fond memory of their rendezvous to keep her warm on cold winter nights. There hadn't been any thought of babies and there hadn't been any thought of marriages.

She put her head between her knees. She didn't want to throw up if he was listening.

"Violet," he said in a whisper that was almost plaintive. "I did not mean…it was just…open this door, please."

"I'm—just a minute," she said, looking around. She didn't even have a robe hanging on the back of the door. Unless she wanted to wrap herself in the shower curtain, she was out of luck. She would feel much better if she could at least cover herself. "Could you go downstairs and get me a Sprite?"

"Ah…yes? Yes," he said again, sounding more sure of himself, and she had to wonder if anyone had ever asked him to fetch anything before. "I can do that for you."

"Thanks."

She exhaled when she heard the familiar creak of the floorboards as he left. Slowly, she opened her door and peeked into her room. Her clothing was scattered all over the place, but aside from that, there was no sign Rafe had been here. That's right. She'd been so turned on, she hadn't even gotten him undressed.

Okay, first things first—she got dressed. She slid her nightgown on and then pulled her light cotton robe over it. Second, she decided to go downstairs. For one thing, the odds of Rafe locating a soda on his first attempt were pretty slim. But more important, it just felt as if it'd be easier to tell him they weren't getting married anytime in the immediate future if they weren't in a bedroom that still smelled of sex.

She padded downstairs to find Rafe staring into the fridge, his eyebrows locked in a confused expression. "Ah," he said in relief when she walked in. "I can't find the Sprite."

"Here," she said, reaching around his body—of course he didn't get out of the way—and plucking the can from behind the eggs.

"Of course," he chuckled. "How did I not see that?"

"I have no idea," she said, trying to be calm.

He shut the fridge door and turned to face her. "Are you well?" he asked, resting his hand on her hip and gently drawing her toward him. His shirt was untucked but still half buttoned.

"Better," she said.

He gave her a hesitant smile, then lifted her free hand up and placed it on his heart. "Your pleasure is my pleasure," he said, pressing her fingers to his chest. "And your pain is my pain. I would never wish to upset you. And if I have done so, I regret that."

"Okay," she said, clutching the cold soda can as hard as she could because the sensation was keeping her grounded in the here and now, preventing her from being swept away by his voice and words again. "Let's get this straight, then, so there's no confusion. It's not really a good idea to tell a pregnant woman that she *will* marry you, okay?"

His eyes crinkled. "That is not done here, I take it?" Then he lifted his hand and kissed her palm again.

She smiled in spite of herself. So he'd freaked her out. But he was also capable of calming her down in a way she couldn't help but be grateful for. "Not really, no."

"Then I shall do better. But there is something between us that makes me lose my head." His eyes twinkled. "Among other things."

She could feel her concerns melting away, but she didn't want him to sweep her off her feet—again—unless things were crystal clear between them. "I don't want to get married, Rafe. I mean, I don't want to say I'll never marry you because, truthfully? You're right. There is something here. But I'm still trying to wrap my head around being pregnant. So can we just agree that we won't talk of marriage for a while?"

He pivoted and leaned back against the fridge, pulling her with him. "I understand, I really do. But you must also understand that it would bring dishonor upon my family and myself if my child were born out of wedlock."

She shouldn't be surprised by this. And honestly, she wasn't. That didn't mean it was what she wanted to hear seconds after one of the best orgasms of her life. She sagged against his chest, the soda can still in her hands. "Do we—will we have to get married? Is that what happens in your country?"

He paused. "In my family…we do not have a choice. We are married for power. Love…"

She closed her eyes. Love. They had talked about a lot of things, but love wasn't one of them.

Rafe cleared his throat. He began to rub his hands up and down her back. "It is something to consider, yes. But I have made you this promise, Violet, and I will continue to make it. I will not force you to do something you do not wish to do."

"Okay." But honestly, did she know him well enough to believe he'd keep that promise? She had no reason not to trust him. Aside from the fact that he'd used a different name when they met, everything he'd done had been up front. "Will you stay in Royal?"

"I will be here for the foreseeable future," he replied. "But I do not think I could leave Al Qunfudhah permanently. It is my home."

She nodded. "I understand."

He leaned her back and stared down into her eyes. "But I would like to suggest that we spend the time getting to know each other. Perhaps," he said gently, pressing his lips to the top of her head for a quick kiss, "it would not be such a bad thing, you and I."

"Perhaps not," she tentatively agreed.

"This is not something I can decide for you," he went on. She wanted to burrow deeper into his chest and feel his honeyed voice surround her. "You must decide that for yourself," he went on. "All I can do is show you that I will be good for you and that I will be a good father to our child."

She leaned back to look at him. "Do you always know the right thing to say?"

That made him laugh. "Based on what happened earlier, I would say the answer is no." He brushed her hair out of her face. "May I stay the night with you?"

She tried to look stern, but didn't think she was successful. "You're not going to propose marriage, are you?"

"Ah, I have many other things I would rather be doing with you," he replied, lowering his mouth to hers.

She sighed into the kiss. Everyone was always telling her what she should do, what was best. When was the last time someone had told her to make the decision?

So Rafe thought they should be married. And given the way he was devouring her, maybe they could be good together. Better than they already were.

She wasn't going to figure it out if she didn't spend some time with him, right? "Stay," she whispered against his skin.

"And tomorrow? I want to know more about you, Violet. I want to know what you do and how you live. I only have a few old stories your brother told me many years ago."

"Mac's out of town for a couple of days. If you wanted, you could ride with me tomorrow." She leaned back and looked at him. "You can ride, can't you?"

That smile—cool and confident, almost cocky. "I can. My family maintains a reputable stable of Arabians, as well as other horses. And I would love to ride with you. But I have some business to attend to in the morning," he said with a rueful smile. "You see, I have made a beautiful woman a promise that I would look into something for her and I would hate to disappoint her."

"Oh." All that languid heat flowed through her again and she thought of how good this could be. "I could meet you here after lunch? We're working calves in the morning, so all we'll have to do in the afternoon is herd the cattle to different pasture."

Something in his smile softened as he touched his fingertips to her cheek. "Mac told me you were a brilliant manager. I would love to see you in your elements, as they say."

She giggled. "In my element," she corrected and he laughed with her.

Oh, yeah, they could be good together. Usually, men said they wanted to "take her away from all this" or some such stupid claptrap, as if she only worked cattle because she had to. As if all she really wanted was to stay home, barefoot and pregnant and baking cakes. As if they could not believe that she, Violet McCallum, might actually be managing this ranch because she wanted to.

And now? Here she was with Rafe, a man who literally could take her away from all of this—away to some distant desert, as the wife of a sheikh—and what did he want? To ride with her. To see her work.

To keep his promise to her.

"Come," he said, taking her hand and kissing it. "The morning is still a long way off."

Six

Rafe, come on in.

Rafe smiled as he pulled the note off the front door and put it in his pocket. Then he walked into Mac McCallum's house as if he owned it.

Soon, he just might.

He had procured the services of a local Realtor, who knew Lulu Clilmer, owner of the Wild Aces. The Realtor had informed Rafe that the Wild Aces, with its 750 acres of prime grazing land, was worth approximately one million dollars but wasn't for sale at this moment in time. She even knew about Mac's leasing arrangements to access the natural springs on the Aces' land.

Rafe had instructed the woman with bouffant blond hair and too-white teeth to offer Mrs. Clilmer two million dollars cash, payable within three days.

Rafe wasn't sure the Realtor trusted him completely.

It would have been better to have a local like Nolan make the offer for Samson Oil instead of Rafe but he was not going to be deterred. And the Realtor was properly motivated by the prospect of an unexpected commission. The only snag was that she wouldn't be able to forward the offer to the owner until tomorrow because she had another closing today.

Which was fine. That gave Rafe another day or so to woo Violet. He made sure he had the box in his pocket—his other errand this morning had been to stop by a local jeweler's. Wedding Violet was almost as important as obtaining the Wild Aces.

In truth, he would prefer to have Violet's promise to wed him secured before he moved on the Wild Aces. His scheme had already undergone enough revisions recently. He did not want to further endanger it.

He stopped inside the front door and listened. Was she upstairs? That was where he had left her early this morning with a kiss and a promise to see her at noon.

Ah, humming—it was coming from the kitchen. And he smelled the scent of fried chicken.

Rafe silently padded down the hall. And there was Violet, assembling their meal. Something in his chest loosened at the sight of her. Her hair was pulled back into a low ponytail. Well-worn blue jeans hugged her hips. She was in her stocking feet and looked smaller, more delicate, than she did when she was in her boots. There was a peace around her that was almost infectious. Most any idiot could see that she was quite happy here.

A series of inexplicable urges hit him. He wanted to be the one that made her that happy. He wanted to walk up behind her and wrap his arms around her waist and kiss her neck and hold her. He wanted…he wanted things he could not put into words, but he could feel, pulling him toward her.

Last night, he had said things that he did not necessarily believe would come to pass. After he exacted his revenge, he had no plans to return to Royal, much less live here. He had told Violet he was considering those options without really meaning it. It had not been a lie—he could consider all his options without choosing to stay.

But this? Coming home at lunch to find her in the kitchen, preparing food? There was something so profoundly normal about it—normal by American standards, at least—that it made him think back to when he was still friends with her brother.

Rafe's childhood had not been one filled with carefree days and playmates. He'd been put through a rigorous education so that he would live up to the iron-fisted expectations of Hassad bin Saleed. And when he failed to meet those expectations, punishment was…harsh. Rafe had quickly learned that failure was not an option, not if he wanted to survive childhood. And although he was unable to save Fareed from any such suffering, Rafe did his best to shield his younger siblings from his father's wrath.

So when Rafe was allowed to venture out of Al Qunfudhah to America to attend Harvard, the freedom had been both sweet and somehow terrifying. It was only when Mac had befriended him that Rafe had started to understand this new world and its expectations.

And those stories… Mac had spoken so often of this house, of the people in it. How his mother still cooked dinner for them all and at least four nights a week, they were expected to sit down as a family and talk. That was such a foreign concept to Rafe. He had only dined with his father during state dinners, when he was expected to follow protocol and remain silent. To imagine a place where the mother and father openly expressed love not only for each other but also their children? Where they did things as a family?

Rafe had so desperately wanted to believe that such a world existed, that such a family existed. And he might have had a better chance to achieve that kind of harmony in his own family if he had not asked Mac to keep an eye on Nasira when she came to visit at Harvard.

In truth, Rafe had thought often of Mac's tales of his home in Royal. But he had not allowed himself to feel this unwanted nostalgia for a dream he had once nurtured and lost.

Not until now. Not until Violet.

Perhaps, if Mac had not betrayed him, this would have been Rafe's destiny. Before the incident with Nasira, they had even made plans for Rafe to make the journey to Royal, Texas, on holiday from university. Rafe would stay with Mac and meet all the people he had heard so many warm stories about—including Violet.

She would have still been in her teens. Would he have felt the beginnings of an attraction for her then? Or would she have just been Mac's irritating little sister?

He would never know. And that thought ate at him.

He slipped up behind her, slid his arms around her waist and leaned down to press his lips to the side of her neck.

"Oh!" She startled in his arms and twisted to look at him. "Rafe! I didn't hear you come in."

"I did not mean to frighten you," he said, pressing another kiss against her lips. "The meal smells delicious."

She grinned and, turning back to her preparations, leaned against him. His hands slid down and cradled her belly. "I hope fried chicken is okay," she said, lifting the chicken out and setting it on a plate to cool. On the counter were a pan of biscuits and a fresh salad.

"It will be wonderful. Here." He pulled the jeweler's box out of his pocket and opened it in front of her. "I brought you something."

She gasped as she saw the pendant. "Rafe—I didn't— I mean—*wow*."

"This is, as I understand, an American tradition. If I have calculated correctly, our child will be born in August," he said, pointing to the light green peridot stone at the center of the pendant. "And you were born in September, correct? So the sapphire is for you."

"And the yellow?"

"Citrine for November, when I was born. It is all set in eighteen-carat white gold."

Violet touched the pendant with a tentative finger. The three stones were strung together with the sapphire first, the peridot in the middle and the citrine on the end. "It's beautiful," she exhaled. "But you really shouldn't have."

"That is nonsense," he said, removing the necklace and opening the clasp. He draped it around her neck and fastened it. "You are carrying my child, a gift I could never hope to match. This is but a small token. There." He adjusted the chain so the pendant lay against her collarbone. "It suits your beauty," he said seriously.

"Rafe," she said and he heard hesitation in her voice. "Is this—I mean, is this really happening? Do you honestly think we can make this work? Or make something work? I mean…well, I don't know what I mean. It's all happening so fast and I just don't want…" Her voice trailed off.

"I take it this was not in your plans?"

"No," she said, giving him a weak smile over her shoulder while she touched the necklace.

"Nor was any of this in my plans. But I think perhaps…" He sighed and let his hands rest against the gentle curve of her stomach again. Within grew his child. No, this was not in his plans at all. "Perhaps this was what was supposed to happen."

"Really?" She didn't bother to conceal her doubt. "You think destiny's been waiting for us to have a one-night stand, huh?"

He grinned against her neck. "Do you know that, at one point, your brother and I had made plans for me to accompany him home on break? We would have met then."

She twisted in his arms, her brow wrinkled. "I would have been, what—fifteen? Sixteen?"

"And I only twenty. Do not mistake me. I would not have made any untoward attempts on you then. I can be very patient. Of that you have no idea. I can wait years for something I want."

Odd, that. He had waited years for revenge on Mac. But what if, instead, he had merely been biding his time for this moment with Violet?

But then, what if he had come home with Mac and Violet had caught his eye twelve years ago? His father would have no sooner allowed a young Rafe to give his heart to a common American girl than he would have allowed Rafe to degrade the bin Saleed name by donning shiny pants and joining a singing group. And if Hassad bin Saleed had discovered that Rafe harbored tender feelings for Violet then, he would have had Rafe married off to the daughter of a political ally within the month and Rafe would never have had the chance to follow his own heart.

But Mac's betrayal had come first.

"I was a different person then," she said, her voice low. "My parents were still alive and I was just a kid, really."

"As was I." She dropped her gaze. He still had her in his arms, but he felt the distance between them. "What is it?"

"Rafe, what happened between you and Mac?"

He supposed that he should appreciate the fact that Violet had phrased it as a question and not an accusation. "It does not signify," he said, his jaw tight. The effort of keeping his voice light was more taxing than he might have anticipated. "What happened was a lifetime ago. I was, as you said, a different person then. It has no bearing on us at this moment."

"But…"

Rafe did the only reasonable thing he could, given the situation. He kissed Violet, hard. She stood stiffly in his arms for a moment but then relaxed into him.

"It does not signify," he repeated, tucking her against his chest. "I am not here for your brother. I am here for you. I am here for our child. Our family."

Odder still that as he said it, it did not feel like a lie.

It felt very much like the truth.

He was surprised to see her eyes fill with unshed tears. "Are you unwell?" he asked hurriedly.

"I'm fine," she said, giving him a watery smile and dabbing at her eyes with the cuff of her sleeve. "It's just the hormones. Okay. Whoo." She exhaled heavily and put on a brighter smile for him. "There."

He was not entirely convinced. "I can still have a private doctor here inside of twenty-four hours."

She waved this suggestion away. "I'm fine," she repeated. "It's just that you have no idea how refreshing it is to know that you don't care about going through my brother."

Ah, yes. His scheme. The one that now hinged on convincing this woman that she wanted to spend the rest of her life with him so that she would turn her back on Mac. He wanted to be impressed that it was going so smoothly, but as she blotted at another stray tear, that was not the emotion that welled in his chest.

"In my country, it is customary to ask permission of a woman's father before you court her," he told her. "Or, if her father is not available, her oldest living male relative."

Violet held her breath. "Oh? You're not going to do that now, are you? I haven't even told Mac about my pregnancy or anything."

"No," he assured her, wrapping his arms around her again and pulling her against his chest. "You forget something."

"What's that?"

"We are not in my country."

Her head lifted and this time, her smile was not forced. "We're not, are we?"

"Not even close. So," he said, cupping her cheek in his hand. "Let us eat this delicious meal and then you can show me what you do. For our child will be a bin Saleed and there are expectations that go along with that, but that child will also be a McCallum and it would be best if they knew how to manage a ranch, would it not?"

Her expression should not make him feel this, well, *good*. Nothing about her except for the sex should make him feel this good. But everything about her did. "It would. And tonight? Will you stay again?"

"I will not leave your side until you tell me to go."

"Good," she said. "Then I want you to stay."

Watching Rafe mount Two Bit was a thing of beauty and quite possibly a joy forever. Good heavens, that man in a pair of blue jeans was the stuff of dreams, Violet decided. She wouldn't have guessed that Rafe could so easily slip into the role of a cowboy but, appearance-wise, he was doing just that. The jeans and the button-down shirt with mother-of-pearl buttons looked completely natural on his athletic form. Hell, he even pulled the hat off with plenty of grit to spare.

Who would have guessed that her sheikh was hiding a cowboy underneath those dark eyes and smoldering gazes? It was hard to disguise the imperial lift of his chin, though.

"Two Bit," he said as he got his seat in the Western saddle. He took up the reins in two hands, but caught himself and switched both to one hand. "That is a quarter of a dollar, correct?"

"Yup. But he's also a quarter horse. All my cutting horses are," Violet said, swinging up onto Skipper's back. Rafe's eyes got wide. "Oh, come on. I'm only a little bit pregnant. Skipper's a good old mare and I've been riding her for years. Trust me, there's nothing dangerous about this. In three or four months, maybe. But I have no plans to ride hell-for-leather today."

"All right," he said doubtfully. "Where are we going?"

"We've been working calves," she explained, gathering Skipper's reins and heading toward the northwest pasture. "We castrate them, brand them and vaccinate them all at one time. But we do that in the morning, when the sun's low and it's still cool. Puts less stress on the animal. So now, we're going to move the calves and the cows from the pasture where we worked them this morning to a different pasture and then round up another group and shuffle them in so they'll be ready to be worked tomorrow morning."

As she talked, she kept a close eye on Rafe's face.

What would he think of her after *that* little lecture? Because thus far, he'd mostly only seen her in dresses at hotels and restaurants. But that wasn't who she really was.

This—crap on her boots, wearing blue jeans and half chaps that covered her thighs—this was who she was.

Could he handle it? Or would his vision of his beautiful, mysterious V be destroyed by a whole lot of cows?

"I gather that being a ranch manager is a hands-on job," he said without wincing at the word *castrate*.

Which was impressive. Most of the men around here—men who castrated plenty of calves on their own—got a look of dread on their faces when Violet said the word out loud.

"It is," she agreed.

"What will you do when you are no longer able to—what is the phrase? Saddle up and ride?"

She shot him a smile. "Good! I've got a good crew. I'll have to hire a few more hands and my crew leader, Dale, will have to take on a bit more responsibility." It wasn't going to be easy to back away from her position like that, but at a certain point when her belly just got too big, she was going to have to accept reality. "We have a Gator, a minitruck I can use to get out into the pastures."

"And when the baby comes?" His tone was not judgmental, nor was he issuing any sort of edicts. Thank heavens for that.

She laughed, but she didn't miss the way it sounded nervous to her own ears. "I'm still working on that. I've only been aware of this pregnancy for a couple of days."

"Ah, yes. I am sorry. One day at a time, correct?"

"Correct."

He was silent for a while and they rode on. Violet pointed out land features as they went. "That's our spring and over there? Those empty concrete pads? That's where our water tanks were," she said. "The tornado ripped our tanks right off their moorings like they were empty pop cans."

"But you could have replaced the tanks, yes?"

"We did. But the spring got messed up. We're not sure what happened—before the tornado, the spring was fine and we had water reserves in abundance. But after the tornado, the cows refused to drink the water and our reserves were gone. Mac thought maybe some fracking that had been happening to our east had something to do with it, but we're not sure."

"But you have water now, correct?"

"Yup. Our tanks are now up on the property line dividing the Double M and the Wild Aces. The Aces has a bunch of springs, including one not that far from the property line. It's the only reason Mac agreed to leasing the Wild Aces—for the water."

Rafe thought this over for a while. "Why did he not allow you to buy the land? You obviously want it."

Violet sighed so heavily that Skipper's ears swiveled back. She leaned forward to pat the horse's neck in reassurance. "I don't know." Rafe turned in his saddle to give her a look. "No, really, I don't. I don't know if he thinks I'm incapable of being on my own or if he just feels more in control of the world if I'm under the same roof. He wasn't here when our parents died and I'm not sure he's ever forgiven himself for it."

"So he did not make a wise business decision because…something might happen to you?" Rafe sounded genuinely confused by this.

"As best I can guess." Rafe was staring at her as if he understood the words, but the meaning was lost on him. "What? Didn't your family try to protect you?"

"Ah," Rafe said in a way that Violet was pretty sure

meant no. "I believe the whole reason my father had children—aside from Fareed, who is the ruler—was to use them to make 'wise business decisions,' as you have said."

Use? Had he really just said *use* like that, like it was this common thing? Sure, her parents expected her and Mac to do their fair share of chores around the ranch, starting when she was three and had the job of making sure the horses' water buckets in the barn were full, but that wasn't the same kind of expectation as being used for business-related purposes. "Really? Didn't your parents love you?"

"My mother, I am sure, felt affection toward us."

Now it was Violet's turn to stare. "'Felt affection'? Didn't she ever tell you she loved you?"

Rafe was silent for far too long and she wasn't sure if the conversation was over or not. Maybe this cultural divide was bigger than she'd thought?

But then Rafe said, "Love is a weakness and weaknesses can be used against you," in such a way that a chill ran down her spine.

"That sounds…awful."

"It was quite normal for us. It is not until you get out into the world and see how other people live that you begin to question your upbringing."

"I never got out into the world," she said quietly. "I've never left home."

"But you will. You will always have a place in Al Qunfudhah as the mother of a royal child."

Another shudder ran through her. Was this what awaited her in this far-off desert country? A royal life with a man who had been raised to believe that showing love—or even affection—to a baby was a weakness?

But how did that mesh with the man who whispered

sweet words in that liquid-honey voice of his, who brought her an expensive necklace symbolizing their birthdays and the future birthday of their baby? A man who had promised he'd look into the Wild Aces for her?

Was that love?

Or was it a wise business decision?

"It was not until I went to Harvard that I saw things could be different," Rafe went on, missing her stunned silence. "I was quite unsure how to understand your brother's closeness to his family, to you."

And then there was that—that unspoken event involving Rafe, his sister and Mac that had destroyed the two men's friendship. Earlier in the kitchen, Rafe had spoken of that time as if it were his fondest memory. It was obvious that Rafe had considered Mac a brother then.

But there were other instances when the mention of Mac's name brought a hard edge to Rafe's eyes—a hardness that Violet couldn't overlook. And she had to wonder what, exactly, Rafe thought of her brother now.

"Were you close to your brothers and sisters growing up?" she asked in a careful tone.

"I did try to protect the younger ones." He gave her a rueful smile. "On that, your brother and I agreed." He turned his gaze away. "To a point."

"And you're not going to tell me what happened? Does it somehow not 'signify'?"

Rafe attempted a careless shrug but, unlike the hat and boots, he couldn't pull it off. She got the feeling that *careless* wasn't in his vocabulary. "In the end, it was for the best. Nasira was promised to a warlord much older than she and, once she was ruined, the warlord released her from her obligations. After that, my father no longer cared what she did, so she was able to leave Al Qunfud-hah and marry a man more to her liking."

Ruined. That was, hands down, the ugliest word Violet had ever heard. And Rafe had said it so easily, as if he now thought less of his sister for what she'd done with Mac.

Was that it? Mac and Nasira had taken a liking to each other and Rafe disapproved because he believed Mac had ruined his sister?

Doubt flickered through her mind. This thing with Rafe was happening so fast—was the attraction between them real or was there something else going on here?

"I'm happy for her," she managed to get out in a tight voice. "I'd love to meet her sometime."

"I shall arrange it. But I do not know if she will come to Texas. She resides in England with her husband. They are quite happy, I believe."

They were silent for a bit longer as they approached the pasture where her cows and calves were anxious to begin the trip back out to the wide-open spaces. "Would it be possible to ride out to this other ranch, the Wild Aces, after we are done here? I would love for you to show it to me."

"Yeah."

Rafe looked out over the spring Texas landscape and sighed. There was something in his face—something that looked more relaxed than she'd seen him yet. "It is your dream, is it not?"

"It is." Violet nudged Skipper into a trot. "So let's get moving."

Seven

Violet's workers greeted her warmly and they all tipped their hats to Rafe. No one questioned her statement that Rafe was an old friend of Mac's visiting. And, Rafe noted, no one questioned her skills.

One of the workers swung open a gate and the calves came hurrying out. Rafe watched with interest as the larger cows and smaller calves all paired off. The noise was something new to him. They did not exactly have herds of cattle wandering around Al Qunfudhah. Camels, yes. Arabian horses, yes. Cattle? No.

"Rafe," Violet called. "To your left—we've got a straggler!"

Rafe twisted in his saddle and saw a cow leaving the group as it was herded north. The animal was moving at a good pace and the distance between it and the rest of the cows was quickly growing.

"What should I do?" he called back. He did not miss

the way several of the cowboys laughed under their breath at him.

Embarrassment burned at his ears, but he kept his attention on Violet. "Try to get in front of the cow," she called back. "I'll be right there."

Rafe touched his heels to the horse's side. He may not know the best way to retrieve a wayward cow, but he would be damned if he allowed this beast to outrun him on horseback.

Two Bit leaped into a flat-out run. Rafe held the reins awkwardly in one hand, but the horse responded to his heels wonderfully. Rafe gave the animal his head and trusted his footing.

Behind him, he heard a loud whoop, but he did not know if it was Violet or one of the men who had laughed at him.

Rafe smiled as he leaned over Two Bit's neck. The wind ripped his hat from his head, but he didn't give it a moment's thought.

Oh, how he loved to ride. His father had kept a stable of prizewinning Arabian horses and expected his children to ride and ride well. Anything less than expert horsemanship would have brought shame upon the bin Saleed house.

Rafe's daily rides were the time of his greatest joys, for then, he was free.

Just as he felt free now. The wind ripped at his clothes as he urged Two Bit to go faster. They shot past the stray cow and then, using only his knees, Rafe got Two Bit turned back. The horse stopped and spun, startling the cow to such a degree that the animal froze.

They all stood there, Rafe and Two Bit and the cow, as if none of them were sure what to do next. He had done as Violet had told him—he had gotten ahead of the cow and the animal had stopped. But now what?

Out of nowhere, a looped rope sailed through the air and landed around the neck of the cow. "Gotcha," Violet said, trotting up.

"You roped that cow in one shot? I am impressed," Rafe said, watching as Violet tied the other end of the rope around the horn of her Western saddle and began to pull the stubborn cow back to the herd.

She shot him a smile. "Get up, Bossy," she snapped at the cow, who reluctantly began to move.

When the cow was safely back with its brethren and she had removed her rope, one of the other cowboys rode up to Rafe and said, "Oowee, man—that was some fancy riding! Didn't expect that from a city slicker—no offense."

He looked at the man with a bemused smile. "None taken. I normally ride Arabians, but this is quite a mount." He leaned forward and patted the horse's neck as he glanced at Violet. "I believe Two Bit is worth far more than twenty-five cents."

Everyone laughed at that—but this time, they weren't laughing at Rafe. And he once again had that out-of-time experience where this whole thing could have easily happened twelve years ago, except with Mac by his side instead of Violet.

He was glad, however, that it was Violet by his side now.

"I trained him myself," Violet said as they spread out along the vast herd of cattle to keep any more from wandering off.

"He rode beautifully. I have not spent much time on other horses besides my own—but it was wonderful."

"Cowboy," Violet said, giving him a look that heated

his blood, "any time you want to come back and ride hell for leather, you just let me know."

It was some hours later, with the sun already setting, when Violet said farewell to her workers. The cowboys all departed, but Violet and Rafe stayed out in the pastures on horseback, riding farther away from the Double M.

"You are quite good at this," Rafe said. They were speaking softly. With dusk closing in around them, the sky lighting up in golds and reds like a tapestry woven of the finest silk, Rafe felt as if the world had been made just for them.

"You say that like you're surprised," she teased, a wide smile on her face.

"I would not have guessed that my mysterious, beautiful V could rope and ride half so good as you do."

"Does this mean you're going to stop worrying about me riding a horse?"

"I shall certainly worry less," he promised. "But no, I do not think I can stop worrying about you."

She seemed to consider this. "Will you be able to come to the appointment with me? It's in twelve days. I think I'll be able to hear a heartbeat."

"I would not miss such a chance. But," he added as they began to climb a low rise, "we must consider beyond that."

Even in the rosy evening light, he saw the color drain from her face. "I don't even know where to begin. Can we wait? Until after the appointment? I just feel like if I have a doctor's seal of approval and everything's okay, it'll be easier to decide what to do next."

"We can wait," he promised her. It was a sincere promise because Rafe had no desire to upset her. But it also played into his scheme nicely. The longer Violet with-held this secret from Mac, the more the betrayal would sting when Violet accompanied Rafe to Al Qunfudhah.

But as soon as he had that thought, a sense of discom-fort overtook Rafe. After spending the afternoon working and riding with Violet on her well-trained horses, he was having a great deal of difficulty picturing her ensconced in his royal home in Al Qunfudhah, with miles of sand surrounding her instead of a sea of waving grass. She seemed as much a part of this land as the grass and sky. It felt wrong, somehow, to take her away from her home. It would be like caging a wild horse and breaking its spirit.

Could he really do that to her? It went against his every urge to protect her and their child.

What muddled his thinking was that she genuinely appeared to care for him in a way that no one else ever had. What if he never found another woman who felt this way about him? What if, by breaking Violet's spirit, he destroyed his last—his only—chance for happiness?

He shook those thoughts from his head. He was not destined for happiness. The past few days with Violet had been nothing but a…a diversion. A pleasant one, to be sure, but a diversion nonetheless. The only wrong he had to concern himself with here was avenging the wrongs done to his family honor. That was all that mattered.

"Here," she said, breaking him out of his reverie as they crested the hill. She reined her mount to a halt. "That," she said, sweeping her hand out over the vista before them, "is the Wild Aces."

Rafe had, of course, seen a few pictures of it. But the beauty of the land, bathed in the glow of the sunset, took his breath away. He could see how the land differed from the Double M—the trees were larger and more grouped and the grasses were a deeper green, especially around the springs that dotted the land. "It is lovely," he said.

"Down there," she said, pointing south, "those are our tanks. And then there? To the north? That's the house."

Rafe looked in the direction she was pointing and saw a grand old home standing in a grove of tall trees. Clusters of yellow rosebushes crowded around the building's foundation; even at this distance, Rafe could see the blooms. A long drive led away from the house and that, too, had trees planted along it. The home seemed as much a part of the land as everything else.

"I love this place," Violet said with a satisfied sigh. "The house needs to be updated, though. Lulu—that's the current owner—has lived there for close to forty years and she's getting on in age. Renovations haven't exactly been on her radar. Plus, she smokes—a lot—so I'd want the whole house cleaned inside and out before I raise a kid there."

A twinge of an unfamiliar emotion took hold of Rafe so suddenly that he had to rub at a spot in his chest that began physically aching. He needed the Wild Aces to complete his revenge on Mac but...

It would not just hurt Mac, what he was doing. It would hurt Violet, too.

Nonsense, he tried to tell himself. First off, Violet would be joining him in Al Qunfudhah—that was the plan, and he would not allow his sentimental feelings for her to change that plan.

The necklace had merely been the first of such gifts. The day after tomorrow, he would bring her a bracelet of diamonds and rubies and then, a ring—diamond, as required by American tradition. If he were still at home, he would not wait a day to bring her jewels, but Violet had shown enough hesitation over their plan that Rafe did not want to rush her too much. More than he had to, anyway.

And besides, once Rafe had the Wild Aces and had broken Mac, well—Rafe would still have the Wild Aces. And he would also have the Double M. There was nothing that prevented him from keeping the land for Violet, just so long as Mac did not benefit from the arrangement.

This realization made the pain in his chest ease. One way or the other, the Wild Aces would be Violet's. Then she would no longer have to rely on her brother's permission to do anything.

"It will be perfect," he told her in all sincerity. And it would be.

All it required was a little more patience.

Patience was, at this exact moment, something Rafe had in perilously short supply. The last thing he wanted to be doing right now was attending some meeting at some club under false pretenses of perhaps joining the club at some point in the undefined future. He had no intention of settling down in Royal, Texas.

Or at least, he hadn't until two days ago.

He wanted to be back with Violet, and the strength of this feeling was worrisome. He had spent two nights in Violet's arms, in her bed—sharing her body and her dreams. That he had been forced to give that up only because Mac returned from his business trip did not improve Rafe's mood.

Violet was pregnant with *his* child. He felt reasonably certain of that, as certain as a man could feel without blood tests. She had agreed that, at the doctor's appointment, they would get the test that confirmed what they already knew—for Fareed and for Mac.

It bothered Rafe that they both needed to operate in

such a manner to prove to their older brothers beyond a shadow of a doubt that the child was theirs. Rafe had vowed to never again be in a position where Mac held sway over him, and yet now Rafe was sitting next to Mac, pretending as if this situation did not bother him in the least.

The Realtor had been in contact today. She would be making an offer on the Wild Aces in the morning. It was the last piece of the puzzle Rafe had been slowly assembling over the past six months, and he was eager to have it in place.

Violet wanted the ranch not only for land or water but because that was where she wanted to make her home. That was where she wanted to raise their child.

With him?

He was still unclear on that. He had foolhardily mentioned marriage while his head had still been clouded with passion on their second night together—and what a mistake that had been. For a man who was actively trying to convince her to choose him over her brother, it was clear that telling Violet what to do would always be a mistake.

No, if he wanted Violet to abandon Mac, he had to convince her that was what she wanted. And to do that…

Rafe had not often awoken with a woman in his arms. But that was exactly the position he had found himself in the previous two mornings when sleep had left him. He had been on his back and Violet had been curled on her side against him.

It should have felt wrong. Or odd, at the very least. But with Violet exhaling her warm breath against his chest, her breasts pressed against his side, Rafe had felt an unexpected calm. It was almost as if she belonged there.

That feeling had only gotten stronger as he had awoken her with a kiss. With more than one kiss, in fact. He had lost count.

It felt as if a sandstorm had been unleashed upon him and he had no way to protect himself. The facts as he knew them spun faster and faster around his mind until he was dizzy and raw.

"...Started admitting women a couple of years ago," Mac was saying as they drove toward the dim lights of Royal. "It's not the same club my father joined, but I don't have a problem with that."

"Is Violet a member?" Rafe asked. What he needed right now was additional information. He wanted to be absolutely certain that Violet was exactly as she said she was. He could not bear the thought that somehow, the McCallum siblings were working together against him.

The trick was to extract the information without arousing Mac's suspicions. It was possible, however. One of the more applicable lessons his father had taught him was to keep your friends close and your enemies closer. And if your enemy still thought of himself as a friend, well, it made things that much easier.

Right now, all Rafe knew of Violet was a collection of disparate facts that did not necessarily add up. Violet was Mac's baby sister, the one he had worried about, the young girl who'd gotten into all sorts of scrapes and hijinks, forever driving their parents to distraction.

She was a cowgirl who trained horses for cutting and roped cattle and pined for a place of her own.

But Violet was also his V, beautiful and passionate, the rare woman who had made Rafe break his long stretch of celibacy. She was the woman who had haunted the edge of his dreams for months now. The woman who had made him consider breaking his promise of one night, no strings, and having Nolan, his lawyer, look into finding her.

And she was the woman, soft and tousled with sleep but still capable of bringing him the greatest of pleasure, who had cried out his name in the morning. She was the woman whose rounded belly contained his child growing within.

The thought of Nolan was a source of pain and Rafe welcomed it. Anything to break his thoughts from Violet. He had come so far, he could not let this...this infatuation with her destroy his scheme.

Nolan had been his friend, his trusted second here in America as Rafe set the wheels of his plan into motion. But Nolan had turned on Rafe just as Mac had all those years ago—Nolan had found a woman and decided that love was more important.

Not that what Mac and Nasira had had was love. Even Rafe understood how lust could drive a man to do things far outside his normal character. But Nasira...

Rafe struggled to remember what his sister had said to him at the time, in hidden whispers on the long trip back to Al Qunfudhah. She had not wanted to marry the man their father had chosen for her—a much older man, a tribal warlord with a reputation for cruelty who had children nearly as old as Nasira herself. She had not wanted to be forced into a marriage. She had wanted to choose. And she was sorry—deeply sorry—that Rafe had been hurt, but his friend had been a better choice than the warlord.

Which brought Rafe's whirling sandstorm of thoughts right back to Violet. Was what she wanted so very different from what Nasira had gone to great lengths to get? The right to choose her husband?

This thought troubled him. It troubled him greatly.

"She hasn't really been interested in joining," Mac was saying. "And truthfully, I haven't really encouraged her. I know what some of those guys are like. They're fine for kicking back and having a beer with in the evening, but I don't want them around my baby sister. They're not good enough for her, you know?"

"You are very protective of her," Rafe said.

"I just don't want anything bad to happen to her, you know? After our parents…" Mac cleared his throat.

Rafe would not allow himself to think fondly of Violet. He would absolutely not allow his baser instincts to override everything else. Instead, he would focus on his reason for being here—avenging his family honor. Nasira. Oh, yes. Rafe was going to make this man pay and pay dearly. How could he sit there and wax poetic about protecting his own flesh and blood after having so callously used Rafe's sister?

"So she does not date among the men from your club?" Mac looked at him sideways and Rafe knew he was treading on dangerous ground. "You did ask me to keep an eye on her. If she is dating someone of whom you approve, I would not want to interfere in that relationship. That is not how things work in my country."

He let the words "in my country" hang in the air. Once, he had tried to explain his culture in general and his family structure in particular to his American friends but it was more difficult than bridging the language divide.

Compared to many other Middle Eastern countries, Al Qunfudhah had an extremely liberal view of women's rights. Women could drive and hold jobs and they had the right to refuse a suitor—well, commoners did, anyway. That had not been true of Nasira or any of the sheikh's children—at least, not under Hassad bin Saleed. His brother Fareed was changing those rules, as well.

But the cultural requirement that a man ask permission of a woman's father or brother before a date in all circumstances did not sit well with most Americans. Perhaps that was one of the reasons Rafe and Mac had been such good friends so quickly—Mac, better than anyone else Rafe had met at Harvard, had understood the impulse to protect sisters.

If Mac believed that Rafe's questions were about Mac's approval or disapproval of his sister's dating, not an effort to ascertain whether or not she engaged with many gentlemen friends, well, that only made Rafe look better. He was supporting his friend's right to rule his family as he saw fit.

"No, no—she doesn't date much. I haven't met the man worthy of her, frankly, and I don't want her wasting her time on losers who are only after one thing."

Well. That certainly lent credence to Violet's claim that in the last year she had only been with Rafe.

This what she was hiding from, the night they spent together. Rafe remembered asking why she was just V— was it family or lovers? And she had not answered the question.

He knew now. She was hiding from family. From the very man Rafe was honor bound to destroy.

This certainly put an interesting twist on things.

Rafe never would have guessed when he made this trip to America that he would be eager to attend a doctor's appointment. His father had never stooped so low as to concern himself with the health of the mother of his children. But Rafe was not his father, thank heavens.

Eleven more days until the appointment, where he

hoped to hear his child's heartbeat, felt a very long time off.

"Here we are," Mac said, pulling up outside a long, low building with immaculate landscaping. "The Texas Cattleman's Club—it missed the worst of the tornado we had last year."

"Mac!" Rafe spun to see a cowboy waving at Mac through the open doors of the clubhouse. "Good to see you, man."

"Hey, Chance. Chance, this is an old friend of mine, Rafe bin Saleed. Rafe, Chance McDaniel."

Rafe shook hands and the two men talked about Chance's new daughter. Rafe looked at pictures of a small, wrinkly baby with rather more interest than he might have otherwise. Was this in his future, a baby like this? "What age?" he asked Chance. He had no experience with babies or even children, for that matter. When his siblings had been younger, they had had nannies and nurses and Rafe had only seen them briefly in the evening, when all the children were brought together and presented for their father's inspection.

"Four months. God, Gabriella's just a natural. I didn't think I could love her more," he said, his gaze fastened on the next picture, which was of a beautiful dark-haired woman holding the baby, who was now wearing a frilly pink dress. "You have any kids, Rafe?"

"Ah, no." He swallowed, uncharacteristically nervous. Until several days ago, there had been no possibility of him having children.

Chance snorted in a good-natured way. "They change everything, kids." He clapped Mac on the back. "I keep telling this guy to settle down, but he's too busy!"

For the first time, the possibility of being a father—outside of wedlock, no less—hit Rafe as a real thing and not just a countermove in his scheme. What would his family think if they found out that Rafe had impregnated Violet? He honestly did not know. His father would have done horrible things in the name of the family honor. Being forced to marry Violet would have been a blessing, compared to what Hassad bin Saleed might have done. But Fareed was a different man and a different ruler.

Still, if Rafe did not marry Violet, he would bring dishonor onto the family, and Fareed would not let that stand.

"Rafe here's thinking about relocating to Royal," Mac said after they had looked at the many pictures of the little girl. "I invited him to a meeting—if he buys some land, he'd be a good member."

"Great," Chance said. Rafe noticed that other men and a few women were all moving back into a larger room. "Oh, shoot—we're late. Come on."

They joined the rest of the group. Mac introduced Rafe around and Rafe shook many hands. Normally, he would be collecting information on each member, examining their connections to Mac. He did recognize several names as people from whom his front corporation, Samson Oil, had purchased land.

But he had trouble focusing because his mind kept returning back to the questions he had yet to answer.

"Case Baxter," a man said, giving Rafe's hand a vigorous shake. "I'll be running the meeting tonight, so if you have any questions, just let me know, okay?"

Rafe nodded and made polite noises of agreement, but his thoughts turned right back to Violet. How could he get her to leave this place with him without breaking her spirit? That was quite a problem—one for which he did not yet have an answer.

"This is my friend Rafiq bin Saleed, a sheikh from

Al Qunfudhah," Mac said to the group. Rafe snapped to attention at the mention of his name. "He's looking to get into the energy business and he might relocate here to Royal. I think it'd be great if we could welcome him into the club!"

There were murmurs, some of approval and some of disapproval. Rafe remembered his American manners and nodded and smiled as warmly as he could while the sandstorm of his mind continued to whirl around winning Violet McCallum.

That would be the ultimate revenge, would it not? First Rafe would destroy Mac's beloved ranch and then his beloved town and then Rafe would marry Mac's beloved sister and whisk her away to Al Qunfudhah, where…

Where Rafe would take her to bed every night. Where her pleasure would be his pleasure.

A voice cut through his reverie. "Rafiq, huh?"

Rafe turned to see a man he did not know standing near the front of the room. His arms were crossed and he looked defensive. More than defensive—he looked dangerous.

This was a challenge, and challenges had to be met head-on. Rafe stood. In times like this, his first instinct was always to do as his father had taught him—rule by force. But Americans were a different breed and Rafe had learned it was best to come at them from the side. "My friends call me Rafe," he said in the congenial tone that worked best with Americans. "And you are?"

"Kyle Wade," the man said stiffly. "Why don't you tell them who you really are?"

Rafe froze. That was the kind of statement that started off badly and only got worse.

Mac interceded on his behalf. "Hey, Kyle—I've

known Rafe since college. We're old friends. He is who he says he is, so maybe ease off a bit on my guest?"

Kyle didn't ease off. Instead, eyes narrowed, he said, "Oh? So you know that Rafiq bin Saleed is the man behind Samson Oil—the company that has been buying up land all around town?" A collective gasp went up from the other members. "Care to explain yourself there, Rafiq? Why have you been buying up property for months?"

Rafe was not the kind of man who panicked. Panicking was a waste of energy that was better spent fixing a situation. Years of enduring Hassad's rages had schooled him well in keeping his features calm and his breathing regular. He resolved to be like the stone that felt nothing.

But if he were capable of panic, he might be feeling it right now. Because suddenly, one huge part of his scheme had exploded in his face, and the feeling of being sucked into a swirling sandstorm was that much stronger. If he were not careful, he would be buried up to his neck in his own lies.

Mac turned to him, confusion and suspicion on his face. At least at the moment, the confusion was winning. "Rafe? Is that true?"

No, he was not panicking. He was a bin Saleed. If anything, he was furious at this Kyle Wade for potentially undermining his plan. Kyle would soon learn not to cross him.

He would, however, prefer not to have any more disruptions to his scheme *today*.

He waved his hand in dismissal and made an effort to look casual. The key to escaping this situation with the bulk of his scheme intact was to play up the cultural differences. "As I said, I'm looking to get into the energy business. Is this not how it is done in this country? Do you not buy land for the exploration of mineral rights?"

"None of that land has any oil left on it," shouted a man from the back of the room. "Why do you think we sold it to Samson Oil? Only a fool would think they're going to strike oil on property we've tapped out!"

Rafe gritted his teeth. He was no fool, and to imply it was to risk his wrath. This was why he had not revealed himself to Mac and the town earlier. Too late, he saw that he should have remained in the shadows until his plans were complete, until he had the Wild Aces and Mac's water had been cut off completely.

In that respect, the man was right—Rafe was a fool who had shown his hand too soon. It would be his last mistake, that was for certain.

But then Mac put his hand on Rafe's shoulder. Odd, really, how that vestigial touch of friendship could still be reassuring. "Listen," Mac said loudly over the growing buzz of people talking. "I vouch for Rafe. They do things differently in Al Qunfudhah, where he's from. If he says he's exploring mineral rights, then…" Mac looked at him and despite this very public declaration of support, Rafe could see the distrust in Mac's eyes. But then a harder expression came over his face and he turned back to the crowd. "Then I believe him," he finished.

Ah, this was excellent. Mac truly had no idea that Rafe was here to destroy him. And the fact that Mac was using his influence to convince other people that Rafe was no danger to them only made the revenge that much sweeter because when Rafe destroyed Mac, the whole town would blame Mac for vouching for his "old friend."

Rafe put his best effort into smiling warmly and shaking Mac's hand and looking as innocent as possible.

Which must have been innocent enough because Case

Baxter called the meeting back to order and everyone sat down. While the group discussed club business, Rafe mentally rearranged his plans. Above all else, Rafe had to close the deal on the Wild Aces as soon as possible. The Double M could not survive without the water from the Wild Aces. And if Rafe had a moment of doubt, a moment when he felt guilty about Violet wanting to raise their child on the Wild Aces…

No such doubt existed, and if it did, Rafe pushed it away. Caring for Violet was a weakness and at this late stage, it was a weakness he could not afford.

He had much work to do.

Eight

Violet's phone buzzed. Of course it did. She was in the middle of branding and castrating calves, for God's sake. It was messy work that required her full concentration and she was glad for that because it had been two days since Rafe had slipped out of her bed at six in the morning and kissed her goodbye with a promise that he would see her very soon.

Apparently, very soon meant something different in Al Qunfudhah than it did here in Texas, because there'd been radio silence for the past forty-eight hours and she was starting to get twitchy.

"Here," she said to Dale, her hired hand. "Hold this calf. I've got to take this call." She managed to get loose of the animal without getting kicked.

Hopefully, this was Rafe. No, she didn't really expect another rose or a love note—not when they'd both agreed that they were going to keep their previous acquaintance quiet for the time being, just until they got things settled a little more.

But again—days of radio silence? The only reason she knew that Rafe hadn't skipped town was that he'd gone to that Texas Cattleman's Club meeting with Mac the night before last.

She got out of earshot from her hired hands and pulled out her phone. It wasn't Rafe, dammit. It was, however, Lulu Clilmer, the current owner of the Wild Aces. "Hello?"

"Violet, honey," Lulu began in her gravelly, two-packs-a-day-for-forty-years voice, "I wanted to call you personally."

"Hey, Lulu, what's up? Are you all right? Do you need me to come over?" For years now, Violet had been helping Lulu out, partly because it was the neighborly thing to do but also because Violet wanted the Wild Aces, dang it all.

"I'm fine, honey. Listen, I know that you've always had your heart set on this place…"

Violet smiled nervously—which was pointless, as Lulu wouldn't have been able to video call anyone if her life depended on it. "Yeah. I've been trying to convince Mac to buy you out, but you know how he is."

"Well, honey—I don't know how to say this but…" Violet held her breath. "I've had an offer."

Violet's breath caught in her throat. Was that what Rafe had been doing? Had he spent the past two days "looking into" the Wild Aces for her? For their family? "Oh?" Violet said, not even bothering to sound cool or calm about it. "Who? Anyone I know?" *Please say Rafe. Please.*

Because if it were Rafe, then—finally—the Wild Aces would be hers. She wouldn't have to go through her brother any longer. God, she could hardly wait.

But if it wasn't Rafe…well, if it were someone else, she'd just have to push Mac harder or head down to the bank and see how much of a counteroffer she could scrape together. She was half owner of the Double M, after all. All that land equity had to count for something, right?

"Naw, honey—I'm sorry. It's some outfit that goes by the name Samson Oil."

Violet's heart plummeted down to around her knees.

"I never heard of them before—they're not local, that's for sure," Lulu continued. If it'd been someone local, there was always the chance Violet could reason with the other buyer. But some out-of-towner?

Wait—Rafe wasn't local. "Did you talk with Rafiq bin Saleed? Is he connected with Samson Oil?" She dug deep, hoping that something might ring a bell with Lulu. "Or someone named Ben, maybe?"

"Honey, no. I had been waiting on you, you know—I was happy to lease the land to you in the meantime—but the money this Samson Oil is offering? I can't walk away from this offer. I'm too old to keep this place up and my medical bills…" She trailed off into coughing.

Oh, God. This was, quite possibly, the worst-case scenario. "How much?" she asked weakly, covering her stomach with her hand as a wave of nausea appeared out of nowhere. She was just getting used to the idea of being a mother to Rafe's child. How much more disruption could she take?

There was a pause, which was followed by Lulu coughing some more. "Two," she said when she finally had her voice back.

"Million?" But Violet didn't have to ask. She already knew.

The Wild Aces was worth close to one million dollars.

Lulu had been willing to let Violet have it for $800,000, but Mac had thought that much money for that amount of land was a waste of resources. Lulu had promised that she wouldn't consider selling the Wild Aces out from under Violet for anything less than $1.5 million.

"I sure am sorry, honey," Lulu said again.

Violet put a hand to her head, as if that could get it to stop spinning. It didn't. "What if—what if I come up with a counteroffer?"

"Sweetie, we both know you don't have that much money lying around," Lulu said sympathetically.

She didn't—but McCallum Enterprises did. The company had plenty of capital. "Can you just hold off for a couple of days? Just give me the chance to make a counteroffer, okay?"

There was another long pause; Violet didn't know if Lulu was having trouble breathing again or if she was going to say no. "This Samson Oil—they want the deal done as soon as possible," Lulu said sadly.

"Just two days. A day, even," Violet pleaded. "Let me talk to Mac one more time. If I can get you $1.5 million, would you consider selling the Wild Aces to me?"

Lulu sighed heavily. "Sure thing, honey. I'll give you twenty-four hours."

Violet knew that it was only because she'd spent the past several years helping Lulu out around the house that the older woman was throwing her that small bone. "Thanks, Lulu. I'll be in touch, I promise." She ended the call and stood there, staring at her phone.

Samson Oil? Who—or what—the hell was that? No—wait. It sounded familiar. Hadn't she heard something about Samson Oil buying up a bunch of land around Royal for the oil rights? She remembered people talking about it at the Royal Diner when she'd gone in for

coffee one morning a couple of months ago. Some folks
had been suspicious, but others had been laughing because some dumb corporation was snapping up nearly
worthless land at insane prices.

Like offering Lulu twice what the Wild Aces was
worth—that was insane. This whole situation was insane.
When had her nice, quiet life gotten so completely out
of control? It was as if Violet's reality had been stripped
away from her and she'd been thrust into some alternative universe where up was down, left was right and she
was living out a soap-opera plot. She looked around, but
didn't see J. R. Ewing and his big hat anywhere.

Suddenly, Violet was mad. At her brother, at Rafe,
at this Samson Oil—at the universe. What the hell had
she done to deserve this? Okay, yes, the one-night stand
with Rafe had led to her pregnancy. Fine, she'd earned
that one herself. But everything else?

She was tired of doing the best she could with what
she got, because what she got was crappy. That's all there
was to it. Her parents dying? That was a crappy thing that
happened when she was at that age where she needed her
mother more than anything. But she went on. She didn't
go to Harvard, didn't go out into the great big world and
find her own place in it, as Mac had gotten to do. Instead,
she stayed home and became a damn fine ranch manager.

But did she get to fall in love? Every boy she'd ever
liked had been chased off by Mac. And now there was
Rafe. She didn't know if this was love or lust or hormones
or what. She liked him. She was definitely attracted to
him. And she was going to have his baby. But was that
love? Or was this just another crappy thing that was happening to her, another thing she was going to have to
muddle through as best she could?

Could she convince Mac that she could handle this,

handle her life? Would he keep trying to shield her from the real world while inadvertently setting her up for the exact heartbreak he was always trying to prevent in the first place?

If he had just bought the Wild Aces when he had the chance...

Angry tears stung her eyes, but the agitated mooing of calves and cows reminded her that she was not, in fact, in the privacy of her room. Instead, she was out on the ranch, surrounded by cows and cowboys, and she was the boss.

That's right, she was the boss. She needed to act like it. She looked up at the sky, trying to get all of her hormone-enhanced emotions under control. She could not fall apart, not now, because if she did, she'd lose the Wild Aces.

Wildly, she thought of Rafe. Where was he? She needed him right now in a way that she wasn't sure she'd ever needed anyone before. For so long, she'd been struggling to show that she was fine, that she could take care of herself. But right now, she wanted Rafe to pull her into his arms and tell her that it was all going to work out, that he'd take care of it—of her. God, she'd never wanted that so much.

And he wasn't here.

"Violet?" Dale asked, worry in his voice. "Everything okay?"

She turned back to where Dale was dusting his chaps off. The other hands were looking at her with confused concern. To them, she was just another cowboy. They didn't treat her like a porcelain doll the way her brother did—but the downside of that was, if she ever had a more emotional moment, they didn't know what to do. It was as if being suddenly reminded that she was, in fact, a woman always freaked them out.

She was not freaking out. She sent a quick text to Rafe, asking him where he was, and then she got her boss face on. Losing the Wild Aces wasn't just a crushing blow to her long-held dream. It could easily be a crushing blow to the Double M. The only reason Mac had agreed to lease the Aces was because they had multiple springs on the property—springs that had remained undamaged from the tornado that swept through Royal last year.

"The Wild Aces might be sold out from under us," she said, keeping her voice level.

Dale whistled and the other cowboys almost visibly relaxed at the revelation that Violet wasn't going to start crying. Because she wasn't. Absolutely no crying in baseball or ranching. "That's gonna put us between a rock and a hard place," Dale said.

"We can…" She had to prepare for the worst-case here—losing the Wild Aces completely. "We can lease Taggert's land and…"

Dale shook his head. "He sold out to Samson Oil a few months back."

"What about—"

"Samson Oil," Dale cut her off. "All of them. The Aces was the last holdout, and Lulu only hung on for as long as she did because she's got a soft spot for you."

"What the hell?" Violet stared down at her phone again, as if it somehow held all the answers. Did Samson Oil own it all? By God, she was so tired of having this crap happen to her. This was the last straw. "I have to talk to Mac."

She would make that man see reason and if they had to shell out $1.5 million damned dollars to get the Wild Aces, then that was his fault for not listening to her the first time. She was the boss. It was high time to show her brother that.

"We've got this," Dale said, motioning her toward her horse. "Go on."

"Thanks, Dale." Violet mounted Skipper and lit out for the house. She was so upset she couldn't even fret about whether or not Rafe would give her a look for riding hell for leather.

They couldn't lose the Wild Aces.

Now she just had to convince Mac of that fact.

"Well, howdy, Violet." Mac's assistant looked up from her desk. "We don't see you during the day much—is everything okay?"

"Andrea—I need help." That was the understatement of the day but Violet's throat closed up and for the second time in the past twenty minutes she was on the verge of tears. Luckily, Andrea Beaumont was one of her closest female friends—not to mention the only person who could get Mac to do anything, basically.

Andrea's face got serious and she stood up, quickly moving around the desk to put her hands on Violet's shoulders. "Oh my God—what?"

As she looked into Andrea's caring face, the corners of Violet's mouth pulled down and her eyes began to water and dammit, she was this close to crying. "I'm going to lose the Wild Aces," she managed to say.

"What? Oh, honey," Andrea said, relief washing over her face. "Good heavens, you scared the heck out of me." Andrea pulled Violet into a quick hug. "I thought there was something seriously wrong. You looked lower than a rattler belly in a wagon rut."

Something was seriously wrong. "I—" *I'm pregnant.* But the words wouldn't come out. She couldn't spill the beans just yet—not without talking to Rafe again. She quickly corrected course. "I'm just worried. We need the Aces for water and if it's sold…"

Andrea sighed. "I wish we could have gotten him to buy it when he had the chance. If you'd come to me first, maybe…"

"Yeah, I know." Mac would never take a suggestion Violet made at face value. He'd only hear her asking for the frivolous things she asked for as a kid—a new pony, new boots, more toys. He never believed that she could have an idea that had merit.

But she'd wanted the Wild Aces so much that, instead of waiting around for Andrea to massage the message, Violet had barged right into all the reasons the Double M should acquire the Wild Aces over dinner. What a mistake that had been.

And now that mistake was going to cost her almost twice the price Lulu would have sold her the Aces for a year ago.

Well, this wasn't all her fault. If Mac wasn't so damned convinced she was nothing but a foolish girl, he'd have seen the logic behind her request and bought the Wild Aces in the first place.

Of course, this was an emergency. There was no time to let Andrea work her magic. She had less than a day to convince Mac that the Aces wasn't just another frivolous thing she wanted—it was part and parcel of the Double M's survival. "Is he in?"

"Yes, let me check." Andrea knocked on Mac's door and stuck her head in. "Your sister is here."

"Come on in," Mac said in the background.

"Good luck," Andrea whispered as Violet edged into the room.

"What's up, sis?" Mac asked without looking up from his computer.

Was there a good way to start this conversation? No, there wasn't. The best she could do at this point was keep quiet about her pregnancy for as long as she could. If Mac found out now—in the middle of this whole thing with Samson Oil—well, the situation would get muddled up beyond all hope. At the very least, she wanted her doctor's appointment to happen before she told Mac.

"We need to buy the Wild Aces," she said without preamble.

Mac sighed heavily, as if she were twelve all over again, an irritating little sister he could barely be bothered to humor. "Again with the Wild Aces, Violet? We don't need to waste money on land we don't need."

"But we need the water, Mac. This isn't about what I want. This is about the Double M. Lulu called—some outfit named Samson Oil offered her two million for the Aces. She'll give me twenty-four hours to come up with at least one-point-five but otherwise, we're out. And if we're out, we'll be out the water."

"Wait—did you say Samson Oil?"

"Yeah, I did. And Dale said they've bought up the Taggerts' land and all the other ranches around ours. If we don't meet Lulu's offer, we're going to be locked out, Mac. We need the water or we'll lose the Double M." She was proud of the way she kept her anger out of it.

Because if he'd just listened to her the first time—or all the other times after that—they wouldn't be in this position.

The blood drained out of Mac's face and he sat back, his full attention on her.

"What?" she demanded. Because he looked a lot more upset right now than he had when a tornado had damaged their wells.

"Samson Oil is—well, it's Rafe. I just found out at the

Cattleman's Club meeting. The other night." He looked flabbergasted. "Kyle Wade told us all."

"Wait—what?" For maybe only the second time in her life, Violet felt faint. The first had been when her parents hadn't come home, but Sheriff Nathan Battle had shown up with some woman Violet had never seen before to tell her that she was now an orphan. It had been perfectly understandable then that Violet had fainted.

But this? Rafe *was* Samson Oil?

Yeah, this was as good a time as any to feel light-headed.

"Hey—hey!" Mac jumped up and hurried toward her. "Geez, Violet—what the heck? Sit down," he said, his voice thick as he caught her under the arms and guided her to the chair in front of his desk. "Andrea, get some water!" he shouted.

"I'm fine," Violet lied, because she wasn't sure of anything anymore, except that she wasn't fine at all. She had just plumb run out of coping, thank you very much. No coping left at all. She couldn't handle one more shock to the system.

Mac grabbed a manila folder off his desk and began fanning her. Andrea rushed in with a glass of water and the two of them hovered over her like protective mother hens. "Should we call an ambulance?"

"For the love of Pete, I'm fine," Violet said, more forcefully this time. She was the boss. Not her emotions and not her hormones. "It's just…he didn't mention Samson Oil when we had dinner."

And that seemed like a rather important fact. When he said he'd look into the Wild Aces for her, for example— that would have been a great time to mention that he was behind the corporation buying up all the land surrounding the Double M at insane prices.

Wait—maybe she was looking at this wrong? What if Rafe had done exactly what he'd said he was going to do?

Hope flared through the mess that was her head. Maybe he was buying the Aces for her, just as he'd said?

"Well, he is Samson Oil," Mac went on. "He didn't deny it at the meeting or anything. Instead, he just said that he was exploring mineral rights." Mac stood back up, frowning. "I don't know, Violet. I mean, it's Rafe—but there's something about this that's not right."

"Dale said we'd be cut off from the water." Just as soon as the hopeful thoughts that Rafe had really bought the Wild Aces for her had emerged, they were sunk under a crushing wave of worry. "Mac," she started, a sense of horror dawning in her mind, "what if he's *not* here because he's checking in with his old friend?"

Just saying those words out loud made her feel ill all over again.

"I don't know if I can believe that either," Mac said, starting to pace. "I mean, he's only been in Texas for, what? A few weeks, tops?"

Violet opened her mouth to correct him because she knew—intimately—that Rafe had been in the area much earlier than that. Four months ago, in fact.

But that's not what she said, at least not directly. "If he's Samson Oil, and Samson has been buying up property all around Royal since last fall, why didn't he come over months ago?"

And that was the $10,000 question, wasn't it? Why had Rafe been in Holloway four months ago? Where had he been since then? And why was he buying up what basically amounted to half the town of Royal, Texas?

"I don't like this," Andrea said quietly. But she wasn't looking at Mac when she said it. Instead, she was staring at Violet.

Oh, no. Andrea wasn't exactly a mother figure, but she was the closest thing Violet had to a big sister. And if anyone could look at Violet and see the little changes that had been happening to her—and put all those little changes together to figure out the one big change—it'd be Andrea. The woman's attention to detail was almost inhuman.

Violet knew her eyes were wide and yeah, she was pretty sure she looked guilty because Andrea's eyes got wide right back. Too late, Violet realized she had covered her stomach with her hands and not in the going-to-be-sick way but the cradling-my-pregnant-belly way. Mac had missed the gesture entirely. But Andrea hadn't.

Oh, *no.* Andrea's mouth opened to say something but Violet cut her off with a shake of her head. They could not have this conversation right now, in Mac's office of all places. Not happening.

Andrea gave her what could only be described as a stern look before quickly nodding her head in agreement. "We'll talk later?" she said quietly.

"Okay," Violet said because really? She wanted to tell someone and of all the people in the world, Andrea was not only the safest option but the one who could most help Violet share her "impending blessing," as Rafe had called it, with Mac with minimal collateral damage. If her mom were here, Violet would have already cried it out on her shoulder. Andrea was the next best thing.

Just not here. Not now.

Her phone buzzed. Numbly, she dug it out of her pocket and saw it was a text from Rafe. When can I see you again?

She stared at the phone. Well, this was awkward. But then, her whole life had become one continuous string of awkward moments. She better get used to it. Where are you?

In Holloway at the inn. Thinking of you.

If she hadn't just been questioning Rafe's every motivation for being in the greater Texas area, she might have been touched by that sentiment. We need to talk.

The problem was how to talk without Mac finding out. It'd been wonderfully convenient that he'd been away on a business trip a few days ago but now? What excuse could she use to get Rafe alone?

Violet looked up at Andrea. "I need Mac to be busy tonight," she said in an urgent whisper.

"Why?"

Violet bit her lip. "I'll explain later."

Andrea gave her that stern look again. "Later, we're going to talk."

"I know. But tonight?"

Andrea sighed heavily, then stood and turned her attention back to Mac. "We need to talk with the other landowners who've already sold to Samson and get an idea of what the terms of the sales were and see if they were all told the same thing or if there are inconsistencies. Once we have a little more information, then we can consider approaching Rafe."

God bless that woman, Violet thought.

Her phone buzzed again. Are you still there?

"Yeah, okay," Mac said, rubbing the back of his neck. "Something doesn't add up, I tell you." He turned his attention back to Violet. She barely managed to get her phone flipped over so her screen was pressing against her thigh before Mac saw. "You going to be okay?"

"I'm fine, really," she said again.

"I want you to go home and take it easy for the rest of the day. Maybe Andrea can come by and fix you some chicken-noodle soup?"

Violet gave Andrea a look, one that Violet hoped said, *Keep him busy.*

"I think I need to come with you," Andrea said carefully. "Violet says she's fine and besides, two heads are better than one. I'll take notes while you talk to people."

"Okay, yeah, that sounds good." When Andrea relaxed into a smile, Violet thought she saw something unfamiliar flicker across Mac's face. "We'll get some dinner and make an evening of it. If," he added, glancing at Violet, "you're sure you're going to be okay?"

Violet stood, casually tucking her phone back into her pocket. "Mac," she said carefully, "I'm not a little girl anymore. If I say I'll be fine, I'll be fine."

For a second, she thought Mac was going to argue with her. But Andrea stepped forward and said, "She'll be fine, Mac."

Mac turned his attention back to Andrea. That look came over his face again and he said, "All right," as if he were physically incapable of taking Violet's word at face value.

God, she loved her brother, but sometimes she just wanted to strangle him.

Violet knew she shouldn't press her luck. She should quit while she was—okay, maybe not ahead, but at least not falling further behind. But they still hadn't resolved the whole reason she'd come here today. "What about the Wild Aces?"

Andrea shot her a warning look. Right. Violet needed to let this drop and she needed to let Andrea work her magic when she and Mac were making an evening of it, so to speak.

"Let me talk to a few people," Mac said, grabbing his hat and firmly cramming it on his head. "But Violet—I won't let it go without a fight. Not if Rafe's got some ulterior motive."

Andrea nodded, and although Violet desperately wanted to remind Mac of how very much they needed the Wild Aces, she let the matter drop.

As soon as Mac and Andrea were safely in his truck, with Andrea already on the phone making calls to everyone who had sold to Samson Oil, Violet texted Rafe back. I'm here. When's good for you?

Now, was the immediate response. Shall I come to you? Or you to me?

She had promised Mac she would go home. And as long as she and Rafe stayed downstairs—with their clothes on—if Mac came home, she could just say, well, Rafe dropped in to chat about all this Samson Oil business.

Can you come to the house? she texted back.

I am on my way.

See you soon.

Soon she would know what he was up to and what part she played and whether or not she was going to get the Wild Aces.

God, she hoped this worked out.

Nine

Rafe paused only long enough to procure another rose for Violet, and even with that small detour, he made it to the Double M in record time.

He did not see Mac's vehicle, which was good. In the two days since he'd left Violet's bed, he hadn't been able to stop thinking about her.

It was discomforting to realize that he missed her. Worse, though, was the fact that he was having conflicting thoughts about the property she wanted, the Wild Aces. The purchase was going according to plan. Despite the issues that kept cropping up, victory was still within his grasp. Once he had the Wild Aces, he could choke Mac McCallum off his property. Revenge served very cold indeed.

Except that he kept thinking back to the grand old home on the Wild Aces, and how Violet wanted to make it over and raise his child there. And how Rafe wanted very much to give her just that—to give her whatever she wanted.

That insidious voice in the back of his head that sounded like his father's angry shouting berated him for even considering letting the Wild Aces—and his entire scheme—fall apart for the sake of one woman.

The family honor. The family name. No one uses a bin Saleed like that and gets away with it.

That was what his father had shouted after he had come to collect Nasira and found her in Mac's bed. Those were the very words he had used to shame Rafe for allowing some common American to take advantage of a bin Saleed.

That was why Rafe was here. That was why he now owned half of this county. He had to avenge the family honor.

In all respects, Rafe had been surprised that his father had not taken even more drastic measures against Mac and his family. But to do so would have continued to draw attention to how Rafe and Nasira had so badly betrayed the family honor. Better to keep the whole incident quiet. At least, that was what Fareed had managed to convince the old man.

Rafe had to do something. The years between when his father had walked in on Mac and Nasira, and the old man's death had nearly killed Rafe in a very real way. All because Mac did not respect Rafe or Nasira enough to keep his lust in check.

Rafe was a bin Saleed.

Honor. Revenge.

Violet…

The diamond-and-ruby bracelet felt heavy in his pocket. It was all part of his new-and-much-improved plan. Wooing Violet away from Mac would complete his revenge in ways he had not even originally considered. He was not letting his scheme fall apart. He was expanding upon it.

As he mounted the steps onto the wide porch, Violet opened the door and he knew immediately that something was not right. "Are you well?" he asked, hurrying to take her in his arms.

"Rafe," she said, not exactly melting into his embrace. Instead, she stayed stiff and he heard the tension in her voice.

And her text came back to him: We need to talk.

He leaned back and looked down at her. And he knew, somehow, that she'd discovered his scheme.

Was it weakness that he wanted to delay that confrontation, even for a moment longer? Was it weakness that had him pressing his lips against hers for one more kiss, because after this kiss, he did not know if he would have another chance to hold her in his arms?

Or was it just the fact that he had failed and he sought the comfort only Violet could provide?

She did not kiss him back. Not as she had kissed him the last time he had seen her.

Suddenly, Rafe was nearly overcome with the urge to fall to his knees and beg her forgiveness. Once, Violet McCallum had been an abstract concept, an afterthought to his scheme. But now? Now she was a living, breathing woman who had shared herself with him, body and soul, and he had been careless with that. With her.

"Who are you?" she said, her voice soft. But that softness did nothing to disguise the anger that she was barely keeping in check. "Who are you, really?"

"Rafiq bin Saleed," he told her truthfully. "I sometimes use Ben. It was…simpler."

"Simpler?" she scoffed, turning away from him.

"Easier to pronounce," he offered, trailing after her as she stalked into her home.

"Or just easier to hide who you really were?"

"That, too."

She spun, her eyes blazing. "Tell me how you're involved with Samson Oil. Tell me why you were here four months ago. Tell me why you suddenly seem to own every single piece of land surrounding the Double M." She began to advance on him and, thankfully, years of conditioned response from being berated by his father had Rafe standing his ground. Cowering was bad enough but to cower before a woman?

"And tell me, Rafe," she went on, her voice getting louder with each word, "*tell me* it doesn't have a damn thing to do with whatever happened between you and Mac back in college. That 'it does not signify.'"

By this point, she was standing directly in front of him and poking him in the chest with one of her fingers.

Tell me you have not failed me. The words were not Violet's but his father's. It had been a trap, because of course Rafe had failed him and Nasira. Rafe had failed the country of Al Qunfudhah by foolishly trusting a duplicitous American.

Some part of him knew that he had failed Violet, that she had had nothing to do with what happened between Mac and Nasira, that she had nothing to do with the hell on earth that had come afterward.

But that part was buried deep beneath Rafe's survival mechanisms. And Violet, while formidable, was not Hassad bin Saleed.

He straightened his back and leveled his best glare at her. He was not the same wayward youth. He would not be dressed down by anyone anymore. Least of all a woman.

Not even *his* woman.

Rafe pushed her finger away from his chest. "Ah, so you have figured it out, have you? I should have guessed that you would put the pieces together before your idiot brother did."

His words had the desired affect—the color drained from her face and, off balance, she stumbled backward. "What?"

Without thinking about it, he caught her around the waist to keep her from falling. He didn't tuck her against his chest, however, nor did he attempt to comfort her. He kept distance between their bodies. "Sit, please. I have no wish to see you hurt."

"Figured *what* out, Rafe?"

"Sit, Violet." This time, it was not a request. It was an order. He backed her up until she hit the chair with the backs of her legs and sat with enough force that Rafe winced. "Take care. Please, think of the child."

Violet looked down at her stomach as if she expected an alien to emerge from her body at any second. "The… child? You still…" Her voice trailed off with the unspoken question.

"Yes, of course I still want the child. The baby will be my flesh and blood just as much as it will be yours." Rafe took the sofa where he had been sitting when she first walked back into his life. She had been ready to flay him alive then. Some things, it seemed, would never change. "Now. Tell me what you know and what your brother knows."

She blinked at him and slowly, he could see her regain her control. "You are Samson Oil."

"That is correct."

"And you've been buying up all the ranches surrounding the Double M for months. That's why you were in Holloway four months ago."

Rafe nodded. "You are correct. I have also bought quite a few other parcels of land."

She looked at him in what he could only call surprise. "Why?"

"So as not to arouse suspicion."

He saw her swallow. "Oh. Of course. And…the Wild Aces? Were you going to buy that, as well, before I told you about it? About how much I wanted it?"

He felt a dull ache spreading in his chest but he held his pose, leg crossed over his knee, arms spread out along the back of the couch. He took up as much space as he could. "Yes."

Pain tightened her features to the point where Rafe fought the urge to stand and pull her into his arms. The jig, as they said, was up. "So you weren't going to buy it for me?"

He let the question hang in the air until he was sure he had his foolish impulses to comfort her under control. "Originally, no."

"Originally?"

"I will keep it for you. In a few years, after this is all settled, you may have it."

He would not have thought it possible for her to get any paler, but she did. "A…few years? And this—what *is* this, Rafe?"

The urge to move was almost overwhelming. No, he did not want to back away or run and hide, but even to stand and pace would be a physical relief. But with his father, any such betrayal of his mental state had always led to not only more beatings, but more severe beatings, as well. So Rafe forced himself to be still. "You are quite bright, Violet. Do not tell me you have failed to guess what 'this' is."

"Mac," she said. It came out almost as a croak.

He nodded his head in acknowledgment. "I can be very patient. Twelve years was nothing to me, not after what your brother did to us."

"But—he didn't," she sputtered. "He told me he found your sister in his bed and that he never even touched her. He always felt terrible about it, but it wasn't his fault!"

Rafe looked at her coolly. "And you believed that, did you?"

Her mouth opened and shut. He could read the doubt in her eyes. "Mac wouldn't lie to me. Not like you do."

"Don't be naive," Rafe said, his tone condescending.

This was not happening. It couldn't be. Maybe... maybe Violet really had fainted in Mac's office. And she was still unconscious. That'd explain this.

The man she was sitting across from looked like the same man she'd met in Holloway months ago. The man she'd taken back to her bed in the past week.

The man she had started to fall for.

But he wasn't. He was nothing but a cold, heartless bastard. "How could you do this to us?" she asked, although she was already starting to get a pretty good idea of the answer. "How could you do this to me?"

Her throat started to close up and her eyes began to water, but she wasn't going to cry. She wasn't going to give him the satisfaction of knowing how upset she was. Besides, she figured a snake of a man like Rafiq bin Saleed wouldn't be moved by a woman crying anyway. That would imply that he was capable of emotions.

He sat looking at her for what felt like a very long time. "Because," he said slowly.

"Don't give me that, Rafe. *Because* isn't an answer. Why are you doing this to me? I never did anything to you or your sister. I never even knew you."

It was only when Rafe exhaled—long and slow, the kind of controlled breath that seemed to say to her he was barely in control—that she realized he might not be quite as calculating as she'd gathered. So she did what she always did—she spoke. Impulsively. "Was this your evil plan all along? Were you waiting for me in Holloway that night for the express purpose of getting me pregnant? Am I nothing but a pawn to you?"

"I understand if you hate me," he said in a much softer voice than she had been expecting.

"Hate you? Jesus, I don't know if I should shoot you or not. And don't think I don't know how," she spat at him. "Talk, damn you."

"You may choose to believe what you wish to, but I have not lied to you."

A bark of laughter escaped her. It was either laugh or start sobbing, and she was the boss of her emotions right now, thank you very much.

"I have, it is true, omitted many things," Rafe went on after she'd settled down. "I did not know who you were—that was the truth. I promised to use a condom, and I did. I promised I would not contact you outside of that evening, and I did not. I promised I would look into the Wild Aces, and I did. Honor is everything to my people, and my family and I have made every effort not to dishonor you through lies."

"You'll excuse me if I don't exactly see the difference between you lying and you carefully not mentioning that the whole reason you were in Holloway and Royal in the first place was to destroy my family."

The infuriating man waved his hand, as if she were

splitting hairs, but he didn't have the energy to argue with her.

"My revenge is complete, with your assistance," he said. He tried to smile, but even in her upset state she could see how forced it was, as if there were something that were pushing him to say and do these awful things. "Surely you can see how Mac and I will be even. He ruined my sister. I merely returned the favor."

Where was her gun? Oh, that's right. Up in her room. She'd never make it up and back before Rafe could get out of range. Dammit.

"For your information, I don't think your sister was ruined just because she chose to get into bed with my brother, and I don't think you ruined me just because I chose to sleep with you—which, by the way, will never happen again."

"As is your choice," he said and there was no mistaking the sorrow in his voice.

"If you think you're ever going to get our baby, you're wrong. I'll fight you every step of the way."

"It does not have to be like that," he said, and it might have been her imagination, but she swore he looked worried.

Well, he could just be worried. She surged to her feet, letting the anger carry her. "The hell it doesn't. I won't let you get the Wild Aces, I won't let you get the Double M, I won't let you get my baby and I sure as hell won't let you get *me*. Now get out."

Rafe stood. "It is too late, you realize. The Wild Aces is as good as mine and soon, your brother will not be able to sustain the Double M."

"It ain't over till it's over," she retorted. "Now leave before I get my gun."

He nodded and walked to the front door. Then he

paused and turned back to her. "You should have been a pawn," he said mournfully. "But you were not. It gives me no pleasure to do this to you."

"Then don't," she said, unable to believe what she was saying. "Don't do it to me. Don't do it to us." And she was horrified to realize that she wanted him to do something—what, she didn't know. Something that would show her that underneath that imperious exterior was the real man she'd almost loved.

"There is no us," he said, turning away from her. "And I have no choice in the matter. I am bound by honor and obligation. But I will hold the Wild Aces for you and for our child. I promise you that, Violet."

She needed to say something—get the last word, put him in his place, but all she could do was watch him open up the door to her house and close it behind him when he went.

Then she sank into the chair and cried.

But not for long. The Double M was her ranch, her home. She was the boss around here. She did not have time for self-pity.

She dialed Mac. "I need you to come home right now," she told him when he answered. "We need to talk."

By the time Mac and Andrea rolled in, Violet had gotten herself under control. She'd texted her best friends, Clare and Grace, because if there was one thing she needed right now, it was backup. She'd splashed her face with water and had a ginger ale and was, all things considered, feeling up to the fight.

"What?" Mac demanded when he walked through the door. Violet stood and faced her brother. "What's so important that you couldn't tell me on the phone? Did you find out something about Samson Oil or Rafe?"

Andrea put a gentle hand on his shoulder and made eye contact with Violet. "What is it, Violet?" she asked, her gaze dropping to Violet's belly.

"Okay, I've got a couple of things to say and I'm going to say them," Violet said, trying to remember to breathe.

"All right," Mac said, looking worried. "What?"

"First off, I'm pregnant."

That might not have been the best way to go about this, but Violet was done tiptoeing around Mac. *"What?"*

"Second off," she said, charging ahead, "Rafe is the father."

"What?" Mac roared. "That bastard! I asked him to keep an eye on you and this is how he repays me? I'm going to—"

Violet held up her hand and Andrea squeezed Mac's shoulder and miracle of miracles, the man shut up. "Third off, I'm four months pregnant. Actually, four months and almost two weeks."

Mac's mouth opened and then shut again. "Wait, what?"

"Rafe was in town months before he showed up here, claiming he wanted to reconnect. I met him at the Holloway Inn in November. That's where..." Mac blanched. Okay, they didn't need to get into the details. "Anyway, I needed a night out. I didn't know who he was and he claims that he didn't know who I was, although obviously we can't exactly take him at his word right now. It was a one-night stand that didn't go quite according to plan."

"Oh, honey," Andrea said.

"I don't think I want to hear anymore," Mac said, looking a little green around the gills.

"Fourth off, he's out to get you and, as near as I can figure, I'm just collateral damage. He made me a lot of promises over the course of the last week and he swears that he'll hold on to the Wild Aces for me and I can have it in a few years after he's put the Double M out of business."

"So this is all—what, exactly?"

"Revenge," Andrea said. "This is revenge."

"She's right. He said he was honor bound to get you back for ruining his sister. Originally, that just meant ruining you. But I guess I provide the ironic twist, don't I?" Her voice cracked and Andrea pulled her into a big hug.

"It's okay, honey," she said softly.

"How the hell is this okay?" Mac shouted. "Some insane sheikh is out to ruin me because his equally insane sister decided the best way to get out of a bad marriage was to be caught in my bed? I had nothing to do with any of this!"

"Mac!" Andrea hissed. "Now is not the best time!"

Mac looked at Violet, who was sniffing violently. "I'm—oh, God, I'm sorry, Violet. I didn't think…"

"It's okay. But I have one more thing I want to say." She straightened up and pushed herself out of Andrea's arms.

Mac eyed her warily. "What's that?"

"This—if you had bought the Wild Aces when I asked you to, if you had listened to me at any point in the last twelve years—we wouldn't be in this position."

The man had the nerve to look hurt. "But Violet—I was just trying to protect you. You've had to deal with more than your share, what with us losing our parents and—"

"It's been twelve years, Mac. I'm not a little girl anymore and I'm not the shell-shocked teenager I was when you got home from college. I'm a grown woman and a ranch manager and soon I'm going to be a mother. Everyone else knows that I can handle myself—even this surprise pregnancy, I can deal with it. But I've spent years tiptoeing around you and asking Andrea to convince you to do things for me because every time I open my mouth, you act like I'm just the cutest little thing playacting at adulthood and I'm sick of it. I don't need your protection. I'm not just your little sister. I am your business partner, dammit, and it's high time you started treating me like it."

Mac gaped at her but, amazingly, didn't tell her he was going to handle it or that it was all going to be okay. "Well, then, what do you suggest?"

Luckily, she'd had enough time to think through the next step. "The only way to cut Rafe off is to buy the Aces out from under him. Lulu said she'd sell it to me for one-point-five million. The very last thing I will ever ask of you is to help me buy it. We need the water and I need my own place to raise my family."

For a second, she thought maybe she'd gotten through to the big lunkhead, but old habits died mighty hard, because Mac's gaze cut to Andrea. Violet rolled her eyes, and she saw Andrea's lips twist into something of a knowing smile.

"She's right," Andrea said. "You know she is."

"Dang it all, I know." Mac took off his hat and rubbed his forehead. "I don't know if we can beat him to the punch. No one knew who was behind Samson Oil at first and the money was too good. He had Nolan Dane doing all his negotiating for him. Kyle Wade is the one who outed him, but I don't think any of us saw this as revenge. Except for you," he added before Violet could correct him. "And why didn't you tell me you were expecting?"

"Because the moment I figured it out is literally the moment Rafe showed back up and I had a lot to deal with, okay?"

Mac put his hands up in the universal sign of surrender. "Okay, okay. Sheesh."

"I need the Wild Aces, Mac."

He nodded—slowly at first, but then more emphatically. "Then I'll go get it for you, partner."

Ten

"I don't know what I'm going to do." It was all well and good for Violet to stand up in front of her brother and tell him she could handle this, but now, far away from Mac, she wasn't so sure.

Which was how she found herself at the Royal Diner, sitting with her best friends, Clare Connelly and Grace Haines, and pouring her heart out while Mac went to try to get the money by liquidating some capital—or something like that. Violet did not handle the money end of things, so Andrea had gently suggested that she get together with her friends for a little girl time.

Violet really did love Andrea. The woman was a peach.

"Honey," Clare said, slinging an arm around Violet's shoulder and giving her a firm hug, "if anyone can handle this, it's you."

"But I'm pregnant." Now that Violet had said the

words out loud, she seemingly couldn't stop saying them. She'd been telling friends, neighbors, Dale—even random people she met in the street. She was pregnant and she was screwed.

"You keep saying that like it's the end of the world, but you know it's not," Grace said. "Heck, I'm suddenly mother to twins. It's a lot but it's *not* the end of the world. You've survived worse, you know."

Violet was too emotionally drained to even wince. "Yeah, but my parents' plane crash was a one-and-done event. This? The father of my child is basically out to destroy the entire town of Royal because he's nursing a grudge against my brother about something that happened over twelve years ago. This isn't a one time trauma. This has the potential to be an ongoing international incident. I mean, he's a sheikh, for God's sake!"

Clare and Grace shared a look. "I'm sure something can be worked out," Clare said. "I mean, look at Grace. First she was Maddie and Maggie's social worker and now she's going to adopt them and marry their father…"

"What Clare is saying is, just because it's complicated doesn't mean you can't find a way to make it work," Grace finished.

"And you know I'll be here with you," Clare said, giving Violet another squeeze. "I love babies! I'll teach you everything you need to know and when your baby gets a little older, we can all have playdates together."

"We?" Violet and Grace both turned to look at Clare. Grace said, "Is there something you're not telling us?"

Clare blushed. "Actually, I'm pregnant. But!" she said quickly, hushing her friends before they could start whooping and hollering. "I'm only a little pregnant. Probably not more than five weeks along, so we're going to keep it quiet for now, okay?"

Now it was Violet's turn to hug Clare. "Oh, honey," she said, and damn the stupid hormonal tears that started up again. At least this time, they were happy tears, right? "I'm so excited for you and Parker!"

As they were comparing due dates, the chimes over the door jingled. All three of them looked up at the newcomer. A woman with long, thick black hair wearing a beautiful gold-yellow suit glided into the diner as if she were walking on rose petals—which was impressive, given her heels. Those suckers had to be at least five inches tall and yet this woman moved in them as if they were a natural part of her feet. The woman paused inside the door and removed her hat—not a cowboy hat, like most of the people here wore, but a short, wide number that was the exact color of her suit, complete with a feather that swept out over the huge brim.

All in all, she looked like someone who might have gotten lost on her way to a royal wedding and wound up in Royal, Texas, completely by accident.

And Violet recognized her immediately.

"Wow," Clare said in a hushed whisper.

"Beautiful," Grace agreed. "Who is that? She's not from around her, is she? I'd remember the hat."

"Rafe," Violet said. Both the women turned to look at her. "I mean, she looks like Rafe. Excuse me."

Her heart pounding, Violet slid out of her booth and approached the newcomer. What was Nasira bin Saleed doing here? Rafe had promised that he would try to arrange a meeting between Nasira and Violet—but Violet was pretty sure Rafe had said he didn't think Nasira would come to America. "Hi—Nasira?"

Because who else could she be? Looking like this woman did—the black hair and olive skin and the same nose and chin as Rafe?

The woman's face registered surprise. "I am sorry," she said in an accent that was similar to Rafe's, but very different. Whereas Rafe's voice always made Violet think of warm sunshine and honey, this woman's voice sounded almost like…like rain and fog and mist. It was not an unpleasant thing, but it was very unexpected. "Do I know you?"

Violet stuck out her hand. "I'm Violet McCallum. I'm Mac's sister. And you're Rafe's sister, Nasira—right? You look like him."

Nasira blushed. "Ah, yes. Violet. Hello. How fortunate I have found you so quickly. I have come to warn you and your brother that—"

"That Rafe's going to buy up the entire town and ruin Mac?" Nasira winced. "Yeah, sorry—it's kind of too late for that."

Nasira clutched at her hat and paled. "Oh, no—I am too late? What has he done?"

Violet decided she liked Nasira immediately. "Why don't you have a seat? Would you like some coffee? Then we can talk."

Clare and Grace introduced themselves and Nasira politely said hello, although she did not shake hands. "Well," Clare said, standing and giving a knowing look to Grace, "we best be running along. But Violet—you call us the moment you need anything."

"Anything at all," Grace added.

And then Violet was alone with Nasira. Once the other women were gone, Nasira sat in the seat Grace had vacated. She sat very stiffly, her back straight and her chin up. She placed her fancy hat on the table next to her and waited silently while Amanda Battle, the owner of the Royal Diner, poured the coffee.

"Anything else I can get you all?" Amanda said, trying not to stare at Nasira.

The Royal Diner was pretty much ground zero for gossip in this town. Violet glanced around. Luckily, aside from a few stragglers, Violet and Nasira had the place to themselves.

"I think we're good," Violet said, smiling warmly at Amanda.

She and Nasira were silent until Amanda was out of earshot. Then, with the most graceful gesture Violet had ever seen, Nasira leaned forward and said, "Tell me what has happened. What has Rafe done?"

So Violet told Nasira what she knew—about Samson Oil, the land grabs, the Wild Aces, everything but her relationship with Rafe. She doubted if just casually blurting out that a person's brother had gotten her pregnant after a one-night stand was "done" in Al Qunfudhah. Violet's life might be a total scandal, but she didn't need to add fuel to the fire if she could help it.

When she'd finished, Nasira sat back—again, her back ramrod straight—lowered her eyes and said, "This is my fault. I am so sorry for the trouble I have caused."

The resignation in her voice alarmed Violet. "What? No way. I mean—okay, so something obviously happened twelve years ago. But I fail to see how that makes you personally responsible for what's going on here."

She was horrified to see Nasira's eyes tear up. "I brought your brother into a family problem without explaining it to him. It was unfair to him and unfair to Rafe."

"Yeah, so what exactly did happen back at Harvard? Mac insists he didn't do anything with you and Rafe won't tell me what he thinks happened either."

Nasira's gaze sharpened, just a little, and she again

looked more like her brother. "Are you and Rafe on good terms, then? Does he talk to you?"

Violet realized she was blushing. "You first," she said, trying to play for time. "Your story happened first, so you tell it first."

"All right," Nasira said again, her voice a little cooler this time.

Oh, yeah, this was Rafe's sister. There was no mistaking it.

After a long pause, Nasira leaned forward again, her voice soft—no doubt to keep anyone from overhearing them. "I chose Mac precisely because I knew him to be an honorable man who would not violate me," she explained. She picked up a packet of sweetener and began to fiddle with it—the first sign of nerves that Violet had seen yet. "I know that may sound unusual to your American ears, but at the time, I felt that letting my father believe I had been compromised by a man such as Mac was the only way I could escape the fate he had chosen for me."

"A man such as Mac? I don't understand—obviously, your father didn't see him as an honorable guy."

A hint of color graced Nasira's cheeks. Really, everything the woman did was grace embodied. "No, he did not. My father barely tolerated Rafe attending an American school, and Mac was not of royal blood. So to be 'defiled' by him—or so my father believed," Nasira hurried to add when Violet opened her mouth to argue with that particular assessment, "was lowering myself even more."

What was it with these people? Ruined? Defiled? No wonder they were so screwed up. Did they ever fall in love and have sex simply because they wanted to?

There had been that night, many months ago, when Violet had gone to bed with Rafe because she wanted to.

She'd wanted one night of fun and freedom and—yes—good sex. And Rafe? He had wanted all those things, too.

But did he now view her as ruined? Defiled? Had he lowered himself by making her pleasure his?

Ugh, she was nauseous again.

Nasira had dropped her gaze to the table, so she missed Violet's reaction. "You must try to understand. I was to be wed to a horrible man, a man I feared greatly. He was well over sixty and had already had two wives who had died in 'accidents' that were not accidents. His first wife died because she only gave birth to girls and his second...well, I do not know why."

Violet gasped. "How could your father marry you off to such a man?"

Nasira looked at her sadly. "I hope you can understand how different our families are. This was all expected when I was a child. I had been promised to the warlord for some time. He was a powerful man and my father wanted to keep him close. It was only when Rafe left for university in America and met your brother..." Her voice trailed off. "Rafe told me such stories, you see. And the way he spoke of his friendship with Mac, of you—of this place—it was almost too good to believe. For the first time in our lives, I envied Rafe."

Violet gave her a confused look. "Wait, what? I mean—you were going to be married off to a monster and you didn't already envy Rafe?" How did that even make sense?

Nasira gave her that sad smile again, one that spoke of pain that Violet could only begin to fathom. "Rafe is second in line for the sheikhdom. In England, he would be the spare, as they say. But we did not grow up in England and my father treated Rafe harshly."

Violet stared at her. Harshly? How harshly?

"But I am getting off the point," she went on. "Rafe was in America and having all of these wonderful adventures, and I was envious. I managed to convince my father that, for my eighteenth birthday, I should be allowed to visit Rafe. Our older brother, Fareed, took my side. It was he who told me what Rafe was doing here in Royal," she added.

"Okay, so Fareed is a decent guy?"

"He is *not* our father," Nasira said emphatically. "He is a just and fair ruler of Al Qunfudhah."

Well, that had to count for something. "So you got to visit Rafe in America and while you were here, you decided to get out of the marriage by… Is *seducing* the right word?"

Nasira's eyes widened in horror and she shook her head. "No, no. I had convinced your brother to kiss me by explaining my situation but, at the last moment, I feared that would not be enough, so I made a foolish choice and snuck into his bed. That was where our father found me." She dropped her gaze again and went back to mangling the sweetener packet. "I regret that choice, but please understand, I also do not regret it. What came after was…terrible." She shuddered and Violet shuddered in sympathy.

"You didn't have to marry that guy, right? That's what Rafe said. He said you were able to leave Al Qunfudhah and marry a man more to your liking."

"Sebastian, yes." There was a note of sorrow to her voice that she tried to hide with a smile. "My life has been much easier than I had ever allowed myself to dream it could be. However, I do not believe Rafe's was." She didn't speak for a moment and, for once, Violet managed not to open her mouth and charge into the gap. "It was a relief when our father died and Fareed

150 A SURPRISE FOR THE SHEIKH

took power," Nasira said quietly. "Rafe was allowed to resume life in the outside world."

Violet felt herself gaping at Nasira like a catfish out of water but she couldn't quite get her face under control. "You make it sound like your father imprisoned him because he didn't protect you. Or your honor, anyway."

"It sounds that way because it was that way." Nasira's words were little more than a whisper. "I believe that, in the years between my actions and our father's death, Rafe held one thought that sustained him. And now that he has regained his power and his wealth by his own hands…"

"Revenge."

Nasira set the sweetener packet down and returned her hands to her lap. Violet could see her composing herself. "For a long time, I've wished that there had been another way. It is all my fault."

What Violet needed was a drink. Of course, she couldn't exactly wander over to the bar and do a line of shots, no matter how much she might want to block out the world for a while. "Well. This certainly puts a new spin on things."

"Oh? And what about you, Violet? You speak as if you know Rafe."

"I do. I…" She took a deep breath. "I don't really know how to say this without it sounding bad, so I'm just going to say it. I'm pregnant and Rafe's the father."

She wasn't sure what she expected Nasira to do with that bit of information, but bursting into tears and smiling at the same time wasn't it. "Nasira?"

Amanda Battle hustled over. "Is everything okay?"

"Um—tissues?" Violet said. Just watching Nasira cry was making her tear up, too.

Amanda hurried back behind the counter, bless her heart, and reappeared with a box of tissues. "Thanks,"

Violet said. Amanda got the hint and retreated back to the counter.

"My deepest apologies," Nasira said, grabbing a tissue and blotting at her eyes. "It is just…well, I am very happy that Rafe has opened himself up. I had believed that part of him might have died after…"

"But you're crying," Violet said gently.

"It is nothing," Nasira said, which was pretty obviously a bold-faced lie. "I am quite happy for you and for Rafe," she repeated.

"But…"

Nasira tried to smile but she didn't make it. "I have long wanted a child of my own and we have not been blessed with one. Sebastian is an honorable man. He wishes to have an heir and I…I cannot. I recently lost the baby I was carrying and now he will not…" Her voice trailed off with such hopelessness that it almost overwhelmed Violet.

"Oh." This time, Violet didn't even try to rein in her own tears. "I'm so sorry. This must be—oh," she repeated numbly. Because seriously, the fact that she got pregnant after one time had to be salt in the wound.

"Please," Nasira said, drying her eyes and putting on a good face, "do not apologize. Tell me more of Rafe. You are aware of his scheme, yes?"

"I figured it out. And when I confronted him about it, he told me the rest. I just…look, I get that he blames Mac. But it's been twelve years. And your father—how long has he been dead?"

"Almost seven years," Nasira said.

"Why is he still doing this? I thought…" Now it was her turn to look down at the table. "I thought he cared for me. But when I confronted him, he told me that Mac had ruined you and he was just returning the favor."

Nasira gasped in horror. "He said that?"

Violet nodded. "And I feel like such a fool because he made all these promises that sounded so good, about how I would always have a place in his country and how our child would be both a bin Saleed and a McCallum and…and it was all a trap. He didn't care for me, but I fell for him."

Unexpectedly, Nasira reached across the table and took Violet's hand in hers. "Do not think such things," she said, a harder edge to her voice. "I know Rafe and I know he does not say such things lightly. He does not allow himself to grow close to people in general and women specifically. That was what was so unusual about his friendship with Mac. I do not think that, before that time, Rafe had had many friends"

"Really? But he's so charming. Too charming," she admitted.

"I shall speak to him," Nasira said decisively.

"What? No, you don't have to do that."

"Please," Nasira said, but it wasn't a request. It was an order, and Violet remembered that, touching moments aside, she was technically sitting across from royalty. "This whole thing began with me and will be ended by me. Rafe has no just cause to treat you like this."

"I just don't want my baby to be this rope in a tug-of-war between me and Rafe," Violet said. "I don't want to keep his child from him but I can't live in fear that he'll take my baby and disappear into the desert and I'll never see my baby again."

"I will not allow it," Nasira said. "And if Rafe attempts such madness, Fareed will step in. You will be the mother of a bin Saleed. That affords you certain rights and protections, both in Al Qunfudhah and I assume here in America."

Violet nodded. "I mean, I guess. I haven't even seen a doctor yet. Everything's happened so fast…"

And what she really needed was for things to slow way, way down. At least long enough that she could get a handle on the situation. Honestly, at this rate, she was becoming numb to the shocks. She wouldn't even be surprised if the ghost of Rafe's dad, the old and seemingly really cruel sheikh himself, floated into the diner. It wouldn't faze her at all.

She glanced toward the door. Well, maybe not too much, anyway.

"Do you know where Rafe is?" Nasira asked.

"He's been staying at the Holloway Inn—it's about thirty minutes from here," Violet said. "That's where we met the first time."

Nasira brought up the inn's information on her phone. "Ah, I see."

"What about you? Do you have a place to stay? Do you want to see Mac?"

Nasira blushed, and in that moment, she looked much younger—probably more like the girl who'd been so desperate for a way out that she'd do anything. "He wouldn't be happy to see me, not after what Rafe has done," she said quietly. "I shall take a room at the inn where Rafe is."

"Will you call me and let me know how it goes?"

"Of course."

They exchanged numbers and Nasira stood to go. "Thank you," she said, putting her hat back on her head.

"For what?" Violet asked, trying not to be jealous of Nasira's style and grace. God knew Violet couldn't pull that level of class off. The one time she'd tried, well, she'd ended up pregnant.

"For caring about Rafe. He needs that more than you

could ever know." Her face took on a battle-ready look. It was a beautiful battle-readiness, but still, Violet decided that, in a throw-down, she'd put her money on Nasira. "I will not let him destroy this chance."

"I don't know that I care for him anymore. Not after all of this."

Nasira gave her a smile that sent a shiver racing down Violet's back. "We shall see."

Then Rafe's sister swept out of the Royal Diner just as quickly as she'd arrived. Violet glanced back to where Amanda was trying hard to look as though she wasn't listening. "Not a word to another living soul," she said.

"Not a word!" Amanda held up the Girl Scout sign. "On my honor!"

Violet sighed. She needed to warn Mac that the plot had thickened yet again. But she sat there for a little bit longer, trying to make sense of everything Nasira had shared. Realistically, she knew it was possible that Nasira was here because Rafe had called her, that she was a hedge against damage control. If Rafe's plan blew up in his face, he'd want a soft, beautiful woman to help with the public relations disaster.

Violet had already been a fool more than once, but she couldn't help but feel that Nasira was being honest with her. The woman's reaction to Violet's pregnancy had been too raw, too real.

And if Nasira was being up front, then it followed that…

Rafe's father had gone far beyond punishment. Rafe had spent literal, actual years planning this revenge. He claimed it was for Nasira's honor but…

She wasn't going to care. Rafe's history was tragic, but that didn't excuse his behavior now. He was single-handedly trying to ruin her family, her business and nearly the entire town of Royal, Texas. Violet needed to focus on protecting herself, her assets and, above all else, her child. Rafe wasn't even on that list.

So why did she hope that Nasira could talk some sense into him?

Yup, she was just that big of a fool.

Eleven

The Wild Aces was his.

True, it had cost Rafe an additional million dollars, but three million was nothing when he was worth a thousand times that. Three million dollars was nothing compared to the satisfaction of having finished what he set out to start.

This was a moment of victory. Years of planning and biding his time had finally come to fruition. Rafe had finally, finally avenged his family's name and honor.

He owned the Wild Aces.

He owned Mac McCallum.

Yet…

As Rafe sat in his car outside the Holloway Inn, he could not help but wonder if this was really what victory was supposed to feel like. That dull pain in his chest was back and had been ever since Rafe had dragged the real estate agent away from her family during dinner and driven madly through the countryside to get to the Wild Aces.

That pain had only gotten stronger when, coughing hard, Lulu Clilmer had told him she'd promised Violet McCallum twenty-four hours in which to match Samson Oil's offer. That was when Rafe had made an offer Lulu could not refuse—provided, of course, she signed the papers right then.

It had taken all of his self-control not to order the woman to sign. But in the end, a warm smile and obscene amounts of money had done the job for him. Lulu had signed.

Rafe should celebrate this victory. But the moment that thought occurred to him, his mind turned back to Violet—to meeting V in the bar of this very hotel and taking her to his bed. Promising that her pleasure would be his and then keeping that promise. Taking her to dinner at Claire's and waking up in her arms. Going for a ride across the Texas grasslands and watching her rope a wayward cow and feeling that, for once in his life, he was at peace. He'd glimpsed what happiness could mean for him—not as a distant, undefined thing he would never know, but a real thing he could hold in his hands when he held Violet close.

He was not at peace now. And he wasn't sure why. This was what he wanted, after all. Exacting his revenge upon Mac was the very thought that had kept him going during those dark years. Ruining Mac's life just as Rafe's had been was everything he had been working toward. His work here was about to be done.

Except that Mac had welcomed Rafe back with open arms, even vouching for him to his friends. Except Nolan Dane had been the closest thing Rafe had had to a true friend since Mac's betrayal. Except for Violet and the child she carried.

What was it about these people, this town, that made him doubt himself? No, this was not doubt. He was a bin Saleed. He did not have doubt and he did not question his motives. His motives were pure. The code he lived by—the code that had governed his family for generations—required this. Rafe had damaged the honor of the bin Saleed name. Retribution was the only way to restore that honor.

It was unfortunate that Violet had become a part of the scheme, he thought dimly as he exited his vehicle. And it was unfortunate that Nolan had lost sight of the larger goal and turned his back on Rafe.

It was unfortunate that they had all turned on him, but it did not signify. All that was left to do here was to confront Mac and let him know that Rafe had been the source of his downfall and that justice was finally served.

Then Rafe would be on the family plane, headed back to Al Qunfudhah. Back to the stretches of sand that backed up against the deep blue of the sea. Back to the family home, where Fareed ruled and Rafe was, once again, an unnecessary second. Back to where happiness was an unknown, unknowable thing that was not for him. Never for him.

It was fine. Rafe would turn his full attention back to the shipping business. Piracy was a growing concern and he needed to take measures to prevent his ships from being hijacked. If he could keep his costs low, he could undercut his competition and increase his share of the market, which would in turn increase the standard of living in Al Qunfudhah. That was how his time would be best spent. That was how he was most useful to his people. His personal happiness and sorrows did not signify. He felt nothing.

The pain in his chest was so strong that he paused outside the sliding doors of the Holloway Inn. Had it only been a matter of months since he had walked through these very doors and seen *her* sitting at the bar, the black lace of her dress contrasting with her creamy skin? Since he had taken one look at her wide smile and beautiful face and decided that he needed her in a way that he had not allowed himself to need another person?

Had it only been that long since he had given a part of him to her—a part he had not realized was his to give?

He rubbed at his chest, but it did nothing to help. He needed to leave this accursed place, he decided. In the morning, he would seek Mac out and then he would leave. He needed to be far, far away from Royal, Texas, and the people in it: people who made him want to care about them, people who seemed to care about him.

None of them did. Mac had not cared enough to keep his hands off Nasira. Nolan had not cared enough to stand by Rafe's side when he met a woman. And Violet...

Well, she had cared. Perhaps too much. More than was wise. And he had made her hate him.

At least she hadn't shot him.

One more day. He would be gone by this time tomorrow and then he could begin again. Perhaps Fareed would have selected a wife for him and he could produce legitimate heirs. That had been the purpose he had been raised for, after all. He would visit his wife when appropriate and the children would be shown to him by their nannies in the evening, as was proper. He would hardly know they were there.

And his child here...

Don't do this to me. Don't do this to us, Violet had

whispered, and he had wanted so desperately to turn back to her, to take her in his arms. In that moment, it didn't matter if it was a sign of weakness, but he could not inflict this pain on her. Not willingly.

But really, what choice did he have?

Still, he did not have to keep hurting her. No, he decided, he would not take the child from Violet. Her only crime was being Mac's sister—that and opening herself to him. There was no just cause to hurt her for that.

A voice in the back of his head—a quiet voice that sounded nothing like his father's—whispered that perhaps there was no just cause to hurt her at all. Perhaps, this soft voice suggested, there was no just cause to hurt any of them. Not Mac, not Nolan, not Violet and not the town of Royal.

Rafe pushed this thought aside. That was weakness talking and he had not come this far only to let doubt destroy everything he'd worked for. He'd spent years planning for this moment. This was not the time to have cold feet, as the Americans said. If anyone knew he was filled with this hollow pain, they would use it against him.

Rafe forced himself to breathe regularly. Years of his father's abuse had taught him that the only way to survive was to be as impervious as stone, no matter what Hassad had said or done to him.

Rafe was that stone now. Nothing could hurt him. Not even Violet's stricken face or the way she had cradled her stomach, seemingly without even being aware she was doing it, while she told him she would fight him at all costs.

It did not have to be that way. He had no wish to treat his child as he had been treated. Just the thought of his own flesh and blood having to survive what Rafe had survived at the hands of his father made his stomach turn.

Rafe focused on the movement of each breath in and out of his body. It would not be that way, not if he had anything to say about it. Perhaps, after some time had passed, he could return for a visit or he and Violet and the child could meet somewhere neutral. New York, perhaps. He could give her the deed to the Wild Aces and see his child and that would be enough for him, to get a glimpse of that happiness again, to be near it. He had made do with far less.

Perhaps he could, perhaps he could not. But could he really do that to Violet?

What happened to him did not matter. It never had. But what happened to her—to their child—could he really do this to them?

There had to be a way. He had to do something to protect her and the child, to show her that he cared for her. Something more than just holding the Wild Aces for her.

He could not destroy her. But this was weakness. If his father were still alive, he would beat Rafe for his weakness until he had no more skin left on his back, but he didn't care.

He had to show her she was not the pawn in this game—that she was something more. Much, much more.

This thought calmed him and he was able to straighten up. He would find a way to shield Violet and, until such time as he did, he would continue on. This happiness with Violet was separate from his revenge on Mac.

Besides, it would not do for Sheikh Rafiq bin Saleed to be seen staggering into a hotel as if his heart had been ripped clean of his chest. He was victorious. He had damned well better act like it.

When he was in full control of his faculties, he walked through the sliding doors of the inn. Habit had him scanning the lobby. He had been doing it for months now—

every time he returned to the inn, in fact. And he was always looking for the same thing—his beautiful, mysterious V.

His gaze came to rest on a woman, sitting stiffly in a cushioned armchair facing away from him. With a start, he realized he recognized that posture, that hair, that regal bearing.

Not V. Not Violet.

Nasira.

His sister was here? He had not seen her in several years, although they communicated via email on a regular basis. He was so stunned by her sudden appearance that he had to pause and think—had he called her here? He remembered promising Violet that he would arrange a meeting between the two women. But that was back when Violet was still speaking to him, and Rafe had been so busy in the interim that he was certain he had not had the time to summon Nasira.

Rafe did not allow himself to feel uneasy about this development. There was nothing to feel uneasy about, after all. This was merely his sister, the woman he had promised to protect. The woman he had failed. The woman whose honor he was avenging at this very moment.

"Sister," he said. He had always called her that instead of using her name.

"Ah, Brother, I see you are looking quite well." She rose gracefully to her feet and smiled. "Texas, it seems, agrees with you."

Rafe was immediately on the alert because he certainly didn't feel quite well. "Sister, why are you here?"

If he had offended her, she did not show it. Instead, she tilted her head to one side and gave him a piercing look. "Are you not glad to see me?"

"But of course I am." He stepped forward to wrap his arm around her shoulders and press a kiss to her cheek. "Does Sebastian know you are here? Are you well? Are you…" He glanced down at her stomach.

That got a reaction out of her. As Rafe watched, he saw her eyes grow flat and he knew that his question had caused her pain. For so long, she had been struggling to have a child with her husband. To ask such a question so baldly was in poor form. "Forgive me," he said gently. "That was unkind."

"Never fear." She put that sunny smile back on her face, but it didn't reach her eyes. "We are much the same. He is aware I am here."

Something about that admission sounded off. "Will he be joining you?"

Color bloomed on her cheeks. "Ah, no."

Rafe and Nasira were not children anymore, but to see her embarrassed in public brought back uncomfortable memories, and an old instinct to shield her from attention kicked in. "Shall we continue this conversation in my room? Or your room—are you staying here? I do not even know how long you plan to be in Royal. I intend to leave tomorrow, but if you are here, I do not see why I should not stay with you. I am sure that Sebastian would feel better knowing you are well cared for."

Again, she tilted her head to one side. "I am sure that Sebastian would appreciate that, if he knew you were here. And as for how long I am staying, that depends, I suppose. But yes," she went on before Rafe could ask what, exactly, she meant by that. "It would be best to talk in private, I believe."

"This way." He led her to the elevator. As the doors closed, he felt another unfamiliar stab of panic. "I must ask, Sister—how did you know where I was?"

"Fareed informed me," she said, but she did not elaborate.

"I am glad to see you. In fact, I had thought about calling you several days ago."

"Oh?" She turned to him. "Was there a reason?"

This was his sister, after all. He was not any more comfortable lying to her than he was lying to Violet. "You were in my thoughts," he said, which was both the truth and not exactly the truth.

She tilted her head. "I am honored."

Finally, the elevator came to a halt on his floor. He led the way down to his room and unlocked the door in silence.

Nasira swept into the room, but she did not take the office chair, nor did she sit on the edge of the bed. Instead, she stood in the center of his room as if it were hers, her hands folded in front of her. "So, brother," she said once the door was shut and he was facing her. "Tell me how you came to be here in Royal, Texas."

What had Fareed told her? "I could ask the same of you."

She waved this away. "I am here because Fareed gave me good reason to think that you are here for less-than-honorable reasons."

"I can assure you, sister, my reasons for being here are entirely honorable." It came out harsher than he meant it to. He did not speak harshly to Nasira. He protected her. He tried anyway.

And wasn't that really why he was here? He had tried to protect her and failed.

She sighed heavily, as if his statement had inspired nothing but disappointment. That was how she looked at him—with disappointment. That hollow pain in his chest bloomed again, burning with emptiness. "It is as we feared, then."

"What is?" He was the stone. He felt nothing because feelings were weaknesses and weakness was not tolerated. He was a bin Saleed.

"It began with me, so it shall end with me." She squared her shoulders and fixed him with a fierce gaze. "I was a virgin when I married Sebastian."

"What?" The statement caught Rafe so off guard that he recoiled a step.

"I never slept with Mac McCallum," she went on, as casually as if they were discussing the weather. "Nor did he even know I was in his bed that day. He had agreed to kiss me in front of our father to help me escape the fate that awaited me, but I was young and foolish and impulsive." She favored Rafe with a sad smile. "So foolish. I was afraid that a mere kiss would not be enough to dissuade our father, so I hatched a different plan. I snuck into Mac's bed when I knew you would be showing Father how you lived."

A strange numbness overtook Rafe's limbs as the scene played out in front of his eyes again.

Nasira had been nude under the covers, all of her clothing in a pile on the floor where they would be impossible to miss. Her hair had been freed of its braid. She had looked exactly like a woman awaking in her lover's bed. "We found you there. In his bed."

"Yes, I had been counting on it. My dear brother," she said in a voice that was almost pitying, "you are not the only one in this family who is capable of great schemes."

"Why are you telling me this? Why are you lying for him again?"

There was no mistaking the pity in her eyes this time. "Why do you persist in believing that I am lying for him?

I tried to tell you on the plane ride back. I did not want to marry that monster Father had assigned me to. I did not want to be forced into any marriage against my will. And to that end, the scheme worked perfectly. But I had not foreseen the other consequences. I did not realize what Father would do to you. And worse, I did not realize that you would do this, Rafe. I never dreamed you would even be capable of it."

"You don't know what you're talking about," he snapped at her. "You have no idea."

"Oh?" She was unruffled by his anger. It only made him madder.

"Everything I have done, I have done for you. For your honor. For our family name."

"That is why I have come to stop you."

"Are you quite mad?" he roared.

"Are you? You are the one who has nursed this perceived hurt for years. Years, Rafe. I understand that you are bitter that Father treated you like a prisoner in our home. I regret every day that my choice led to such dire consequences for you. That is a burden I carry with me everywhere I go."

He opened his mouth to say something—what, he did not know, but something, dammit all, that made her realize that *bitter* did not even begin to describe him. But she held up a hand, cutting him off with all the commanding manner of a member of the royal family. "But I have never given up hope for you, Rafe. You are not our father. He is dead and I am glad of it. You no longer have to do as he would do. You no longer have to prove that you are as cruel and heartless as he was."

"This is not cruelty," he shouted, unable to get control of himself. "Cruelty is being thrown in a dungeon and beaten because I allowed my friend to defile my sister."

"Cruelty," she calmly responded, "is destroying a man and an entire town because you were beaten. Cruelty," she said, her voice rising in pitch, "is destroying a woman who cares about you, a woman who carries your child even as we speak." Her voice cracked, the first true sign of emotion since his words had wounded her earlier. She put her hand on her heart. "Cruelty is being given the gift of love, of a child, and doing everything within your power to destroy those gifts."

He would not be moved by her sorrow. "Mac betrayed me!"

"No, Rafe. No." She shook her head and regained her composure. "The only person who has betrayed you is you. Well," she added in a casual tone, as if she had not just swung a hammer of words at his stone heart and broken it to small bits, "you and our father. But then, he betrayed us all, did he not?"

Rafe stared at her, unable to form words in his mind and equally unable to get his tongue to say them.

"Fareed is worried about you," she went on in a quiet voice. "We all are. We had hoped that, with Father's death, you would have been able to find peace. You have a chance for that, Rafe. Do not be the man Father demanded you to be. Be the man you want to be."

She moved a chair out of the way and walked toward him. No, not toward him—toward the door. When she reached him, she said, "Please forgive me for my part in your pain. It was never my intention to see you hurt. But believe me when I say this—I will fight to protect your child from you, if it comes to that. The choice is yours."

She stepped around him. He heard the door open and then shut. He knew, at least on some level, that he was alone.

But he was not. Ghosts of the past—and the present—

cluttered his vision. He saw Nasira in bed, looking shocked to have been discovered. But now he remembered that she had disappeared from their group only a few minutes before that—thirty, at most. Not nearly enough time to have slept with Mac in his bed.

And Rafe remembered Mac's shock at coming into the room and finding all of them there like that—Nasira in his bed, Rafe standing next to it, Hassad raging at both of them. At the time, Rafe had taken that shock as confirmation that Mac had not expected Hassad to find him with his lover but...

Was it possible he had been just as shocked about seeing Nasira in his bed?

And then it had all happened so fast. Within hours, they were on the family jet, flying back to Al Qunfudhah.

"Tell me you have not failed me," Hassad had said in that dank dungeon, in between blows. And Rafe had known there was no hope. He could not defend himself, for his father would call him a liar and beat him more. And he could not admit defeat because his father would beat him for being a coward.

And Fareed—he was there, as well, sneaking down to the dungeon with extra food or wine, with medicines that took the edge off the pain or a blanket to make the stone floor more comfortable or books to read so that Rafe did not go out of his mind. "I will convince him," Fareed had promised. "This is not your fate."

And Rafe had been so beaten down that he had not bothered to correct his brother. This was his fate. He took his father's anger so Hassad did not treat his other children this way. That had always been Rafe's fate, ever since he was a child and had defended Nasira, his closest sibling, from Fareed's teasings and had gotten slapped across the face for daring to speak against the future sheikh of Al Qunfudhah.

Rafe had not gotten to see Nasira get married to Sebastian, a man who did not beat her and did not use her poorly. He had not gotten the chance to meet the man for years.

And Nolan Dane—his ghost was here, as well, looking at Rafe with distrust and something verging on horror.

Then there was Violet—his beautiful, mysterious V, his tough, quick cowgirl. She was carrying his child. She had been haunting his every thought for months. Did he honestly expect that he would return to Al Qunfudhah and not see her everywhere he went?

And woven in with all of these visions were past versions of himself. Of the boy who took the beatings so his siblings would not have to. Of the young man who attended to his tutors closely and dreamed of leaving Al Qunfudhah behind. Of the man who was ripped from his studies and his friends. Of the scarred man who refused to cower in the face of the abuses heaped upon him by the one person who was supposed to have defended him. Of the determined man who watched and waited and schemed.

Of the man who'd seen a beautiful woman who had sparked something in his chest, something that had not been there before. Something that made his heart cry out for pleasure, for something *more*.

Something more. That was what Violet was to him. More than just revenge. More than the stone wall he hid his heart behind. More than what his father expected and demanded.

With a cry of pain, he realized what he had become. Mac, Nolan and Violet—most especially Violet—they had opened their arms to Rafe, embraced him as friend and family. He had never been a sheikh's second son, not to them. He had always been Rafe and, for the first and only time in his life, just being Rafe was enough. More than enough.

Rafe would never be enough for Hassad bin Saleed. He could keep trying and trying and trying but the old man was dead and gone, and just as Nasira had said, Rafe was glad of it.

But he had been wrong. He thought that with Hassad's death, he had been freed of the old man. But he saw now that he had still carried Hassad with him, allowing his father's perverse sense of honor to warp Rafe's thoughts and actions.

Mac had been blameless. And in the name of a dead man's honor, Rafe had bought almost half an American county's worth of land to ruin his old friend.

Nolan had offered Rafe friendship but the moment he got too close, Rafe had shut Nolan out and driven him into the arms of a woman who would love him.

And Violet... She was beyond blameless. Yet Rafe had used her poorly. Cruelly, even.

What had he done? Hassad was dead. Yet he still controlled Rafe. Perhaps that had always been the old man's scheme, his plan to live from beyond the grave.

Well, no more.

Rafe had much work to do.

Twelve

Only one window at the McCallum house spilled light out into the night. It was not Violet's window—of that, Rafe was certain. Did that mean Mac was the only one home?

It did not matter. Rafe was here to make things right and if that meant he had to go through Mac, then that was what must be done.

Rafe shut his vehicle off and got out. Before he even closed the car door behind him, the front door of the Mc-Callum house burst open.

Ah. He would have to go through Mac. Fitting.

But as Mac came down off the porch, Rafe drew back in alarm. He had never seen Mac this visibly angry before. His hands were balled into fists and, for the first time, Rafe thought his old friend could physically harm him.

The question that remained unanswered was, would Mac pummel him for what he'd done to Mac—or to Violet? It did not matter much. Either way, Rafe was deserving of this fury.

Despite the rage that poured off Mac in waves, Rafe held his ground. Years of habit had trained Rafe not to fall back or seek cover. Instead, he awaited his fate.

"Give me one good reason," Mac growled as he advanced in long strides, "why I shouldn't shoot you where you stand." Though he didn't have a gun that Rafe could see, the threat hung heavy in the air between them.

Because if Mac had a gun and pulled the trigger, Rafe would not survive. But he would not fight back.

The family honor, his father's voice whispered insidiously. *No one uses a bin Saleed like that and gets away with it.*

But this time, Rafe pushed the thought away. He did more than push it away. *No one uses a bin Saleed like you used me*, he thought back. *And I am not your instrument any longer.*

Mac was staring at him, rage and confusion blending into one hard mask of hatred. Rafe had earned that. "Well?" Mac demanded.

"You always were a man of honor," Rafe said, not bothering to hide a smile.

"Not like you, you dog. You and Violet? And the land? Why?"

Rafe took a breath. He suspected he had only one chance to get this right. "I have come to beg your forgiveness."

"I'm not buying that load of bullshit." Rafe did not flinch. That instinct had been beaten out of him years ago. "All this happened because you thought I slept with your sister. But I never even touched her, dammit."

"So she has told me."

The confusion in Mac's eyes overtook the rage a bit. "What?"

"She is here. Well, in Holloway. My brother told her

what I was doing. She came to make things right." Odd, that after so many years of trying to protect his siblings, they were now the ones doing the protecting. Except that, instead of protecting Rafe from their father, they were trying to protect him from himself.

"I don't understand."

"She has explained to me what happened the day we found her in your bed," Rafe went on, still trying to make sense of the day's events. "And I have realized something."

Mac fell back a step. "Yeah?"

"I came here for revenge." There was no cushioning that truth with soft words. "But I did not come here to avenge her. I thought I had. I thought I was meting out justice for the shame you brought upon my family's honor and our name. But that was a lie, I see now. A lie that justified my actions."

Mac took another step back. "So why are you here? Why did you come?"

Rafe found himself looking up. The stars were clear and bright here. When his father had him trapped in the dungeon, he had hardly seen the night sky for years. *Years.* "I came here to avenge myself."

"I didn't do a damn thing to you," Mac said. "And I'm not going to let you destroy Violet. I'd sooner rot in prison than see you ruin her."

Rafe smiled at this. "A man of honor," he repeated quietly. "I understand. For, you see, I did the same thing."

"What?"

Rafe had that weird out-of-time sensation again, the same one he felt when he had gone riding with Violet and slept in her bed with her. "I think it was always supposed to be this way," he told Mac.

"I don't know what you're talking about."

He grinned. "I am in love with your sister."

Before Rafe could protect himself, Mac stepped forward and punched him in the jaw. Rafe was knocked sideways as pain bloomed in his face, but he kept his feet underneath him. All told, he deserved that punch.

"You have one hell of a way of showing it. You hurt her, you ass. I've done everything I could to protect her and you waltz in here and…" His voice shook. "And you hurt her. She doesn't deserve that."

Rafe straightened. "No, she doesn't. But you can't get revenge for her." He took a deep breath. This was right. This was peace. "You can only get revenge for yourself."

"What?"

"I have hurt you, Mac. We were friends—I considered you to be a brother. Which makes the way my entire family acted toward you all the worse." Rafe bowed his head before Mac. "Please accept my apologies on behalf of my sister, my father—and myself. You did not deserve to be used like you were."

Mac stood there, his mouth open wide as he gaped at Rafe. "I—you—"

"I would like to speak to Violet now." Rafe reached for the deed to the Wild Aces. "I want to give this to her and tell her I love her."

But as he moved, Mac tensed and reached behind his back. Someone screamed.

And a gun went off.

"That bastard is here." Those had been Mac's exact words as he'd grabbed his pistol, shoved it in the back of his waistband and run out the door before Violet could do anything else.

Rafe had come back? That man must have a death wish. If Mac didn't get him, Violet would.

Lulu had called. She was sure sorry, but three million—well, she knew that Violet would never be able to come close to that. The money was too good. She'd signed the papers.

Tears silently streaming down her face, Violet had ended the call.

Gone. It was all gone. All because Rafe had his facts wrong.

Bastard wasn't a strong enough term.

Still, she didn't exactly want Mac to shoot Rafe. At the very least, he shouldn't kill Rafe. A flesh wound might be okay.

No, that was just the anger talking because if Mac shot Rafe, Mac would wind up in prison and Rafe's family would want to know why and there would be an international incident. And the very last thing Violet wanted right now was an international incident.

So she hurried out through the kitchen and crept along the side of the house, sticking to the shadows. When she could peek around the porch, she saw that Rafe and Mac were standing only a few feet away. Oddly, Mac wasn't holding his gun. Odder still, the two men were talking.

"…And tell her I love her," she heard Rafe say as he reached into his pocket.

Mac tensed and reached around his back—for his gun.

Oh, God—he was going to shoot Rafe. And Rafe had just said that he loved her? Hadn't he?

One thing was clear. Mac couldn't kill Rafe. He couldn't even wound him.

But that wasn't stopping Mac. He had the gun out of his waistband. She tried to shout a warning—but she couldn't even get the words, "Don't kill him!" out before a shot was fired into the darkness.

Violet screamed so loudly that the world went blue on the edge of her vision and then, just as it was going black, she saw both men turn in her direction.

Rafe was the last thing she thought about before she blacked out.

"Violet," she heard a silky voice say. For some reason, it made her think of sunshine and honey, warm and sweet. "Are you well? Please open your eyes," the voice pleaded. "Please be well."

"Here," another voice said. This one was gruff and tight. It was her brother, Mac.

"Ah," said the liquid sunshine voice. *Rafe*. Rafe was here. Oh, thank God.

Then something wet splashed on her face and she startled. Her eyes flew open and she saw the night sky and Rafe's face close to hers and Mac's hovering behind him. "What happened?"

"Someone scared the hell out of me," Mac said. He sounded mad, but she could see the worry lines on his face. "And I pulled the trigger."

"I fear the car will never be the same," Rafe said. He managed a small grin at her.

"You're not dead? I'm not dead?"

"No one is dead," he assured her. "You, however, fainted."

"Dammit." This was embarrassing.

"Yeah," Mac replied. "She's shooting her mouth off again. She's fine. Help me get her up."

"I have her," Rafe said. He pulled Violet into his arms and cradled her against his chest. Then, as if she weighed nothing at all, he stood. "If you could be so kind as to find the paper I dropped…"

"Sure. What is it?"

"The deed to the Wild Aces." He said it casually as he carried her into the house.

"What?" she gasped.

"The Wild Aces. It is yours." He sat down on the couch, but he did not let her go. Instead—in the middle of the living room, in full view of her brother and anyone else who might wander through—he pulled her onto his lap. "Whatever you choose, I will accept. But the land—and the water—it is yours."

She blinked up at him. "Are you serious? You're just going to *give* me the Aces? You spent three million dollars on it!"

"I would pay twice that if that was what it took to give you a beautiful home where you can raise our child. I want you to give him or her the kind of life that you have had, surrounded by family and love."

"I don't understand." It came out confused and weak, and she didn't want to be weak in front of him. She tried to shove herself off his lap, but his arms closed around her and there was no escaping him.

"I am sorry," he said. "I beg your forgiveness, Violet." He gave her an oddly crooked smile. "If my father could see me begging a woman for forgiveness…"

"Don't," she said. "I don't want to ever hear his name again."

"A sheikh of Al Qunfudhah does not ask for forgiveness. And begging is unthinkable. But that is what I am doing now, Violet. I treated you poorly and there is no excuse."

There was something else going on here and it wasn't just that he'd been crazy enough to tell an armed-and-dangerous older brother he was in love with her.

It was the same *something else* that Violet had seen in Nasira's eyes when Nasira had said that their father had imprisoned Rafe. At the time, she had hoped that the other woman was speaking metaphorically or Violet had misunderstood because of the language and cultural differences between them, even though Nasira spoke perfect, if British, English.

What if…what if she hadn't been speaking metaphorically?

Rafe bowed his head over her. "My father was…a difficult man."

Violet waited. She had the feeling that he was getting to the truth of the matter and she could not rush him.

"He held me responsible for what had happened to Nasira. He washed his hands of her and she was able to move to London. In that, I had succeeded in protecting her. Her life has been much better for it. But as for my father, I had failed him. And he made me pay for that failure."

"What do you mean, he made you pay? Nasira said…"

The sorrow on Rafe's face made her eyes tear up. "He locked me in the dungeons."

"Oh, God." She blinked, but the tears refused to go away.

"For years, until he died, I was a prisoner in my own home." His voice wavered and he closed his eyes, but only for a moment. When he opened them again, he looked almost unmoved by what had happened. But she could see now that it was a lie. He wasn't incapable of emotions. He was just hiding the pain. "Fareed is the only reason I am still alive. He snuck me food and medicines and did his best to convince our father to free me—or at least treat me better."

Violet's heart about broke. *Oh, Rafe.*

"It does not excuse my behavior," he said sternly. "But during those years, there was but one thought that sustained me. I had lost everything. My freedom, my life, my friend. And I believed that it was because of Mac that everything I loved had been taken from me."

She didn't know what to say. So instead, she hung her arms around his neck and held him to her, as if that could take the pain away.

Rafe went on, "I told myself that I had to avenge the family name, I had to make us even for Nasira's honor. That was what my father beat into me. But I see now that it was never that. I suffered greatly. And I wanted to make Mac feel the same hopelessness I had felt."

Violet's throat closed up and she had to choke down a sob. So that was it. His father hadn't delivered a metaphorical beating—hell, it wasn't even a single beating. The horrible man had treated Rafe like a whipping boy.

She couldn't stop the tears that traced down her cheeks. All those times when a shadow had crossed his face—was he remembering what his father said or did to him?

This wasn't fair. He was making her feel things for him and she didn't want to. She didn't want to feel anything but hate because he had been prepared to take everything she loved away from her. She absolutely did not want to feel this urge to pull him into her arms and hold him tight and tell him that as long as she lived, no one would ever do that to him again. A silly girl's silly promise—Rafe was a man now, and more than capable of taking care of himself. But, as silly as it was, she wanted to say it to him. She wanted to tell him that she would never let anyone treat their child like that either.

She wanted to keep him safe. After all these years of being guarded and protected, this sudden urge to defend Rafe was almost overwhelming.

Stupid pregnancy hormones. She had no idea if she was mad or sad or upset or so, so happy because Rafe really did love her and he had come back to apologize. He wasn't going to destroy her.

He wasn't going to destroy the two of them.

"All those years ago, Mac had entranced me with stories of your happy family and your beautiful ranch and your town. And for years, I waited for a way to destroy those things. But when I was with you, it all came back to me. And I felt like… I feel like I had finally come home again."

"Oh, Rafe," she gasped. "Why couldn't you see it sooner? I would have been your family. We all would have been. This could have been your home—with me." She lifted his hand and put it against her stomach. "With us."

That look of sorrow passed over his face again, then he cupped her cheeks in his hands and touched his forehead to hers. "I understand. My treatment of you has been unforgivable and I will regret until my dying day that I hurt you so. The Wild Aces is yours, but I know that it can never truly make up for my actions. I will leave tomorrow and I will not trouble you again."

She froze, a feeling of horror building in her chest. "Wait—what?"

Rafe gave her a sad smile. "I wish to stay—I wish to be with you. You are my only happiness. But to do so would bring dishonor upon my family name. But more than that, it would dishonor you and your family. I cannot do that, not anymore. I cannot destroy what I love."

"I swear to God, if you ever talk about doing something stupid out of honor again, I'm going to shoot you myself."

At this announcement, Rafe's eyebrows jumped up so high they almost cleared his forehead. "What?"

"You keep talking like it's too late—well, I've got news for you, buster. Just because you hold a grudge for over a damned decade doesn't mean I have to."

"But—my actions—I have hurt you."

"You're damn right you have." She glared at him, trying to put her thoughts into something that resembled order. "But you've also faced down my brother to apologize. You survived a horrific childhood and yet here you are, trying so hard to do the right thing that you're about to go and screw it up again." She threw her hands up, almost hitting him in the chin. "God! Men!"

Rafe was staring at her, a puzzled look on his face. "What are you saying?"

"You begged my forgiveness. That's what you said, right?" He nodded. "Well, I forgive you. I forgive you, Rafe."

The impact of these words hit Rafe as hard as if she'd actually shot him. He fell back against the couch, clutching at his chest. His eyes went wide and he turned a scarily pale color.

Violet panicked. "Rafe? Are you okay?"

"You—you forgive me?" He said it in such a way that it was clear that the thought had never crossed his mind. Forgiveness hadn't been an option. "I nearly ruined your life!"

"But you didn't," she reminded him. This was right, she decided. She could hold this misguided attempt to rule the world against him—but that would be punishing the son for the sins of the father. And Rafe was more than that.

He was the father of her child. And she would not let those sins ruin them all. "I forgive you, Rafe. I hope you can forgive yourself."

He was physically shaking. She really had no choice but to wrap her arms around him and hold him tight— tighter than she'd ever held anyone before.

"I do not deserve you, Violet. I am not worthy of your love."

"Is that what *he* told you—that bastard of a father of yours? Because it was a lie, Rafe. You are the man I want—when you're not trying to be what *he* wanted you to be."

Rafe looked at her with so much longing and pain in his eyes that she had trouble breathing. "Violet…"

"Found it," Mac said, walking into the room. He took one look at the two of them curled up on the couch together and groaned. "Am I going to have to shoot you or not?"

"In my country," Rafe said without flinching at all, "when a man wishes to marry a woman, he would ask permission of her father or her oldest male relative."

Mac's mouth opened, but Rafe didn't let him get a word in. "However," he said, his gaze never leaving Violet's face, "we are not in my country, are we?"

Violet's heart—the same heart that had very nearly stopped beating only a few minutes ago—began to pound. "No," she said, quietly. "We aren't."

"Lord," Mac scoffed. "I will shoot you if you do anything stupid to deserve it ever again."

Rafe laughed. "I have a feeling you won't have the chance."

"You're nuts," Violet said. "Both of you. Now, Mac— if you don't mind, I think Rafe was trying to ask me something?"

"I don't want to know," he muttered, turning on his heel and stalking out of the room. The last thing Violet caught before the front door slammed was, "…little sister—gross!"

She laughed and Rafe laughed with her. "I'm sorry my brother almost killed you."

"I deserved it. I have no right to ask this of you and you have no obligation to say yes—but Violet McCallum, would you do me the honor of becoming my wife?"

She wasn't sure she remembered how to breathe, but it didn't matter. All that mattered was Rafe was here and there were no more lies between them. "Are you sure we can make this work? You've got to admit that nothing about this has been a normal relationship."

"You have shown me there is another way." Rafe rested his hand on her belly. "I want nothing more than to spend my days riding by your side and my nights in your bed. I want to hear our child's heartbeat and be there when you bring him or her into this world. I want to do all the things my parents did not do, all the things Mac spoke of that gave me hope. Dinners and birthday parties and movies with popcorn and love. I want your love, Violet. I do not deserve it but—"

He didn't get to say anything else because Violet had pulled him down to her and covered his mouth with hers.

"Do you love me?" she asked, pulling away before she lost what little control she still had. "Really?"

"I have never loved anyone before, but I love you. You grace my thoughts during the day and haunt my dreams at night, my beautiful, mysterious Violet. I love you more than I can hold inside me. I think I always have," he whispered against her forehead.

"It was always supposed to be this way," she said, remembering his words. She leaned into his touch, curling her hands into the fine cloth of his shirt and holding him to her.

"I was always supposed to be yours," he agreed. "I just did not realize it until it was too late."

"It's not too late," she told him, throwing her arms

around his neck and hugging him. "But no more shocks, okay?"

"No more shocks. You know the worst of me. All I can hope to do is show you the best of me. Your pleasure is my pleasure," he said into her hair. "And I swear I will spend the rest of our lives giving you nothing but pleasure."

"I'm going to hold you to that," she cautioned him. "Because your pleasure is my pleasure, too."

He cupped her face in his palm and stared into her eyes. "I love you, Violet McCallum. Marry me. Be my family. Because I want there to be an *us*."

Us. He might have torn them apart, but he was going to put them back together. "I love you, too. Stay with me, Rafe. Let me protect you."

"Only so long as I can protect you. This is your last chance, Violet. If you say no, I will leave, peacefully and quietly. I will support our child, but I will not interfere with your life again."

For some reason, she thought of their conversation in the elevator their first night together. He'd given her a chance to say no then, too—but she hadn't. "And if I say yes?"

His grin grew wicked. "If you say yes, you will be mine, you understand? And I will be yours. For always and forever."

"Then I better say yes. I am yours, Rafiq bin Saleed."

He touched his forehead to hers. "I am yours, Violet McCallum."

And that was all either of them said for quite some time.

* * * * *

Henri needed to touch her, to wrap her in his arms.

She was sexy—a tangle of tousled hair and pure fire. And in this setting—in the middle of the garden in that peach dress—she looked like a nymph those classical artists were always capturing.

He could sense the answering awareness in her, a heat she'd denied too often these past months. Now, extending a hand, he trailed it along the length of her lithe arm. Gentle pressure, the kind that used to drive her wild with anticipation. She turned to face him, leaning into his light touch.

Reaching for her hand, he threaded his fingers through hers, locking them together in that one, small way. He was holding on to her.

Could he hold on to them?

* * *

Reunited with the Rebel Billionaire
is part of the Bayou Billionaires series:
Secrets and scandal are a Cajun family
legacy for the Reynaud brothers!

REUNITED WITH THE REBEL BILLIONAIRE

BY
CATHERINE MANN

First Published in Great Britain 2016
By Mills & Boon, an imprint of HarperCollins*Publishers*
1 London Bridge Street, London, SE1 9GF

© 2016 Catherine Mann

ISBN: 978-0-263-91856-4

51-0416

Our policy is to use papers that are natural, renewable and recyclable products and made from wood grown in sustainable forests. The logging and manufacturing processes conform to the legal environmental regulations of the country of origin.

Printed and bound in Spain
by CPI, Barcelona

USA TODAY bestselling author **Catherine Mann** has penned over fifty novels, released in more than twenty countries. A RITA® Award winner, she holds a master's degree in theater and enjoys bringing that dramatic flair to her stories. Catherine and her military husband live in Florida, where they brought up their four children. Their nest didn't stay empty long, though, as Catherine is president of the Sunshine State Animal Rescue. For more information, visit www.catherinemann.com.

One

Fiona Harper-Reynaud was married to *American Sports* magazine's "Hottest Athlete of the Year" for two years running.

She hadn't married the New Orleans Hurricanes' star quarterback for his looks. In fact, she'd always been drawn to the academic sort more than the jock type. But when that jock happened to be visiting an art gallery fund-raiser she'd been hosting for her father, she'd been intrigued. When Henri Reynaud had shown an appreciation and understanding of the nuances of botanic versus scenic art, she'd fallen hook, line and sinker into those dreamy, intelligent dark eyes of his. His eyes were the color of coffee and carried just as strong a jolt.

Still, she'd held back because of her own history with relationships, and yes, two broken engagements.

Held back for all of a couple of weeks. And ever since then her life hadn't stopped spiraling out of control.

Sure, they'd eloped because they'd thought she was pregnant. But she'd loved him so intensely, so passionately, reason scattered like petals from a windswept azalea. They hadn't realized until it was too late they had no substantive foundation in their marriage when difficult times came their way. And what little base they'd built upon had crumbled quickly.

Especially right now.

In two short hours, Fiona would be greeting the elite community of New Orleans for her latest fund-raiser, purely in a volunteer capacity. Any time a foundation offered to pay, she donated the funds back to the charity. She believed deeply in the causes she supported and was grateful to have the wealth and time to help.

But the pressure of the high-glitz affair wasn't what rattled her. The doctor visit today had her scared, and more determined than ever she couldn't continue a marriage built on anything but love. Certainly not built only on obligation.

She switched her phone to speaker and placed it on the antique dresser, one of many beautiful pieces in the home she shared with Henri in New Orleans's gracious and historic Garden District. Her eyes lingered on the crystal-framed photograph of her with Henri from a trip they'd taken to Paris a few years back. Their smiles caught her off guard.

Had her life ever been that happy? The version of herself in the photograph felt like a stranger now.

She'd been so focused on the photograph, she almost forgot she was on the phone with Adelaide, her future sister-in-law and longtime personal assistant to Henri's half brother Dempsey. At long last the two were engaged. Their love had taken longer to bloom, unlike Henri's impulsive proposal to Fiona.

Blinking, Fiona shifted her attention back to the conversation. To her family. She internally laughed at that thought. Family implied closeness and solidarity. Instead of that, she felt numbingly alone and isolated.

And there was no reason for that. The Reynaud family was large and the majority of them resided right here in New Orleans. Two of her husband's brothers lived in a private compound of homes on Lake Pontchartrain. And they'd be at that compound tonight for the fund-raiser.

Star athletes, celebrities and politicians would gather and mingle for Fiona's newest cause. Conversation would fill the air. And if her past events were any indication, she would raise the funds necessary to open up the new animal shelter.

She perched on the delicate Victorian settee at the end of her four-poster bed. She pulled on one thigh-high stocking as she listened to her future sister-in-law rattle off the wines, liquors and other beverages delivered.

Still caught in the past, when she'd fallen hard for Henri Reynaud, she rolled the silk socking up her other leg. Henri had chased her relentlessly until she'd begun to believe him when he said he adored her mind every bit as much as her body.

Her body.

Hands shaking, she tugged the band on her thigh into place. She couldn't afford to think about those days before their marriage turned rocky, only to have him stay with her because of her health. She respected his honor, even as it hurt her to the core to lose his love. But she couldn't accept anything less than honest emotion.

Which meant she had to keep her secret. She tugged a wrinkle from her stocking and continued her phone conversation with Adelaide. "I can't thank you enough for helping me out with tonight's fund-raiser."

"Glad to lend my help. I wish you would ask more often."

"I didn't want to impose or make you feel pressured before when Dempsey was your boss." She'd known Adelaide for years, but only recently had they all learned of her romance with Dempsey Reynaud.

"But now that we're going to be sisters-in-law, I'm fair game?"

"Oh, um, I'm sorry." Her mind was so jumbled today. "I didn't mean that the way it came out."

"No need to apologize," Adelaide said, laughing softly. "Truly. I was just teasing. I'm really glad to lend a hand. It's a great cause. You do so much for charity—it's an inspiration."

"Well, I would have been an inspiring failure if not for your help today setting up the party at the compound." The main family compound on Lake Pontchartrain was larger and more ornate than Fiona and Henri's personal getaway. They'd purchased the place for privacy, a space she could decorate in her own antique, airy style in contrast to the palatial Greek Revival and Italianate mansions that made up the bulk of the family compound. She was grateful for the privacy right now as she readied herself for the party and steadied her nerves.

"Emergencies crop up for everyone. Did you sort

things out with your car?" Traces of concern laced Adelaide's voice.

Fiona winced. She didn't like lying to people, but if she admitted to seeing the doctor today that would trigger questions she was still too shaken to answer. After years of fertility treatments, she was used to keeping her medical history and heartbreak secret. "All is well, Adelaide. Thank you."

Or at least she hoped all was well. The doctor told her she shouldn't worry.

Easier said than done after all she had been through. Worrying had become her natural state, her automatic reflex lately.

"Glad to hear it. I emailed you the changes made to the menu so you can cross-check with the receipts."

"Changes?" Anxiety coiled in Fiona's chest. Normally she rolled with last-minute changes. They presented her with an opportunity to become more creative in the execution of the event. Every event she'd ever run had called for an adjustment or two. But her mind was elsewhere and her deeply introspective state made dealing with these external changes difficult.

"There were some last-minute problems with getting fresh mushrooms, so I made substitutions. Do you want me to go over them now?" Keys clicked in the background.

"Of course not. I trust your taste and experience." And she did.

"If you need my help with anything else, let me know." Adelaide hesitated until the sound of someone else speaking then leaving the room faded. "I'm comfortable in my work world, but my future role and responsibilities as a Reynaud spouse will be new territory to me."

And Fiona's time as a Reynaud wife was drawing to an end, even if the family didn't know it yet. Her heart sank. "You are a professional at this. You could take any event to a whole new level. Just make sure to find what you want your niche to be. The men in this family can steamroll right over a person." The words tumbled out of her mouth, and her cool, collected front began to crumble.

"Fiona…" Concern tinged her voice. "Are you okay?"

"Don't mind me. I'm fine. I'll see you soon. I need to get changed." She couldn't attend the event in stockings, a thong and a bra. No matter how fine the imported Italian lace. "Thanks again." She disconnected and slid her sapphire-blue gown from the end of the bed.

She stepped into the floor-length dress, the silk chiffon a cool glide over her skin, the dress and underwear strategically designed. The fabric fit snugly in a swathe around her breasts and hips, with a looser pleated skirt grazing her ankles. A sequin-studded belt complemented her glinting diamond chandelier earrings.

No one would see her scars. No one other than her husband and doctors knew.

Double mastectomy.

Reconstruction.

Prophylactic—preventative. In hopes of evading the disease that had claimed her mother, her aunt and her grandmother.

Fiona had never had breast cancer. But with her genetics, she couldn't afford to take the risk. She pressed the dress to her chest and tried not to think of the doctor's words today about a suspicious reading on her breast MRI that could be nothing. The doctor said the lump was almost certainly benign fat necrosis. But just to be safe he wanted to biopsy…

The creaking of the opening door startled her. Her dress slid down and she grabbed it by the embellished straps, pressing it back to her chest even though she knew only one person would walk in unannounced.

Her husband.

America's hottest athlete for two years running.

And the man she hadn't slept with since her surgery six months ago.

Henri's hands fell to rest on her shoulders, his breath caressing her neck. "Need help with the zipper?"

Henri took risks in his job on a regular basis. Sure, his teammates worked their asses off to prevent a hard tackle from his blind side, but he understood and accepted that every time he stepped onto the field, he could suffer a career-ending injury.

Fans called him brave. Sports analysts sometimes labeled him reckless. The press branded him fearless.

They were all wrong.

He'd been scared as hell every day since the doctors declared Fiona had inherited her family's cancer gene. It didn't matter that their marriage had been on the rocks. He'd been rocked to his foundation. Still was.

Henri clenched her shoulders so his hands wouldn't shake. Even the smallest touch between them was filled with tension. And not in the way that made him weak in the knees. "Your zipper?"

With a will of their own, his eyes took in the long exposed line of her neck, her deep brown hair corralled by a thin braid so that lengthy, loose curls cascaded in a narrow path down her back. He looked farther down her spine to the small of her back that called to him to touch, to kiss in a lingering, familiar way. But he'd lost the right. She'd made that clear when he'd tried to reconcile after the doctor's prognosis.

"Thank you. Yes, please," she said, glancing over her shoulder nervously and pulling her hair aside, the strands so dark they almost appeared black at night. He hated seeing that sort of distance in her amber-colored eyes. "I'm running late because of, um, a last-minute snafu with the caterer."

"Adelaide said you were having trouble with your car, so I came home early. But I see it's in the garage. What was wrong?"

Whipping her head away from his gaze, she muttered, "Doesn't matter."

It was becoming her trademark response. It didn't matter.

That was a lie. He could tell by the way her mouth thinned as she spoke.

He let out a deep sigh as his gaze traced over their room. Or should he say—their *former* room. He'd taken to sleeping in the guest bedroom of the restored home. Away from her. They'd even lost the ability to lie next to each other at night. To show up for each other in that simple way.

In front of him was the first gift he'd ever bought Fiona. It was a handsome jewelry armoire that doubled as a full-length mirror. It was a one-of-a-kind antique piece. Whimsical and light. Just like Fiona in her jewel-colored dress. Looking at the gilded mirror framing the reflection of his exquisite wife reminded him of how far they'd fallen. Damn.

This whole room was a mausoleum to what had been.

He wanted her to lean on him. Even if it was just a little bit. This wasn't what he wanted. "Anything else I can do to help?"

"I've got it under control." Finality colored her words.

"You always do." It came out harsher than he intended. But dammit, he was trying. Couldn't she see that?

She spun around to face him, her petite frame filling with rigid rage as the silk of her gown whirled against his shins. Raising her chin and her brow, she pressed her lips tight, primly. "No need to be snarky."

Sticking his hands in his pants pockets, he shrugged, his Brioni tuxedo jacket sliding along his shoulders. "I am completely serious."

Fiona's sherry eyes softened, the amber depths intoxicating. She took a deep breath and stared at him. A breeze stirred the stale air of the room, filtering through the window with the sounds of foot traffic and car horns. It was a grounding sound, reminding him of when they'd first bought this house—when they'd been a team. They'd spent months working together on every detail of restoring the historic Victorian home, a celebrated building that had once been a schoolhouse, then a convent.

And they'd done it together. They'd transformed this deteriorating five-thousand-square-foot house into a home.

"Sorry, I didn't mean to start a fight. Adelaide was

a huge help during a really long day. Let's just get through the evening. It's harder and harder to pretend there's nothing wrong between us."

Something was off with her today, but he couldn't tell what. It was clear enough, though, that she was trying to pick a fight with him.

"I don't want to fight with you, either." He didn't know what the hell he wanted anymore other than to have things the way they were.

"You used to love a good argument with me. Only me. You get along with everyone else. I never understood that."

"We had fire, you and I." It had been a sizzling love. One that warmed him to his damn core. And he knew there was still a spark in the embers. He couldn't believe it was all gone.

"Had, Henri. That's my point. It's over, and you need to quit making excuses to delay the final step." Ferocity returned to her fairylike features. A warrior in blue silk and sequins.

"Not excuses. You needed to recover. Then we agreed we wouldn't do anything that would disrupt the start of the season. Then with my brother's wedding on the horizon—"

"Excuses. Divorce isn't the end of the world." She pinned up a curl that had escaped the confines of the delicate braid binding the others into place.

Everything about her these days was carefully put together so that no one saw a hint of the turmoil beneath. For months he'd respected that. Understood she was the one calling the shots with her health issues. But how could she deny herself any help? Ever? She'd made it clear he didn't know how to be the least bit of assistance.

And now, divorce was the recurring refrain.

"Our family is in the spotlight. A split between us would eat up positive oxygen in the press." He needed her to take a deep breath. They needed to figure out everything. He needed to stall.

She turned back around, using the mirror to smooth her dress. "No one is going to think poorly of you for leaving me. I will make it clear I'm the one who asked for the divorce."

Anger boiled, heating his cheeks. "I don't give a damn what people think about me."

"But you do care about your team. I understand." He picked up on the implication of her words. That he didn't care about *her*. And that couldn't be farther off base. She was still trying to pick a fight. To widen the gap between them.

"We're going to be late." The tone of his voice was soft. Almost like a whisper. He wanted to calm her down, to stop this from turning into an unnecessary fight. Something was upsetting her. Something major.

As much as he wanted to understand her, he couldn't. The party was about to start and he didn't have the time to unwrap the subtle meaning of all her words.

All he wanted was to have their old life back instead of silently cohabitating and putting on a front for the world. He longed for her to look at him the way she used to, with that smile that said as much as she enjoyed the party, she savored their time alone together even more. He ached for their relationship to be as uncomplicated as it once was when they traveled the country for the season, traveled the world in the off-season. They both enjoyed history and art. Sightseeing on hikes, whether to see Stonehenge or the Great Wall of China.

Tapping the back of her dress, he met her gaze in the mirror, holding her tawny eyes and reveling in the way her pupils widened with unmistakable desire. Settling his hands back on her shoulders, he breathed against her ear and neck. "Unless you would like me to take the zipper back down again."

Her lashes fluttered shut for a second and a softness entered her normally clenched jaw. In that brief moment, he thought this might be how they closed the gap.

Instead, her eyelids flew open and she shimmied out from underneath his hands. "No, thank you. I have a fund-raiser to oversee. And then make no mistake, we need to set a firm date to see our attorney and end the marriage."

family about. So many more health heartaches they hadn't shared with his family.

After her very public miscarriage in her second trimester, he'd bought them the house in the Garden District to give them both space from the Reynaud fishbowl lifestyle. Their emotions had been bubbling over far too often, in good and bad ways.

Living here? It was just too difficult. Spanish moss trailed like bridal veils from live oak trees on either side of the private driveway leading into the Reynaud estate on Lake Pontchartrain. It was in an exclusive section of Metairie, Louisiana, west of the city. Pontoon boats were moored in shallow waters while long docks stretched into the low-lying mist that often settled on the surface, sea grass spiking through and hiding local creatures. The gardens were lush and verdant, the ground fertile. Gardeners had to work overtime to hold back the Louisiana undergrowth that could take over in no time. The place was large, looming—alive.

She glanced at her too-damn-handsome husband as he steered their sports car up the winding drive toward the original home on the family complex, the place where Henri and his brothers had spent time in their youth. Gervais, the oldest brother, and his fiancée lived here now, and the couple had allowed Fiona to host her event on the property.

Henri's tailored Brioni tuxedo fit his hard, muscled body well. His square jaw was cleanly shaved, his handsome face the kind that could have graced a *GQ* cover. Her attraction to him hadn't changed, but so much had shifted between them since their impulsive elopement three years ago. While she didn't care about missing out on a large wedding, she did wonder if things might have turned out differently if they'd waited longer, gotten to know each other better before the stress piled on.

Now they would never know.

He bypassed the valet and opted to park in the family garage. The steel door slid open to reveal a black Range Rover and a Ferrari facing forward, shiny with polish, grills glistening. He backed into an open space, the massive garage stretching off to the side filled with recreational vehicles. The boats and Jet Skis were down in the boathouse at the dock. This family loved their toys. They played hard. Lived large. And loved full-out.

Losing Henri already left a hole in her life. Losing this family would leave another.

She swallowed down a lump as the garage door slid closed and he shut off the vehicle.

"Fiona?" He thumbed the top of the steering wheel. "Thank you for keeping up the happy couple act in public. I know things haven't been easy between us."

"This fund-raiser means a lot to me."

"Of course it does." His mouth went tight and she realized she'd hurt him.

How could they be so certain things were over and still have the power to hurt each other with a stray word? "I appreciate that your connections make this possible."

He glanced at her, smoothing his lapel. "You throw a great party that wins over a crowd not easily wowed."

"I owe Adelaide for her help today."

"When your car broke down."

She nodded tightly, the lie sticking in her throat.

He reached out to touch a curl and let it loosely wrap

around his finger as if with a will of its own. "You look incredible tonight. Gorgeous."

"Thank you."

"Any chance you're interested in indulging in some make-up sex, even if only temporary?"

The offer was tempting, mouthwateringly so, as she took in the sight of her husband's broad shoulders, was seduced by the gentle touch of his fingers rubbing just one curl.

"We need to get inside."

His mocha-colored eyes lingered on her mouth as tangibly as any kiss, setting her senses on fire. "Of course. Just know the offer stands."

He winked before smoothly sliding out of the car and moving around to the passenger side with the speed and grace that served him well on the ball field. Her skin still tingled from the thought of having sex with him again. They'd been so very good together in bed, with a chemistry that was off the charts.

Would that change because of her surgery? It was a risk she'd never been able to bring herself to take.

Just the thought had her gut knotting with nerves. But the next thing she knew, her silver Jimmy Choo heels were clicking along to the side entrance and across the foyer's marble floors. The space was filled with people from corner to corner, chatter and music from the grand piano echoing up to the high ceiling. The party was in full swing. The place was packed, people standing so close together they were pushed up against walls with hand-painted murals depicting a fox hunt.

Once upon a time she'd lived for these parties. But right now, she wanted to grab the banister and run up the huge staircase with a landing so large it fit a small sofa for casual chitchat in the corner.

Her hand tucked in Henri's arm, she went on autopilot party mode, nodding and answering people's greetings. She and Henri had played this game often, fooling others. She had to admit that while women chased him unabashedly, his gaze never strayed. He was a man of honor. His father's infidelities had left a mark on him. Henri had made it clear he would never cheat—even when the love had left their marriage.

No, she couldn't let her thoughts go there. To the end of love and of them. At least, not while they were in public. Too many people were counting on her. While planning this fund-raiser had served as a distraction from the widening gap between her and Henri, the whole event still had to be properly executed.

Time to investigate her handiwork. Excusing herself, Fiona walked over to the favor table. Turquoise boxes with silver calligraphic font reading "Love at First Woof" lined the table. Laughing inwardly, she picked up one of the boxes. This one was wrapped in a white ribbon. She opened the box, pleased to find the pewter dog earrings staring back at her. Satisfied, she retied the bow, set the box on the table, and picked up a box wrapped with black ribbon. To her relief, the pewter paw tie tacks were in there, as well. Good. The favors were even cuter than she had remembered.

Fiona's gaze flicked to the service dogs from a rescue organization. They sat at attention, eyes watchful and warm. Glancing over her shoulder, she saw the plates of food in the dining room. People were gathered around the food, scooping crab cakes and chicken skewers onto their plates.

Convinced that everything was more than in order, she surveyed further, walking into a more casual family space with an entertainment bar and Palladian windows overlooking the pool and grounds.

No detail had been missed thanks to the highly efficient catering staff she'd hired and Adelaide had overseen. Smiling faintly, Fiona peered outside at the twinkling doghouse situated just beyond the luxurious in-ground pool. The doghouse was a scale replica of the Reynaud mansion, and it was going to the shelter after tonight. But for now, it lit the grounds and housed hand-painted water bowls for the shelter dogs. Four of the shelter dogs walked around the pool, enjoying all the attention and affection from the guests.

People were spread out. Laughter floated on the breeze, and so did snippets of conversation. A small Jack Russell terrier was lazily stretched on Mrs. Daniza's lap. A fuzzy white dog was curled up, fast asleep, beneath Jack Rani's chair. The dogs were winning over friends with deep pockets.

Everything appeared to be in order. But then again, Fiona knew firsthand the difference between appearances and actual reality.

Sadness washed over her. Grabbing a glass of water from a nearby beverage station, she continued on as Henri went to speak to his brothers. Movement was good. Movement was necessary. The busier she stayed, the less her emotions would sting through her veins.

And it was as if the world knew she needed a distraction. As she slipped out onto the pool deck, she saw two of her favorite Hurricanes' players—wide receiver "Wild Card" Wade and "Freight Train" Freddy. Not only did they inspire her with how much of their time they donated to worthwhile causes, the two men always made her laugh.

It seemed that tonight would be no exception. Freight Train was in a black suit, but his tie had dog butts all over it and his belt buckle was a silver paw print. He and Wild Card were posing for pictures with two of the shelter dogs. Their energy was contagious.

Directly across from Freight Train and Wild Card were the Texas branch of the Reynaud clan. When fund-raisers or troubles arose, despite the complicated and sometimes strained relationships, they jumped in. The two Texas boys were sipping wine and talking to a Louisiana senator. The cousins were supporting their relative who played for the Hurricanes. Brant Reynaud wore his ever-present small yellow rosebud on his lapel.

Everyone was out in full force to support her latest cause. She would miss this sense of family.

Landscape lighting highlighted ornamental plantings and statues. She checked the outdoor kitchen to one side of the pool to make sure all was in order. The hearth area was unmistakably popular, a fire already ablaze in the stone surround. Built-in stone seating was covered with thick cushions and protected by a pergola with a casual wrought-iron framework. The Reynaud brothers were there. Well, at least two of them. Fiona watched as Gervais waved Henri over.

One of the things that amused Fiona was the sheer amount of posturing the boys did when they were around each other. They loved each other—there was no doubt about that. But the brothers were all driven and natural-born competitors.

They were all tall, with athletic builds, dark eyes

and even darker hair, thick and lush. While Gervais, Henri and Jean-Pierre were full brothers, Dempsey was the result of one of their father's affairs. The brothers had each gotten their mother's hair coloring, while their father had donated his size and strength.

The semicircle of the Reynaud clan was an elegant one. Gervais, the most refined of the brothers, was at ease in his role as oldest, leader of the pack. Erika, his fiancée, laid a gentle hand on Gervais's forearm as she leaned into the conversation. The light from the hearth caught on her silver rings and cushion-cut diamond engagement ring. One would likely never guess Erika had served in her home country's military, although her princess bearing was entirely clear.

To Gervais's immediate left stood Dempsey, ever-present football pin on the lapel of his tuxedo, with lovely, efficient Adelaide at his side.

Fiona told herself that she was lucky not to have to work. That she made a positive impact in the world with her volunteer philanthropic efforts. Not holding down a regular job outside the home also enabled her to travel with her husband. She helped organize outings for the other family members who traveled with the Hurricanes, as well. Keeping the players and their families happy kept the team focused and out of trouble.

She looked around at the packed event, a total success. Anyone would think she had a full life.

Except she couldn't bring herself to have sex with her husband. She'd been so certain the surgery was the right decision. She'd gone to counseling before and after. Her husband had been completely supportive.

And still the distance between them had grown wider and wider these past months, emphasizing how little they knew about each other. They'd married because of infatuation, great sex, a shared love of art and a pregnancy scare that sped up the wedding date.

Now that the initial glow of infatuation had passed and they didn't even have sex to carry them through the rough patches, a common love for gallery showings wasn't enough to hold them together. Their marriage was floundering. Badly. She needed to keep in mind how dangerous it would be to let her guard down around a man who had worked hard to take care of her through her decision.

And with a cancer scare looming over her today, she couldn't bear the thought that he would stay with her out of sympathy.

Henri wasn't in much of a party mood, no matter how much his brothers elbowed him and teased him about his latest fumble. His Texas cousins weren't cutting him any slack, either.

He'd been thinking about the divorce his wife insisted on pursuing.

While the love had left their marriage, he'd heard plenty say that marriage had ups and downs. He wasn't a quitter. And damn it all, he still burned to have her.

His gaze skimmed the guests around the pool, landing on his wife. Her trailing curls and slim curves called to him, reminding him of the enticing feel of her back as he'd tugged her zipper up.

She smiled at whomever she spoke to—a man with his back to the rest of the crowd—and nodded as she walked away. The man turned and Henri's breath froze in his chest. He knew the man well. Dr. Carlson was a partner in the practice Fiona used to see before they'd transferred her to another physician for the surgery.

Fear jelling in his gut, Henri charged away from his brothers and cousins, shouldering through the crowd to his wife.

"Henri—"

He grasped her arm and guided her toward the shore of Lake Pontchartrain. "In a moment. When no one can overhear us."

Lights from yachts and boats dotted the distance. Along the shoreline, couples walked hand in hand. Henri opened the boathouse door and stepped inside. Moonlight streaked through the windows, across Fiona's face. Confusion and frustration stamped her lovely features.

He angled them beneath a pontoon boat on a lift. The boat was still wet from use, and water tapped the ground in a rhythm that almost matched his pounding heart. Inhaling deeply, he caught the musty scent of the boathouse mixed with the cinnamon notes of Fiona's perfume. He'd bought it for her on a trip to France before all of these difficulties had really gotten out of control.

"Enough already, Henri. Would you please tell me why we're out here?"

He clasped both of her shoulders. "Are you okay?"

"What do you mean?"

"I saw you talking to Dr. Carlson." He looked in her sherry-colored eyes, trying to read her. Something flickered there, something he could have sworn was fear, but then she looked away, her lashes shielding her expression.

Staring at the floor, she chewed her bottom lip for

an instant before answering, "We were discussing a fund-raiser and party for the pediatric oncology ward. The planner had a heart attack and they need someone to step in and help."

Okay, but why was she looking away? "You're sure that's all?"

She hesitated a second too long. "What do you mean?"

Fear exploded inside him. "Are you feeling all right?" He clasped her shoulders. "Physically. Is there something wrong? If so, you know I'm here for you. Whatever you need, just tell me."

She squeezed her eyes closed, shaking her head, tears sliding free.

He reached to sketch his knuckles along her cheeks and capture the tears, hands shaking. "Oh, God, Fiona, is it…" His throat moved in a long swallow. "Do you have…"

She touched his mouth. "You don't have to worry about me. I'm fine. Thank you, but you have no reason to feel obligated."

"Obligated?" He kissed her fingertips. "You are my wife, my responsibility—"

"Please, Henri." She took his hands from her face and clasped them briefly before letting go. "You are a good man. I've never doubted that. This is an emotional time for both of us, and let's not make it worse with confrontations. Let's just return to the party."

He wouldn't be dismissed so easily. "What were you laughing so hysterically about?" Anger edged through the fear. "And would you like to clue me in on the joke? Because right now I could use something to lighten the mood."

"No joke," she said with a sigh, meeting his gaze. "Just so ironic."

"Then what are you hiding?"

"Henri." She chewed her bottom lip again, her gaze skipping around evasively before she continued. "Um, he asked me out for a drink to discuss the fund-raiser."

Henri saw red. Pure red. "He asked you out for a drink? As in a date? Not because of the fund-raiser?"

"Because of the fund-raiser, but yes, he clearly meant a date, as well." She pulled at her curls, color mounting in her cheeks.

Henri had to stay calm. Had to make it through this conversation. "And what did you say?"

"I told him I'm still married, of course." Gaze narrowing, she launched the words at him like daggers.

"Clearly that wasn't a problem for him, since you are wearing my ring."

She shrugged her shoulders, chandelier earrings swaying. "That didn't bother him in the least."

Henri turned toward the door, ready to return to the party and deck the guy straight into the pool.

Fiona placed a hand on his shoulder. "Stop, Henri. He mentioned hearing we're splitting up. He thought I was available."

"How would he have heard such a thing?" His mind went back to the original concern. "Were you at the doctor's office where he's a partner?"

She swallowed hard. "You seem to have forgotten his brother is our lawyer."

"Not anymore."

"I was thinking the same thing, actually." She picked at her French manicure. "We should get separate attorneys."

Dammit. This conversation was not going the way he intended. He just wanted to pull her into his arms and take her here. Now. To say to hell with the past and future. No more jealousy or discussion about...hell.

He just wanted her. "This is not the time or the place to talk about lawyers. Enjoy your party and your success." He cupped her face in his hands, his thumbs stroking along her cheeks as he stepped closer, the heat of her lithe body reaching to him. "You've raised enough seed money for the shelter tonight. They can start their capital campaign for a whole new building. Let's celebrate."

She swayed toward him for an instant, as if she too was caught in that same web of desire. Her gaze fell away from his for a moment, roving his broad-shouldered body, then returned to meet his hungry gaze. There was something there still. He could feel it in the way her lips, slightly parted, seemed to call him to her.

Stepping back abruptly, she grasped the door latch. "Enjoy?" She shook her head, a curl sliding forward over her shoulder. "I don't think that's possible. There's too much left unsettled for me to think about anything but getting my life in order."

In a swirl of French perfume, she walked out the door and raced along the dock back to the party. The forcefulness of her reaction left him wondering what he was missing, but the speed of her departure closed the door on finding out.

She couldn't go back to the party. Not with her emotions in such a turmoil. She hadn't expected the brief conversation with Tom Carlson to lead to a showdown with her husband. But Tom had seen her come through the office earlier…and he had asked her for a drink. She'd shut him down hard. Even if she weren't married, she was not in a place emotionally to be in a relationship right now.

Life was getting too complicated. She longed for simpler times again.

Peace.

Family.

So she sought out the last remnants. She loaded a plate of party food onto a tray with two glasses of mint iced tea and went upstairs to Grandpa Leon's suite. His Alzheimer's had progressed to the point that he required a round-the-clock nurse to keep watch over him so he didn't wander off. His nighttime nurse's aide sat in the study area off his bedroom, reading on her phone. A brunette in her midthirties, she had a warm expression on her face at all times. The perfect temperament for at-home care.

She looked up quickly and set her phone beside her. "Good evening, Mrs. Reynaud. Mr. Leon is on the balcony enjoying the stars over the lake."

They'd glassed in the balcony so the temperature could be regulated year-round, and he could safely sit outside without fear of him falling—or climbing down as he'd tried to do one evening.

"Thank you," Fiona said. "Please do feel free to join the party while I visit with Gramps."

"That sounds lovely. Thank you. I'll step downstairs for a snack. I'll be back in a half hour, if that's all right?"

"Absolutely. Take your time." Fiona loved her grandfather-in-law and treasured this time with him.

His disease was stealing him away and she would soon be gone. Her heart squeezed tighter as she stepped through the open French doors leading to the enclosed balcony.

"Grandpa Leon," she said softly, adjusting the tray and settling it on the wrought-iron table between two chairs. "I've brought you a bite to eat."

The older man turned, his shock of gray hair whiter every day as if each lost memory stole more of his youth along with the color in the once dark strands. "They don't like me going to parties anymore. I believe they're afraid of what I might say."

"Everyone loves having you there. I'm sorry you feel that way, though." The family was just trying to protect him from embarrassment.

"It's not your fault my memory's failing. The boys are just trying to protect me and my pride." Spearing a bit of shrimp scampi on his fork, he looked up at her gratefully. "This is good, especially for party food. Filling. Not a bunch of those frilly little canapés."

"We have plenty of those, too. I just know your preference."

"And I appreciate that. My tastes are the only thing not failing in my mind. But I imagine you knew that. You were always a perceptive girl. I am going to miss you."

Her head jerked up. What did he know? He couldn't possibly have guessed about the divorce. "Grandpa Leon, I'm not sure what you mean."

He tapped his temple. "When my illness takes over. Even in my fog, I feel the sense of loss. I feel it here." He tapped his chest. "The people who should be a part of my life. But I can't recall who belongs to me and who doesn't."

Fiona didn't even know what to say, so she covered his hand with hers and squeezed. "I do love you and I won't forget you."

"And I love you, too, sister dear."

She blinked away a tear. She shouldn't be surprised any longer at these moments he mistook her for someone else. Still… She shoved to her feet and started for the door.

Turning to look back at the man who soon wouldn't be her grandfather anymore, Fiona said, "Do you want seconds on anything?"

He stared back at her, a confused look in his java-brown eyes. "Seconds?" He stared down at his empty plate. "What did the chef make for dinner? I can't seem to recall."

She struggled for what to say and then realized specifics didn't matter so much as peace. "Tonight's menu included your very favorite."

He smiled, passing his plate to her. "Of course, my favorite. I would like more. And dessert—pie with ice cream."

"Of course."

Would he even remember he'd asked for it when she returned? She would bring it all the same and savor her last moments as part of this wonderful family.

Would she still be welcome here to visit him after the split became known to the rest of the family? Would she even be able to come here without losing her mind? The pain would be…intense. Especially at first. And later? She could barely think into the future. She'd been so afraid to dream years ahead for fear there were no years for her.

Today had reminded her all too well of those fears.

Three

Always hungry—which was the fate of an athlete—Henri pulled open the door to the Sub-Zero fridge, rummaging around shelves big enough to park a car—his personal choice in the kitchen remodel. It was three in the morning and no way would he make it until dawn. Though the food at the party had been decadent, he needed to put proper fuel into his system. In season, he put his body through the wringer and there was a helluva lot at stake.

He pulled out a carton of eggs and placed them on the granite counter. Running a hand through his hair, his mind drifted back to the fund-raiser.

From an outside perspective, the event was a complete success. Seven figures had been raised, more than enough seed money to launch a capital campaign to build a new shelter. His wife's fund-raising goal had been surpassed. And he was damn proud of her. Even if things were difficult right now, he admired her spirit. He'd practically had to drag her out of the fund-raiser as the cleanup crews arrived. Fiona had wanted to make sure that everything was perfect, that things were easy on the housekeeping staff.

Of course, by the time they'd returned to their house, she'd bolted from his company and retreated to her room. Par for the course these days.

Opening a cabinet drawer, he pulled out a frying pan and sprayed it with olive oil. He switched on the gas of the massive gourmet cooktop and adjusted the flame. Once the pan began to hiss to life, he cracked two eggs, reveling in the sound and the promise of protein.

Cooking was one of the things that he actually liked to do for himself. And for Fiona. He'd made them de-licious, flavorful and healthy meals. That was one of the reasons they'd spent so much time restoring this kitchen. It had been a space where they had bonded.

They had jointly picked the decorations in the room, visiting high-end antiques stores in the French Quarter and finding beautiful pieces. Like the big turn-of-the-century clock that occupied a prominent spot on the south wall. The clock was an intricate work of angles and loops. The antique vibe of the wrought iron had reminded them both of Ireland, which was one of the first places they'd traveled to together.

The room contained an eclectic mix of items—nothing matched, but the pieces complemented each other, pulling the room together.

With a sigh, he slid the eggs out of the pan and onto a plate. After he'd fumbled in the drawer for a fork, he grabbed the plate and made his way to the large window in the dining room. He sat at the head of the long cherrywood table, bought for entertaining the whole family. A gilded mirror hung over the side-board laden with Fiona's well-polished silver. Even though they'd built this haven together, if they split, he would be booted out on his ass and moving back to the family compound with his brothers. He loved his family, but this place was home now, deep in the heart of New Orleans.

The thought of leaving made it too damn hard to sit at this table—their table. Pushing his plate of half-eaten eggs away, he shot to his feet and wandered to the window.

Sometimes the contrasts of this city just struck him, the historic buildings jutting up against contempo-rary trends. It was a place between worlds and cul-tures. The New Orleans moon hung in the late night sky, just peeking through sullen clouds that covered the stars. He'd always enjoyed the moodiness of this place, his new home after growing up in Texas. This fit his personality, his temperament. He'd thought he had his life together when he met Fiona. Perfect wife. Dream career. Jazz music that could wake the dead and reach a cold man's soul.

His brothers would laugh at him for saying stuff like that, call him a sensitive wuss, but Fiona had un-derstood the side of him that enjoyed art and music. It cut him deep that she said they didn't know each other, that they had no foundation and nothing in common.

She minimized what they'd built together, and that sliced him to the core. It hadn't helped one bit that men were hitting on her at the party, already sensing a divorce in the wind even if they hadn't announced it to a soul.

He was used to men approaching his wife. She was drop-dead gorgeous in a chic and timeless way that would draw attention for the rest of her life. But tonight had been different. He spent so much time on the road and she usually traveled with him. But even when they weren't together, they'd always trusted each other. The thought of her moving on, of her with another man, shredded him inside. He didn't consider himself the jealous type, but he damn well wasn't ready to call it quits and watch her move on with someone—anyone—else.

Without his realizing it, his feet carried him past the window, past the living room. And suddenly, he was upstairs outside Fiona's room.

Her door was wide open. That was the first thing that jarred him. He'd become so accustomed to seeing that closed door when he passed by her room at night. Fiona had literally shut him out.

So why was it open tonight?

Not that he was going to miss the opportunity to approach her.

The soft, warm light from her bedroom bathed the hall in a yellow glow. Curiosity tugged at him, and he peered into the room.

She was curled up in a tight ball on the settee at the foot of the bed, her sequined waistband expanding and contracting with her slow, determined breaths. He was surprised to see her still in her party clothes. Even with disheveled, wavy hair she was damn breathtaking. Her shoes were casually and chaotically tossed to the side.

For a moment, he thought she was asleep, and then he realized…

Fiona was crying.

A rush of protectiveness pulsed through his body. Fiona had been so calculating and logical these days that this spilling of emotion overwhelmed him. Damn, he didn't want to see her like this. He *never* wanted to see her like this. It made him feel helpless, and that was a feeling he'd never handled well.

Once when Henri was younger, he'd walked into his mother's room to find her crying. Tears had streaked her face, mascara marring her normally perfect complexion. She had been crying over the death of her career as a model. And his father's infidelity. She'd been so shattered, and all Henri could do was watch from the sidelines.

She hadn't been the most attentive or involved parent, but she'd been his mother and he'd wanted to make the world right for her.

He'd felt every bit as useless then as he felt now.

"Fiona?" He stepped tentatively into the room.

Startled, she sat up, dragging her wrist across her tears and smudging mascara into her hairline. "Henri, I don't need help with my zipper."

"I was on my way to my room and I heard you." He stepped deeper into the room, tuxedo jacket hooked on one finger and slung over his shoulder. "Are you okay?"

"No, I'm not," she said in a shaky voice, swinging her bare feet to the floor and digging her toes into the wool Persian rug they'd chosen together at an estate auction.

Something was different about her today. She was

showing a vulnerability around him, an openness, he hadn't seen in nearly a year. And that meant there was still something salvageable between them.

For the first time in a long time, they were actually talking, and he wasn't giving up that window of opportunity to figure out what was going on in her mind. He didn't know where they were going, but he sure as hell wasn't willing to just write off what they'd had. "It's tougher and tougher to be together in front of people and pretend. I get that. Totally. That's what you're upset about, isn't it?"

"Of course," she answered too quickly.

"Why am I having trouble believing you?" He draped his jacket over a wing-back chair by the restored fireplace. "We didn't have trouble with trust before."

"It's easy to trust when you don't know each other well, when we kept our life superficial." The words came out of her mouth almost like lines from a play. Too calculated, too rehearsed.

He leaned back against the marble mantel. "You're going to have to explain that to me, because I'm still bemused as hell as to where we went wrong."

Sighing, she smoothed the silk dress over her knees. "We forgot to talk about the important things, like what would happen if we couldn't have kids. What we would have bonding us besides having lots of sex and procreating."

Sifting through her explanation, he tried to make sense of her conflicting signals, her words and body language and nervous twitches all at odds. "You only saw sex between us as about having children? Is that why you've been pushing me away since your mastectomy and hysterectomy?" Because of the genetic testing, the doctor had recommended both, and Henri hadn't been able to deny the grief they'd both felt over the end to any chance of conceiving a child together. But the bottom line was, he'd cared most about keeping his wife alive. "You know I'm here for you, no matter what. I'm not going to leave you when you need me."

Her expression was shuttered, her emotions hidden again. "We've discussed this. Without kids, we have nothing holding us together."

Nothing except for their passion, their shared interests. Their shared life. She couldn't be willing to discount that so quickly.

"And you're still against adoption?" He was stumped about that, considering her father was adopted. But she'd closed down when he brought up the subject.

"I'm against a man staying with me for the children or out of sympathy because he thinks I'm going to die." She shot to her feet, a coolness edging her features. "Could we please stop this discussion, dammit?"

Was that what she thought? That he had only stayed because of her cancer gene? They'd discussed divorce before then, but only briefly. After? She'd dug in her heels about the split.

He couldn't deny he wouldn't have left a woman facing the possibility of a terminal illness, but their relationship was more complex than that. He shoved away from the fireplace strewn with Wedgwood knick-knacks, strode toward her and stopped just short of the settee.

He clasped her shoulders. "You said we never talked enough. So let's talk. Tell me."

Henri needed her to talk. To figure this out. Because

even now, even with the smudged makeup and tousled brown hair, she was damn beautiful. The heat of her skin beneath his hands was familiar and intoxicating.

He still wanted her. Cancer or no cancer. Kids or no kids. Though his hands stayed steady on her shoulders, he wanted to send them traveling on her body. To push her back on the bed.

Their bed—before she'd sent him to his own room after they'd returned from her surgery overseas. She'd said the surgery left her in too much pain to risk being bumped in the night. And somehow over time, she'd kept the separate rooms edict in place. He didn't know how so much time had slipped away, but day by day, he'd been so damn afraid he would say or do the wrong thing when she was in such a fragile state. He'd gone along with her request for space until the next thing he'd known their lawyer was drawing up papers.

He was done waiting around. He was a man of action.

After a moment of hesitation, she shrugged off his hands. "Talking now won't change us splitting up. You have to understand that."

"Then let's talk to give each other peace when we walk away." If he could keep her talking, they were still together. She wouldn't be closing the door in his face.

She chewed her bottom lip before releasing it slowly, then nodding. "Speak then."

He sat on the settee and held her hand, tugging gently. She held back for a moment before surrendering to sit beside him. He shuffled at the last instant so she landed on his lap.

"That's not playing fair."

"Then move."

Indecision shifted across her heart-shaped face, then a spark of something. Pure Fiona spunk. She wriggled once, causing a throbbing ache in his groin an instant before she settled.

He raised an eyebrow. "Now *that's* not playing fair."

"I thought you wanted to talk."

"I did. Now it's tough to think." He tapped her lips. "But I'm trying. We could start with you telling me what really made you cry."

She avoided his gaze as she said, "I had a long talk with your grandfather this evening. Seeing him fading away made me sad." Resting her head on Henri's chest, she took a ragged breath. Grandpa Leon and Fiona had always been close.

"I understand that feeling well. It's hard to watch, hard to think about. I miss him already." Pulling her closer, Henri softened as she wrapped her arms around him. Lifting a hand, he stroked her dark brown hair, releasing the braid that confined her curls. This was what he missed. Being close like this. Feeling her against him. "Are you really prepared to walk away from this family? My brothers, Adelaide…everyone?"

Fiona stayed against his chest, fingers twirling around the back of his neck. Shocks of electric energy tingled along his spine. His hand slid down the side of her body, gingerly touching the silky fabric of her dress, making him itch for more. The light smell of her perfume worked his nerves. It had grown silent between them. The only audible noise was the click-click-click of the ceiling fan.

"Perhaps they will still like me afterward." The words came out like a whisper.

"Of course they will." It was impossible not to like her.

"But I understand it could be awkward for everyone, especially for you when you move on." Again, she cut into his core.

"You already have me in a relationship with someone else? That's cold." He hadn't had eyes for anyone but her since they'd met. He'd been head over heels for her from the get-go.

"I imagine the women will be flocking to you the instant they hear you're free."

Fiona's face was close to his now. Her mouth inches from his. The breath from her words warmed his lips.

"But I only want you." He tilted his head, touched the bottom of her chin and kissed her fully, his tongue meeting and sweeping against hers.

The familiar texture of her lips, the taste of her, awakened a deep need in him. They knew each other's bodies and needs. He knew just where to stroke behind her ears to make her purr.

Fiona kissed him back, wrapping her arms around him, pulling him close against her. Her fingers slid into his hair, caressing along his scalp and grazing lower, her nails lightly trailing along his neck, then digging into his shoulders with need.

His hands roved down her back, the ridge of her zipper reminding him of earlier when he'd slid it up, link by link. Every time, touching her set him on fire. The silk of her dress was every bit as soft as her skin.

And he had once made it his personal mission to learn the terrain of every inch of that skin.

His fingers played down to her hips, digging in as he tugged her even closer on his lap. The curve of her ass pressed against the swelling ache of his erection, making him throb even harder. He nipped along her ear, then soothed the love bite with the tip of his tongue. Her head fell back and her lips parted with a breathy sigh that prompted his growl of approval in response. He kissed down her neck, to the sweet curve of her shoulder. His hand skimmed up her side—

And just as quickly as it had started, she pulled back, sliding off his lap and stumbling to her feet. Her hands shaky, she smoothed the lines in her dress.

What the hell? He struggled to pull his thoughts together but all the blood in his body was surging south hard and fast.

She stared at him, eyes full of confusion. "You need to go." Before he could speak, she made fast tracks to the door, holding it open even wider. "You *need* to go. I'll see you in the morning."

And even with the lack of blood to his brain, he knew. There was no arguing with his wife tonight.

Kicking at the cover, Fiona tossed in her king-size bed, trapped in the twilight hell between having a nightmare and being half-awake. The torture of knowing she should be able to grapple back to consciousness but unable to haul herself from the dream that felt all too real.

In the fog of her dream, Fiona pushed open the door of her childhood home, making her way across the kitchen and into the living room. Her father, a dignified-looking man with salt-and-pepper hair, sat on the overstuffed chair in the corner of the room, clutching the newspaper in his hand.

Something was wrong. She could hear it in the rattle of those papers clutched in his shaky grip. See it on his face when his gaze met hers over the top of the *New Orleans Times*.

"Dad?" The voice that puffed from her lips seemed distant. Younger.

He shook his head, his mouth tight as if holding back words was an ungodly tough effort. Panic filled her chest. She needed to find her mother.

Spinning away, she started roaming the halls of the three-story house, opening the doors. Searching for her mother. Chasing shadows that crooked their fingers, beckoning, then fading. Again and again.

At the last door, she was sure she would find her mother, a willowy woman, a society leader who stayed busy, so busy Fiona had attended boarding school during the week to be kept out of the way.

On her weekends at home, there just hadn't been enough hours to spend together. Her memories of her mom were few and far between.

Fiona opened that very last door, the one to the garden where her mother held the very best of parties. The doorknob slipped from her hand, the mahogany panel swinging wide and slamming against the wall so fast she had to jump back.

Petals swirled outside, pink from azaleas, purple from hydrangeas and white from larger magnolia blooms, all spiraling through the air so thickly they created a hurricane swirl she couldn't see through. Her mother must be beyond the storm.

Fiona pushed forward, into the whirlwind, flower petals beating at her body in silken slices that cut her skin. Left her with scars on her body and soul.

The deeper she pushed, the more the realization seeped in through those cuts. The painful truth sank in deep inside her. Her mother was gone. The cancerous hurricane had taken her mom, her grandmother, her aunt, leaving Fiona alone. The world rattled around her, the flap of petals, the crackle of newspapers, the roar of screaming denial.

Water dripped down her cheeks. Tears? Or rain? She didn't know. It didn't matter because it didn't change the ache of loss.

The garden shifted from her childhood home to the historic house she shared with Henri. Grandpa Leon sat in a wrought-iron chair, his fading memory darkening the storm clouds slowly into night. No matter how much time passed, she felt the pain of her shrinking family. The pain of so many losses. The loss of her unborn children. All of her failed attempts at stability and happiness paraded down the pathway. Losing her mother young, her aunt and grandmother, too, until there were no motherly figures left to steer her through her shaky marriage. Hopelessness pushed at her, wound her up as the darkness of the windswept garden became too oppressive. She catapulted herself forward, sitting upright in her bed.

It took a moment for Fiona to gain her bearings and to realize she was in New Orleans.

Sleep was anything but peaceful these days.

Taking a deep breath, she considered calling her father. They'd never been close and it had been a while since they'd spoken. But still, the nightmare had left her completely rattled. All of the pressures of her current situation were bubbling over.

She had to leave, sooner rather than later. She realized that even though she'd been protecting herself from the pain of having Henri stay with her out of pity, she was also protecting him from watching her fade away if the worst happened.

Her dad had never been the same after her mother died. The loss of her mother had shattered him. Though there was distance between Fiona and Henri, she still cared about him.

It was best to walk away. It was simpler to walk away than get more attached.

Morning runs had a way of clearing Henri's mind. And man, did he need some perspective after last night.

Sweat cooled on his neck as he pulled into his driveway, the muggy, verdant air mixing with the funk of his own need of a shower. He'd driven to the Hurricanes' workout facility and ran harder than he had in weeks. There was a renewed energy in his steps. Something that felt a bit like hope. Which was exactly why he was back at their restored Garden District house now. He'd been in such a rush to make it home before Fiona woke up that he hadn't even bothered with a shower. He'd simply discarded his sweaty clothes in favor of a clean T-shirt and basketball shorts.

Deep down, he knew he had to focus on the upcoming home game. It was huge for the team in a year that could net them a championship. But everything that was going on in his personal life was taking his head out of this season.

Henri shoved out of his car, waving at the security guards who were on duty. The two nondescript but well-trained men responded with a curt nod as he entered the old home through the back entrance.

As he turned the knob on the door, thoughts of Fiona filled his brain. There was something between them still. The kiss confirmed that. There had been passion on both ends of their kiss last night. Having her pressed against him felt so right. Natural. Normal. He needed to get her to see that they fit together. Bring her back to his bed, back to him.

Stepping into the kitchen, he found Fiona cooking, the scents of butter and caramel in the air. Her chocolate-brown hair was piled in a messy bun. Her sleep shorts hugged her curves, revving his interest. Glancing over her shoulder, she flashed him a small smile.

He wanted her now more than ever. But how to convince her that they needed to get back to what they had?

"You don't have to cook for me. I do want you for more than your body and awesome culinary skills." He eyed the Waterford crystal bowl of fresh blueberries next to her. An intriguing—undeniable—notion filled his mind, and he pressed himself against her as he reached for them. They'd always done best when they kept things light. That might well be the way to go with her today.

With slow deliberation, he popped a few blueberries into his mouth, eyebrows arching.

For a moment, she looked visibly riled. Damn, she was sexy.

Then she glanced away quickly and kept her focus on the task at hand. "I don't mind. I love to cook. At some point soon, I'm going to have to figure out what to do with my life."

"If you insist on going through with the divorce, you know I'll take care of you." It was all he wanted to do. To be the one to support her no matter what.

Setting a plate down on the island, she gestured for him to sit. He looked at her handiwork—a whole-wheat crepe filled with various fruits. A protein shake was already there, waiting for him.

"Eat your breakfast and stop talking before I pour cayenne pepper in your protein shake." She shook the spice at him before she carried over her own plate and the cut-crystal bowl of blueberries and sat down at the island.

Sunlight streamed into the room, filling the space with warmth.

"I'm a bad guy if I say I want to provide a generous alimony settlement?"

"I appreciate the offer. It's the verbiage about taking care of me that rubs the wrong way. Like I'm…"

"You're far from a child. Believe me, I get that." He scooped up another handful of berries, pitching one at a time into his mouth, the sweet juice bursting along his taste buds.

"I have a degree."

Henri nodded. "And you've sacrificed your career so we could travel together. I appreciate that. I thought you enjoyed our time on the road—"

She held up the cayenne.

He yanked his shake away, nudging her playfully with his shoulder. To win his way back into her bed, he needed to keep things light. "Changing the subject."

"Thank you." She set down the red pepper. "Enjoy your breakfast. I certainly intend to."

"As do I." He tapped the bowl of berries. "These are incredibly fresh."

"I haven't tried them yet." Fiona reached for the

berries, but Henri snatched them away, that devilish smile playing on his lips.

Nudging the bowl toward her, he stepped closer, closer still. He plucked up a particularly fat berry and fed it to her. Her lips nipped at his fingertips, sparking his awareness. And she seemed to be enjoying herself, as well.

"That kiss last night—"

She coughed as the food went down the wrong way. Once she cleared her throat, she asked half-jokingly, "Are you trying to choke me to death to avoid alimony?"

"That's not funny. At all."

"You're right. Bad joke born out of nerves." She looked down, her cheeks flushing with embarrassment. "Your breakfast deserves to be enjoyed."

"Thank you. We've had some incredible meals together, just us. I'm going to miss these times with you."

"You're accepting it's over?"

"You're making it tough not to." He eyed her over his fork. Frustrated. Determined. "Any chance we could have one more night together for old times' sake?"

"That's not going to happen."

He wished he understood why. The doctors had told him to give her space to process the shock of learning she carried the cancer gene, time to accept the long-term implications. They'd claimed that she would get over the self-consciousness, the grief over what she'd lost. But God, they'd spent so much of their marriage on a roller coaster of emotions. Trying for a baby. Miscarriages. Losing a baby in the second trimester. Then when the doctor pointed out how the fertility treatments could put her at risk with her maternal family's history of cancer.

Then her hysterectomy. Her double mastectomy.

So damn much to process.

He wished he had someone to talk to for understanding it from a female's perspective…but her mother and grandmother were gone, her aunt, too.

The realization dawned on him. There were women in his family. Strong, spunky women who could help him win Fiona back.

Because come hell or high water, he wasn't giving up.

Four

If Fiona had to be in the middle of a fund-raiser crisis, she'd at least found some peace that the crisis was unfolding in the sunroom of their restored Victorian home. The presence of the garden stilled her frantic heart, reminded her to breathe.

In a lot of ways, the sunroom had become her unofficial office. She came out here to think or to read old-fashioned paperback books from the library. She felt, in a manner of speaking, very turn of the century.

She let her eyes rove above the half wall, her gaze pushing past the intricate wrought iron on the windows to the garden proper. Lush trees and bushes nestled against a winding brick paver path. Taking a moment to appreciate the view, she reorganized her thoughts.

Sitting in an oversize wooden chair, she surveyed the table in front of her. It was a mess—iPads, laptops, cell phones and sticky notes littered the farm-house-style table. She was up against a deadline for the next fund-raiser to step in with emergency help for the children's oncology ward event since the other planner had had a heart attack. The concert hall she'd originally booked had backed out last minute due to a terrible fire. It hadn't seemed very likely that the hall would be fully operational again in time, so she'd made a few calls and switched the location.

Making this fund-raiser a success felt exceptionally personal. The proceeds from the event were going to cancer research. It was a cause she felt deeply about and she couldn't bear to see the children's event canceled or even postponed. Fiona did what she did best—she threw herself into her work.

Fiona watched how Adelaide worked on the iPad, intensely focused on the screen in front of her. She was logging a lot of hours on Fiona's project. It was even more impressive because Adelaide was in the process of launching her own sportswear line.

"You have such a full plate of your own. I don't know how to thank you for your help." Fiona was truly humbled by Adelaide's support, especially on the last two events. She'd stepped in, no questions asked.

"Being a part of the Reynaud family gives great opportunities to effect change. You know how poor I was growing up. The thought that I could improve other people's lives? I don't take that opportunity lightly. I just haven't figured out how I want to make my mark yet. So if you don't mind, I'll just hitch my philanthropic wagon to your star for now." Turning away from the half wall, she smiled warmly at Fiona.

"Then I'll gratefully accept the help."

"Well, I trust you can help me plan my wedding. You have the best eye for things, Fiona," Adelaide said, examining the way her engagement ring caught the sunlight, sparkling with the brilliance of the ocean on the sunniest of days.

Fiona put on her best face, schooling her features into happiness, though such a task took some effort. She could feel the edges of her composure wobble under the pressure.

"It is such a lovely ring, and you will be an even more beautiful bride." Tucking a loose strand of wavy hair behind her ear, she gave her future sister-in-law the biggest smile she could manage. "Truly beautiful."

The light reflected off Adelaide's ring paled in comparison to the emotion that lit her love-struck eyes and tugged pink into her cheeks.

Her future sister-in-law began to chatter. And Fiona would have listened on, equally joyful, if she didn't notice the text message that blipped across her screen.

It was a courtesy reminder of her upcoming doctor's appointment. They had results to give her and more tests to administer.

Suddenly, despite the bright, airy nature of the sunroom, she felt claustrophobic. Anxiety wrapped her in a grip she didn't know how to shake. An acute tingling sensation rippled through her arms, and the world felt farther away from her than it ever had before. Everything—her impending divorce, her uncertain health, the loss of family—crashed into her at once.

She recognized that Adelaide was still talking, but the words were lost on her.

Fiona must have looked as bad as she felt, because her future sister-in-law stopped talking.

Setting aside her iPad, Adelaide pensively tipped her head to the side. "Is something wrong?"

"Why would you ask that?" Fiona placed her cell phone facedown on the table. It was time to focus on tangible things, to push herself back into the present moment. Concentrating on Adelaide's concerned words, Fiona let herself notice the warmth of the phone and the coolness of the table.

"You just don't seem like yourself." Adelaide held up a hand. "Never mind. Forget I asked. It's none of my business."

Fiona decided what the hell. She should dive in and be honest—or at least partially open. And yes, maybe she was acting out of fear, because Henri's kiss had rocked her resolve to move on with her life. "It's no secret in the family that Henri and I have had trouble. We've struggled with infertility. There's more to it than that."

"I'm here if you want to talk." Adelaide walked closer to her, lowering her voice, her southern accent full of earnest concern.

"What happens if I'm not part of the family anymore? Your loyalties will be here, and I understand that."

"It's that bad? You're thinking about splitting up?" An edge of surprise hitched in Adelaide's voice.

It had been a giant mistake to say that much. The last thing Fiona wanted to do was burden anyone. It was suddenly clear that she wasn't ready to discuss this, not with Adelaide. Now she had to refocus, get them back on track. Ignore the pain in her chest and move forward. That's what she was best at, anyway.

Moving forward. Stacking a few papers into perfect order, she inhaled deeply, closed her eyes and spoke.

"Let's focus on the party. I need to get through the next couple of weeks and salvage this event for the fund-raising dollars—and for the children in the hospital looking forward to their party."

"If that's what you want." Adelaide didn't seem particularly convinced, but she also didn't press her further.

"This event is important to me. More so than the others." Scrolling through a web page, she gestured at the band options. "I need it to be perfect. This disease has taken so much from so many families." Not just other families. Her family. And now it threatened her, too. In a small voice, she added, "My mother died of cancer when I was young—my grandmother and aunt, too."

"I didn't know." Adelaide reached across to squeeze Fiona's hand. "Apparently there are a lot of things I didn't know and I'm so very sorry for your pain."

"Henri and I aren't ready for people to know about the divorce until the end of the season, when the papers will be ready to be filed, but I'm thinking now we aren't going to be able to wait that long. I imagine our secrets will be out in the public soon enough if the press gets wind of things."

"The lack of privacy is difficult."

"We've worked hard to keep things private."

"Perhaps too much so, from the sound of how little the family knows of what's going on. Family can be a support system." Adelaide patted her chest. "I consider myself part of your family."

"Thank you, but if we split..." She swallowed hard.

"Most of my family is gone. I only have my father left and, well, we're not close." Since all of her friends were tied to Henri's family and the football world, that left her facing a looming void.

"Fiona, I'm here for you if you need me, regardless."

"I envy your career and independence. I need to find that for myself."

"What would you like to do with your life?"

Fiona cheeks puffed out with the force of her sigh. "I'm an art major and I throw parties. If only I had an engineering degree to tack on to the end of that, I would be a hot commodity on the job market."

Before Adelaide had a chance to respond, Princess Erika stepped into the sunroom. She was Gervais's beautiful Nordic fiancée. Her pale blond hair was gathered over one shoulder, intricately woven into a thick fishtail braid.

"Sisters," she said, rubbing her hand along her pregnant stomach. Her announcement—and engagement—had caught the whole family by surprise since the couple hadn't known each other long. But their love was clear. "I rang the bell but you didn't hear me. The cleaning lady let me in on her way out. What are we doing here and can I help? I am at loose ends until after the wedding, when I begin school. And of course newborn twins will keep me busy. The calm before the hurricane."

The hurricane? Erika had a way of twisting idioms that was endearing. Fiona would miss that and so many other things about this family she'd grown close to during her marriage.

Adelaide shook her head. "Only you would think preparing for a wedding isn't enough to keep a person busy."

The princess shrugged elegantly, wearing her impending motherhood with ease. Fiona swallowed down an ache that never quite went away. She'd had such plans for her life as a wife and mother. She'd wanted a family, a big family, unlike her solitary upbringing. Maybe Henri's large family had been part of the allure, too.

Regardless, there would be no family for her. It hurt that this woman got pregnant with twins without even trying while Fiona couldn't bear a child no matter how hard every medical professional worked to bring about a different result. But that wasn't the fault of anyone in this room.

Fiona kept her gaze firmly off Erika's stomach and on her face. "Thank you for your offer of help. We would love to have you keep us company."

"Does that mean you will share your beignets?" Erika said with a twinkle in her blue eyes. "I cannot get enough of them."

The lump in Fiona's throat became unbearable. She loved these women…but it hurt. She knew it was selfish and small, but watching them get their fairy-tale endings just served as a reminder that she was far from having that. And Erika's pregnancy was so difficult for her to watch.

Tears burned as thoughts of lost dreams threatened her ability to hold it together. And she absolutely would not lose it in front of Henri's family. Her pride was about all she had left.

Henri's body ached from practice, but he still burned to talk to Fiona. So he did the sensible thing:

he went to the sunroom. Her operation station, as he liked to call it.

He turned the corner into the sunroom, only half surprised to see Adelaide and Erika working alongside Fiona. Adelaide, iPad in hand, pointed out something on the screen to Erika.

Everything was under control. A smile tugged at his lips. It felt good to see some bit of normalcy in the house.

Not until he saw the tears welling in Fiona's sherry-colored eyes did he realize there was something truly wrong. She was on the verge of falling apart.

In one swift motion, she grabbed her phone and opened the door to the garden. It rattled behind her as she walked into what she'd often called her land-scaped haven.

Every part of him screamed to life. He should fol-low her. Had to follow her. Feet moving of their own volition, he started toward the door.

But something stopped him. What would he even say to her?

It was time to call in reinforcements. With a heavy sigh, he sat in the chair by the table.

"Ladies, I need your help. Adelaide, can I count on you for some assistance?"

"The party is well in hand. Your wife is a master-ful organizer." Adelaide gestured to the scattered pa-pers on the desk. Each stack was color coordinated with sticky notes.

Tapping his fingers on the desk, he looked up at her. "My wife and I are going through, a, uh, rough patch. I could use some ideas for bringing romance back to the marriage."

"I'm very sorry to hear that," she said with undeniable sympathy. But he could see she wasn't surprised.

How had she known? Had she sensed it? Or had Fiona said something?

Erika clasped her hands. "Of course we are willing to help however we can. You and Fiona are my family too now."

"Thank you. I mean that. I'm hoping you can offer some advice, ideas."

Adelaide eyed him curiously. "What kind of time frame are you looking at?"

"I need to move quickly. Fiona is…not happy." That was an understatement. If he could just find a direction to go in. Some clue.

Erika scrutinized him with a sharp look. "Should you be speaking with her about this?"

"Never mind." He shook his head and turned on his heels. "Forget I asked."

Erika called out, "Wait. I did not mean to chase you away. I am happy to share what I can, although I do not know her well. You want your marriage to work, yes?"

"I do."

Adelaide ticked off ideas as if she was running through one of her iPad checklists. "Help her remember that you appreciate her, that you still desire her. Don't assume she knows. And remind her of the reasons you got married in the first place."

He heard her and felt as though he'd already done as much. Of course he'd put Adelaide and Erika on the spot, since they didn't really know the depth of the problems. He was asking them to shoot in the dark. But he and Fiona had guarded their privacy so intensely and now he couldn't share without making her feel betrayed.

Maybe there was a way around it without telling them everything. He and Fiona needed to get back to the early days of their marriage. Back to fun and laughter. Yes, the romance he'd mentioned. Fiona had a point that they hadn't dated long.

They'd gotten married because they thought she was pregnant, and it turned out to be a false alarm. They'd both wanted kids so much they'd focused on that goal—until suddenly surviving surgeries became their whole life. "Let's just say we've fallen into a routine and this old married man needs some concrete dating ideas."

Erika leaned forward, expression wise and intense. "That is very dear of you."

Adelaide quirked an eyebrow. "And to think America's hottest athlete is asking me for dating advice."

He spread his hands. "I'm all ears."

And he was. Because the thought of returning his marriage to the early days, before life grew complicated, had never sounded more appealing.

On her hands and knees, Fiona rooted around the flower bed, decompressing after a restless night with little sleep. Henri had locked himself in his study last night after her future sisters-in-law left. God, the man was full of mixed signals.

She carefully separated the butterfly ginger plants from the aggressive weeds that threatened them. The butterfly ginger was a sweet plant, and the invasive species that shared the flower bed threatened to snuff them out completely. She'd made a habit of maintaining balance in the garden. It provided her a sense of peace.

Especially these days.

She was so fixated on the weeds in the flower bed she barely registered the sound of footsteps on the brick pavers. Casting a glance over her right shoulder, her gaze homed right on the muscled form of Henri approaching. His lips were in a thin line, strain wearing on his face as he went underneath the ivy-wrapped arbor, passing the golden wonder tree and the forsythia sage plants. He still looked like the man she fell in love with and married three years ago.

And that was what hurt the most. She was broken, in her heart, unable to let him or anyone get close. She didn't know how to push past the icy fear.

Henri said nothing. He simply knelt next to her and started helping her. As they sat in silence, the woody scent of him filled her head with memories, each more painful than the last. Of what they were in the beginning. Of when things were good. Of how terrible things were now.

"I think it's time we surrender to the inevitable." Her heart was pounding so hard and fast, she thought it would shake her to pieces.

"What are you talking about?" he asked, his voice raspy.

"Seriously? You have to know. But if you can't bring yourself to say it, I will. Our marriage is over."

Shaking his head, he said, "You're wrong."

"Why?"

"Excuse me?"

"Tell me why I'm wrong."

"Because we got married. We said till…um, forever." He yanked a weed out of the ground.

"You can't even say the word. *Death*. I'm not dying. You don't have to feel guilty over walking away."

Frustration crept into his features, hardening his face. He tossed a weed on the ground. "Dammit, that's not at all what I said."

"But I can hear it in your voice. You feel protective, and that's not enough for us to build a life together." She shook her head. He had to see what was going on.

"We got married because we loved each other."

"We got married because we thought I was pregnant and we were infatuated with great sex. It was a whirlwind romance. We didn't know each other well enough before trouble hit. We're not okay and we never will be."

"I'll go back to the marriage counselor. I'll listen. I wasn't ready then. I am now."

"Thank you, but no. I've had enough." She couldn't stay and have her heart continually fracture and break.

"Stay until the end of the season."

"What good would that do?" Leaning back on the ground, she stared at him.

"I can't file for divorce in the middle of the season. It may be simple for you to just call it quits, but I can't walk away that easily."

"Because of the bad press." It was a low blow, but she delivered it anyway.

"Because I'm not a machine and I can't risk the stress screwing with my concentration, especially not when we have a real shot at going all the way this year. You know how much I have riding on me. How rare it is for a team to have all the right parts assembled the way the Hurricanes do this year."

The request sent her reeling. "Seriously? I'm supposed to put off my life because you want to chase a championship ring?"

"Seriously. It's not just about me, Fiona. You know that. How many people look to me to lead these guys? How can I ruin their chances at being part of a once-in-a-lifetime team? Those opportunities don't come around twice. And there are endorsements to think about, commentator jobs. So many things ride on this season."

Since she traveled with the team, she'd organized family support for the wives and kids when the guys were on the road. She couldn't deny she felt a commitment to that community. Guilt stung over throwing this at him when she knew how much those guys looked up to him. While Henri was blessed on many levels with talent and wealth, many of the guys he played with definitely weren't. The running backs could well be out of football in two years, given the short life span of their careers. Some of the linemen had been raised by hardscrabble single mothers who gave up everything to help their kids succeed.

She would be putting the season at risk... Still, she couldn't stay with him indefinitely.

"When you retire from football, you don't have to work." That was the truth. The Reynaud wealth went far beyond football and Henri played for sport, not to put food on their table. He would have enough money to be just fine if he quit tomorrow.

"Yes, I do. I'm not the type to take on pet projects. I need a full-time job. That's who I am."

Pet projects? Is that how he saw her non-paying fund-raising? It sure felt like a dig at her.

"What's wrong with a life devoted to philanthropy?" She reached for straws, pushing him hard with both hands because he'd edged closer to the truth, the hurt beneath the facade, and she felt so damn vulnerable right now. She was hanging on by a string.

"That path is one you chose, but it's not the one for me."

Indignation blinded her. "Are you calling me a dilettante? Deliberately picking a fight?"

"No." His dark eyes were clear. Focused. "But I think you might be."

Her defenses crumbled and he saw right though her. Panicking, she didn't even know what to say as he brought all that masculine appeal her way.

"You're sexy when you're riled up." He stepped closer. "No matter what we've been through. No matter how many problems we've had or how much distance, know this. I want you in my bed every bit as much as I did the first time I saw you."

Five

Anticipation sent his awareness into overdrive. Henri needed to touch her, to wrap her in his arms.

She was sexy—a tangle of tousled hair and pure fire. And in this setting—in the middle of the garden in that little muted peach dress—she looked like one of those beautiful nymphs that classical artists were always capturing.

Every bit as alluring. And every bit as elusive, too.

But he'd gotten this close to her and he could sense the answering awareness in her, a heat she'd denied too often these last months. Now, extending a hand, he trailed it along the length of her lithe arm. Gentle pressure, the kind that used to drive her wild with anticipation. She turned to face him, leaning into his light touch.

Reaching her hand, he threaded his fingers through

hers, locking them together in that one small way. He was holding on to her. To them.

He pulled her closer. Mouths inches apart. Temptation and need mounting.

Her lips parted. For a moment, things felt normal. The air was charged with palpable passion.

And then it happened. She swayed back ever so slightly. Henri could see the desire flaming in her eyes even as he spotted the *no* already forming on her lips.

So he pulled back instead, releasing her fingers to tap her on the nose. "Lady, you do tempt me."

She flattened her hands on his chest, her fingers stroking, her amber gaze conflicted. "Passion between us has never been an issue. But it will only make things more difficult when we split for good."

He tried not to take that personally, forcing himself to focus on the action over at the tall Victorian bird condominium the landscaper had installed in the garden. Taking a deep breath, he tried to haul in some calm from the backyard his contractor had promised would be a haven for years to come.

"Why do you keep talking like we're over the border and a quickie divorce is already a done deal?"

Fiona's hands clenched in his shirt with intensity. "Why won't you accept that we might as well be? Why are you making this so hard? It's not like we've even uttered the word *love* in nearly a year."

He should just say the word if that's what it took. But for some reason he couldn't push it past his lips. He was saved from a response when a squabble broke out in the birdbath nearby.

Her smile was bittersweet while she watched the little wrens fly off to leave the bath to bigger birds. "You know I'm right. People get divorced even when there aren't big issues at hand. We've been through a lot with the infertility, miscarriages, my surgery, the stress of your high-profile job, as well. It's just too much."

Did she have a point? In some ways. But at least she spoke in tangibles now, delivering more straight talk than she'd given him in a damn long time.

And in a strange way she was making sense. They had been under an immense amount of stress. He hadn't even considered that his job added to the stress of all she'd been through. He had food for thought, and even though she was still attempting to push him away, he felt a bit closer to achieving his objective of reconnecting with her.

"Fiona, I hear what you're saying now, and I understand that—"

"Please, I'm not sure you do." She rested her hand on his. "I'm sorry, Henri. I need to move on with my life."

God, she was stubborn, and that turned him on, too. "You've made that clear. We're ending our marriage after the season—"

"After my next fund-raiser. *Or now.*"

"Okay, not arguing. In fact, I'm suggesting the total opposite. We agreed we need new lawyers. That will happen after your fund-raiser so we don't taint the event. We used to have fun together. Let's use this time to relax. The pressure is off. No expectations. No doctors."

She flinched.

He hesitated. Had he missed something? Before he could ask her, she seemed to relax again.

With a slow exhale, she took a few steps toward the

simple white swing that hung from a huge old live oak that spanned most of the yard. "All right. No pressure. Explain what you mean."

Seeing his chance, he needed to proceed carefully. Not push for too much.

"Let's just be friends." The closer he was to her, the more opportunities he would have to woo his way into her bed and into her heart, back to a place where they understood each other. Where their world would still make sense. "Like we used to be. People will ask fewer questions. We can take a deep breath."

She bit her lip as she trailed a hand over the wooden scrollwork on the seat back of the swing. "But some of the family knows there are problems and the rest of the family already seems to be guessing."

Henri shrugged. He didn't care what they thought. He needed to make it right with Fiona. That was the number one priority. "Then let them unguess for now. We'll deal with the rest later."

"Don't you want their support?" She stilled, a light breeze sifting through her dark hair and teasing it along one arm.

He remembered the days when he'd just sweep her off her feet and carry her to his bed when the mood struck—which was all the damn time with her. When was the last time they'd sprinted to the bedroom to peel each other's clothes off like that?

Shaking off thoughts that would only be counterproductive in his new approach, he picked a few daisies out of the rock garden for her instead, needing to keep his hands occupied with something that wasn't her.

"I want some peace for both of us right now, and something tells me you want that, too." He gathered one simple bloom after another, hoping maybe, just maybe, this peace could bring them back together. The fact that she was considering being friends spoke volumes.

"Why would you say that?" She stepped closer to him, watching him as he wound a too-long stem around the rest of the stems to hold the flowers together.

"We've been married for three years. Call it intuition." He passed her the bouquet, remembering she far preferred simple, garden-variety flowers to anything he could have found in their hothouse.

"I didn't know men believed in intuition." An all-too-rare smile—the ghost of one, anyway—lifted the corners of her mouth.

"I do. What do you say?" He gave her his best bad-boy smile. "Wanna go play?"

The cherry-red 1965 Mustang purred as they wound through the Garden District. The midday sun loomed large, warming the leather of the seats. In the vintage pony car, she felt more alive—more aware—than she had in years.

Fiona couldn't remember the last time they'd done something spontaneous like this. Or the last time they'd chosen the Mustang over the sparkly high-end automobiles at their disposal. She was happy with the choice, though. It blended into downtown seamlessly, attracting less attention and making them seem more like a regular couple.

For now, she could forget about the suspicious lump that might or might not be anything. She could forget about the biopsy scheduled for tomorrow.

And she absolutely would not allow herself to think of the worst-case scenario.

Today, she would play with her husband.

As the car passed through the streets, Fiona gazed out the window. Sometimes she forgot how truly beautiful this place was. Old Victorian homes lined the street, boasting bright hues of red and yellow. Wrought-iron gates encircled the majority of the homes.

What she loved most about New Orleans was the way the streets and sights felt like a continuous work of art. The cultures pressed against each other, yielding brilliant statues and buildings unique to this small corner of the world.

Pulling her thoughts away from the road to downtown, she cast a sidelong glance at Henri. His head bopped to some snappy song from the 1960s. He noticed her looking at him and he flashed a small smile.

He wore a plain T-shirt, cargo shorts and aviator glasses, his dark hair gleaming in the sun. Just looking at his beard-stubbled face made her cheeks sting as if he'd already kissed her in that raspy masculine way that brought her senses to life. Today he was rugged. Rough around the edges. Hot.

And a far cry from the normally polished quarterback the press couldn't get enough of.

As he turned the car down a narrow street, she couldn't help but notice the way the muscles in his arm bunched, pressing against the T-shirt.

Anticipation bubbled in her chest. The day reminded her of when they first met—from the impromptu backyard bouquet to the impulsive drive around town. "The suspense is making me crazy. What are we doing?"

Grabbing a baseball cap from the dashboard, he

gestured to the downtown district. "We're going to play tourist today."

Wind rushed over her, stealing her cares if only for a little while.

"But I've lived here all my life." She gave a half-hearted protest.

"And sometimes the more a person lives somewhere, the more that person misses seeing what's right under their nose. There's a guy on the team who used to live at the beach and he said he hardly ever hit the waves."

"Okay, I see your point. Let's go for it. Let's 'travel' to our home city."

"I thought you'd say that." He pulled into a parking spot and was out of the car before Fiona even had a chance to unbuckle her seat belt. He opened the door, extending his hand. She took it and a surge of desire seemed to ignite in her.

What was it about those easy words of his back in their garden that had given her permission to have fun today? Without worrying about mixed signals or holding strong to her defenses around him, she felt as though maybe she could relax again. Just for a little while.

Because when was the last time they had dated each other? It had been so long, so many months ago. Her heart raced as they made their way down Bourbon Street.

Trying to see the city as a tourist forced her to approach the street differently than she ever had. She began to notice the small details—the way the air seemed spicy, alive with the Creole seasonings of the various restaurants. As she concentrated on the smells, she started to notice what stores were garnering the most attention.

The street was bustling with people. Street musicians played with such artistry she felt moved by their passion. Her hand moved toward Henri's. Giving it a quick squeeze, she breathed in the moment.

Eyeing the carriages, Henri stopped walking. "How about we do this right? Horse-drawn carriage through the city. It's the best way to see this place, after all."

"I'd like that."

"Excellent. You pick the ride that will turn this town magical."

Henri gestured to the line of horses in front of them. Fiona studied a large bay draft horse in the middle of the pack. She liked the way he stood—tall and at attention.

"That one." Fiona pointed to the bay.

"Done." Henri went to talk to the driver, and they climbed into the carriage. There wasn't a lot of room, and Fiona found herself pressed against Henri. The simple touch of their legs against each other felt electric. She wanted him to take his hand and rub her leg. Her thoughts wandered over his body as she looked at him.

The jerkiness of the carriage caused them to fold into each other. Henri was wearing an older cologne—the one he'd worn when they went abroad a while ago.

Instantly, she was transported to the UK. It had been her favorite vacation.

"Remember when we went to Stonehenge?" Fiona peered up at him through her lashes.

"You were convinced you were going to travel back in time."

Nudging him with her arm, she laughed. "Those rocks hum."

"You've been listening to too much voodoo lore and vampire stories." He tapped her nose playfully.

Laying her hand on her chest, she poured a bit of theatrical flair into her voice. "I'm a native of New Orleans. You're a transplant. Give it time."

"Hey, I'm the New Orleans golden boy."

"Because you have a golden throwing arm. It's like you fast-tracked your way into being a native."

"Then good thing I have you around to make sure I stay authentic." He stretched his arm around her, the warmth of his touch pulling on her heart. She nestled into him, leaning into his embrace. Head on his shoulder, she was content to take in the scenery and keep pretending for now the real world wasn't ready to intrude with a biopsy needle in less than twenty-four hours.

So far, the no-pressure day was going far better than he could ever have hoped for. They were connecting. It was the first time in months that they'd been so open with each other.

So honest.

Shuffling a bag of tourist trinkets to one hand, he reached into his pocket for his leather wallet. Pulling out a few crisp bills for the vendor, he nodded at the woman's child as the imp put a handmade bead necklace into the bag. The fact that these mass-produced tourist trinkets were bringing Fiona and him closer together than the diamond jewelry he'd bought amused him.

The vendor was a rangy woman with too-bright red

lipstick, but she was friendly enough. She tossed a few chili peppers in the bag. The lagniappe. It was one of the things about New Orleans he'd liked since he was a boy on vacation—the gesture of the lagniappe always made New Orleans feel like a welcoming city. Which was why he'd felt drawn to this place when he was younger.

Henri scooped up the bag along with the others as they wound their way out of the store crowded with kitschy ghost memorabilia and wax figures of famous jazz musicians. "My grandparents used to bring us here on vacation when we were kids."

"You never mentioned that before. You always talked about the jet-setting vacations."

"My family's in the boating business, after all." That was putting it mildly, really, since they'd made their billions off shipping and the cruise industry. "Gramps combined business trips with a stop here, checking out the latest route."

"That sounds like fun." She ducked under his arm as he held the door for her, bringing the scent of her hair in tantalizingly close proximity to his nose.

"It's no secret my parents weren't overly involved in our lives, so my grandparents didn't have the luxury of just playing with us. My grandfather included us in work so he could see us. I like how you've worked in the same way for the team families." Fiona's capacity to include and integrate people was something he admired about her. No one ever felt left out if Fiona was involved. She had a knack for making people feel that they mattered.

"It makes sense. The ultimate educational experience for children is to travel along. Study the world as they see it. What did you like most about New Orleans as a kid?" She flicked her ropy ponytail over her shoulder as she continued to scan the streets, drinking in the sights while the heat of the day faded along with the sinking sun.

"The music. Street music." He smiled at the memory. "I would sing along. Jean-Pierre would dance. Damn, he was good. He's always been more nimble on his feet."

"What about Gervais?"

"He just quietly tapped his foot."

She snorted. "Figures. And Dempsey?"

"Those trips had stopped by the time he joined our family." Those days had been tough, integrating their half brother into the family fold. They were tight now, and Jean-Pierre was the one who'd left. Henri shook his head and focused on the moment. "Let's get something to eat. What are you in the mood for?"

"Someplace simple in keeping with our tourist day. Somewhere open air. And someplace where you will keep talking."

"Can do." He pointed to Le Chevalier. Ivy snaked around the outside of the trellis. It was casual and intimate—the perfect combination. "How about gumbo?"

Fiona clapped her hands together. "That sounds perfect."

Her French-manicured nails looked ever so chipped. Unusual for her. As though she'd chewed the edges. He shook off the thought and focused on the moment. On her.

Henri led them to a table in the corner of the outside patio. He pushed in her chair for her and then sat beside her.

Menus in hand, the blonde waitress bustled over to them.

"Are you enjoying New Orleans?" The lilt in her accent was particularly musical.

"Oh, yes. This trip has really made us fall in love with the city." Fiona played along, clearly enjoying the feeling of anonymity as much as he did. Since they were outside, he could keep on the baseball cap and sunglasses. His disguise was intact and his wife was engaged in actual conversation with him.

"Well, that's wonderful, loves. Take your time and let me know when you need something. I'll start you with some waters."

"We'll also go ahead and order gumbo." Henri smiled, handing the menus back to the waitress.

"Excellent choice," she said, writing the order onto the pad. And then the waitress turned on her heel and walked away.

"I love that we blend in here. That there aren't hordes of people vying for our attention." Fiona rummaged through the pile of bags from their purchases.

"See? What did I tell you? It's a no-pressure date day. It does wonders for the soul."

"Mmm." Fiona nodded, piling the trinkets onto the table. A little purple jester doll stared back at him.

He surveyed the stack of souvenirs. A masquerade mask brilliantly decorated in feathers. A T-shirt for him. A bamboo cutting board in the shape of Louisiana. A cartoonish, floppy toy alligator. The necklace with bright blue beads that would look lovely against Fiona's pale skin.

"Aha." She held out the voodoo doll. "Here it is. Best purchase of the day."

"You really are such a native," Henri teased.

"Hey, now. Watch out, mister. Or you'll be under my control." She wriggled the doll at him. Then she took its right arm and made the doll tap its own head.

In a gesture of good faith, Henri tapped his own head, mirroring the doll. She gave him a wicked grin.

"Your spunk amazes me." A rolling laugh escaped his lips.

Picking up the necklace, he watched how the sunlight caught in the blue beads. The glass was cut with the intention of splaying light.

"May I?"

"You may." Lifting her hair up in one hand, she turned her back to him.

His fingers ached to touch her. Sliding the necklace over her head, he worked at fastening the tiny clasp. He rested his fingertips on her neck, enjoying the softness of her skin. Breathing in the scent of her perfume, he leaned in, pressing his lips to her neck.

But instead of leaning into him, she recoiled away. She wrapped her arms around her chest and folded into herself.

He sat back in his chair, watching her, trying to understand. "Why don't you want me to touch you? It can't be the scars, because I've seen them and you know it doesn't matter to me." Couldn't she see that he wasn't bothered by any of that superficial nonsense? It was her that he cared about.

"That time we tried to have sex, you were different. It still is between us." Her voice was low, audibly conflicted.

"Of course it's different. You had major surgery."

"But you still touch me, treat me, talk to me like I'm going to break." She picked at her manicured nails absently.

"You're the strongest woman I know. You made an incredibly difficult decision and faced it with grace. I'm so damn proud of you it blows my mind."

"Thank you." She took a sip of her water, brushing off the compliment the way she always did.

He needed to make her see that it wasn't just talk.

"I speak the truth."

"I don't feel strong. I grew up pampered and spoiled by my father, who was afraid I would die like my mother. I don't mean to sound like a spoiled brat now—a kept woman who's whining because her husband wants to baby her." She chewed her thumbnail, then quickly twisted her hands in her lap.

"I fully understand you gave up a career so we could travel together, and you fill every other waking hour doing good for people when you could be like some sports wives and spend your days at a spa. Instead you're putting together six- and seven-figure fundraisers. You're organizing family adventures and educational activities for the children who travel to see their dads play."

"Why are you saying all of this?" Suspicion edged her voice.

A long sigh escaped from his lips. "To let you know I noticed all your hard work and your thoughtfulness. Your kindness. You're an inspiration."

"Then why can't you treat me like I'm strong? Why can't you trust me that I *am* strong?"

Trust?

He was caught up on that word, turning it over in his mind like a puzzle. Why was it that he could read the nuances of a complicated defense strategy, spotting the weaknesses and potential threats with uncanny accuracy, yet he couldn't begin to interpret this simple word from his wife? He lacked the right awareness for people, the right emotional frequency. He was grasping at straws.

This stumped him. He'd felt that he'd been protecting her, not treating her as though she was delicate crystal.

Damned if he knew the answer to her question.

Six

Opening the car door, Fiona swung her legs out, her feet hitting the garage floor with a tap. Before she could thrust herself up and out of the Mustang, Henri was in front of her, offering support.

Clasping his hand, she rose, their bodies closer than she would have guessed as she straightened fully. After the distance of the last months, it was as if her measurements of personal space were all off. Their breath seemed to mingle in the space between them. A faint flush warmed her cheeks and her stomach tumbled in anticipation—and nerves.

"I just need to put the cover on the car." Henri's voice was a dull murmur as he dropped her hand.

He strode to the corner of the garage and picked up a fabric drape for the vehicle, the cover crinkling in his hand. He always had a knack for keeping things safe and secure. The need to protect was part of his nature, and one of the things that was undeniably sexy about him.

The garage windows let the last rays of the evening sun pour into the space, bathing the walls in a twinkling amber light. She'd always loved this time of year—the way the autumn colors of the trees seemed impossibly brighter and sharper as New Orleans went from summer muggy to beautifully temperate. Even from her perch leaning against a sleek tool bench, she couldn't help but appreciate the way the wind whipped through the trees, gusting and causing them to rattle.

Fall was here. The time for dead weight to trickle from branches, even in the South, time for things to change. The hair on the back of her neck stood on end, goose bumps rippling down her body.

Her marriage was going to be one of those free-falling things. A beautiful leaf cascading from a tree. Perfect, vibrant—but not built to weather the harsh winter.

Holding herself together, she forced her eyes back inside the garage. Back to Henri as he tucked the car in for the night. His dark hair curled around his ears ever so slightly. He'd set aside the sunglasses and ball cap in the car on their drive home. Now, he stood before her in his plain, somewhat faded T-shirt. Perfectly casual. He wasn't America's poster boy or the team's golden boy. He was any man. He was hers.

And he was completely sexy.

Hitching herself up onto the tool bench, her leg swaying, she took in the way his muscled arms filled the sleeves of the T-shirt to capacity. But she also noticed the faint bruises that seemed darker on his tanned skin. The result of hours on the field, training with a resolve that had always made her proud. Henri's family had done well enough that he didn't have to work. And yet he poured his soul into his team.

As he stretched the cover on the Mustang, the car let out a low hiss. A tick of the vintage automobile.

Their date had turned quiet after their deep discussion at dinner. Had it been a good idea or bad? It was certainly the kind of subject matter their former marriage counselor would have encouraged.

In the brief time they'd attended therapy, they'd both alternated between quiet and boiling angry. Then they'd ended the appointments. She drummed her fingers against the cement tool bench, wondering if they had taken more time—tried a bit harder in therapy—would they be here right now?

Meanwhile, her looming biopsy had her stomach in a turmoil. She'd thought she had until the end of football season to ease out of her marriage, but the latest health scare put a whole new timetable on their relationship. If she didn't end things soon, Henri would absolutely dig his heels in for all the wrong reasons, staying by her side to help her battle for her health. Honorable, yes. But in no way related to love as a foundation for their relationship.

So this was possibly her last night to be on somewhat even footing with Henri. Their last night to be together.

Yes, she would have to get past the awkwardness of showing him her scars, but he'd helped her dress in the hospital more than once, seen the incisions. They'd even had that one failed attempt at lovemaking. He knew the extent, and certainly the scars had faded.

The plastic surgeon had reconstructed her body, and while he'd been the best of the best, the surgery had left her feeling less than normal.

But after the day she and Henri had shared, she found none of that mattered to her tonight. She'd married a sexy, generous, caring man and she'd never stopped wanting him. Spending the day together only reminded her how much.

This would be their last night to indulge in the passion she'd been fighting for months on end. She ached to reach out and touch him, to press herself against his tanned, toned body once more. To be with him. And after tomorrow...well, things might never be the same. So she'd put this on her terms. She'd go for this now and damn the future.

Fluffing her hair over her shoulder, Fiona inhaled a sharp breath, tasting the air. The scents of falling leaves and gasoline filled her nostrils. It was now or never.

"Henri, let's walk outside, savor the sunset."

He cocked his head to the side, his forehead creased with confusion. "Sure, sounds like a nice idea."

"We're blessed to have flowers longer in the season because of the greenhouse." And their garden was her own special haven, the place she felt most at peace. "Restoring that was the most thoughtful gift you ever gave me—other than those daisies."

They began outside. She took unsure steps, wending toward the greenhouse. Brilliant oranges and yellows flamed out on the horizon. A few birds trilled in the distance, chattering over something that sounded urgent.

"I'm glad to know there are happy memories for

you." His eyes wandered over their yard. Their home. The place they'd restored with a kind of passion she wished they could have applied toward restoring *them*.

She slid her hand in his, testing the waters for seduction. "There are many happy memories. I want to treasure those."

He squeezed her hand. "Me, too."

Henri's thumb ran gently across her knuckles. Slow and deliberate.

Opening the greenhouse door with one hand, Henri led them inside. The chill in the air was replaced by temperate warmth. The scents of rosemary and sweet flowers hung heavy in the air.

It was a stark contrast from outside. The plants in here hadn't succumbed to the change of fall yet. No leaves were hanging by threads; the flowers still bloomed. All was alive with possibility in this sheltered environment.

"Mmm. Do you remember the time we went to New York City?" Her voice was open and lithe as she allowed herself to look back through their entwined history.

"I haven't thought about that trip in forever. One of the best away games of my career."

"And?" she pressed. They continued into the greenhouse, heading for the back wall where there was a small clearing and some patio furniture.

"And also one of the best art galleries I've ever stepped foot in. Then again, having a built-in guide helps that."

He sat on the lounge chair, sinking into the plush cushion. Beckoning her, he patted the space next to him.

Folding herself onto the lounge beside him, she took a deep breath. "Well, my art degree is good for things like that."

"It certainly helps. It's probably why you are brilliant at assembling fund-raisers—you approach problems with such creativity." His voice trailed off as he stroked the back of her hair.

The simple touch sent ripples of pleasure along her skin, all the more potent for how long she'd denied herself those feelings. Those touches. She wanted to tip her head back to lean more heavily against him, to demand more. But after all the times she'd pulled away from him these last months, she wanted to be clear about what she wanted.

Spinning around on the lounge, she faced him. Scooting close to him, she slung her arms around his neck, drawing closer.

"Henri, I can't deny that I want you." She saw the answering heat flash in his dark eyes, but she forced herself to continue. "Please don't read anything more into this than there is, but right now, I just want us to finish this day together. To make another memory regardless of what tomorrow holds." She hoped he understood. That he wouldn't turn her away even though she wasn't sure she deserved him on those terms. "Say something. Anything."

"You've surprised the hell out of me. I'm not sure what to say other than yes." He stroked his fingers along her cheek. "Of course, yes."

Relief eased the tension inside her for all of a moment before another feeling took hold of her. His hands stroked up her arms. Over her shoulders. As the sun set, dim lights flickered on overhead via auto sensors. The warm glow added a romantic aura to the verdant space.

His fingers found the nape of her neck. Twisting her hair in his hands, he pulled her to him, their mouths barely touching. The feeling of warm shared breath caressed her lips.

Anticipation mounted in her chest. This moment was everything. She'd almost forgotten how fast he could turn her inside out with just a look. A touch.

And then his lips met hers, his mouth sure as he molded her to him. Tension and longing filled his kiss. It was in the way he held her. How he touched her. How he *knew* her. She melted into him, her body easing into his in a manner she hadn't allowed herself in forever. His tongue explored her mouth, making her rediscover a rhythm—a way of breathing. She dragged in air scented by hothouse flowers and Henri—his skin, his sweat, his aftershave, all of it intensified in the muggy greenhouse air.

Her hands sought his back, roving over the impossible cords of muscle as the passion between them picked up in intensity, as desire developed a course of its own. She wanted him more than ever. How could she not? This was a constant between them, burning hotter than ever.

Henri pulled back. The absence of his lips shocked her for a moment, and she blinked at him. Unsure.

A small, wicked smile played along his lips.

He held her hand, pulling her into him. His breath was hot against her ear. "Let's go inside, to the bedroom."

"Let's not. Let's stay here, together." She bunched

his shirt in her eager fingers, pulling it over his head as his grin widened.

"I always have appreciated your adventurous spirit."

His hand went beneath her dress. Nimble fingers teased up her leg, setting her desire into overdrive. He caressed a spot behind one knee, lingered along the curve of her hip as he kissed her, driving her crazy for more of him and his touch. She scooted closer on the lounger until she was almost in his lap, and he finally fingered the edge of her panties and slid his hand beneath the lace. Hunger for him coiled in her belly and she pressed herself to him harder. He pulled her lace panties down, discarding them on the floor.

Her whole body hummed with anticipation.

Taking a moment to appreciate his honed body, she edged back to run light fingers over the bruises on his arms. They were purple and dark, the result of sacks he'd taken and defensive players continually trying to chop the ball out of his sure hands. She carefully avoided putting a lot of pressure on them.

She looked at his bruises, suddenly aware of her own scars again. What would he think of them? She looked up to find him staring at her. Waiting.

"No spun glass. I am strong. A survivor." She needed to remind herself even as she wanted him to know it.

"I understand that. And before we go farther, I want you to know I do know what the scars look like now. More than just seeing you. After we talked to the doctor about surgery, I asked the plastic surgeon. I wanted to understand the during, the after, the years to come."

Frustration chilled her skin and the moment. "So

you wouldn't be shocked, turned off for life after seeing me in the hospital?"

He cradled her face in his hands. "I've never been turned off. Only concerned. I wanted to support you. And sure, I didn't want to look surprised or sad for you. I didn't want to risk hurting you, especially after what you'd gone through."

Some of the tension eased. She knew he meant it. And she refused to let some superficial insecurity steal this night from her. From both of them.

She turned her cheek into his palm and gently nipped his finger. "And now what do you think?"

She'd been afraid to ask before.

He skimmed his knuckles along her cheekbone. "That I'm glad you're safe. I pray every day you'll stay that way."

She clasped his wrist, stilling his hand. "Pity? Fear? Those are *not* turn-ons."

She needed to be clear on that point.

"Caring." He palmed her breasts. "It's about caring. You know me."

Delicious shivers of awareness tingled through her, her body wakening to life.

He eased off the rest of her clothes. Slowly and deliberately. With practiced hands, he unhooked her bra. The rays from the fading sun and dim interior lights danced against her bare skin, illuminating her completely. Scars and all.

Self-consciousness whispered through her no matter how much she told herself she knew the surgical lines had faded to a pale pink, barely visible. And her breasts were, if anything, perkier than before, although she had opted for a smaller cup size, going down from D to C. But he knew that already.

And she couldn't stop her thoughts from rambling.

As he took her in with his eyes, an unmistakable heat lit his gaze and a sigh of reverence passed his lips. He swiped a flower from a nearby pot. The stem snapped easily.

"You are so beautiful." He traced her scars with the petals of the flower, the timbre of his voice lowering an octave. The silky petals tingled against her skin, sparking desire in her bones. "Every inch of you."

"You don't have to say that." She deflected compliments so often.

"Have I ever been anything but truthful?"

"Not that I know of."

"Believe me then. Trust me. I look at you and I see beauty. Even more than that, I see strength, which is so damn mesmerizing it's the greatest turn-on imaginable."

A renewed commitment to this moment surged in her. Her hands snaked toward his bare chest. With gentle pressure, she pushed him back on the lounge chair. As the light from the sun faded behind the horizon, she surveyed the way his muscles expanded. He inhaled deeply. His eyes were fixed on hers, her need mirrored in his face.

Hooking a finger in his shorts, she edged them down and off. Climbing forward, she straddled him, pressing her hips into his. Feeling more alive than she had in months.

Henri didn't have a clue what had caused her change of heart, but after more than six months of being shut out by his wife, he wasn't passing up this opportunity to be with her. To taste and love every inch of her beautiful body.

Holding back from her every day had been hell. In the early days, of course, right after her surgery, it had been easy to give her space and time to heal. But after that, once she looked as strong and healthy as ever, he'd had to employ a ruthless amount of restraint to keep his distance.

And now, by some freaking miracle he didn't even understand, she was his again. Right here. In his arms.

He cradled her breasts in his hands, stroking, caressing, savoring the feel of her every bit as much as he enjoyed the sighs of pleasure puffing from between her lips. Everything about Fiona was sexy. Her wordless demands. Her hungry sighs. Her endlessly questing hands. He'd missed those touches. Hell, he'd missed the scent of her long, dark hair against his nose when they made love.

So now, it was sensory overload having her bare skin glide over his. She restlessly wriggled against him, the moist heat of her sex rubbing along his throbbing hard-on, driving him to the edge of frenzied need after so long without her.

He didn't see the scars, not in any way that mattered. He saw her. His strong beautiful wife, a survivor, who faced life head-on with bravery and strength. He thought of her giving heart, her philanthropy and the help she always gave to the other team wives.

What would it be like to travel with her again? To have her by his side in Arizona for his next game? Even though they couldn't travel on the same aircraft since he had to fly with the team and the spouses traveled separately, being with her, really being with her on the road, was something he'd missed. Having her in his bed at night was more than just a show of support. He missed talking to her, decompressing with her, telling her about the game he was passionate about.

He'd missed all of that as much as this. But this?

He felt as if he'd won the freaking lottery by taking her out on a date tonight. She braced her hands on his chest. He cradled her hips in his hands, lifting, supporting, guiding her...

Home.

The hot clamp of her body around him threatened to send him over the edge then. She felt so good.

So right.

Every glide was perfection as she rolled her hips and he lifted her up then back down again. Damn straight, sex between them was amazing. But he hadn't even remembered how incredible. Wasn't sure something this special could be captured in a memory.

Only experienced.

Their bodies kept time with each other. They pressed together, his mouth finding her lips. Her shoulder. Her hands twined in his hair. Her breath hitching, faster and faster, let him know she was close, so very close to her release. He knew her body well and intended to use that to bring her to a shattering orgasm while holding back his own for as long as possible. No way in hell was he going without her.

His hand slid toward her and he tucked two fingers against the tight bundle of nerves between her legs. Her husky moan gusted free, her head falling back. Her hair grazed her back as she rode him harder.

Damn straight, she wasn't a fragile flower. She took

him every bit as soundly as he took her. He reveled in the sight of her, her breasts rising and falling more quickly, her gasping breath, the flush spreading over her skin until…yes…a cry of bliss flew free from her mouth, echoing through the greenhouse. A bird fluttered in the rafters and, finally, he allowed himself his own release.

He thrust upward, deeply, his orgasm hammering through him. His heart slammed against his rib cage. The power of being with her was…more than he remembered. If he could even form words or a coherent thought. He could only feel each pulse of pleasure throb through him.

Her back arching, she fell forward against his chest. Her sigh puffed over his skin, perspiration sealing them together, connecting them further even as they stayed linked, his body in hers.

This moment had been what he was trying to construct for months. A moment of connection. Something real between them. Something built on emotion and trust.

Finally, after months of confusion and frustration, he felt alive with the possibility that this might be salvageable. Their trip to Arizona for his game would be like old times.

Lying in Henri's arms on the lounger, she planned what she wanted to do to his body through the night. Of course they would have to gather their clothes first, because running through the yard naked was out of the question. Even in the privacy of their garden beyond the greenhouse, there was always the risk of the media snapping a shot with a telephoto lens.

Nothing, nothing at all, could steal this evening from her. She had to make the most of this time with him, because this was likely all they might ever have. She couldn't even go to Arizona with him because of her biopsy.

If she even dared to tell him, it would only distract him from the game. Deep down, she knew he needed to stay focused. And she didn't intend to tell him regardless, though the excuse of work made her more comfortable in her decision to withhold information.

All of which she would deal with later.

His breath caressed the top of her head. "I've missed you."

"I've missed this, too. We've been through a lot, suffered lost dreams. Maybe if things had been easier for us..."

"I'm sorry, Fiona, so sorry I couldn't make this right for you. We can have children, adopt, foster—it doesn't matter to me."

As much as his words tempted her to throw caution to the wind and dive into the promise in his eyes, she couldn't escape the specter of fear that loomed inside her.

"It wouldn't be fair to bring them into a shaky marriage, anyway."

"You didn't say no to adoption outright, though. Not initially. Did you back out because you don't trust me? The marriage?"

"It was more than us. I wouldn't be honest if I didn't admit that my genetics have scared me lately. All the women in my family have died of breast cancer or ovarian cancer. As much as I worried about dying, the thought of a child losing her mother..." She swallowed hard. "That scares me to the point where I don't know what to think. So yes, adoption is something I've thought about. I wasn't sure how you felt."

"We really didn't talk about the important things in life, did we?"

As much as she wanted to share with him now, she couldn't bring herself to tell him about her biopsy tomorrow. She understood he would expect her to travel with him this weekend, to be there for him at his game. It was going to be hard as hell to push him away.

But for better or worse, she had to do this alone.

Seven

They made love in the greenhouse, the shower, again in their old bed.

Memories of their night together slammed into Fiona as she lay beside Henri in their four-poster bed. They'd spent the night entwined with each other. They'd slept naked. Well, he'd slept naked. Sleep had eluded her. She'd pressed up against him, too full of fluctuating emotions to actually drift off.

As morning crept closer, sleep was farther from her than ever. Instead, she watched the minutes tick by. Each successive change on the clock pulled at her heart.

She'd passed the night watching the steady rise and fall of Henri's chest as he slept. His rhythmic breath was raspy, his expression relaxed while she contemplated his bed-tossed dark hair.

She felt a pang in her heart. He was so damn sexy and last night would be the final night she would ever spend with him.

Even if the biopsy turned out all right, what about the next time? Fiona wanted to freeze this moment in her mind, to carry the essence of him with her for the rest of her life. The unraveling of their marriage was painful, and while a part of her loved Henri, she knew she was doing them both a favor by leaving.

So she did the only sensible thing she could. Fiona memorized him, noting all the small details that make a person complete. She watched the unsure morning light filter into the room. The muted sunshine seemed to get caught in his stubble, highlighting his square jaw. His long, thick lashes fluttered slightly.

Guilt and anxiety tickled her stomach. When he learned that she wasn't going with him, he would be devastated. The knowledge that last night hadn't changed anything between them would rock him to his core. She hadn't meant to rattle his focus before a game, knowing too well how hard that made things for him on the field. But there was nothing to do about it. Her mind was made up.

The sheets rustled and Henri shifted beside her. His even breaths hitched and he cleared his throat as he rolled closer to her. A growl of appreciation rumbled up from his throat an instant before his eyes opened to meet hers.

He slid a hand up to cup her neck and draw her to him. He sketched a tender kiss along her cheek, his bristly face scratchy and delicious. "Good morning, sunshine."

She pressed her face to his for an instant and allowed herself to savor every last sensation. "Good morning to you, too."

His arms extended out to either side. He stretched in a way that forced her to roll onto his chest. Ending the stretch, he wrapped his muscled arms around her naked body, pulling her close. A deep sigh filled the air as he cocked his head to the side to glance at the rising sun through the part in the curtains.

"God, it's later than I thought." He patted her bottom. "We gotta get moving. I have a plane to catch. I know yours is later, but wanna grab a quick bite of breakfast before I go? I know you have to pack—"

"Henri." She cut him short, unable to let him go on any longer. "I won't be flying with the other wives to Arizona."

He sat up slowly. "You're busy stepping in at the last minute to salvage the fund-raiser. I understand."

She wanted to use the excuse he'd handed her on a silver platter, but she could see now they'd let this play out too long. "Henri, last night was incredible—" she cupped his face "—a beautiful tribute to what we shared. But it was also goodbye."

Shock, then anger, marched across his face. "I don't know what's going on with you, Fiona, but you're wrong, dammit. Last night made me more certain than ever we are not finished."

She crossed her arms, pressing the sheet to her chest. "You can believe what you want, but my mind's made up. We can put off the official announcement to the public, however, we can't keep playing the charade at home and with our families. It's not fair."

Jaw tight, he studied her silently.

It hurt so much to see him hurt, and things would

only be worse if he guessed her secret. "Henri, you're going to miss your flight."

Exhaling hard, he turned away and flung aside the sheets, striding out of her room.

And out of her life.

The Hurricanes always traveled in their team jet, but today proved to be an exception. Their usual aircraft had been grounded for maintenance. Instead, the Hurricanes made their way to Arizona in a chartered luxury jet.

Henri wasn't having much luck enjoying the plush leather seats and open floor plan that made the jet feel less like a plane and more like a living room, the quarters as nice as anything his family owned. His thoughts stayed locked on Fiona. On last night and how damn close he'd been to winning her back. Yes, he'd made it into her bed again, but as always, one night wasn't enough.

Distracted as hell, he barely registered the interactions of his teammates. Freight Train Freddy tossed a football back and forth across the seats with Wild Card Wade. They hooted and hollered, pumping up the other guys with adrenaline. Even the veterans trying to play a card game in the corner were getting in on the action, fielding passes that came their way and taunting the guys on the other side of the jet.

Normally Henri would be leading the pregame amp-up charge. But today, he sat next to Gervais, the team owner, with a few of the other front-office members. Their seats up front kept them out of the fray.

Their Texas cousin Brant Reynaud, who also played for the Hurricanes, made his way from across the cabin. His yellow rose lapel pin glinted in the warm light of the cabin. He paused briefly to lean against the cognac leather chairs by Gervais and Henri, phone in hand.

"Did you see the Twitter feed? Our fans are loving us—all those pictures from the airport are viral." He gestured to his smartphone. "Someone on the media relations staff is doing a hell of a job connecting us to the public."

Brant clapped Gervais on the shoulder before continuing toward an empty chair by Freight Train Freddy, seamlessly reeling in a one-handed catch on his way.

The words barely registered with Henri. Pointedly fixing his gaze on the intricate chandelier in the center of the cabin, he wondered what the damages were going to be to replace the thing when someone hit it with a bad throw. Gervais pulled out his own phone to investigate the latest posts.

Gervais's face hardened as he thumbed through the Hurricanes' Twitter feed. A number of fans had rushed Henri and the other Hurricanes players in the airport. These types of things were normal. Fans always wanted autographs and photographs.

Today, however, had been a little different. Gervais's eyebrows skyrocketed as he flashed the six-inch screen of the smartphone to Henri.

Henri leaned over, hands resting on his thighs. Damn. The blonde from the airport who had gotten a little handsy with Henri had posted a photograph—one that had the potential for scandal. Not that it took much these days. People's marriages and careers had been ruined over less.

The thin blonde fan was dressed in high-waisted

shorts with a sheer chiffon crop top. She'd popped her leg and planted a kiss on Henri's cheek, anchoring herself by hooking their arms together. The image, out of context, didn't show the way Henri had tried to remove her and redirect her to a more appropriate pose.

A part of him longed for simpler, less connected days. Seeing how quickly the pictures in the airport circulated on Twitter left a sour taste in his mouth. This viral information was overwhelming, even when it was good news. When things looked slightly less than legit…viral information had a way of becoming deadly.

While Gervais was largely concerned with the team's image, he also no doubt worried about his brother. "Do you think that's safe, or even wise, given the current state of your marriage?"

Stomach plummeting, Henri ran his fingers through his thick, dark hair. "I wasn't encouraging her. I was working like hell to get away."

His brother nodded, but the stern expression didn't leave his mouth. "Oh, I know that. But you're in a career that puts you in the public eye. One picture. One sound bite. That's all it takes."

"And you think I don't realize that?"

Gervais didn't know the half of it.

"Just be careful, brother. Your marriage doesn't appear steady enough to weather this kind of pressure."

"What did Erika tell you?" In that moment, Henri regretted asking Erika and Adelaide for advice.

"No one has to. I know you." Turning the screen of his phone off, Gervais folded his arms over his chest.

"All marriages go through rough patches."

"Hmm." Gervais rubbed his chin in that wise big-brother way while saying absolutely nothing in the way of big-brother help.

"Don't pull that enigmatic bull with me."

Gervais gave a quick shrug of the shoulders. "You don't act the same around each other. You don't touch each other."

"You're in that newly-in-love stage, seeing hearts and stars." Henri tried not to snarl the words, but damn. Gervais's view of his marriage hit too close to home.

"You saw hearts and stars?" Honest surprise laced Gervais's voice as he unfurled his arms, leaning forward.

Henri jutted his chin in answer to that question. But the truth? He had seen stars. God, he'd been so in love with her then. What had happened? Or better yet, how had they gotten to this point?

"We're brothers, so I'm just going to say this and if it makes you mad, then I'm sorry. But here it is. We've seen with other couples in sports how infertility can put strains on even a rock-solid marriage," Gervais said softly. Sometimes he could be so matter-of-fact, peeling back the layers most people danced around.

Infertility clearly wasn't an issue with his brother, whose fiancée was already expecting twins after one weekend encounter. And Henri couldn't deny that stung. "I'm happy for you and Erika, but honestly, brother, do you think you're the one to talk to me about the strains of infertility on a marriage?"

"Point taken. Life isn't fair."

Bitter reality pulsed in Henri's veins as he shook his head. "Don't I know it?"

"Have the two of you talked about adoption?" Gervais didn't even turn when the chandelier finally took a hit, sending the glass medallions clanking together without breaking. He stayed focused on their conversation while Dempsey, the head coach, stood to call the group to order before the next pass broke the fixture.

"It's about more than not having kids. During a round of tests after another miscarriage, she found a lump in her breast." He'd carried the weight of those secrets long enough. And clearly, he hadn't been doing a good job of it, given how much Gervais had guessed.

"Damn. Didn't her mother and grandmother—" Gervais's voice had fallen an octave lower than normal.

Henri finished the sentence for him, nerves alight and fraying. "Die of cancer? Yes. She got tested for the gene and she's a carrier."

"I'm so damn sorry."

All the pressure and secrecy from the last few months came pouring out. Once uncorked, Henri found he couldn't contain the reality of his situation anymore. Fiona wouldn't be there in Arizona. Very soon, she wouldn't be part of his life at all. And that thought…it was too damn impossible to come to terms with. "We didn't just go to Europe for a vacation six months ago. Fiona had a double mastectomy and a hysterectomy while we were over there."

"God, Henri, I am so sorry. Why didn't you tell us?"

"She didn't want to."

Gervais gripped his shoulder and squeezed. "You didn't have to bear that burden alone. I would have been there with you."

"We didn't want to run the slightest risk of the press getting wind of this. Our privacy was—is—important." Still, it meant something to have his brother's support. He knew all of them would be there for him—and for Fiona, too, if she ever allowed anyone to get that close to her.

"Your call. Your decision. But I'm here if you need me, and there's nothing wrong with needing someone. You both lost your mothers young. That's difficult as hell." One thing about Gervais that no one could question was his fierce loyalty to his family. They were his tribe.

But that didn't negate the truth. A truth that still made Henri angry as hell. "Her mother died. Mine ran off because she was mad at Dad for not keeping his pants zipped."

"Death is tragic. Betrayal hurts like hell, too, like how our mom bailed on us even though her issue was with Dad's cheating. I can see how that would make it tough for you to trust. I've wrestled with that, too, in the past."

"Fiona isn't my mother." Not by a long shot.

"But she's leaving you." He paused, tapping the screen even though the image had faded to black. "Or maybe you've pushed her away?"

"That's crap," he quickly snapped. Too quickly? "I'm working my ass off to win her back."

"If you say so." Gervais looked away, reclining his seat.

"I thought you were here to help me," he couldn't help grousing.

Scrolling through his contact list on his smartphone, Gervais stopped at Erika's entry. He waved the phone at Henri. "For this mission, I'm calling in ground support from a certain extremely efficient princess I know and adore."

And just like that, Gervais asked Erika to deliver Fiona flowers from Henri.

Maybe he did need some more help winning back his wife after all.

The pain from her biopsy had nothing on the pain in her heart. The ache that was caused by a chapter of her life ending—the end of love.

She'd taken a taxi to the appointment because she didn't want to risk having the Reynaud chauffeur telling anyone else she'd been to the doctor.

Lying on the table during the procedure, she'd wished she had someone's hand to hold—Henri's hand. Not that they would have allowed anyone in with her anyway. Possibly having him in the lobby waiting could have brought comfort...but she'd made her decision and had to stick to it.

Now Fiona had sought sanctuary in the library, amid the books and art collection. She sat in an oversize Victorian chair, curled up in a throw blanket that featured famous first lines of novels in the design. She hoped the collective power of literature and art alone would seep into her veins and make her feel whole.

Settling into the chair, she had nearly become comfortable.

Until a knock at the front door sounded. Mustering energy and some bravado, Fiona made her way to the door, brown hair piled high on her head in a messy bun.

There were a lot of things Fiona was prepared for today. Company was not one of them. Her soul ached to be alone and to mourn her wounds and losses.

When she opened the door, Fiona's face fell. Erika was in front of her, armed with a card, a bouquet of lilies and baby's breath, and a decorative box of Belgian chocolate.

"Erika, what a surprise." Fiona forced a smile.

The Nordic princess braced her grip on the flowers and candy. "May I come in? Oh, and these are from your husband." She thrust the treats into Fiona's arms. "I won't be long. I have to catch the plane with the other wives."

"Of course, right this way," Fiona mumbled, urging her inside. She appreciated the gesture but somehow she knew full well this hadn't been Henri's idea. And it also meant their problems were becoming more public.

And she felt like a wretched ingrate. Forcing a smile, she thrust her face into the flowers and inhaled. "They smell lovely. Thank you."

Fiona set the crystal vase of lilies on the entryway table beside an antique clock. "Let's have a seat and you can help me eat the chocolates. How does that sound?"

Laughing softly, Erika patted her stomach. "The babies definitely need a taste of those chocolates. And they send their thanks to Aunt Fiona."

"Then let's dig in." Fiona led the way back down the hall to the library, taking comfort in the smell of old books and vintage art. This room was a place where everything was still in order—where things didn't have the pesky habit of uprooting and shaking her world.

Fiona tugged the red satin ribbon on the box of Belgian truffles. "Erika, you're glowing."

"Thank you. Double the babies, double the glow, I guess." She plucked a raspberry-filled truffle from the box with obvious relish. "Mostly, I just want to sleep double the time and eat double the food. Not very promising for a romantic honeymoon."

Erika's self-deprecation fell flat on Fiona.

"I'm sure Gervais understands." Fiona sat in a wing-back chair, cross-legged, the chocolates in her lap.

"He does. He has been incredibly patient." Erika looked around the library, absently rubbing her stomach as she chewed her candy. The motion played on the tendrils of Fiona's heartstrings. As if she could hear the pain in Fiona's heart, Erika looked up suddenly. A pale blush colored her cheeks. "I am sorry. I do not mean to babble on about myself."

"You don't have to hold back your joy." Fiona chewed her bottom lip, studying Erika's face. "Someone told you, didn't they, about Henri's and my fertility troubles?"

"I do not mean to pry." Erika dropped into a wing-back on the other side of the fireplace.

"You aren't. It's…well, I'm working on finding my comfort zone in discussing this with others in the family. It's painful, but that doesn't mean I can't celebrate your happiness. I love children and want to enjoy them." Fiona popped a creamy truffle into her mouth, but the high-quality chocolate tasted like dust. She set the box carefully on the end table beside her chair, leaving it open for her future sister-in-law.

"Want to?" Erika tilted her head, trying to understand what she was saying.

"I do. It's been a difficult road."

"Would you like someone to listen? We are family." Erika laid a strong hand of support on Fiona's forearm.

"We may not be family much longer."

Erika frowned and leaned forward to give Fiona's

hand a quick squeeze. The grace of royalty filled her expression. She spoke deliberately, a commanding reassurance filling her words. "I am so sorry to hear that. The offer to listen does not expire."

"Thank you." She reached to clasp her hand. "I hope you and Gervais are finding time to be together in spite of the busy season. That's important. Time slips by so quickly."

"I appreciate the advice." Erika inclined her head but—thank goodness—didn't call her hypocritical.

"And I appreciate that you didn't throw it back in my face, considering I have no children and am on the brink of divorce."

"You care about my future, Gervais's, the babies'. I can see that and appreciate it."

"I do. Henri and I rushed to the altar so quickly we didn't have much time to get to know each other."

"It is not too late to change that." Erika got up and straightened the books on the shelf, peering over her shoulder.

"How can you be so sure?"

"You are still here. So there is still hope, still time. Regrets are so very sad."

Regret. It was so damn hard to live with that hanging over her head.

Fertility was only half of the issue. And maybe, just maybe, she'd get the other half off her chest once and for all. The last thing she wanted was to live with regret, without ever giving her situation the dignity of a thorough examination. She'd already confided in Erika this much. Might as well see the situation all the way through.

"How are the wedding plans going?"

"Well, very well. We have a wonderful wedding coordinator."

"Is there anything I can do for you?"

"Just enjoy the day." She rubbed the swell of her stomach. "These two babies are growing so fast I may have to choose a new wedding gown."

"You will be a lovely bride."

Erika pointed to the couch at the end of the library. Taking a seat, she patted the space next to her, staring directly at Fiona. With kind eyes and a steady voice, Erika pressed on.

"You have something else on your mind. I can see that in your eyes. Since English is not my first language I tend to read eyes and emotions more clearly these days. Please speak freely."

"It's not my business, really." Fiona sat next to Erika, avoiding direct eye contact. Instead, her gaze fell on a Victorian-era depiction of the Greek goddess Artemis. Far easier to focus on art than the reality of her situation.

"Does it have to do with your difficulties with Henri?"

"I'm not even sure how to say this." A rush of dizziness pushed at Fiona's vision. Speaking this aloud would be one of the hardest things she'd ever done.

"Simply say it." Grasping her hand, Erika held on tightly, giving her reassurance and encouragement. Fiona couldn't meet her gaze.

But the words did tumble out of her mouth. "Henri and I got married quickly because we thought I was pregnant. I may have been and had an early miscarriage—or maybe Henri already told you this?"

Erika stayed diplomatically silent, just listening, which encouraged Fiona to pour her heart out.

God, how she needed to. "Since I had the one positive pregnancy test, I assumed…well…my point is, we rushed to the altar and didn't take the time to get to know each other. We have paid a deep price for that."

"I did not know the details. I am so sorry."

"Even if you go through with the marriage as scheduled, take time to be a couple. Your children are important, but having parents with a solid marriage will reassure them."

"Are you suggesting Gervais and I should not get married?"

"That's a personal decision. I'm simply sharing my experience and wanting to make sure you are certain. That's all. I hope I haven't offended you."

"Not at all. I insisted you tell me your thoughts and they are valid. My family pushes for marriage. You are the first to present the other side of the argument." She patted Fiona's wrist. "But please be assured. I have thought this through. I am in love with Gervais. I want to be his wife for the rest of my life."

"Then I am so very happy for you." And so very heartbroken for herself.

It was going to be a long weekend before the biopsy results came back, and either way she wasn't sure how she intended to handle things.

alone, but Fiona knew there really wasn't an option. No doubt she'd distracted Erika enough from her impending wedding and giving birth to twins without saddling her with this, too.

Blinking back tears, Fiona wondered how long it would take for the pain medicine to kick in. Desperate for relief, she needed a distraction. Immediately. Glancing at the clock, she realized the Arizona game had already started. Had she really slept in that late, dozing off and on through naps?

Clicking on the remote, Fiona channel surfed until she arrived at the Hurricanes game.

Sitting up against the headboard in a sea of pillows, she situated the oversize nightshirt. One of Henri's shirts, actually, that still carried the scent of him. She'd allowed herself this small indulgence as she watched the game. Her fingers, seemingly of their own accord, fled to the loose cotton bra and bandage combination that shielded the places where she'd been pierced by the needle. Checking. Since she'd come home, the biopsy was a constant source of anxiety.

A long rumble sounded from the deepest point in her belly and she realized she hadn't really eaten anything. Easing carefully out of the bed, her bare feet hit the soft Persian rug, then the cooler wooden floorboards. She walked gingerly downstairs and riffled through the freezer—a woman deserved ice cream on a day like this. The best medicine a girl with an ailing body and a broken heart could get. She opted for a pint-size container of plain vanilla then plopped some of the chocolates Henri had given her on top. Taking a heaping spoonful, Fiona swallowed with bliss and made her way back upstairs to her bedroom to rest.

The flat screen mounted on the wall still echoed with the game. The daisies he'd given her earlier brightened the TV-lit room. Fiona had left the lilies he'd sent yesterday downstairs in the library in an attempt to spread out the reminders of what she was about to lose.

A heaviness pressed on her chest. This particular pain had nothing to do with the biopsy needles. It had everything to do with the large part of her that wished she'd gone to Arizona.

How she wished to be there cheering with the other wives, or even just waiting for him in the hotel room. To celebrate after the game. Her mind wandered back to the way her body had somehow, after all this time, synced to his two nights ago. Fiona wanted to have sex with him again, to pretend that none of this pain and suffering was real.

Scooping another large bite of ice cream into her mouth, Fiona turned her attention back to the game. Just in time to see the camera pan to the sell-out crowd, pausing on an older couple in matching football jerseys. The fans seated around them waved signs that read *Happy Sixtieth Anniversary!* and the smiling couple turned to one another to share a tender kiss on national television before the announcers moved on to comment about Arizona's offensive drive.

But her mind was stuck on that kiss. That celebration of a lifetime of love. Her mind rushed back to the gentle way Henri had cupped her head in his hands before kissing her. She tried to remember exactly the way his lips felt against hers—that gentle pressure of their kisses. The way his tongue had explored her mouth, leaving her breathless and ready for more.

And as she thought about him, the broadcast shifted to a close-up of her quarterback husband.

Soon-to-be ex-husband, she corrected herself. More ice cream.

Her gaze raked over him in his shoulder pads and away-game jersey, his features visible even behind the bars of his face mask. He was barking orders after the huddle, waving his arms toward the strong side of the field, reading the defense and making adjustments right up until the last minute in the way only he could.

He was one of the finest in the league and this season could be his best shot at finally earning the Super Bowl ring that he deserved to wear. She regretted not being a part of that. Even more, she would regret it if their breakup distracted him from that goal in a year when Dempsey and Gervais both agreed the Hurricanes had all the right pieces to win a championship.

But this was the business of breaking up. It was painful—the undoing of a person.

Suddenly wrought with grief—for her husband as much as for herself—her soul needed some reassurance. She reached for her cell phone and thumbed through the contacts, pulling up her father's new number in his retirement beach community in Florida.

One ring. Two rings. With each successive ring, she felt more uneasy about calling her father. What if he didn't answer?

She'd almost decided to hang up and abandon her idea to reach out to him. But on the fourth ring, as her heart pounded in her chest, she heard the phone pick up.

"Daddy?" She elbowed the pillow to nudge herself up higher on the bed.

CATHERINE MANN 117

"Fiona? Is something wrong?"

"Why does it have to be bad news for me to call my father?"

The lie slipped off her tongue. For a moment, she felt bad about being so damn practiced at lying about this terribly scary aspect of her life.

"Forgive me, let's start over. Hello, dear. How are you doing?"

Not well, and of course he was 100 percent on target that she'd only called because she was upset, but she had no intention of admitting that. "I just had some time on my hands and thought I would give you a call to catch up."

"Why aren't you at the Arizona game?"

Panic gripped her. She needed a reasonable excuse. Pushing the chocolate into the ice cream, she stumbled toward a feasible explanation. "I, um, have a cold, so it was better for me not to fly. Sinuses and all." Lame excuse. But better than the truth that would undoubtedly freak her father completely out.

"The game is a close one."

"You're watching? I don't mean to keep you."

"I can hear the game playing at your house, as well. Strange time for us to talk." His gravelly voice revealed nothing. Her father had always been tight-lipped. Well, at least since her mother had passed away.

"I'm sorry, Daddy. If you need to go…"

"No. Still plenty of time left in this quarter. I can watch this part on replay. So tell me. What's the reason for the call?"

Leave it to her practical accountant father to cut right to the point. Although that had made his meltdown over her mother's illness and passing all the more difficult to take. "Dad, what did we do for vacations before Mom got sick?"

"What makes you ask that?"

She was feeling her mortality? "Her birthday is near. I've been thinking about her more than normal. But the memories are starting to fade from when I was a kid."

The sigh coursed through the phone. "We'd take you to Disney. All you wanted to do was go there when you were small. Your mom would plan the whole trip— character breakfasts and character lunches. She loved Disney because it made you glow from the inside. Your mom would always take a bag of glitter with us and she'd sprinkle it on you before we'd walk through the main gates. Called it pixie dust and told you if you believed enough, your dreams would come true."

"I barely remember that." A sad smile played on her lips as she gripped the phone with a renewed intensity.

"Fiona? I'm not good about remembering to phone, but I'm glad to hear your voice. I'll miss your mother for the rest of my life. It was nice to enjoy that memory with you."

Sometimes, Fiona was struck at the way the memory of her mother elicited so much emotion from her father. He was normally so stoic, so practical. It always caught her off guard when he fell into telling stories about his bride, who'd been called back to heaven far too young.

Fiona hung up the phone not feeling any more assured about her life. Her heart swelled with the knowledge of too many deaths and too many people who had to deal with the memory of loved ones claimed by cancer.

Rather than feeling comforted, Fiona felt a new kind of sadness settle into her veins. Hearing the strain in her dad's voice as he recalled his late wife affirmed the logical reason that she had to leave Henri. If she left now, he wouldn't be hurt the way her dad was.

But that also meant she had to face this alone. Selfishly, that scared her to her core.

Henri had a lot of reasons to feel out of sorts. The Arizona game hadn't panned out for a few reasons. Though the one that continued to be the real source of agitation was the fact that Fiona had been states away from him.

Grabbing his duffel bag, Henri left the chauffeured car and headed through the front gates and up the walkway toward their Garden District home. The old three-story Victorian loomed ahead of him, jutting against the storm clouds brewing in the background.

Clicking open the door, he was greeted by silence.

Setting his keys down on the kitchen counter, he noticed the lilies he'd sent were in the middle of the kitchen island, card askew next to the vase.

While he had no idea what he was walking into, he was certain that he had to see Fiona. The need to be there for her—no matter how hard she pushed against the idea—gave him purpose.

He took the minimal amount of texting between them as a good sign. Though they didn't talk on the phone, they had still communicated. For Henri, as long as a line of communication was still open, he harbored hope for them. Believed they could work this out.

To allow his mind to wander to the alternative was

absolutely not an option. It admitted defeat, made him a quitter. And Henri was not about to do that when it came to his wife.

Quietly, he made his way up the stairs to her room, hoping to find her lost in a good book.

Instead, when he gingerly nudged the door open, he saw she was asleep. Out cold, really.

Something about her sleeping form seemed off. She was paler than normal, wearing a loose night-shirt and couched by pillows on both sides. Her bare leg was thrown over one of the pillows, which made his thoughts wander back to their night together. How damn amazing it had been to be back in bed with her again. It had been even better than before, because now there was no way in hell he would ever take for granted the gift of being with her.

Inside her.

Except then his mind hitched on the fact that some-thing was off in her position, the way she lay with all those pillows. Her inexplicable paleness struck him as deeply odd. It registered in his brain, but he didn't know what to do with the information. So he tucked it away, saved it for later. He was too tired to analyze that now.

Unable to pull himself away from her, he slumped into the fat wing-back chair by the fireplace. The cush-ions were comfortable and he relaxed. His eyes grew heavy, until he was barely able to keep his lids open. And then they closed completely, and he drifted off.

His dream took him to a memory of when they'd just met. He'd whisked her away to watch him play a game in Philadelphia. The Hurricanes had had their

first major win, and all he'd wanted to do was celebrate with her.

In the hotel room postgame, the passion that had
danced between them was a palpable energy.

"How about a double victory?" she'd breathed coyly
into his ear, hands traveling slowly down his chest and
stopping at his waistband. Her hair had been longer
then, wilder. There'd been an unquenchable desire in
her eyes, and he'd wanted to do his damnedest to give
her everything, all of him. They were young—lives
and potential sparking before them.

The next day, they'd made themselves at home in
Philadelphia, ducking in and out of museums and art
galleries. While most people assumed Henri was incapable of appreciating culture due to his occupation,
Fiona had simply rolled with his interest. Being an art
major, she could have easily made him feel inferior or
assumed that he was showboating.

But Fiona would never do something like that. The
appreciation of art, she'd always said, didn't take a
degree—it took appreciation for the human soul. And
so, they'd stolen hours in that city, getting to know
each other, body and soul.

On that trip, he'd known there was something that
bound them together, a passion that twined them together. Yes, there was an undeniable physical compo-
nent, but that was only half of it.

They'd returned to the hotel after debating the
meanings of paintings and other fine points of culture. Back in the hotel, he'd begun to learn the way she
liked to be touched, exploring the fire that burned beneath her skin. He needed to capture her as she was in
this moment. And so, in the dream, he began to brush

paint over her, to make her immortal on canvas. And what a muse she was for a man who'd never even considered himself an artist.

But then the dream shifted, as they often did. Fiona's surety and fire had been dulled, replaced by a self-consciousness he understood but couldn't fix.

He watched her fade in his arms, become ashen. The paint he'd used to capture her beautiful lines and curves ebbed away. In their stead, her body on the canvas was covered in scars.

Sweat pooled on his brow and he woke up with a start. Eyes adjusting to reality, he came to terms with the fact that he was dreaming.

He stayed in the chair because if he moved closer he wouldn't be able to resist touching her, making the dream a reality.

Casting a glance at Fiona, he was relieved to see her there. In the moment between sleep and alertness, he'd been afraid that she might be gone, fading away even now.

She tossed to her side, facing him now. His eyes roved over her, and he wanted to reach out and hold her. There had to be something—anything—he could do to win her back. So she missed a game. In the grand scheme of things, that didn't have to make or break this.

Maybe he'd take her to the new exhibit at the art gallery.

His thoughts on the gallery were short-lived. As he studied her, he noticed something dark against the white nightshirt.

Something that looked an awful lot like blood.

* * *

Fiona found it hard to stay asleep. The pain medicine had worn off, making it impossible to find a comfortable position.

Eyes fluttering open, she blinked into focus. Out of the corner of her eyes, she noticed a man in the wingback chair. Momentary panic flooded her mind until she was fully awake.

Henri. He was back and in their room, his face stoic and hard.

Very slowly, she sat up. Pain pulsated. Fiona did her best to hide the wince that tore through her.

"Welcome back. Congratulations on a good game."

"We lost," he said briefly, curtly.

She understood how upset he could be over a loss. She leaned back against the pillows. The pain meds had her so woozy she wasn't sure she trusted herself to walk. "Defense wasn't at their best. You can only do so much. You threw two touchdown passes and ran another. But then you don't need me to recap what happened. I'm sorry."

"Are you?" Crossing his arms, anger throbbed in his voice.

"What do you mean?" She sat against the pillows, breathing through the pain that rocked her body.

"Are you sorry?"

"Of course I'm disappointed for you. I know how much a win means to you. Just because I knew the time had come for me to stop attending, that doesn't mean I won't be following the team's progress."

"Sure." His voice was sullen and she noticed, in the half light from the lamp by the wing-back chair, that his lips had thinned into a hard line.

"Henri? What's with the clipped answers?" She was too foggy from pain meds that weren't doing enough to dull the ache to sort through these mixed signals from him. "I understand you're unhappy with my decision to not attend the game—"

"I'm not happy with your decision to keep me in the dark about the real reason you stayed in New Orleans."

How had he found out? She followed the line of his gaze and realized he was looking directly at her left breast where…

Oh, God. Her biopsy incision was leaking spots of blood.

Nine

A jumble of emotions played bumper cars in Henri's mind. The blood on her left breast…the way she tried so hard to push him away.

How could she keep this from him? Frustration—and, hell yes, fear—seized his jaw. He ground his teeth, feeling something that felt a bit like betrayal.

That she had kept him from knowing something major—and potentially life threatening—was too much to digest.

His fingers pressed into the arms of the chair as he tried stabilizing himself. Part of him wanted to run over to her side, to hold her tight against him. But knowing she was sick and in recovery, the possibility and fear of injuring her made him stay firmly planted in his chair.

Scared as hell.

"What's going on?"

"I think you've already guessed." She tugged at the white covers on the bed. But she didn't look directly at him.

A lump grew in his throat. Terrible possibilities ran through his mind. "Were you even going to tell me at all?"

She tipped her chin upward. "Not if I didn't have to. No need for both of us to worry."

They'd fallen so far apart that they didn't share something as huge as this? He'd been by her side every step of the way through medical treatments, and now she was trying to cut him out of her life. Completely. Excise him like cancer.

No. Not a chance. "Details," he demanded softly, but firmly. "I want details. We're still married. We owe each other that much."

"It's just a biopsy of a lump that's likely fatty tissue dissolving. The oncologist is almost certain it's nothing to be concerned about."

She said it as casually as someone reporting the weather. He felt the distance spread between them like an ever-collapsing sinkhole.

Oncologist? But no, it wasn't serious. "If it was nothing, you would have told me. This is why you didn't go to the game. I would have understood."

She pushed her tousled hair back, her eyes fuzzy with what appeared to be the effects of pain meds—and sure enough, a bottle rested on her bedside table. "You would have been distracted. You would have gone crazy worrying. Look at how you're reacting now."

"I am in control. Here for you, always." Why couldn't she see that?

"That's good and honorable of you to say, but it's not the reason I want you staying with me."

"So if I hadn't seen the spots of blood you wouldn't have told me at all?"

Drawing a pillow in front of her chest, she let out a small sigh. "If the worst happens, then of course you would find out. Otherwise there was no reason to upset you."

The way she discussed her health with such nonchalance rubbed him raw. As if the only reason he would care to know if she was sick was bound up in some sense of honor and duty. That did him a disservice, minimized their bond. He did not stay with her merely for appearances' sake or to come across as honorable. Dammit, why couldn't she see that?

"Did it occur to you I would want to know, to be there to support you?"

"Thank you. But you don't have to do that anymore." She smoothed a wrinkle on the pillow and gave him a pointed stare.

"I'm your husband, dammit." He reined in his temper. "I'm sorry. I didn't mean to snap at you. Could I get you something to drink? Or an ice pack for the biopsy site?"

"You know the drill." She slumped back on the pillows, her eyes sad.

"I do. Is that so wrong?"

"I don't want you feeling sorry for me."

He ignored that. Couldn't even imagine how to make her understand his desire to care for her had nothing to do with pity.

"When will you hear from the doctor?"

"Next week."

"I have one question. How long have you known?"

"Since the day of the pet rescue fund-raiser."

He inhaled sharply. He pressed his fist to his mouth—he'd hoped she had only recently found out, that it had been some sort of emergency operation. That would be much easier to swallow.

"You weren't late because your car broke down. You've been lying all week."

"I've been protecting you and protecting my privacy."

The bedroom started to become suffocating as he looked around, seeing the life they had jointly built. It all felt like a lie. Some kind of story he'd been telling himself.

More frustration piled on top of the old, building up inside him when he was already exhausted and on edge. He knew somewhere in his gut that getting out of this room was his only option. Before he said something he'd regret.

"Right." Shoving the chair out from underneath him, he sprung to his feet. From the threshold, he called over his shoulder, "I'll get you that ice pack."

With every step, Fiona drew in sharp breaths. The movement pounded in her chest, causing pain to spiderweb through her shoulder.

Of all the ways she'd envisioned Henri finding out about the biopsy, this hadn't been one of them. With slow, determined steps, she made it to the first-floor landing and caught a glimpse of her reflection in the hallway mirror.

The mirror was expansive—and Victorian. Cherubs with lutes and lyres danced down the frame, twisting and turning in endless patterns. She'd found it at a flea market years ago and fallen in love with the distressed glass.

As she examined her reflection, depression edged her vision. She was a mess. Tempest tossed. Those were her initial assessments.

Her brown hair was swept up in a high ponytail but was completely disrupted from troubled sleep. All her tossing and turning had loosened it. Her pallid complexion and tired eyes did nothing to improve matters. Pulling on the corner of her clean oversize shirt, she felt like a shadow.

Clutching her favorite Wedgwood bowl full of ice cream, she charged into the kitchen. When she rounded the corner, a wave of nausea overcame her. A by-product of the pain medicine. Taking a moment to regain her balance and calm her stomach, she eyed Henri nervously.

He was leaning against the kitchen island with his back to her. He fumbled with the ice pack, but his head was cocked to the side, examining the news story on television.

It was entertainment news, overhyped coverage of celebrity outings and gossip.

Spinning into focus was a photograph of Henri with another woman. Her body was pressed against his.

Old news. That had already popped up on Fiona's radar. She knew such a photograph didn't mean a damn thing. Fans were sometimes aggressive and pushy. Henri might be a lot of things, but a cheater? Not in his wheelhouse.

Still, sadness swept over her as her toes curled against the cool tile floor.

This photograph might not be real…but after their divorce was finalized? Well, then these types of photographs might actually be evidence of a new relationship for Henri. Her heart fell ten stories in her chest as she stared at him.

Bad enough to end a marriage and know that your ex would probably move on and find someone new. That dynamic would be much more intense for her. Henri, rising star quarterback, would be front and center in the news. She'd be forced to watch him fall in love with someone else.

The thought hit her like a ton of bricks.

He must've felt her eyes on him. He whirled around, face flushed, pointing at the screen. "That's not what—"

"I know it isn't." She steadied herself on the coffee bar.

"You do? You trust me even now?"

"I trust that you wouldn't sleep with another woman while you're still married to me." Knowing that made it all the tougher to walk away from this man. He was a good person. He deserved better from life than he'd gotten in their marriage. She knew she wasn't easy to live with and her ability to deal with stress—well, here they were.

"Thank you for trusting me." Some of the stiff tension in his shoulders eased, although she didn't think for a moment he'd forgiven her for holding back.

"I believe in your honor, your sense of fair play." That had never been a question.

"I've never wanted a woman as much as I want you, always."

Her hands wrapped her body in a protective cocoon. Tears pushed at the edge of her vision. "But I'm not the woman you married."

He stepped toward her and wrapped his hands around her waist. Pulling her into him, he whispered into her hair, breath hot on her ear, "You're every bit as beautiful. No matter what else happens between us, the attraction hasn't stopped."

"Even with the surgeries?" The words squeaked out, finding vulnerable life in the small space between them.

"I still see you." He lowered his face to hers.

Fiona wanted to believe him. Wanted things to just stop spinning out of control. But…but there was physical evidence that she could never be the same.

"But there are scars. Even with the best plastic surgeon money could buy. And there's always going to be the specter of another lump and biopsy."

"I married you for what's inside. And I'd like to think that's what you wanted me for, too." He stroked her back with warm, strong hands. "Even if there had been no reconstruction at all, I would want you. You know that."

"I do. And it makes it all the tougher to resist you."

"Then don't resist me." Tipping up her chin, he gently pressed his lips to hers.

For the briefest moment, she indulged herself in the kiss. Let herself melt into his lips and the beautiful familiarity of being in his arms, of letting the musky scent of him fill her senses. After the fear and stress of the past day, she took comfort from his strong arms and the hard wall of his chest. The steady beat of his heart was echoed by hers; they were in sync. They'd been that way once, so in tune with each other. God, she hadn't imagined all of it, had she?

She deepened the kiss, loving the taste of him and the hint of toothpaste. She gripped his T-shirt in tight fists as she nipped his bottom lip. Henri's hands fell gently to her shoulders.

"Careful, Fiona," he whispered, brushing his lips along her mouth, then her cheek.

It was a tender, lovely moment…and yet there was something off. In the way he held her, maybe? His touch was far too light.

She angled back to study his brown eyes awash with molten emotions. "Henri? What's going on? This feels suspiciously like you're treating me as if I'm some fragile glass figurine. Like spun glass. Like when I got the operations six months ago."

His eyes went so dark the ache was downright tangible. "Damn straight I'm being careful with you. You're bleeding, on pain meds, and I wasn't there with you. How the hell else am I supposed to treat you?"

His pain reached out to her until she could barely breathe from the weight of it. Images filled her mind of her father, frozen in his reading chair, newspaper upside down in his tight-fisted grip as tears streaked down his face. Her grandmother and aunt shushing her, guiding her from the room. Later helping her pack for boarding school. Then college. Then they were gone, too. The women's husbands had all stood like hollow shells at their funerals.

Oh, God, it was too much. She needed space. Air. More space. She couldn't think clearly. She was about to shatter like the glass he seemed to think she was made of. And of course he would pick up the pieces no matter how those shards stabbed at him.

Breaking contact, she laid a hand on his chest. "I think you should stay at your family's place tonight."

Lips thinning into a stoic mask, he took a deep breath. His jaw grew taut. But his emotions stayed hidden. She'd seen him do that often in the past, protect her from anything unpleasant—or anything real.

Stepping away from her, he folded his arms over his chest. "We're not divorced. And I'm not leaving you here alone when you're recovering."

She also knew that look well. An entire line from an opposing team wouldn't stand a chance of sacking the immovable force he'd become.

Fiona filled her morning with forced movement. She needed to stay busy, to bounce back from the biopsy and from the impending fracturing of her heart.

Henri had left for the gym early in the morning. She'd been awake when she heard him make his way down the stairs. Part of her wanted to crawl out of bed to talk to him. Fiona knew better, though. She had to guard her heart. He'd only briefly come to the doorway and told her he wasn't comfortable with her being alone on pain meds, so he'd arranged cleaning help for the day and a car to drive her if she wished to go anywhere.

The stony look on his face didn't leave room for argument. And he was right. She needed help and should be grateful. In her need to protect him from hurt she was still causing him pain, and she couldn't seem to work her way out of the messy maze she'd made of her life.

So she'd stayed in bed waiting until she heard his car drive away before she got up and dressed herself.

Pulling her thoughts back to the present, she tried to focus on the sensation of sun on skin. She and the other Reynaud women were lounging by the oversize pool at the main family complex on Lake Pontchartrain. Giggles surged through the air—the family was at peace. Several team wives were there as well, getting to know Erika better, which was part of the reason Fiona had felt she needed to be here. Hell, she wanted to be here.

But it was tougher than she expected, watching them joke with each other, all so happy and healthy.

All of them except for her.

Though fall was settling in, the heated pool provided sanctuary from the light, chilly breeze. Fiona watched the sunlight dance in the pool as Erika dipped a toe, testing the water.

Fiona sighed, listening to the chatter of bugs and birds as she tried to appear normal. Such a difficult ruse, especially since she'd had no choice but to make use of the chauffeur if she'd wanted to join in the outing. And she had wanted to, so very much. Still sore from the biopsy, she'd forced herself here. Determined to embrace the world.

A loose but elegant navy dress clung to her body, positioned just right to hide the scars.

Adelaide tossed her head, easing herself onto the first step of the pool. A wicked grin warmed her eyes. "We should go lingerie shopping."

"What?" The suggestion snapped Fiona back into the moment. Lingerie shopping would be pretty damn difficult in her state.

Swirling her foot in the water, Adelaide continued, "The new bride will need new lacies. We can call it an impromptu lingerie shower." She whipped out a gold credit card. "Lunch is on me."

Erika's rich peal of laughter resonated on the patio. "I am getting very big very fast. I will not be able to wear the underthings long."

Adelaide winked, emerging from the pool to sit next to Erika. "If you're doing it right, he'll tear them off your body and you'll only be able to wear them once."

A faint blush colored Erika's snow-pale skin.

One of the linebackers' wives spoke in a low rasp. Macie's gray-streaked auburn hair framed her angular face, her crow's-feet crinkling as she sipped on a bottle of water. "I wore bikini panties under my belly for the whole pregnancy."

"I wore thigh-high stockings and a cute little thong. Drove my man wild."

Adelaide nudged Erika with her shoulder. "I've got one! This isn't pregnancy related, but Dempsey goes nuts when I wear these black strappy heels. Does it every time. I'm half inclined to think they are magic."

Erika's moonlight-blond hair rippled as she laughed, and then put her hand to her stomach. "Fiona? So spill. What does that sexy man of yours like you to wear?"

Adelaide turned to face Fiona, brows raised in anticipation.

How to answer that? Sitting up, she choked on the words. Nothing came to her lips.

The stress of the past few months had taken an additional toll on Fiona. She'd unintentionally lost weight. What she hadn't realized was how much weight.

As she shrugged, attempting to brush the question off, the shoulder of her dress slipped down her arm.

Revealing the bandage from the biopsy. And the very edge of the scar just under her breast line from the mastectomy and reconstruction.

The laughter from the other wives stopped. All attention and eyes rested on her.

There was no use in pretending anymore. The charade had finally bested her. In vague horror, she watched their gazes trail from her torso to her face. Watched the transformation of pity in their eyes.

"When? How did no one know?" Erika breathed, rising to her feet. With slow, waddling movements, she made her way to Fiona's side. Sitting down with royal poise, Erika searched Fiona's face while the other team wives stayed diplomatically silent.

"We didn't want anyone to know. We just…took one of our trips and had the surgery done."

Adelaide plopped on her other side, putting a hand on Fiona's back. She ran her hand in small circles up and down her back. "But you have this whole big family here that would have wanted to be there for you. I know they would. The team family, too."

Flashes of her childhood drama and trauma scrolled through her mind. Somehow containing the pain and emotion had seemed easier this time. Had she been wrong? She didn't know. She only knew she and Henri had made the best decision they could at the time. "I'm not certain how to explain it other than to say so much of our lives was in the spotlight, we just wanted to crawl off and be alone."

"Did that help?" Leave it to Erika to be direct. But Fiona preferred that to being treated like a glass mannequin. Looking back and forth from Adelaide to Erika, Fiona noticed that they didn't seem to feel pity. Just concern.

"I thought so at the time. But now I think it could have helped Henri to talk to his brothers. Even if their advice stunk, just to lean on them. Maybe I was being selfish."

Adelaide's voice came out like a wind-tossed whisper. "How so?"

"Wanting him all to myself. I had no one else." She rubbed her temple. "I never really thought of it that way until now." Her eyes stung with tears and regret.

Giving her hands a quick squeeze and a gentle smile, Erika asked, "So you made the decision all on your own to keep it quiet?"

A dark laugh escaped Fiona's lips. "Sounds like you already know the answer to that one. Henri was emphatic about not wanting the press involved. He wanted things quietly handled."

"Even kept from family?" Adelaide asked in a quiet voice. "That was your decision to make. I'm just sorry we didn't provide the support we all would have wanted to give you both."

Fiona had been so concerned with handling this discreetly, she had never stopped to consider what Henri might have needed. So focused on her own needs, on her own wounds, she had been blinded.

In this small moment, as the afternoon sun streamed onto the pool patio, she began to understand that she had deeply hurt Henri. Which was the one thing she had been desperately trying to avoid doing.

The world started spinning. She felt distant from her surroundings. Had she really made the wrong choices?

Ten

"I owe you an apology," Fiona said softly as she stepped into Henri's in his childhood home at the Reynaud family compound. Not the home they shared on the lake. For whatever reason, Henri had chosen to stay at Gervais's house. It had been tough to find him, but she'd tracked him down.

Now she wondered if that was wise, but there was no leaving.

She felt as if he'd put as much distance between them as he could by coming here, staying under his brother's roof instead of at their second home just up the lane. Could it have something to do with the fact they'd once lived there together? Or maybe it was the nursery they'd decorated for the child they'd lost—a room they'd never changed back. Her throat grew tight, so she blocked that thought. Maybe here was best after all.

Heart pounding, she stepped across the threshold, eyes still adjusting from the bright sun of the fall day.

Blinking slowly, she scanned the room.

The small suite, filled with trophies and photographs of her husband's high school and college careers, felt like a shrine to Henri's past. She hadn't set foot in here for a long time, but she'd always been fond of the large, gold-framed photograph of the Reynaud brothers and Grandpa Leon. The brothers had all still been in high school at the time of the photograph, and Grandpa Leon had had plenty of energy then.

The photograph pulled at her already raw heart. Refusing to become sidetracked by Grandpa Leon's state, she pressed on into the room, leaning on one of the oak poles of the four-poster bed. Henri's eyes stayed fixed on the bed where his suitcase lay open. With a sigh, he yanked another shirt from the suitcase and slung it into an open dresser drawer. Without looking at her, he asked, "How are you feeling?"

Apparently he wasn't in the mood for an apology. Sitting on the edge of the bed, she felt awkward, as if she was forcing her way into this space.

But she had to try. "A little sore but otherwise okay. I didn't even have to take a pain pill today."

"Glad to hear that. I hope you're resting enough," he said in a quiet voice, almost a monotone. Noncommittal.

"It was a biopsy. I'll be fine."

"Just be careful." For the first time since she'd walked into the room, he looked at her. His dark eyes were full of concern.

"In case I need to be prepared for something worse?"

He shrugged, leaning against the dresser. The subtle pressure caused one of his childhood baseball trophies to shift. "You're the one who said that. Not me."

He picked up an old football off the dresser. It was signed by all of his college teammates. Tossing it lightly from one hand to another, he grimaced.

Putting her fingertips to her lips, she took a moment to compose her thoughts, noting the hurt in Henri's expression.

"And that's why I'm here to say I'm sorry for not telling you about the lump and the procedure. Even though we're separated, we're still married. We share an intense history."

"Thank you for acknowledging that." As he folded his arms across his chest with the football still clutched in one hand, she noted the tension in his clenched jaw.

"You've been kind. You've been understanding. You deserve better than the way I treated you."

"You've been through a lot. I understand that." He set the ball down carefully on the dresser again.

"Please take this in the spirit intended, but it's damn hard to be married to the perfect man."

Henri let out a choked laugh, dark hair catching the glow of the lights. "I'm not sure what spirit to take that in at all—and I'm far from perfect. Just ask my brothers."

Her head to the side, she linked her hand with his. "So you'll accept my apology for not telling you about the biopsy?"

"I'm still upset, but yes, I can see that you're sorry…" His voice trailed off and he looked down.

"But?"

"But I'm certain you wouldn't do things differently. Even though you're sorry, you would still shut me out."

He held up a hand. "Don't say anything either way to agree or deny."

He hauled the suitcase off the bed, headed to the ornate closet door. Etched molding that resembled Grecian columns framed the door. Whenever she came here, the details always caught her off guard. Every visit yielded a new dimension of awareness. She'd lived in their Italianate monstrosity across the road. She should have been able to call all this home, but when had she ever taken the time to settle in?

That lack of awareness, it seemed, extended to her understanding of Henri. Now, as he put the empty suitcase in the closet, she began to understand his point of view a bit more clearly.

"We have problems. Big problems. Obviously. I just want us to find peace."

"I agree." He turned to take her by the shoulders, his whole hulking body radiating pain. "You'll be sure to tell me the second you know the results of the biopsy?"

"Of course. Right away." And she could feel how much he cared, really cared. That tore at her, left her feeling conflicted all over again. Just when she was sure she could walk away, doubts plagued her as she felt how much he cared for her. How deeply she was affected by him.

She stroked her hand over his hair, sketching her fingers along the thick, coarse strands. "I truly am sorry I hurt you. I wish our lives could have been easier. That we didn't have to face biopsies and infertility."

"Life isn't guaranteed to be easy." He leaned into her touch.

"I don't know if things would have been smoother if we were chasing a cute little toddler around now."

The tears of loss and regret stung. "A little girl with your brown eyes and feet that never stop because she loves carrying around your football."

"Fiona, you're killing me here." He put his arms around her, careful to avoid her left side.

She let herself enjoy the warmth of his embrace. She couldn't bring herself to step away. Keeping distance between them the past months had been torture and right now she couldn't recall why she had to.

Pressing her ear against his chest over the steady beat of his heart, she slid her arms around his waist. She took in the musky smell of his soap and a scent that was 100 percent Henri. Her husband. Her man.

She heard the shift in his breathing at the same time her own body kindled to life. She shouldn't be feeling this way right now. Turned on. Aching to make sweet tender love to him.

Henri nuzzled her hair. "You should rest."

Angling back, she met his gaze dead-on. "I don't want to sleep. I want you to make love to me. Here. Now. No thinking about tomorrow or what we'll say after. Let's be together—"

He kissed her silent, once, twice, holding the kiss for an instant before speaking against her mouth. "You won't hear an argument from me. I want you. Always. Anywhere, anytime."

He walked her back toward the bed, sealing his lips to hers every step of the way until her legs bumped the footboard. He angled her back onto the mattress, cradling her body with arms so strong, so gentle. She sank into the puffy comforter, reaching for Henri only to have him drop to his knees at the foot of the bed. He bunched her skirt up an inch at a time, nibbling along the inside of her left leg, stroking her other leg with his hand.

He made his way higher. Higher still. Until…

Her head pushed back into the bed as she sighed in anticipation. His breath puffed against the lacy silk of her panties, warming her.

"Lovely," he murmured.

"I went shopping."

"I was talking about you." He skimmed the panties off and his mouth found her, pressing an intimate kiss to the core of her.

She felt his hum of appreciation against her skin. She grabbed fistfuls of the blanket and twisted, pleasure sparking through her. His tongue stroked, circled, teased at the tight bundle of nerves until her head thrashed restlessly against the bed. Her heels dug into his back, anchoring him, but also anchoring herself in this oh-so-personal moment. She ached for completion. And one flick at a time he drove her to the edge of release, backed off, then brought her even closer, again and again until she demanded he finish, now, yes, now… And he listened with delicious attention to her need.

Gasps of bliss and, ah, release filled the air as ripple after ripple of pleasure shuddered through her. Her back bowed upward and her fingers slid down to comb through his hair as he eased her through the last vestiges of her orgasm.

Gently, he slid her legs from his shoulders and smoothed her dress back into place. He stretched out beside her, carrying them both up to recline against the pillows.

She traced her fingers along his T-shirt. "That was

amazing. Thank you. This may sound obvious, but it feels so good to feel good right now."

"That was my intent."

She pressed her mouth to his. "I want us both to feel good again. Make love to me."

"But you're recovering…"

"There's no reason we can't have sex as long as you're gentle." A smile tugged at her lips. "Ironic and a little funny, but I'm actually asking you to treat me like spun glass."

"I'll take you any way I can have you, lady. You're perfect, you know that, right?" He pressed kisses against the curve of her neck.

"Far from it, but thank you." She angled her head to give him easier access.

"I mean it. You're beautiful and giving and smart." His hands moved reverently over her long dark hair, skimming low, lower still and then back up again to rest on her shoulders.

"What brought this on?" She touched his face, reveling in his stubble, in his dark eyes.

"I just wanted to make sure you know. I think I get so caught up in gestures, I forget to give you the words." Gentle fingers traveled from her lips to her neck, causing shivers to run wildly down her spine. Sparks lit her nerves, the tingling then gathering at her core.

"Well, thank you for those lovely words. I appreciate it. I do understand that I am not defined by my breasts," she said.

Kissing her collarbone, he pulled her flush against him. "I'm glad you realize that."

Her heart filled again with something that felt like hope.

* * *

With Fiona asleep in his bed, he felt better than he had in weeks. Hell, better than he had in months. The scent of her on his linens was something he didn't take for granted. He'd missed this. Missed her. And looked forward to devoting even more attention to persuading her to stay right here.

But still…he felt compelled to move. To walk about the house to process the 180-degree change he saw in Fiona.

He slid out of the silk bedsheets, his feet landing on cool marble tile. On tiptoes, he made his way out of the room.

When was the last time he'd spent any time out at the lake, trying to ferret out an answer to a complex problem? He couldn't remember. He and Fiona had spent so much time trying to give themselves privacy, he'd forgotten what it was like to share space with his brothers. To ask for help.

Now, staying in this wing of his childhood home, he could see his older brother's stamp on the place. He'd made changes to personalize the home, yet he'd kept so many things from their past, too. Leaving Henri's old bedroom untouched had been a welcome surprise.

For the most part, he barely registered the mammoth house anymore. Greek Revival wasn't his style— it felt too rigid and restrictive. As he walked through the house, he found himself appreciating the quirky charm of his home in the Garden District. The eclectic Victorian space he and Fiona had reconstructed.

Needing to talk, he searched for his brother. After all, Gervais had pushed him down this path by sending his fiancée, Erika, to deliver flowers to Fiona.

Catching sight of his brother's silhouette by the pool, Henri opened the sliding glass door. Gervais stood, back to the house, on the path that led from the pool to the dock.

Gervais's shoulders were slumped. Heavy as the boughs of the live oak trees. Fragrant ginger and bushes lined the paths around the pool, next to a round fire pit surrounded by a low wall of flat rocks. A glider swing with a seat as big as a full-size bed anchored the space, which was draped in breezy white gauze threaded with a few tiny twinkly lights overhead.

His brother's hands were linked behind his back. As Henri drew closer, he could see that Gervais was squeezing his hands so tight they were turning white.

Surveying the landscape in front of them, Henri watched the dying light bathe the wooden dock in rich oranges. At the end of the dock, the pontoon boat was hoisted out of the water. They'd spent many nights out on that pontoon boat—and the yacht off to the left—when they were younger. As he looked at the pontoon boat, he felt a wave of nostalgia wash over him. Things felt simpler then. But he knew that wasn't actually true. Nothing about his family had ever been simple.

These past few months had been a strain on Henri's relationship with his family. Everything between his brothers and him had been placed on autopilot. Nods and lies became the default modes of communication.

Had those months of evading serious conversation come at the high cost of neglecting to see that his brother had been struggling? Impending marriage and managing the team were enough to test anyone, even his collected and cool older brother.

Henri tried to imagine what was on Gervais's mind:

owning the New Orleans Hurricanes, having a winning season, even what was going on with their baby brother Jean-Pierre's career as a New York quarterback.

And smack-dab in the middle of all that, Gervais was trying to plan a wedding to a princess and keep it out of the public eye, all while facing fatherhood. And Dempsey was engaged. Life was moving forward at full force.

"What are you doing down here?" Henri asked.

"Reliving the old days." Gervais's chest expanded as he breathed deeply. A football lay at his feet. He gave it a shove with his shoe.

"Do you miss it?" Henri gestured to the pigskin.

"Sure I miss playing sometimes. But I'm not you, living and breathing for the game. Honestly. I like being the brains behind the larger operation."

"Impending marriage and fatherhood has made you philosophical."

Gervais shook his head. "Practical. Focused."

"I'm so damn tired of people questioning my focus."

"People?" Cocking his head to the side, Gervais stared at his brother. It was a knowing kind of glance, one that chided him to be more specific.

"My family." He practically spat the words from his mouth.

"You *are* staring at a possible divorce." Such a blunt statement. As if Henri wasn't aware of the state of his marriage.

"So are half the guys out there playing."

"But you love your wife."

Henri stared hard at the lake, his voice growing quiet, the words feeling like ash as he spoke them. "I thought I did."

"You do, you big idiot."

Henri shoved Gervais's shoulder. "I hate it when you pull the wise big brother act."

"Then do something about it—you're the Bayou Bomber, for God's sake. You run the Hurricanes' offense from the quarterback position, slinging record-setting pass yardage with an arm destined for the Hall of Fame. You can't do better than this in your personal life?"

Henri let out a bitter laugh. "Brother, no offense. But this marriage thing is a helluva lot harder than it looks."

Gervais scooped up the football and tossed it to him. "Our family is too quick to anger and rifts."

"What are you talking about? We're tight." He stepped back, putting some distance between them before flinging the football back at his brother.

"Seriously? Are you delusional?" Gervais caught the pigskin, surprise coloring his face.

"Look at us now." Henri gestured between them and to the sprawling buildings of the family property.

"Look at our history," Gervais retorted. "Our dad didn't speak to the mother of his son for over a decade. We find out we have a brother we never knew about and Mom leaves, never to be heard from again. We have a brother in New York who barely graces our doorstep unless we're in crisis. We have one uncle who doesn't speak to us at all. And another in Texas who only shows up to support his son who plays on the team. This family doesn't have a problem cutting and running."

"I guess when you put it that way, it doesn't sound like a close-knit clan." Henri mused over his brother's words, balancing them against the security their lake-side spread had always given him. The mere presence of the Reynaud family homestead had anchored him, made him believe they were close and as stable as the Greek Revival construction. Gervais's words shook his foundation.

"Families have their problems, sure, but ours has more than a few. And I just don't want to see you fall victim to the pattern of cutting someone off rather than working through the tough stuff."

"You're referring to Fiona and me." Nodding in understanding, he tossed the football again.

"Yes, I am. You two are good together. Quite frankly, this break scares the hell out of me as I look at tying the knot myself. You two were the perfect couple."

"There's no such thing as perfect."

"Truth. So why are you expecting perfection?" Gervais lobbed more than just the football at Henri that time.

"Who says I'm the one who wants the divorce?" Gervais was out of line. Henri didn't want a divorce, didn't want things between Fiona and him to be over. His passion burned for her and her alone. Life without her... It was an impossible thought for him to even finish.

"If she's the one who wants to walk, then why aren't you fighting for her?"

"I'm giving her space." Space had been what she wanted.

"Space... Like I said, our family gives space all too easily." Gervais slammed the football to the ground, turning away from Henri to look at the compound.

His philosophical brother struck a chord in Henri. His words reverberated in his chest, stirring a renewed commitment to winning Fiona's mind, body and soul. Passion had never been a problem for him and Fiona. That burned bright and true. But this was more than getting her back into his bed. He wanted her back in his life. Full time.

He refused to be another Reynaud who cut and run.

She'd been dreaming about Henri.

In Fiona's imagination, they'd been together in Seattle, exploring the city's art district during one of the Hurricanes' trips to the West Coast. It had been the early days of their marriage, and they'd run through the rain to dart from one private studio to the next, trying to meet some of the city's up-and-coming artists just for the fun of it.

In the car on the way back to the hotel, they'd been sopping wet and laughing. Kissing. Touching with a feverish urgency. Almost as if they'd known their time together was limited and they needed to live on fast-forward.

Why hadn't she tried to slow things down? To build the bond that they'd need to get them through a lifetime instead of floating on that high of incredible physical intimacy?

Even as she thought it in her hazy dreams, she became aware of a strong hand on her hip. Stroking. Rubbing.

Alertness came to her slowly. Or maybe she just didn't mind lingering in that dreamy world between wakefulness and sleep. The real world had disappointed her enough times in the past year and a half.

She would gladly take her touches with her eyes closed for just a little while longer.

Her body hummed to life at Henri's urging, skin shivering with awareness at his caress.

"Fiona." Her husband breathed her name in a sigh that tickled along her bare neck right before he kissed her there.

Slowly. Thoroughly.

What was it about a kiss on the neck that could drive a woman wild? she wondered. Or was it only Henri's kisses that could turn her inside out like this?

Still lying on her side, she reached for him, knowing where he'd be. She palmed his rock-hard chest. He was so warm. So strong.

"Open your eyes." His soft command made her smile.

"Since when do you give orders in bed?" she teased, keeping her eyes closed.

"Since I need you to see me." His words, spoken with a starkness she hadn't expected, forced her eyes open.

"Is everything all right?" She moved her hand from his chest to his face, her eyes adjusting to the last rays of daylight filtering in through the blinds.

She'd napped for longer than she realized.

"Yes. I just needed to see you." He skimmed his hand up her side, following the curve of her waist to bring her closer to him in the bed.

"You're sure?" She crept closer still, remembering how good she'd felt in her dream. No, how good he'd made her feel just a few hours ago before she'd fallen asleep.

"Positive. I just want you to know I'm here." He dipped a kiss into the hollow behind her ear.

She sensed more at work, but she was content to lose herself in the moment. In the touches she'd denied herself for too long. No matter what the future held for her and Henri, she wanted to savor these moments in a way she hadn't known to do in the past. For too long, she'd been focused on their problems. For now, she wanted to remember the things they'd done well.

The things that made them both happy.

Threading her fingers through his hair, she sifted through to his scalp, down to his neck and over his powerful shoulders. He halted her touch midway down his arm. He gripped her hand to kiss her wrist and then continue down the inside of her forearm, surprising her with how ticklish she was there.

Their shared laughter felt like a rare gift, the moment so oddly poignant she wasn't sure if she should cry or jump him. Their eyes met. Held.

And she had her answer.

She needed this. Him. Melting into his arms, she kissed him, nipping his lower lip and stroking his tongue with growing urgency. He stripped her naked, removing every barrier between them while she poured all the longing of the last months into that kiss. His hands molded her gently, cruising over her curves and paying homage to every inch of her that wasn't in pain.

"I've missed you." He said it so softly she thought it was her own thought for a moment. "I know I've said it before, but I mean it."

"I know. Me, too," she admitted, glancing up to meet his eyes. Needing to say the words, too. "I've missed you, just being together, so much."

That's why she needed him so much right now.

He must have understood—of course he understood, since he knew her so damn well—because he shifted her thighs with his knee. He made a place for himself, gripping her hips and steering her where he wanted her. Close to him. So close.

She was ready for him, but he took his time brushing featherlight caresses up the hot, needy center of her until she had to threaten him with dire sexual payback if he didn't come inside her.

She could feel his smile against her mouth when he kissed her and the heat of him nudged inside her. His smile faded when she thrust her hips hard into his, taking all of him and holding him tight. She could feel his heart pound hard and fast against her chest on the right side where he allowed himself to make contact with her.

Arms looped around his neck, she trusted him with her body. Knew he'd be careful with her and make her feel amazing at the same time.

And oh, did he deliver.

With his powerful thrust, he could have delivered heart-stopping pleasure to her all night long. He was tireless in pursuit of her pleasure. And while normally she liked to ensure he was every bit as swept away as her, tonight she simply let the desire build. Allowed the sensations to build however he wanted. Gave herself over to him completely.

"Henri." She whispered his name more than once as he took her to one dizzying high after another.

She clung to him, raining kisses down his impossibly strong torso, savoring the shift of muscle beneath her hands with his every movement.

When he finally reached that point of no return, she met his gaze again, remembering that he wanted her to see him.

What she saw sent her crashing into blissful completion as much as any skillful touch. Wave after wave of pleasure shuddered through her, undulating over her body. She felt his release, too, not just inside her, but under her hands as his back bowed and his muscles tensed.

She held him for a long time afterward, stroking his hair and remembering every moment they'd spent together. But most of all, she thought about what she'd seen in his eyes in that shattering moment before she'd hit her peak.

Her husband still loved her. Deeply.

And she was terrified of what that meant for both of them.

Eleven

Between her jumbled feelings for Henri and waiting for her biopsy results, the past days getting ready for the fund-raiser had zipped by in a blur of emotion. She'd spent every spare moment attending to different details. Making sure the event would go off without a hitch.

Making sure she didn't have time to think about the confusing mess she'd made of her life.

The lingering aftereffects of her biopsy still caused a dull ache in her chest and throughout her shoulder. The pain didn't slow her down, though. Her recent diagnosis of the cancer gene filled Fiona with a renewed sense of commitment to the cause. This event wasn't just in memory of her mother, aunt and grandmother. No, Fiona needed this event to work—to outperform any event she'd ever done—because she needed, down to her bones, to be a part of eradicating this disease that took too much from people and their families.

So she'd spent hours on the phone, personally reaching out to all her contacts to woo them into sponsoring the event. She found creative ways to pay for a memorable gala without taking an extra penny from the client's budget. No detail was too small for her to tackle full force.

She couldn't deny that another factor contributed to her increased productivity. Henri. Her failing marriage. The reality of life without him.

The thoughts were too real, too hard for her to deal with. Fiona threw herself into the fund-raiser because it filled her with purpose and direction. Things she desperately needed in her life right now.

After another day of dogged dedication, Fiona felt suffocated by the walls of her lonely home. It was time to get some fresh air and, she did need to get some paperwork she'd left at the Reynaud compound.

Not that she was looking for an excuse to run into Henri.

A quick drive later, she arrived at the sprawling cluster of buildings…the Greek Revival main house, the Italianate home, the carriage house, the boathouse…the dock.

Her gaze snagged on a figure at the end of the dock. Gramps sat on the bench overlooking the water, and while she knew he was likely fine, she also worried about him wandering off in a fog.

She set out toward the dock and the water, each step closer filling her lungs with the familiar scents of this place that had once been her home. The lake air had a way of breathing life into her.

The Friday event would irrevocably change the course of her life. And Henri's. As much as it pained her, she knew it was time to cut the ties between them. She could not—no, she would not—be the source of pain for him anymore. He deserved more. He deserved children and a wife who wasn't so sickly. Leaving would shelter his heart from any additional pain if those results—due any time now—turned out for the worst.

Though Henri had wanted her to stay with him through the rest of the season, she couldn't put them both through that. Too much pain. Too much exposure to the electric passion that hummed between them. And after the last few days…well, she couldn't lead either of them on like that.

After the charity event on Friday, Fiona would create her own timetable for leaving Henri. One that minimized damage to both of them.

A season of difficult choices was upon her. Henri planned on attending the event on Friday before leaving Saturday for Indianapolis, where he'd play his Sunday game. The running assumption was that she'd join him, take her place in the wives' section of the stands.

But maybe…maybe the better call came in the form of a clean break after the event. Leaving him to travel alone.

Alone?

Revulsion settled in the pit of her stomach. Alone. Could she really let him be unsupported during a season that could finally be the one he deserved? A season that might allow him to achieve all his professional dreams? As he'd pointed out, it wasn't just his dreams that were on the line this year, either. So many of the Reynauds were bound up in the Hurricanes' future. Could she live with herself if she was the cause of their championship run falling apart?

Before she could explore the ramifications of her idea, she got to Grandpa Leon. He clutched a glass of juice and balanced on his lap a dinner plate that contained specks of spiced sausage and rice.

His state continued to shock Fiona. Every time she saw him, he looked less and less like himself. The disease seemed to steal more than just his mind. The effects were rendered visible on his skin, his face. Even his smile had shifted, changed.

Glancing at her, he motioned for Fiona to sit next to him. "The boys used to like boating. But I don't see them use the yacht that often. Or maybe I am forgetting that, too. It just seems everyone is so busy working."

Sitting down beside him, she laid a hand on his tissue-paper-thin skin. "You would be right about that."

"I used to work, too. A lot." Grandpa Leon's sight turned inward. Fiona wondered what he remembered in this moment. If they were real memories or imagined.

"Yes, sir, you did."

"So I guess I'm to blame." Taking a swig of his juice, he spoke into his crystal glass.

Fiona shook her head, gathering her hair in her fist and pulling it over her shoulder. Grandpa Leon had stepped up for Henri and his brothers. Set a good example about the value of hard work and family. "They're adults. We all are. We make our own choices."

Flashing her a dentureless smile, he tapped her temple. "I've always liked you. When I remember who you are, of course."

"And I adore your sense of humor in the face of what has to be… Well, I enjoy your humor."

"Thank you, dear." His gaze returned out toward the yacht. Toward the past and what had been. Swirling around the last few drops of his juice, he let out a small sigh.

"Could I get you a jacket or a pillow?" she asked just as she saw Henri walking toward them. Her stomach twisted into knots and she wanted to run into his arms, but that would mean giving him answers to questions she wasn't ready to face yet.

Gramps extended his juice glass, staring absently ahead. "Just more juice."

Springing to her feet, she grabbed the glass from him and made fast tracks for the house, racing past Henri.

So much for a conversation with Fiona. She was dodging him like the plague.

Though Henri knew Fiona was busy with her fundraiser, he felt that her disappearing act over these past few days had more to do with what was unresolved between them.

Henri had caught sight of her from the pool patio, sitting with his grandfather, looking out on the lake. She'd always been so good with Grandpa Leon. Nurturing. Kind. And as the disease claimed more and more of his memory, Fiona never lost her temper, but took it in stride, displaying patience even saints would envy.

Making his way out to her, Henri felt anticipation quicken his steps. She'd practically run into him, glass in hand. Her face was solemn, and she was quiet as she made her way back to the house.

Grandpa Leon turned his head, looking over his shoulder at Henri. Recognition washed over his expression.

Good. These days, Grandpa Leon's ability to process who was in front of him had waned. To be recognized was a rare blessing.

Gramps clapped Henri on the back as he sat down. "Nice figure on your girlfriend there, Christophe."

Henri's stomach fell. Watching his grandfather grasp at memories would never become easy. Grandpa Leon thought he was Christophe, his father's brother.

The Texas branch of the family was deeply involved in the Reynaud shipping empire and the cruise ship business. They owned an island off Galveston that was a self-sustaining working ranch and an optional stop on many of their cruise itineraries. Guests could ride horseback on the gulf beaches or take part in one of the farm-to-table feasts that made use of the organically grown vegetables. They hadn't visited their Texas cousins in years due to a family rift. Leon had publicly cut his oldest son, Christophe, out of his will long ago, but Uncle Christophe still retained his title as a vice president of global operations and, along with his oldest son, was very much a part of the family business.

Grandpa Leon's greeting was a small slipup. It didn't mean anything. Henri coughed, stepping closer to his grandfather. He scratched the back of his neck, hoping his grandfather would recognize him now. "Um, thank you."

Leon tapped Henri's ring finger. "You're married?

Married men shouldn't have a piece on the side. It's not right."

Offering a small smile, he sat down next to his grandfather. "Grandpa, I'm Henri, and Fiona's my wife."

Fog settled on his grandfather. He pursed his lips, weighing the information. Looking down at his feet, he shook his head. "Oh, right. Of course you are, and she is. I just never expected you to go for the kind who've, um, had surgical embellishments."

"I'm not sure what you're talking about."

Grandpa Leon's eyebrows shot up. Cocking his head to the right, he gestured to his chest and lifted upward a hint.

Just in time for Fiona to come back with his re-filled juice.

Henri's voice fell low. "How do you know that?"

"I have a keen eye for the finer things in life. I just am not so sure why such an already perfect woman would alter anything about herself."

Handing the glass to Henri, Fiona leaned in to kiss Grandpa Leon's cheek. "Grandpa, you're amazing. Love you."

The older man reached up to touch the side of her face. Henri saw how the simplest movements tired his grandfather.

Dropping his hand away from Fiona, Grandpa Leon peered back and forth between Fiona and Henri. He pursed his dry lips.

Handing his grandfather the glass of juice, Henri looked at his wife, trying to ferret out what she was thinking.

Grandpa Leon took a big swig of his juice and

popped his lips. Shakily, he rose to his feet, stretching his arms out above him.

"You two kids have fun. *Jeopardy* will be on soon and I can't miss that." He winked at Henri, shuffling toward the house.

"Do you need help, Grandpa?" Henri asked earnestly.

Waving Henri off, Grandpa Leon shook his head. "No. No. You two stay here. Enjoy the sunset."

As Leon walked to the house, Fiona made her way to the dock. Sitting on the edge, she let her bare feet dangle over the water, swinging them to unheard music.

Henri strode over to join her. He was itching to speak to her. To win her back still, even though she'd been avoiding him over the last few days.

Taking a seat next to her, he remembered all the times they'd sat here when they were first married. They'd talk here for hours. About literature and art and football. Everything.

Fiona twisted her rope of long dark hair draped over her shoulder. "How strange that your grandfather knew I'd had surgery all this time and never said a word. I might have expected a man to notice if I'd opted for larger, but since I went down a cup size... I'm just surprised."

"You and I instituted the code of silence on this. Maybe he sensed that, too." His grandfather had always been intuitive, if a bit eccentric.

Leon hadn't given Henri and his brothers the most traditional upbringing once he'd stepped in to take charge of his four rowdy grandsons, but he understood boys. He'd brought a fifties-era Harley-Davidson to the Texas ranch to give them a lesson in engine rebuilding. The motorcycle had been in crates when he bought the beat-up old thing. By the end of the summer they'd reveled in seeing how fast it would race on the private ranch roads. They'd even collected a lot of bruises along the way.

Memories of his youth and his grandfather flooded him. Watching as Alzheimer's consumed Grandpa Leon's mind tore at Henri. It was as if the lines connecting the flowchart of Grandpa Leon's memories had been erased.

"All this time I thought I was the one holding back. But it's you, too. You're scared," Henri said to Fiona.

"I meet with the doctor tomorrow. I'll know one way or another. Odds really are that it's nothing."

"I want to be there…" He paused. "But I can see in your eyes I'm not welcome."

"It's not that. I'm just not sure I can…" She shook her head. "Hell, I don't know. I just need to do this on my own."

Silence pooled around them, filling the spaces between them. It cut deeper than any fight or argument they'd had.

At least when they were fighting, he felt a connection. That their relationship had a chance because there was an active struggle. This silence felt like a killing blow.

As the sun sank farther into the lake horizon, he felt the weight of their situation sink onto his shoulders. He was losing her.

Pink balloons covered the entire ceiling of the new wing of the hospital soon to open as an updated children's oncology floor. Fiona clutched a glass of champagne, taking in the mass of people that flooded the ward.

Success. Her biggest one yet. Despite the tiny budget and last-minute assignment, the event was packed. In one corner, people bid on silent auction items, which were always a strong source of donations at charity events. A few casino games provided more entertainment and allowed attendees to contribute while having fun.

But the event was mostly family oriented. Nearby, a troupe of storytellers in elaborate costumes held the attention of a glitzed-out crowd. She watched the emotions play out on the faces of the audience.

Across the room from her, Henri handed out footballs signed by the entire Hurricanes team. She watched the way the women in the crowd ogled him. A surge of jealousy sank into her veins.

The event should make her feel fulfilled. At the very least, accomplished. But as she surveyed the pianist and TV star-turned-pop singer Daisy Dani, she felt hollow. She smoothed her crepe skirt, fingers catching on the sequins that outlined a paisley pattern that managed to be elegant and bohemian at the same time. While the deep purple skirt shone with metallic highlights, the dark silk blouse on top was simple and secure. No more shoulder-baring costume mishaps for her.

Hearing Henri's laugh from across the room ignited her feet to move. Things had been strange between them over the past few days. A new sort of strain had settled between them. She'd tried texting him earlier, but phones were forbidden during practice.

The results of her biopsy had come in today. She'd

promised to let him know the results and she had. Right away.

The biopsy had revealed nothing. No cancer. Such news ought to fill her with relief and promise, but the risk of the cancer gene would always be part of her existence. Just like her scars. Permanent marks on her mind and body.

Fiona had told Henri via text that she was in the clear. Everything from the test had come back normal. No reason to worry.

As she made her way to Henri, she bumped into the doctor who had asked her out. Had that really only been a few weeks ago?

So much had changed since her last fund-raiser. Her relationship with Henri had cooled and heated…and now? Well, now it was an utter mess.

Things with the doctor were cordial, platonic. At least on her end. Avoiding a drawn-out conversation, she almost couldn't believe her eyes.

She blinked, stunned. Jean-Pierre had arrived at the party. He and Henri hadn't exchanged more than a few words in months. Things in the family had been strained since Jean-Pierre had left New Orleans. But having him show up added to the pro ball appeal of the event, and would give the fund-raising a generous boost.

As the youngest Reynaud, Jean-Pierre had inherited his love of the game from his father and his grandfather, the same as his brothers. But Jean-Pierre had gone to college playing the quarterback position, the same as Henri. And since Jean-Pierre wasn't the kind of man to play in a brother's shadow, he hadn't wanted a spot on the Hurricanes. He was a starter and an elite player. When the New York Gladiators had made him an offer, he'd taken it.

Fiona shouldered through the masses of people to her brother-in-law.

"Jean-Pierre, how did you know we could use the extra help for this? It's wonderful to see you, but why are you here?"

"Henri told me you had to salvage this event so he called me." He grinned, leaning in to give her a hug and a kiss on her cheek. "Access to the family's private plane has its perks. I had some time, so I was able to swing it."

"Thank you." She was touched. Not just by Jean-Pierre's quick flight and visit, but that Henri had thought to ask him.

Jean-Pierre acknowledged greetings from a few friends, and now the whole room was buzzing with all the star power. When his fans had shuffled past, his eyes returned to Fiona's. "Not a problem. The Gladiators' PR guy thought it was a good idea. I'm off to sign a few more autographs. Nice party. You did a great job."

She thanked him again before he melted into the crowd, moving slowly since he was signing autographs as he made his way, shaking hands and making time for everyone who wanted to see him.

With no one else vying for her attention, Fiona edged her way to Henri. He looked so handsome in his tuxedo, as he always did. But she could see the way he stiffened as she approached, as if bracing for the next hit. The tension in his jaw pulsated as she drew near. Hurt still colored his face.

Tugging at his blue shirtsleeve, she leaned into him,

her heavy sterling silver bracelet sliding down her arm. Placing her hand on his chest, she tried to memorize his scent and the way he stood. Pain ached in her joints. Everything would change after this conversation.

She just hoped she'd make it through the hardest conversation she'd ever have.

"Let's step outside. Just us." The words formed on her tongue like a prayer or a plea.

Rather than answering her, he placed his hand on the small of her back. Shivers rolled up her spine as he led them outside. Laughter and music filtered through the doors as they sat on the bench in the garden patio.

In the distance, the night hummed with the sound of expensive cars being parked by the valets. A few feet away, a water feature gurgled and multicolored lights glinted. A few patients who'd been medically cleared to attend were brought out in wheelchairs and chatted with guests. One teen in particular caught her eye, a thin girl with a party hat—a cloth jester cap—on her bald head. Streamers glittered from her chair and her mother leaned down to whisper something while her father set plates of food down on a nearby bench.

Fiona tore her gaze away before the image dragged her under, and focused her attention back on Henri. There was a buzz of activity here, but not the press of a crowd like inside. Here, they could speak privately, seated on another bench, one of the three she'd donated in memory of her mother, her grandmother and her aunt.

Henri's mouth thinned for a moment. She could see the ragged edges of his nerves, the stress she'd caused. The hurt. Her fingers clutched the edges of the stately concrete bench, sturdy, made to survive far longer than her mother had. Her breath hitched as she fought harder to tamp down the tears, the emotion.

Henri gently pried her hand free from the bench—her mother's bench—and linked fingers with her. She tried to hold onto the feel of his rough calluses from years and years of training and practice.

His wedding band glinted in the halo of patio lights. "Thank you for letting me know about the doctor visit. I'm glad the scare's over. And that you're okay."

Chewing her lip, she could only think of this party, everything surrounding her reminding her of what she needed to do no matter how much pain it caused her.

"Except the scare will never be over, Henri. There will always be a next time. You'll worry every time I go for a checkup." Words exploded from her mouth like gunshots. He needed to hear this. Needed to understand everything. "Look at you. Even when I say that now, you look like you're going to throw up."

"Because I care about you, dammit."

"I care about you, too." She couldn't deny the truth any longer. "In fact, I'm still in love with you."

"You love me? Then why the hell are you divorcing me?" he barked, confusion swimming in his dark eyes.

"Because I can see how this is tearing you apart. Even your grandfather sees me as I am. A woman with a high risk of contracting cancer one day. I pray if I do that it will be curable. But I don't know. I do know *I* can live with that possibility." She looked around her, at the patients in the wheelchairs. And she looked at their families with their haunted, exhausted and scared eyes. "But I can't live with watching how afraid it makes you."

"You were fine with us having sex and being together these past few days when you thought it was day by day." He leveled the accusation at her. His gruff voice seemed to shake the night air. "Then, once you had to think about forever, you shut me out."

"That's not fair. You're not listening."

"I am listening. I've been listening. And you know what I hear?" He turned sideways on the bench, drawing his face close to hers. Tucking a loose hair behind her ear, he breathed. "I keep hearing none of this is fair to either one of us."

Desire. Hurt. Longing. The three warring emotions beat in her chest, threatening to disrupt her course of action. But she had to focus on why she was here. To end things before either of them suffered a loss they'd never recover from. She had to be brave, to face this head-on.

Pulling away from his touch, she lowered his hand to his lap. "We shouldn't be discussing this two days before a game. You need to focus."

"Impossible." Resting his forehead on his hand, rubbing his temples, talking more to the ground than to her, he said, "There's never going to be a good time for this conversation."

"Henri, please, what are you hoping to accomplish?"

"To make you admit what we had was real." He tipped his head to look sideways at her. "But you checked out of our relationship."

Tears clogged her throat, even stinging her nose. But she wouldn't cry in front of him. She'd shed so many tears over the mess she'd made of their marriage. "Fine, you wanted this conversation now, we'll have it. I admit it. I can't deal with being married to you. I'm scared as hell, every single day when I wake up, that

I'm going to get sick, and just the thought of you grieving over me dying rips my heart out again and again."

Fiona knew how to pick a moment. Art had taught her as much. She knew what leaving looked like. Her mother, her aunt, her grandmother. Knew what it was like to be left behind, to suffer with a loss that ravaged the bones.

With tender fingers, she stroked the side of his face, tracing the faintest stubble with her fingertips. His lips parted slightly. Leaning into him, she inhaled his cologne and musk. Her lips found his. Pressed a kiss from her soul to his.

Their last kiss.

Twelve

Henri had thought football was his world. Until he met Fiona.

Love for her had slammed into him hard and fast.

As hard and fast as the Indianapolis linebacker plowing toward him—

Damn.

His body hit the ground in a crunch of shoulder pads, grunts and smack talk. Well deserved. He was losing this game for his team. His mind wasn't in the game. Hell, his heart wasn't in it.

Crisp fall air stung his lungs as he viewed the world from the ground. How damn symbolic. Dazed, he blinked into focus. Eyes scanning the crowd, he saw the disappointment on the faces of his teammates after what should have been a straightforward third-down conversion. He clenched his teeth.

This game should have been a simple win for them. The Hurricanes had a better record against better opponents. Their key players were all healthy. But instead of posting big numbers for their team and calling in some guys off the bench, they were fighting to stay in the game, and that was clearly his fault.

The world spun, but not just from the impact of the 230-pound rookie with the speed of a track star. Henri's eyes trailed to the wives' section, where he half expected to see Fiona, decked out in team colors and a scarf.

But she wasn't there. Hadn't bothered to get on the plane. She'd said she was still in love with him and for that precise reason, she needed to leave him.

Nothing made sense anymore.

He'd spent too much time knocked down lately. Pushing himself off the turf, he launched into the air, landing on his feet.

The Hurricanes fans peppered through the crowd cheered as he rose to his feet. At once believing in him and completely oblivious to the metaphorically shaky ground he stood on. They wouldn't cheer if they understood why his game was off.

Brushing the dirt from his shoulder, he started to walk toward his team. But two of the team trainers were already there, ready to help him off the field.

"I'm fine." He waved them off.

He could hear the offensive coordinator in his ear through the microphone in his helmet. "You're off the field, Henri."

"What the hell?" Henri straightened his helmet that had been knocked askew, talking to the trainers and his offensive coach at the same time. "I'm fine."

He could see his brother Dempsey, the head coach, waving him off the field from the sidelines. His backup had already sprinted to the huddle.

Benched? What in the hell would that accomplish? Henri's pride bristled. It was not as if they were punting it away. The Hurricanes were going for it on fourth down, trying to take that yardage he'd failed to grab in the last play.

"You're going to lose if you take me out." He could still recover the game. The tackle left him with new clarity.

Adjusting his ball cap, Dempsey shook his head, eyes firm and impassive as Henri reached his side. "And you're going to risk breaking your damn neck out there. I'm not ending this day with you in the hospital." He shoved his microphone aside to talk to Henri without an audience on their headsets.

Nearby, the offensive coordinator stepped up to run the show as the clock kept ticking.

"So what, I get tackled once and suddenly I'm a candidate for ICU?" Henri barked back, tugging off his helmet to keep this conversation as private as the fishbowl of a stadium would allow.

Dempsey ripped off his own headset, too, turning a shoulder to the field. Away from the inevitable cameras focused on them.

"We both know that's not what's going on here. Fiona isn't here and your rocky marriage has compromised your focus like we all damn well warned you it would. You are getting your ass handed to you out there," Dempsey said flatly.

"To hell with that. I can handle the field," he shouted back at his brother, rage coursing in his veins.

Henri's teammates nearby exchanged glances. Outbursts of emotion weren't his normal MO and no one talked back to the coach—family or not.

Dempsey leveled a glare at him. "This isn't the backyard. And you might want to think about what you say next." He slammed his headset back into place and turned his attention toward the field where the backup QB had just run for the yards they needed.

A much-needed Hurricanes first down and it hadn't come from Henri. He tried to hide his bitterness, knowing damn well a camera would be closing in on his face right about now.

Henri's cousin and Wild Card approached him, providing a wall of shoulders between him and the cameras.

"Hey, man. Just sit out a few. We'll do you proud, brother." Wild Card clapped him on the shoulder, walking out a stinger in his knee from a previous play.

"Yeah, cuz. We're a family here. Let someone else step up and take care of business. You take care of you," his cousin said with his Texas twang. No judgment, no fuss. They were good men. Good friends.

Deep down, Henri knew that. He seethed anyway.

Sitting on the bench, he watched his second family execute play after play. They moved like an extension of each other. Synced. In tune.

The longer he sat on the bench, the more Dempsey's words rang true. Dempsey had called it. Henri's performance had been poor. He'd been asking for an injury, asking to feel something other than numb.

Pulling him from the game was the right call. But then, Dempsey wasn't calling the plays because he was a novice. His older half brother had as much at stake this season as he did. More, maybe.

Henri had to get his head together for real. Because in marriage, he didn't have any backup. It was just him and he was screwing it up big-time. This was about more than football. It was about his wife. His life.

His love.

Guilt flooded through Fiona.

She should have gone to Henri's game. He'd come to her fund-raiser and, yes, the night had ended with a fight. The worst kind. The forever kind.

The longer she spent alone with her ice cream in her garden, the more she realized she needed to talk to him. She needed to shake him out of his family's habit of cutting people off—his family that had Texas cousins who mostly never spoke. And then there was the California branch that owned vineyards she'd maybe heard mentioned once. It was insane. The Reynauds had so many branches, so many healthy, thriving parts, and yet they didn't even function as a family. Didn't they know how fortunate they were?

Her phone buzzed on the wrought-iron patio table. An incoming text lit up the screen. She swiped her finger across and found a photo from the night before. A photo of the teenage cancer patient who'd worn the jester hat, her mom and dad leaning in on either side of her with matching smiles.

The text scrolled: We're making memories for a

lifetime with every moment. Thank you for an awe-some night!

A second photo came through of the girl with Henri and Jean-Pierre: So excited to meet football idols. She texted the photo to all her school friends. Thank you again.

The joy on the teen's face, on her parents' faces, blew Fiona away. They weren't just brave. Somehow they were happy in the moment. Something her family had never quite managed.

Something she'd never managed.

She'd walked away from her marriage because she didn't know if she could deal with Henri's fears. But had she even tried to manage her own? Could she honestly live with herself if she cut them both off without trying to get a handle on those fears? Her finger traced the faces—genuinely happy faces—and wondered how she'd missed that joy for herself. She kept telling Henri she was strong. But maybe she hadn't been strong enough to truly live in the moment.

It was time to quit assuming Henri would fall apart the way her father had. It was time to stop fearing she would follow her mother's path.

She'd already chosen a different path with her surgery. A hopeful path. She could embrace the day and be her own person, no matter what that future held. It was time to accept the happiness waiting for her.

Snatching up her phone and wallet, she wasn't wasting another moment. She rushed to the closest airport where the family kept their jet. She called Gervais on the way, needing to clear it with him before she used it, but he not only gave his approval, he also managed to put a pilot on site to greet her with the flight plan filed for immediate takeoff. What a godsend to have the support system of family. Why had she spent so much time pushing them away with both hands?

Fiona's stomach was a bundle of nerves as the Gulfstream touched down in Indianapolis. She'd watched the rest of the game on the jet's television, catching the final few plays in a streaming app on her phone.

Henri had been benched even though he stood up after that hard hit in the backfield. He didn't seem to have been treated for concussion symptoms, but maybe they'd say as much in the press to dance around the fact that he simply hadn't played well.

The Hurricanes barely won, and only because the game had been put into the rest of the team's hands while the Bayou Bomber sat one out. Dempsey's strategic coaching had coaxed a win out of the backup quarterback and the rest of the starters, so she suspected Henri wasn't going to be in any kind of mood to see her and talk about their problems.

Again.

But she'd come too far now to back off. And thanks to Gervais's help again, she'd landed at the airport and hopefully would make it to meet them before they left. The jet taxied over to the parking area. She peered out the window, praying she had enough time to get to the stadium. Were any of the parked jets theirs? Surely if they'd left, Gervais would have let the pilot know their flight was in vain.

Just when she was about to grab her phone to call him and check, she caught sight of a chartered bus

CATHERINE MANN

driving toward one of the other planes. The sort of bus the team would usually travel in collectively to the airport. Her stomach did cartwheels.

Could she have been that close to missing him? Yes, they could have spoken later, but now that she'd figured out what she'd been missing—the happiness she'd been robbing them both of—she couldn't bear the thought of waiting a second longer to see Henri.

Her jet stopped wonderfully close to the path of the bus—bless the pilot and Gervais. Eons later—or at least it felt so—the steps were in place on the Gulf-stream so she could disembark. Cautious feet found purchase on the stairway leading out of the jet. Wind gusting her hair back, she had to bring her hands to her eyes to make out the New Orleans Hurricanes team inside the bus. But then the charter bus's door opened, and the players exited one after the other.

Heart beating hard in her chest, she scanned the team for Henri. Dempsey. Wild Card. Freight Train.

They were all there. But where was Henri?

She felt far away from her body as he came into view. His broad shoulders and wind-tossed dark hair. Sunglasses that shielded his eyes even though night had fallen. Did he see her?

She couldn't wait for him to notice her. Here she was. Ready to gamble, to leap. Gathering her voice, she yelled his name.

She half tripped down the steps of the jet, her ballet flats pounding the asphalt as she ran toward him, still calling out.

"Henri? Henri!" she shouted, her feet picking up pace, her dress wrapping around her legs.

Henri's back was to her now, but his muscular frame was easy to pick out in his tailored charcoal-colored suit.

No matter what he wore, he was still as sexy as the day she'd met him.

He glanced over his shoulder. He cocked his head to the side, then as the distance closed between them she could see him raise an eyebrow. Luckily Dempsey waved away security and Henri broke ranks.

Henri's arms went wide and without hesitation she flew into them. That easy. That right. She was his. He was hers.

He looked over at his brother. "Dempsey, can we have a moment?"

Dempsey laughed. "Now you ask permission?" He gave his brother a shove in Fiona's direction.

Henri took her by the elbow and guided her back into the Reynauds' private jet. "Why are you here? Wait. Never mind. Who the hell cares? You're here."

He hauled her into his arms and kissed her. Really kissed her in a way he hadn't done in…she couldn't remember when. It was something more than the kisses of their early romance. Something more than the kisses of their newlywed days. This was the kiss of a couple tested in fire. More than the fire of passion, but the fire of life.

She eased back, sweeping her hand over his hair that curled after a fresh wash. "I'm here to say I'm sorry. To say I want to try if you'll forgive me for being afraid to face the future. Living in the day was so much…safer."

"God, I lo—"

She pressed a hand to his mouth. "I know. You've

shown me in a million ways with your patience, but I want to be the one to say it first. I love you. I want to spend every day of my life with you. I want to live for each day and focus on that. The joy, the beauty, the art. Our love. And yes, our family. I want to focus on the positive every day for however many days we have." She traced his lips. "I hope you understand that while half the fear was for me, the other half was fear of hurting you."

"Losing you these past months has hurt like hell." His arms found her waist, snaked around her hips. He pulled her closer, as if she'd blow away in the wind if he didn't. She'd missed the feel of his arms around her. Had forgotten what being together—truly together—was like.

"I'm sorry. Who would have thought dreaming of a future would be so scary?"

"I do understand, but you'll help me be strong, won't you?" His smile was light but his dark eyes were serious.

"We'll help each other. I hope there will be countless days. It's not about how much time we have, but how beautiful we can make each day together."

"Not that I'm going to tempt fate here, but I am curious. What made you change your mind? Did my family hound you? Because if they're being pushy just let me know."

"Actually, they've been incredibly helpful. Gervais even set up the plane. Looking back, I'm rethinking our decision to keep them in the dark these past months." She glanced at the window, at the bus full of players waiting patiently as the exhaust puffed into the night air. "I learned my lesson from a photo the mom of one of the patients at the party texted me. I can show you later. It's…beautiful."

"I look forward to seeing it." He brushed a kiss across her lips. "I want us to talk more, share more, spend more time together. I've decided I should quit the team."

Shock pulled at her heartstrings. She had to have misheard him. Football wasn't just a job for him. Passion for the game ran as deep as her passion for art. "What?"

"At the end of the season, I'm through."

"What about your contract?" Another gust of fall wind ripped past them, carrying the smell of oil and decomposing leaves past them.

Pushing the hair from her eyes, he kissed her forehead, his lips gentle and warm in the cool atmosphere.

"I'll buy out. Money's not an issue."

"You love the game. I don't understand." Fiona shook her head, processing the logic of his words.

"I love you more, and I'll do whatever it takes to win you back. We'll take more time to get to know each other, at home or traveling, or starting a fund-raising foundation. I'm committed to making this work. No half measures. I want you as my wife, my love, my life." He spoke in earnest. She could see that in the way a faint smile tugged at the corner of his lips and how his gaze intensified as he stared into her eyes.

But Henri without football? That didn't seem right. The game twined with his soul, his purpose. They had to reach a point where they accepted all of each other, no holding back, no reservations. They couldn't pick and choose parts to love and parts to neglect. That road had led them to ruin.

Time to begin again. To take bigger chances and risks together.

She rested her head against his chest, listening to his pounding heart. He offered her complete devotion and she appreciated the sentiment, needed to hear he'd move heaven and earth for them. But she didn't need Henri to give up his job to fix them. They'd do that together.

"Henri, you don't have to give up your job for me."

"I do if it means I could lose you again."

She repeated her thoughts from earlier out loud. "I'm yours. You're mine. When I talk about the joy of living, I mean embracing every part of who we are. I love the game, traveling, seeing you play. We can figure out the details together. If we need to, we can truly talk with the counselor rather than racing straight to the lawyer. Are you okay with that?" Communication. That's what they needed. Old-fashioned communication.

"Whatever it takes. I've made that clear." He kissed her nose. Her temple. Her neck. Her mouth. Each kiss affirming his commitment—a promise imprinted into her skin. Into her soul.

Enjoying the feel of him, she asked, "What if I say counseling and you keep playing?"

Her fingers traced designs on the back of his neck as their eyes met.

"I think you're letting me off too easily, my love."

She rolled her eyes and arched up to give him a quick kiss. "Oh, I don't think this is going to be easy at all. Not if we dig in deep with counseling."

"I can face it if we're together." He intertwined their hands. Raised their joined fists to his lips. Kissed the back of her hand while staring into her eyes.

"Together, as a team." She stepped closer, their clasped hands against her heart. "That sounds like a winning game plan to me."

* * * * *